Full Circle

Seasons' Turn Book I

E. E. Kellogg

Full Circle by E. E. Kellogg

© 2018 E. E. Kellogg

Cover Design: SelfPubBookCovers.com/dejuand

DEDICATION

Dedicated to my late parents, William Bradford Kellogg and Marguerite Graham Kellogg, who gave me the love of books in infancy, to my best friend, Jessica O'Connor, without whom this book would never have been written, and to my husband, Llewellyn Evans, who gave me the jump-start I needed.

INTRODUCTION

Welcome to Haven Point

S unlight hits the eastern coast; white cliffs made whiter with the brightness. It glints over the rippling water of the harbor, darts among the anchored boats.

Near the south-western end of Maine's Bold Coast, on one of the peninsulas which, together with its many islands, give Maine more miles of shoreline than California, sits the town of Haven Point, incorporated in 1792.

Our story begins in a decade not far removed from our own. Little has changed in Haven Point between then and now; there is still no reliable cell phone service, minimal wifi coverage. Many farms and small businesses are run very much as they were a century or more ago. Power outages are regularities during storms; many houses are heated with wood; many are equipped with generators.

The town extends for roughly the bottom third of the peninsula, a little longer on the western side. Route 226 runs south to the point from east and north again to the west, although the eastern section was fully extended to the main coastal road many decades after the western leg was cut.

The western coast is granite cliffs and waterfront property. The older families who now return as 'summer people' built their houses here. The principal and most northern is still called 'The Van Leyden House' in Haven Point, though by the time our story begins, Julia Van Leyden, only child of John and Emily Van Leyden, has been married to Peter Lord for several decades (theirs had been *the* Boston-society wedding that season), and the graceful 1789-built stone home which stretches over serene land like a blessing has been hers and her husband's since her father's death.

Peter and Julia Lord had two children; they now have one. Geoffrey Van Leyden Lord, tragically dead, far too young, and Elizabeth Van Leyden Lord, just turned 23, with a B.S. in Chemistry and working on her Masters and Doctorate simultaneously.

North of the Van Leyden / Lord residence is the Van Leyden Granite quarry, which still produces income for Julia Lord and her family.

* * *

Jan and Liesbeth Van Leyden had been Loyalists during the Revolution, residing in the city of New York. In 1782, finding the social climate increasingly hostile, they carefully and secretly sold as many of their possessions as possible. They headed for Canada in a wagon with their four children, gold, silver, a few clothes. Blankets. Guns and ammunition, as many and as much as they could obtain. Long and hard miles, they traveled. Lost their way. Lost two children to sickness as weather chilled. With winter almost on them, they found what is now 'Gray Way,' and the Grays and the Hardies. Both families were patriots.

But they were Christians. The Van Leydens were a test of their faith, and they took it on—and the Van Leydens, who were fellow Anglicans, in. In return for silver, which the Van Leydens pressed on them, and the Grays and Hardies accepted. Shelter, food—at least dried salted fish and meat, root vegetables, apples they had. Hard coin was scarce. The Hardies had four bedrooms and two children, compared with the Grays' three bedrooms and five children, and the Van Leydens sheltered with the Hardies for the winter. The Grays chipped in with shared food from their cellar. Jan Van Leyden slept with a gun beneath his pillow, fearful of the temptation his gold might be, but never was his rest in fact (as opposed to fancy) disturbed on that score. He did not know that Ian Hardie slept with a gun beneath his own pillow, against the possibility of a plot to take over his home, perhaps by the slaughter of his whole family. But Ian Hardie, like his guests, never had his sleep disturbed by violence.

Over a century ago, Christopher and Muriel Endicott of Boston and Endicott Bank built a summer home in Haven Point on what is now called the 'old' side of the peninsula. It was inevitable that they made the acquaintance of Stefan and Catherine Van Leyden; that they might become good friends was not, but they did.

The two families discussed their children's prospects; the outcome was parental encouragement of a match between Lucas Van Leyden and Marianne, the elder Endicott daughter. Lucas and Marianne were dutiful children, and liked each other well enough. The surprise was Nicholas Endicott and Helena Van Leyden, who fell in love, and brought this fact to their parents before the engagement of Lucas and Marianne was announced. Both marriages were happy ones.

Thus, the Endicotts and Van Leydens joined in business as

well as family, and the younger Van Leydens (and their descendants) lived in Boston for much of the year. But to this day, no Van Leyden has ever been allowed to forget that they owe their very existence to the town they helped found, and most especially to those residents named Hardie or Gray.

The easterly coast is limestone. Van Leyden Granite operates a limestone quarry here; the company provides more local jobs than any other single concern, although several of the fishing industries, most particularly lobstering, provide many more overall.

On this coast are also newer-built summer homes, including scores of smaller rentals, set on twisting roads cut to reach denser-built properties. This coast has better harborage, and several boatyards operate near the point, which holds the principal harbor. Summer sees enormous motor yachts, and, once in a while, Peter and Julia Lord's immaculately maintained antique 200-foot sailing yacht, the 'Liesbeth,' anchored there. Lobster boats bob, Paul Hardie's five among them.

The interior of the peninsula, from the north end of Haven Point to about five miles from the southernmost point, is mostly local-owned farmland.

Just across to the west of Route 226 from the road labeled simply 'Van Leyden' runs Gray Way. Down this road are three farms. These days, Jake and Ann Gray's son Jason, eldest of three children, farms 20 of his father's 60 acres and sells what deadfall from the woodlot isn't used for their fireplaces and woodstoves. Jake himself operates the local garage, in town, down the point. Ann Gray runs an in-town second-hand clothing and tailoring shop near the eastern end of Main Street. Her elder daughter, Joanna, helps in the shop, and hates it. She is taking a course in nursing. The younger Gray girl, Melody, is in high school. The Grays were the first family to settle in the peninsula's in-land, a decade before the Revolution.

East of the Grays are the Hardies, who settled several years after their neighbors. Paul Hardie's property is called 'farmland' for courtesy and a nod to history; Paul is one of Hayden Point's more prosperous local businessmen (with one exception, the Hardies have been respectable and financially sound), employing quite a few locals in his lobster boats. What is grown these days on Hardie land, besides 65 acres of wood, are a handful of dwarf peach and two dozen apple trees, and the roses Madeleine Hardie planted around the house before separating herself (physically but not otherwise) to Hollywood some nine years ago. Paul finds tending them restful and sweet-nostalgic. Cleared land of some 15 acres surrounds the Hardie home. Just enough trees exist between Paul's land and the Grays' for privacy.

Ernest John (Jack) Hardie means to be a lobsterman like his father, his father's father, and several generations before that. He's at home on the water. As soon as he is out of high school, which graduation is imminent, he will captain one of his father's boats full-time; Jack can't wait. Gwendolen Marie (Gwen), a little less than two-and-a-half years younger, is a straight-A student, in the same class as Melody Gray.

Madeleine Hardie once played Gwendolen Fairfax in Oscar Wilde's play, 'The Importance of Being Earnest,' and insisted on naming her children for the lead characters. She gave her daughter, also, the name of the Blessed Virgin. Madeleine was raised Roman Catholic but adopted her husband's high-church Anglican practice upon their marriage.

Both Jack and Gwen think it icky that they are named for a romantic couple in a play. But 'Jack' is better than 'Algernon.' And 'Gwen' is okay. Gwen Hardie does not like to be called 'Gwendolen.' She does like cooking, reading, and running or riding, horseback or bicycle, on the cliffs, through the woods, with Jack and her 'other brothers,' as she calls them, the sons of the Hardies' eastern neighbor, Hank Greenlaw.

Gwen is already perhaps the best non-professional cook in Haven Point, having insisted on preparing her family's meals since she was nine years old. She's inherited a taste for literature from her mother, whom she resents very much for what she would consider constructive abandonment, if she associated legal terms with her feelings.

The 40 acres east of the Hardie land, now divided almost evenly between wood and farmland, are owned by Hank Greenlaw. In the 1870s, Martin Hardie had grand notions, and had tried to set up a fish-canning plant on his farmland. The structure still stands.

The utter failure of this enterprise, coupled with the extravagant construction costs of the large-roomed northern addition to the house, necessitated the sale of these acres to Samuel Greenlaw, a dour and diligent family man new to Haven Point, who farmed his land with eventual success. Samuel's descendants have been a mixed bag. Some have increased the farm's value, some have decreased it. Hank Greenlaw is one of the latter; we must hope that his sons, Seth and Benjamin, may do better by the land and for themselves than their father has.

Seth will graduate from high school soon, along with Jack Hardie. He trains horses, like but also unlike his father, and gives riding lessons. Thanks to the income Seth brings in, the Greenlaws own three of the horses in their deteriorating barn. Four years ago, they had one. He has a reputation as a mechanic, too; many locals have had the useful life of old farm equipment extended through his skill.

Ben, five-and-a-half years younger than his brother, by now has thoroughly perplexed and confounded his middle-school math teachers; he looks forward impatiently to working the same on the high-school instructors who will soon have to deal with his racing mind. College professors, as well, too far into the future to suit Ben. Pick their brains, get every scrap. Like eating lobster, claws and all. Take and *make*.

Ben likes making things, *different* things, useful or not; he *knows* himself superior to his brother, who has been an uneven student, and—Ben thinks—only repairs what others have built. He also knows his inferiority to Seth.

Ben remembers being thrown by a horse at age 8, and refusing to let his brother coax him back into the saddle. It was Seth who rode the horse to exhaustion, saying that leaving the horse having thrown its rider could ruin it for use, as well as leaving the rider ruined for riding. He'd been right. Ben had 'froze scared,' as Seth said he would; the horse had been just fine.

Ben itches for a world as unlike Haven Point as possible. Seth, like Jack and Gwen Hardie, does not.

And here we begin.

CHAPTER 1

Memorial Day 19____

A gray day. Clods thudded on the coffin. Not even June yet, and already a summer-season funeral. Paul Hardie blinked back tears. Hank Greenlaw had had his faults, no question; but the Greenlaws and the Hardies had lived in each others' pockets for over a century.

Hank's boys stood quiet across the open grave, in ill-fitting, hastily bought second-hand suits. Seth, five months shy of 18, tall and too thin, his face bleaker than any boy his age ought to look. A quiet boy, watchful from behind wide dark gray-blue eyes, too intense for most people's ease around him. Dark heavy hair, never tidy.

Ben, just turned 12, huddling close to his brother. It was too soon to be quite sure, but it wasn't likely he'd be as tall as Seth. Darker than his brother, hair and eyes almost black. Wiry-built.

Ten years, wasn't it, since their mother had passed. Poor orphans.

Paul's own children, Jack and Gwen, at his side in proper black. Gwen, 15, slim-framed, bright coppery hair half-hidden under her black beret, wept quietly, looking at the Greenlaw boys.

Jack, fair, stocky, middling in height and six months older than Seth Greenlaw, shifted uncomfortably on his feet. At that age, it was hard to face that nothing you could do would help.

Paul had stood firm that the Greenlaw boys not be taxed with hosting mourners after the funeral; they gathered at the Hardie home. Gwen had raided the larder, swiftly setting out a spread of ham, chicken, salads and bread she'd prepared the day before. Lobster, too, brought in from deep water in Paul Hardie's boats.

"Mr. Hardie? Could you give me a minute, sir?" Paul looked up into his young neighbor's dark blue eyes. Nodded, and led Seth into his study.

"Sit, Seth."

"I'm okay, thanks." The boy took a deep breath. "Before Dad died, he told me they'd be trying to take Ben away, put him in care. Is that right, will they do that?"

"I don't rightly know. They might. He's 12, and you're not out of high school 'til next month. They might think you're too young to be fit for his care."

"Can't let it happen, sir. It'd ruin his future, you know it would. Ben's so smart, they're saying brilliant. He needs his chance, and I've got to see he gets it."

Both knew the threat to brilliant, racing, unused minds in a slow country town. They had a good, a god-awful example already in Philip Cortwright, once thought to have a great future in something, anything, now Haven Point's saddest and angriest drunk. No money for college, no scholarships.

In his worst states, Philip might fling himself in attack upon slow-moving cars downtown.

It was as unthinkable to Paul Hardie that Ben Greenlaw follow that route as it was to Ben's brother.

"If they try, would you speak up for me? Mr. Gray's got a

job for me at the garage, I'm starting as soon as I graduate. I'll still train, give riding lessons, I can clear a few more acres and farm them. Ben'll help out. I can do it, Mr. Hardie. Would you tell them that, sir?"

"I'll do better than that. I'll tell them I'll keep an eye on the pair of you. I'll make it official, if I need to. We'll get Ben his chance. But—what about yours, boy? Hell of an undertaking, this."

Seth spread his hands, looked at them. The boy had good hands, no question—they could coax ancient farm equipment into working order, gentle-break almost any horse. And make that cheap second-hand guitar of his sit up and beg.

"I know that, sir. I'll wait a while for mine. I guess." Paul's heart ached. A man's determination in the thin young face; a boy's pain in the voice.

A quick knock on the door, and Gwen Hardie darted into the room. "Daddy, Seth, the Lords want to take leave, some others, too. You'd better come."

She turned to Seth, spoke his name, hugged him hard. Paul Hardie watched the boy's thin arms fold around her, head bending until his cheek rested on her hair.

"Come on, you two. Company's waiting." Gwen darted out again. Paul saw Seth's gaze follow her. *Oh, Lord.* If he yearned for Paul's sweet, pretty daughter, Seth Greenlaw would find himself with another bitter cup set on his table.

CHAPTER 2

Early August, 2 Years Later

Should he wake them? Paul Hardie wondered. The Greenlaw boys had become fixtures at the Hardie table since Paul had vouched, two-plus years back, for Seth's fitness for custody of his younger brother. That awful proceeding. People who neither knew nor cared deciding for people who did know and care.

Paul had overridden Seth's pride, asserting his own semi-official responsibility. Seth salved that pride with offerings of game and produce, which he brought to Gwen.

Gwen had cleared their places. Seth's head drooped first. There they were, both of them, heads on folded arms, fast asleep on the cherrywood table. Seth's breath was quiet and steady; Ben snored a little. Lines of exhaustion making old the young faces. Seth, his 20th birthday over two months away, looked closer to 40.

"Daddy." Gwen touched her father's hand. "I'll make up a couple of beds, they can sleep here, can't they? Please? I can't bear seeing them so tired."

Jack added his voice to Gwen's, and Paul assented, relieved. It wasn't much, but he could do that. "You're a good girl, Gwen." He stroked her shining red hair, so like Madeleine's.

Paul Hardie missed his wife. Filming on the other coast. Per usual.

He'd watched, and would continue watching, over the boys to the extent Seth allowed. Stubborner than any mule, that boy. Proud as Lucifer. And, yes, in love with Paul's Gwen, if you knew to look close. Gwen beamed at Seth with a sister's confiding love. She loved him better, Paul thought, than her real, blood-kin brother.

She'd smiled, too, though—shyly, diffidently—at Mark Sinclair this season; the Sinclairs didn't spend every summer in Haven Point. And the Sinclair boy had taken notice.

Paul sighed. Whatever he thought of, or felt for, Seth Greenlaw, no father could wish his daughter tied to waiting for a boy who looked in a fair way to working himself to death before he was thirty. Who'd be in no position to take a wife until near that age, if he didn't.

Mark Sinclair was another matter. The Sinclairs were solid, if not rich. There was a trust fund for the children, gossip had it; how much it was, or would amount to—stretched over three boys and two girls—Paul didn't know. Assuming there actually was a trust fund, that gossip hadn't got it wrong. But some money, certainly. And Mark, the middle son, seemed a nice young man—respectful, excellent manners, no apparent summer-people snobbery toward a local lobsterman's daughter.

Mark smiled back at Gwen, had begun to single her out, with all the propriety any father of a young girl could wish. And Gwen quietly but clearly adored him—Mark Sinclair was so blondly handsome, the surprising deep voice so smooth and mellow, his address to her so considerate.

It was early days, anyway, for Gwen, who was headed to Boston and college, in a few weeks. Jack was different, he wanted nothing but to follow in his father's footsteps. No college needed for that, and Jack had been C-average at best.

Paul was proud of his daughter's straight-A record, but she'd wept at the idea of leaving Haven Point. Paul was firm, and Madeleine Hardie had insisted one of her children, anyway, would take advantage of the college fund her film and television earnings had built.

But Paul knew his Gwen, and how little-focused any ambition she had really was. College would be for finding her focus, or at least a good husband, he hoped. She might even find a career that would bring her home, or a young man who had such a career himself, and wanted to live here with her. But that was so long a shot as not to be worth a penny-bet. Haven Point would lose his lovely girl, as it lost so many of its young people, for better, more varied opportunity elsewhere. And Paul could not wish otherwise, for her sake.

He heard Gwen's quick step on the massive, carved oak stair. That third step had a creak in it he'd never been able to fix.

Paul nodded to his son. Jack was tired, too. He was out before light in the boats, like Paul, and hadn't had the years of accustoming to the hours.

Ben woke easier than his brother, and Jack took him upstairs. Paul and Gwen, together, helped Seth, still half asleep or more, from the ancient table. Paul kept an arm around the boy as they navigated the stairs.

"Thanks, Mr. Hardie," Seth whispered.

"Gwen's idea."

"Gwen." He stumbled, would have fallen but for Paul's arm.

She'd made up one of the bedrooms in the original portion of the house. The furniture was of the same pre-Revolutionary period. Twin walnut-wood low beds, fresh sheets turned down.

Oil lamps converted to electricity, whitewashed plaster walls. Paul—and his daughter—loved the old rooms best.

Ben, already tucked in, slept soundly.

Seth sat on the empty bed; his head dropped toward his knees. Gwen knelt, unlacing and pulling off his boots, quickly, neatly. Paul got the boy into bed, pulled up the covers.

Gwen bent over Ben, kissing his cheek, patting his shoulder lightly. Turned, and sat down beside Seth. Smoothed the tangled hair, kissed his forehead tenderly.

"What can we do, Daddy? There must be something?"

"I don't know, Gwen. We'll do what we can, when we can— like this. But he's set on making his own way, and Ben's, too. You know him. Too proud for his own good."

Gwen's eyes filled with tears. "You'll see they're okay, won't you, Daddy? When I leave? No—I can't go! What will they eat, if I'm not here to cook for them? What will you and Jack eat, for that matter? Can't I stay? Please? I don't want to go away, I don't!"

"Now, Gwen. You know better than that. What would your mother say, if I said yes? Let them sleep, now. Time we were all in bed."

CHAPTER 3

Mid-August, 2 Years Later

Gwen Hardie, not quite 20, sat on the crazy-quilt covering the hand-hewn bed so many young Hardies had slept in, over the decades and centuries. Looked at her dress, laid out for tomorrow. Her mother's mother's mother's white lace, taken in to fit. The antique lace veil, so fine she could see the details of the wallpaper's faded roses through it. Tomorrow, her father would give her to Mark in church. She'd be happy forever. God willing, and the creek don't rise, she smiled to herself. But God would be willing, and the creek wouldn't rise.

She was so lucky. How many girls got to be Cinderella in real life? Not really 'Cinderella,' not the 'cinders' part. But, still, she'd gone off to the ball at the castle of college—Gwen had been allowed to skip Freshman Comp, having demonstrated sufficient writing skill; she'd got past her language (French), science (Chemistry), and math (Geometry—she liked the theorems and written proofs) requisites, and could concentrate on literature.

It was a blast. *Exciting.* She'd been a little scared of being 'found out'—found to be less intelligent than she'd thought.

What she'd found were professors delighted with her ideas— insights, they said.

Gwen had been so busy at first, with acclimating to dorm life—she still couldn't get used to the noise, but there were places she could find quiet, libraries, quiet corners on the campus—she hadn't been too disappointed when Mark Sinclair hadn't got in touch. She hadn't been certain he would.

Just before that first Thanksgiving, as she'd packed for her trip home, the knock on her door.

And wasn't he Prince Charming to the life? So romantically handsome, so graceful. And that beautiful voice.

"I said I'd call on you—did you not believe me? I thought you might need a little time to find your balance—a very different environment from what you're used to."

Gwen wasn't sure she'd found that balance; at that moment, wasn't sure she needed to. Mark was a lovely precipice. It might be sweet to fall.

He'd taken her to dinner at a good, unpretending restaurant, discussed her school reading list and books they'd read in common. Mark took her breath away—his understanding was so rapid—her own was quick, but not as his was. His ideas were akin to hers, but light years ahead. Or so she thought.

Mark's odd—to the world, but not to Gwen— uncompensated 'profession' was just another instance of his princeliness. He was on a quest, understanding was his grail. His dedication piqued her mind and touched her heart.

And it seemed she'd somehow touched his. They dated regularly after she returned, more frequently following Gwen's Christmas break. She fell; he caught her. Mark had spent the summer in Haven Point, spoken with Paul Hardie and, after agreeing to a year's engagement, proposed.

They still weren't lovers. Mark told her they should be circumspect; Gwen was very, very young. She might, he cautioned, change her mind. As if she *could.*

That, too, was romantic of him.

She had not changed her mind, nor he his, and tomorrow, the fairytale would come real.

Today, though—well, it wouldn't really *be* a proper day if she didn't spend at least a little time with Seth, who had not come to dinner. Ben had shown up, with Seth's apologies—he was 'working on' something, Ben said.

"What?" asked Gwen.

"That's all he told me."

The table had been almost full as it was; Paul and Madeleine Hardie, Jack, Gwen and Mark, her future in-laws, Margery and Charles Sinclair, and Ben. Gwen felt Seth's absence as a black hole.

Mark had kissed her goodnight, gone back with his parents to the house they'd rented for the summer. He made her feel as light, as shimmery, as perfect as a soap bubble—the ones in a plastic jar, that kids blew in summer. Gwen laughed aloud at herself—it was a ridiculous simile. But true.

Well. It wasn't very late—she could easily walk the couple of miles to the Greenlaw house, talk a while with Seth, and be back before midnight. She'd take Jack's creamy Lab, Buddy, and go straight through the woods. Perfect.

She changed her dress for her favorite old jeans and a sweater, laced up sturdy boots. Carefully took the stairs, making as little noise as she could manage.

Buddy came to her low whistle; she scratched the pale-furred head, clipped on his leash, and slipped out the kitchen door, across the field to the wood.

At its edge, Gwen looked back at the home she was

leaving—a leaving more final than for college alone. With all her heart, Gwen wished Mark wanted to move to Haven Point, live here year-round. At least, he'd promised to consider it, once she graduated.

The big, awkward house—misfit styles and periods in the newer wings pulling the old, four-square stone of the oldest building in conflicting directions. Hardie's Folly, they'd called it when that ill-advised patriarch, Martin Hardie, had built the larger, north-east wing, which threw the whole so off-kilter. Among other follies. How Gwen loved it. She still made her father repeat tales of its history over and over—not that he minded. Paul Hardie loved his home as much as his daughter did.

She ducked into the woods, switched on her flashlight. She didn't really need it, she could walk this stretch of wood blindfold. But better to use it. She'd prefer not to run into a coyote in the dark, especially tonight.

Old dead pine needles whispered beneath her feet, breathing a ghost of fragrance into the cool late-summer night. Tall pines and firs, mixed here and there with hardwoods, loomed and receded as she walked. An owl hooted, something scurried. The smell, the sounds of home. Buddy sniffed the air, too, looked up at her. Jack unclipped the leash for this walk. "Not tonight, Buddy, sorry." She'd never be able to find him if he ran off.

The wood opened to cleared Greenlaw land; the small woodframed farmhouse, paint peeling, roof drooping in at least three places Gwen could see, showed one light upstairs, one down. Closer, she heard the tuning of Seth's guitar; from the sound, he'd be on the back porch. She quickened her step, eager—she hadn't heard him play since she'd started college. Since before that.

Faltered, as the notes twanged out, almost angry. Stopped

dead as he sang into the night, low and bitter.

Singing a life of work and pain and dead dreams, no end in sight.

He sang on, grimmer, bleaker, the notes flowing in the dark like poisoned water. She couldn't bear it, called his name to stop the sound. It worked—voice and instrument went silent immediately. She rounded the corner, to the sagging porch, where Seth sat on the rough wood steps, cradling his guitar. A half-empty pint of cheap whiskey beside him. So that was what he'd been 'working on.' Why? Seth almost never drank, a beer or two with her father or Jack at most.

Or so it had been—Gwen realized she didn't know whether drink had become a habit with him. She didn't see enough of him anymore to know, although she came home every chance she got, and called Seth from Boston at least once a week. Gwen needed him as air to breathe, water to drink, as much as Jack, as much as her father, even. More—if she were truthful—than her mother, who might be home for Gwen's wedding, but would fly back to her television show as soon as Mark and Gwen left on honeymoon.

"Seth," she said again.

He stood up, carefully. "Shouldn't be here. Go home, Gwen." Words a little slurred.

"I walked all this way just to see you." She moved closer, reached out to touch his hand. Which he snatched away as if she'd burned him.

"Don't want you to. You don't want to. Go home."

"Seth, what's wrong? What is it? Please—tell me, I'll help any way I can."

He laughed; it was an unhappy sound. Shook his head. "Want to help me? Just—go home, Gwen. I'm drunk, I'm sorry, I'll be okay tomorrow. Just go, now, Gwen. Please." His voice broke on the last word.

She was stunned, didn't move. Seth shook his head again, impatiently, turned away from her, made for the house, guitar in hand. Turned back for the whiskey bottle, repeated, "Go home." Slammed the door behind him.

* * *

A fair, sunny day, and Paul's fair and sunny girl spoke her vows in response to those of her fair and sunny young man.

Sunlight through St. Aidan's dusty stained glass painted colored shapes on their faces. Father Trundy pronounced Gwen and Mark Sinclair man and wife, proscribed humanity from splitting them.

Mark kissed his radiant bride, exquisite in her white lace, Madeleine Hardie's pearl circlet (cultured, not real) holding her veil in place. Gwen looked exalted, angelic; Mark looked at her with profound tenderness and satisfaction.

She'd chosen well enough, Paul thought. He'd been concerned. Gwen was so young, Mark five years older. Madeleine had not been—as she pointed out, she'd been younger, herself, when she and Paul married, and Paul had been older than Mark was. Parents, he thought, were always protecting children from what they had done themselves.

Not that there was any use standing out against it. When Gwen set her heart on something . . . it would take a harder heart than Paul's to break hers.

He had asked her, seriously, about Mark, before giving his blessing. The two had dated, in a limited, casual way, in Haven Point, as early as the summer before Gwen went to college. Mark Sinclair had *seemed* very respectful, but had brought her home late more than a few times.

"Daddy, Mark doesn't treat me like a little girl. He treats me—like a person. A smart person. We talk about books. And films, and stuff. I've never had someone even close to my age I could do that with. He wants to know what I think about—art. Ideas, even.

"He thinks I have—that what I think is—worth *his* thinking about, worth talking about. I've really only ever had you and Mom to talk even just books with. And you don't read many of the same ones I do.

"Mom's worse. Trying to talk about books with her always feels like I'm taking an oral exam.

"But *Mark*, Daddy, it's exciting, talking with him. You know those times we got home a little late? You didn't believe me when I said we were talking and lost track of time, but that was what happened. I mean, we did kiss, but he never tried to go beyond that. And mostly, we really did just talk."

Paul believed her. Mark Sinclair, he had discovered, was both gentlemanly and genuinely eccentric. Not eccentric in his manner, certainly not in his looks or dress, but in his ambitions and intentions. He had graduated from Harvard two years ago, dissatisfied with the experience and determined to obtain a satisfactory education by reading and writing himself into an understanding of life he could live with. Gwen thought this madly noble, and perhaps it was.

An open-ended plan, which would manifestly provide no income for years, if ever; but the trust fund distributions (there really was one, set up initially by the Sinclair children's great grandfather, and growing in value) had kicked in three years back, when Mark turned 21.

Mark Sinclair had been frank—it would bring them some $30,000 or so annually. Little enough to live on in Boston, to be sure, but many couples started out with less, and Gwen had found work in the kitchen of a well-rated restaurant, working shifts around her classes. She was a prep cook now, but Paul thought her talent might earn promotion, when she could work full-time. Gwen showed off her new knife skills delightedly in the Hardie kitchen. When she came back to Haven Point, which she would do less often, in the future. Her home, now, would be with Mark in Boston, not in her father's house.

St. Aidan's parishioners (and many who were not) filed out of the church behind the young pair. Gathered again at the Hardie home. Gwen had wanted to cook, but Madeleine was right—it would be ridiculous for her to cater her own wedding. And Amy Mason, Haven Point's principal caterer—aside from the Haven Point Inn, which provided food and drink for any event held there—had prepared the good home-style cooking that had made her name.

Madeleine had ordered the cake from an excellent bakery two peninsulas to the east. The topper was well done—a small, delicate bride with flaming hair, a tall, slender blond groom, faces nicely detailed to suggest the new couple.

The guests fell on the food, and upon Gwen—every man present kissing the bride, from Peter Lord down to Ben Greenlaw. Paul didn't see Seth among them. No, Paul found Seth in his own study, otherwise empty of humans.

"Sorry, Mr. Hardie. I wanted—I needed . . ." *To be alone,* Paul thought. Seth had been looking better the past year. He'd got used to grueling hours of grueling work. No more growth spurts; he'd stopped at around 6'2". Hard muscle now wrapped the long, thin bones. But today, Seth looked sick—wax-pale, a trace of red around his eyes. Paul knew the signs. Hung over. Couldn't find it in his heart to blame the boy—who was not, really, a boy any longer.

He rested a hand on Seth's shoulder. "Let it go, son. Let her go."

Seth made a helpless gesture. "Oh, she's gone. I know that." Seth had suspected Paul Hardie knew how he felt about Gwen, though neither had spoken of it before this. Good of Mr. Hardie, really, not to have banned him from the Hardie house for it, Seth thought.

"Plenty of time to find a girl of your own, Seth."

"Not while she's alive." Quiet and final.

"Make an effort, son."

"Almost wish I wanted to."

He had to ask. "She doesn't know?"

Seth shook his head. "And she won't, if I can help it. My word on it." He got up, heavily. "I should congratulate the groom. Wish her all the happiness she deserves. That's what's done, isn't it?"

Seth found Mark Sinclair outside, looking off toward the woods that separated the Hardie and Greenlaw properties.

Kept his voice steady, as he said the proper words. And the improper ones he needed so badly to say. "Make her happy, treat her right. Or I'll kill you."

Sinclair seemed unfazed. And spoke gracefully. Seriously. "A sacred trust. I do know how *very* lucky I am."

That was fair enough. With effort, Seth took the hand Mark Sinclair extended.

He returned to the house. The next part would be harder.

Found Gwen—surrounded, of course, but she moved out of the crowd to meet him. Seth took her hands, carefully; they gripped his, tight and trusting.

"Be happy, Gwen. Be very happy." He bent to kiss her forehead.

"Thank you, dearest, *dearest* Seth! The whole world should be so happy!" She moved to hug him, but he stepped back, dropping her hands.

"You'll get makeup all over me." She always pressed her cheek against his chest when she put her arms around him—but rarely wore makeup. He was grateful for the excuse to avoid those encircling arms. "I'm going home now."

"Oh, don't! I haven't had a minute to talk with you, yet." Gwen protested, "We haven't even cut the cake!"

"Save a piece for me. Ben can bring it. Be happy," he repeated.

And left her troubled and wondering.

CHAPTER 4

Christmas-Time, One Year Later

Gwen was coming home for Christmas. Paul Hardie had extended an invitation to the elder Sinclairs—and their other children—to join them in Haven Point. There were enough bedrooms in the sprawling house for a real, old fashioned house party, and Paul would have welcomed a houseful of his daughter's in-laws. Mark's wife for a little over a year, now, Gwen was as radiantly happy as she'd been on their wedding day. They'd spent their first Christmas with Mark's family.

The Sinclairs wrote back, declining with thanks.

It was snowing lightly; Paul hoped Mark drove carefully. They should be here soon, any minute—starting half an hour ago. Madeleine Hardie moved, and moved back, an embroidered cushion on the ancient horsehair settee in the old parlor. Jack poked up the fire in the huge brick hearth, black with ineradicable layers of the soot of centuries.

The sound of a motor, and its shut-off. Light rushing feet on the front step, in the hall, Gwen crying, "Daddy! Merry Christmas!" as she flung herself into Paul's arms, red hair flying. "It's so good to be home!"

Mark, behind her, set down bags of presents, shook hands with Jack, and kissed the cheek offered by Madeleine, who beamed at him. She highly approved of her son-in-law's graceful manner and address. Mark shook his father-in-law's hand with both his own, when Gwen finally released Paul.

Gwen hugged her brother, kissed him. "It's so strange, not seeing Buddy by the fire. You doing alright?" Jack's cream Labrador retriever had died, old age, this past spring. Just in time for Jack's birthday. They'd both cried when he called Gwen to tell her.

"I'm okay." Basically.

She kissed her mother's cheek with more reserve than her husband had. "Merry Christmas, Mom." Paul sighed, inwardly. He wished Gwen might, someday, forgive her mother for so much absence from her daily life, for so much of that life.

"Where are Seth and Ben?" As she and Mark hung up coats, removed boots.

"They'll be here tomorrow night, for Christmas Eve and the Lords. And spend Christmas Day, or most of it," Jack told her.

"I never heard of such a thing." Gwen was at the telephone in a flash.

"It was very proper of them to give your family one night with you first," said Madeleine, who was less fond of the Greenlaws than the rest of the Hardies were.

"Nonsense, Mom. *They are* my family." Punched a number she didn't have to think about, one she knew in her fingers.

"Ben Greenlaw, I can't believe what I'm hearing! I could just weep! I haven't been home for nearly seven months, and two of my brothers can't be bothered to give me the time of day until tomorrow *night*? It's enough to break my heart! You go grab Seth, and get yourselves over here this minute, or I'll come and get you." She listened, laughing. "Okay, but not one second longer. I mean it."

"Ben says half an hour. *Then* we'll all be here." She curled up beside Mark on the settee. "*All* my family," kissing her husband's cheek, snuggling against him.

Paul smiled at his daughter. Gwen would be graduating in the spring, with a useless degree in English Literature and a full-time job at Farmhouse Table, which had just been awarded a Michelin star.

Marriage hadn't changed her, nor college, nor work, nor big-city Boston life. Not much, anyway—she was more confident, perhaps, since she'd found a potential career. Mark guarded her well, Paul thought, contentedly; Gwen remained unspoilt. *Untouched* whispered through his mind; he wondered why the word troubled him.

Getting fanciful in his old age, that was all it was. Paul Hardie had been 34 when he'd fallen, scandalously, in love with beautiful Madeleine Pelletier, then 18; to everyone's astonishment (none greater than Paul's), she had returned his love, and married him, washing scandal into respectability.

Star of the senior play, and already audiences rolled in the aisles. She'd easily gotten roles with the un- and very badly-paying local and regional theater groups. Had been 'discovered' by an agent on holiday, one summer.

That part had taken a decade; Gwen had turned six that September, as her mother screen-tested three thousand miles away. Most of the rest was well-known history, and for the 15 years since, Madeleine Hardie had been celebrated as one of the finest comediennes working, sitcoms to Shakespeare. More awards than Paul could count. He'd stopped attending the ceremonies, but he loved his wife dearly, and she him, as they always had.

Perhaps it was odd, but they'd made it work, as best they

could. Both had felt deeply that raising children was better done in Haven Point, Maine, than in Hollywood, California, and so they—Paul—had done. Madeleine's interviews were negotiated to preclude discussion of her private life, her family. She came home at every opportunity, telephoned at least three times each week while work kept her away.

"The tree looks beautiful, Daddy." Gwen broke into his reverie, and Paul shook himself back to the present. "I wish I'd been here to help trim." Balsam fir, standing twinkling with lights in the front window. Topped with the worn spangled felt and styrofoam angel Gwen had made in grade school, almost brushing the old ceiling beams. Hand-made and hand-me-down ornaments, decades and centuries of Hardie history, Hardie tradition. Gwen set swaying with her fingers the newer, intricate silver-wire shapes Ben Greenlaw made for friends and neighbors—and, more recently, for sale. Seven of them, one each year since he'd begun. Only ten, he'd been, with hands as clever as his brother's. At different things.

"Mom. Did you get everything on my list? From the right places? Or do I need to run around tomorrow to fill in?" Without waiting for an answer, Gwen went to check the larder.

Spun right round at the sound of Seth's pickup. Such a happy smile, Paul thought. Running to the door, throwing it open -

"*Seth*, Ben! *Now* it's *really* Christmas."

* * *

"And I didn't tell you the best part! I've been staging for Gail, so I'll be ready to hit the ground running, come June, and she told me yesterday Henry's leaving Farmhouse Table—isn't the name great—to open his own restaurant. He's been her sous for years and years, and she talked him into staying on 'til I graduate, and then *I'll* be her sous chef—can you believe it? I can't, I keep pinching myself." Gwen laughed happily.

"I told you, darling, Gail Winthrop's not a fool. Perhaps she ought to clone you, you'd be an adorable hostess, as well as a splendid sous chef," Mark teased his wife, smiling with pride.

"What about your work, Mark?" asked Madeleine. "What are you reading now?"

"Matthew Arnold. I rather liked 'Culture and Anarchy.' I can't quite get on board with his idea that being good makes one happy, and that this proves God exists. I've seen too many good people unhappy, for one thing. But I do believe it is better to consider carefully before taking action—which is what the argument of 'Culture and Anarchy' boils down to, roughly speaking."

"Sounds like sense to me," Seth agreed.

Paul had hoped he'd see Seth finally past caring for Gwen— at least, in the way that could bring him nothing but unhappiness.

For almost five minutes, Paul had thought perhaps he *was* past it. Seth had smiled, hugged Gwen close, looked at her exactly as he ought to, and appeared to be in good spirits. It had been a better than decent year for him. Relatively speaking, of course. Seth had turned a corner, working smarter, though still far too hard. He'd set himself to the math (not his best subject), had figured out that the job at Jake Gray's garage took too much time for the money it paid.

He had 'considered carefully,' as Mark put it, and given notice. Set up on his own, on his land, with his old tools and a shed and, although he had no mechanic's license yet, made three times the money in half the time. Jake Gray hadn't been pleased when his best mechanic had quit to set up his own shop, but he understood the need for more money. Almost every year-round resident of Haven Point understood that.

Horses were becoming popular among the summer people. Seth Greenlaw, reputed to have the best hands in three counties, had had as many of them to train this past summer as he could handle. Group riding lessons had mostly replaced individual sessions, bringing in more money. If he'd had a decent barn, Seth could have boarded those summer-horses for the winter—precious income in Maine's hardest season. He was setting aside what little he could, what wasn't earmarked for Ben's college fund, which would be needed all too soon, to repair and extend the one he had.

Seth had grown into himself, over the past couple of years. The off-beat features were now coherent and arresting; the long, wide dark blue eyes held a hard glint, faintly amused. Paul had seen high-school girls giggling—and not the way girls did in mockery. Seth would always be very lean, but he'd added a bit more muscle. He was, quietly, confident. He had taken on what should have been an impossible battle. And he was winning.

After initial greetings and hugs, Gwen had looked up at Seth. "You're such a grownup, now, Seth. And so handsome. I feel a little shy of you." Which she'd immediately given the lie to by hugging him again. And Paul saw the faint flicker that shut Seth's face for an instant. No-one who didn't know and care would have caught it. Gwen cared, of course, but she did not know. Paul knew, though, and he, too, cared.

Seth had rejoined, "*You* haven't changed any. Maybe you're a mite sillier."

Gwen, drawing herself up to her full 5'4" in mock hauteur, replied, "I beg your pardon. I have always been *exactly* this silly." He'd laughed, so had everyone, and ruffled the red waves of her hair. "Don't!" she protested, laughing back at him.

Ah, God, what life was. *And what fools it makes of us*, Paul thought.

Madeleine had gone up to bed, citing "beauty sleep." She had no cause, Paul thought, to worry, she was still so beautiful, taller and much more poised, more elegant than her girlish daughter.

Mark, too, retired to read. Seth said he and Ben should be going.

"Why don't you two spend the night?" Gwen asked Seth. "We could walk over in the morning, and I'll help with morning stables, I'm dying to see your new stock. Maybe we could even ride, after? If you can spare the time," she added, a little wistfully. "It seems you're always so busy when I come home, I hardly see you."

"Not much going this time of year, Gwen." He should say no. He couldn't. "Ben? Want to stay? If it's no bother," turning to Paul.

"Always welcome here, you know that, Seth."

Ben shrugged assent. Gwen hugged Paul, whispering, "Thank you, Daddy," and ran upstairs to make their beds.

Seth smiled wryly at Paul. "Just like the bad old days."

Gwen soon returned. "Same room as you used to have. I've put out fresh toothbrushes and towels in the bathroom."

Ben, tired and a little bored, went up to bed. Gwen kissed her father and Seth, and she too, went up to join her husband. Out of the corner of his eye, Paul saw again that tiny flicker in Seth's face.

"Come out with me a bit," he said. "I want a pipe, and Madeleine hates the smell. Can't smoke in the house when she's here."

The two men shrugged into coats—Paul's new parka, the

old airman's jacket Melody Gray, Jake and Ann Gray's younger girl, had picked up at St. Aidan's annual church fair and saved for their neighbor. Lined with sheepskin—slightly stiff with age, but warm. It fit well enough.

The snow had stopped hours back; the night air was clean and frosty. Paul packed his pipe, lit it. Seth looked up into star-spangled black.

"Look out for yourself, son. I'd hate to see you hurt worse."

"How'm I supposed to say no to her? When she looks at me like that."

"She does love you."

"Best thing in my life."

"Timing . . . if things were different . . ."

"They're not. I won't trouble her happiness, Mr. Hardie."

"Isn't it about time you called me Paul, son?"

* * *

Paul was an early riser, his work demanded it. But Christmas Eve morning he found his daughter and Seth Greenlaw already over coffee in the big, old kitchen. One or both had lit the fire in the old hearth; it crackled merrily.

Consciously or otherwise, Gwen's clothes echoed Seth's—worn jeans, heavy white wool sweaters with fraying cuffs, sturdy, laced-up boots. Paul remembered that old sweater of Gwen's; she'd left it behind when she went off to college. And marriage. He wondered where she'd found it. Got himself coffee. Gwen's was so much better than his own. Or Madeleine's.

"How soon do you plan to start out?"

"No rush," Seth responded. "They'll keep another couple of hours." It wasn't full light, yet.

"Are you sure?" Gwen asked. "Then I could make everybody breakfast—we'll walk and work and ride it off, after all."

Two men who'd been eating their own cooking after being used to Gwen's were not about to object.

Gwen stripped off her sweater. Found an apron. Gathered eggs, buttermilk, bacon, sausage, cream cheese, butter, herbs from the refrigerator. Stuck two more sticks of butter in the freezer, prowled for flour and baking powder, murmuring, "At least she got the list okay." Lit the oven to preheat for bacon and biscuits. Put cast-iron skillets over flames, one low, one medium-hot. Crumbled sausage into the hotter pan, stirred vigorously as it browned, and drained it, reserving the grease. She spread slices of bacon on a rack, lined a sheet pan with foil to catch the drippings, slid it all into the hot oven, and began her biscuits.

Tempting smells wafted upstairs, wakened sleepers, and soon the chairs around the big, round old oaken table were filled with hungry expectation. Paul and Seth had laid the table; Jack, the next to come down, had, under Gwen's orders, squeezed oranges into a cold pitcher. Gwen had put on another pot of coffee, and a third.

"Mark, Seth, can you give me a hand with these?" And Paul, with a mixture of mild amusement and mild alarm, watched the two men who loved his daughter help her set out the skillet of eggs, scrambled with cream cheese and sprinkled with chives, plates of bacon and hot biscuits, a big boat of sausage gravy.

"Help yourselves. Mom, you did okay on getting the right things. Thanks."

Plates filled rapidly. Ben, forgetting Gwen's one rule, reached for salt and pepper. Gwen, a little sharply, said "It's seasoned. Taste first."

"You don't *know* how good this tastes, Gwen," Seth

murmured.

"It's just breakfast, but thanks. At least, it's mostly local stuff."

Seth turned to Mark Sinclair. "Gwen's going to walk over with me, help with stables. I don't guess you'd have any interest in that, but we'll take out a couple of horses for a bit, after. If you want a ride."

Paul saw Gwen look up, puzzled. Maybe faintly disappointed. But her face cleared, and she said, "Sure, Mark— you used to like riding. Come along, it'll be fun."

Mark smiled, "Thanks for the offer, Seth, it's very good of you. But I seem to have dreamed up an idea or two in the night, and I want to get them written while they're fresh."

"You change your mind, call. I'll check messages before we go out. We'll wait."

"If I do, I will. Thanks again. Wrap up warmly, darling."

Mark and Paul walked out with Gwen and Seth, watched them cover the snow-dusted distance toward the wood.

"Am I a fool? Or a fraud? I'd rather not be a farce." As his father-in-law turned, Mark, who had not realized he'd spoken aloud, said, "An impressive young man."

"He is that."

"She speaks of him a great deal. There's a very strong bond, there." *You have no idea*, thought Paul.

But, "How long have you known he's in love with her?" Mark continued, and Paul gaped at his son-in-law. Could think of no better response than "How long have you?"

"Since the day I married her. Something he said, that any devoted brother might have said. But I knew, then. Your turn."

"Longer than that. I saw it the day we buried his father. He was 17. I don't know when it started."

"Was it a mistake, marrying her so young? She *is* very

young, younger than her age, in some ways. *Can* she have known what she really wanted? Does she know now?"

Paul had no answer for him.

"My great passion, Paul, is for understanding. For my work, if I may call this possibly—probably—frivolous pursuit of mine work. There may be a book, or books to be got out of it. I hope so, but I can't be sure yet. It's disappointed my parents, and I'm sorry for that, but I don't feel I have a choice.

"I do love Gwen, *very* much. She's—*conjured*—a love out of me, with her own, that I thought I would—could—never feel. But she's not my greatest passion. I've taken care of her, kept her happy, I think you'd agree. And I'll go on doing so, and be grateful to do it.

"I *would* rather not be a farce, though. And it would be farcical if a man whose great passion is for understanding didn't recognize an equally great passion for his own wife in another man. If Gwen made a wrong choice, if she'd be happier, her life richer, having something I can't give her, she must have the chance to find it out."

He turned and went into the house. Paul looked after him. Gwen said, always, that Mark was noble. If the man she regarded as her favorite brother was impressive, so, too, was the man she'd married.

In fact, Paul realized with astonishment, the two had more than a little in common. You would not think it, to look at them, the one so Boston-polished, the other Haven-Point-local rough. Yet it was true. Both were observing, both quiet. Intelligence, certainly, both had, though Seth's was unrelated to book learning. And Seth, too, was an *understanding* man. In very different ways, of very different things. Both were aware of life's irony.

And both, young as they were, were men, doors shut on

boyhood. His own son, Jack, older than Seth by some months, was a boy still. A good boy, a responsible, hardworking boy, and clever enough where he needed to be. But a boy. Had Paul over-protected, over-sheltered his almost—effectively—motherless children?

He didn't know. He'd done the best he could.

* * *

Jack Hardie would have found that question puzzling, if anyone had asked him. How could they be over-sheltered when they'd run wild all their childhood?

It had ceased to puzzle him that he felt more like Gwen's younger brother than her elder. That had solidified long since. Before he'd reached the age of twelve.

Hanging with Seth Greenlaw meant playing "follow the leader;" whether this derived from any need of Seth's to lead or inclination of his own to take a back seat, Jack couldn't have said.

By the summer Gwen was eight, she was first to follow where Seth led. Sometimes darting ahead, once the path was set. Much the fastest of them over the rocks along the coast, sure-footed and fearless. Turning back to laugh at her slower brothers.

Strong personalities, strong wills, both of them, and a few clashes. Mostly over Gwen's discounting of hazard. But nothing shook the love and trust between them.

People assumed Jack and Seth, born not quite six months apart, in school together year on year, were best friends who let younger siblings tag along. That wasn't how it was.

It hadn't bothered Jack. Not much, anyway. Things were how they were, and he accepted that.

He loved them both.

* * *

"She's a real beauty, Seth. Can I ride her, when we go out? What's her name?" Gwen stroked the almost pink-and-white muzzle; the horse nuzzled her. *Pretty redheads*, Seth thought.

Shooing Gwen away from the stall door, Seth replied, "Her name's Belle—it does fit, doesn't it?" He scratched Belle's forehead. "She'll do for you." He let the three-year-old strawberry roan out into the field he'd fenced around his barn. She was one of the two newest of the six horses Seth now owned. Two sorrel and two chestnut mares, and the new ones— Belle and the blood bay stallion. Several of the summer people he'd trained for had asked whether he'd considered breeding for sale, and Seth was considering it.

He'd start repairing the barn as early, come spring, as he could. Fix the stalls which were unusable, add onto the barn and build more. Boarding horses for winter would boost income. And he'd breed Minister (Seth didn't like the name, but he did like the horse, who was as beautiful an animal as Belle) with his mares. See what happened. If people he trusted enough wanted the foals, he'd sell them. As semi-trained yearlings, or fully trained and ready to ride by three or four, not any raw weanlings. Which would bring their price up nicely.

The horses had had fresh water and buckets of grain and nuts before he'd let them out. Now, Seth shoveled, and Gwen went behind him, sweeping out. Good fertilizer for his crops. Armfuls of fresh hay went into haynets. Water buckets were refilled.

He brought bags of sawdust and wood chips. Gwen joined him, kicking it round the stalls.

"Want coffee? I should see if Mark called."

Gwen insisted on making the coffee. "How come it's better when you make it? It's the same pot, same coffee, same water."

"Simple. I bet you measure what it says on the can. Double it," Gwen grinned at him, and Seth smiled back.

Mark had not called.

Alone in the house with her. He should have told her no. He wanted—so much it hurt—to kiss her, open her mouth, put his hands into that pretty hair, put his hands under her clothes, make love to her. Seth had longed for Gwen, and not in celibacy. He knew what he wanted from her, with her. Knowledge, the Bible called it, and that was right. He wanted *that knowledge* of Gwen. He did not imagine what it would be like with her; he wanted to *know.* Making up some story about it would be like accepting that he'd never know her, never have her. And he didn't accept that, not as final. Life took funny bounces.

But it wouldn't be now. She was happy with Sinclair. She trusted Seth—he *would not* see his betrayal of that trust in her eyes. Or Paul Hardie's. Fine payment for his kindness that'd be.

"Seth? Can we saddle up? I swear, since you said yes, I've been doing happy dances inside."

"Sure. Get your coat on."

As she zipped her parka, "*Thank you*, Seth. You do *not* know how much I've missed you, since I went to Boston."

They walked out toward the barn. "I've missed Haven Point *al*together. Life's just not the same, there."

"I *said* you were getting sillier. What did you expect?"

"I don't know. I mean, it's wonderful, of course, all the museums, the restaurants, the stores. Seems like hundreds of movies. Mark likes the libraries. I wish I could spend more time in them—they're quiet." Gwen shrugged, "I just—get homesick for going outside barefoot, walking in the woods, climbing down the rocks to that cove over up northeast—remember? I miss *grass.* I miss snow that isn't black in a *day.*"

He'd feel pretty much the same, in Boston. In any city. Seth saddled Belle for her, put his own saddle on Minister. That horse needed hard exercise. Seth could use some, himself, just now.

Gwen had used the mounting block while he'd saddled up, and sat astride Belle. He glanced over her gear. "Let me shorten those stirrups."

When he'd done that, and double-checked the girths, snugging one a bit, Seth swung easy onto Minister's back. Gwen leaned forward on Belle's neck, cooed into her ear.

"Come on, pretty girl, show me what you've got." Glancing sidelong at Seth, mischief and delight, she kicked Belle's flanks and flashed away. Wind in her hair. Trailing notes of laughter.

Jesus Christ. At that moment, Seth Greenlaw hated his Maker blackly.

He kicked his own mount, and followed her. Not too close.

* * *

The old parlor was warm with woodfire, warm with Christmas-cheery company. Warm with the bourbon glow of excellent eggnog in glass cups. Warm with pleasant memories of roast pheasant, shot by Seth Greenlaw, cooked by Gwen Sinclair.

Firelight danced over the walls and ceilings, the twinkling tree, hair and faces.

There could be little question that Julia Lord and Madeleine Hardie were the most beautiful women 'of a certain age'—of any age (since Elizabeth Lord was so rarely in Haven Point, and so briefly when she was)—Haven Point boasted. Julia Lord's elegant bones would keep her beautiful to the day she died. Her fine, dark hair, threaded with undisguised silver, was knotted in an intricate twist at the nape of her long neck. She was around Paul Hardie's age; Peter Lord, her husband, was tall and spare, greyer than his wife and a decade her senior.

Contrary to the general way of summer people, the Lords either stayed or re-opened their house for the winter holidays. Holiday visits among the Van Leyden, Hardie, and Gray families were a tradition over 200 years old, with the Van Leyden New Year's Eve gathering the high point and close. Peter Lord had married into the Van Leydens with his eyes open. One got with the program fast, if one were wise.

"I'm afraid Liz may not be here at all," Julia Lord was saying. "They say all flights out of Chicago will be grounded for at least Christmas morning, possibly all day. And she was off to New York on Boxing Day, as it was. It's too sad."

Everyone in the room thought of a flight in nasty weather, years back, and the crash that had killed young Geoffrey Lord.

"Liz has been so nice to me, since I've been in Boston," Gwen broke the brief silence. "I think she might have put in a word with Gail Winthrop, when I applied. Do you know if she did? I'd like to thank her, but I don't want to put her on the spot if I'm wrong."

"I don't know," Julia responded, smiling, "but she might have. Shall I see if I can find out? I know she's fond of you. She's a good girl."

Julia either did not see, or ignored, the carefully un-met eyes, the ever-so-slightly raised eyebrows of those around her except Gwen, who smiled back. Elizabeth Lord was brilliant, daring, and a notorious rake. Her exploits had been gossip-fodder since she tossed away her virginity at age 14 like last year's math workbook.

Liz had kept her activities low-key in Haven Point (the men were very slim pickings, to her mind), but stories traveled from Boston, and she'd been reported on in the tabloids regularly for years. Liz loved it—it would be pre-made publicity, when she was ready to use it. Her mother did not stoop to recognize that such publications existed.

The idea of her being 'a good girl' would have sent Liz into fits of laughter. Gwen knew; it was an alien mindset to her, but it wasn't her business, and she liked Liz Lord.

Time for presents—one each tonight. Of course, the Lords' gifts were to be opened. Gwen handed presents around. "Would anybody mind if I open two? I've been staring at this one all day."

'This one' was a white package, stenciled with sparkling interlocking stars of purple, green, red. Tied with green twine, a 'bow' of fresh balsam cones—that lovely blue-purple—and holly leaves. A little tag read 'Gwen,' and she knew Greenlaw handiwork when she saw it. Ben's stencils (how that boy loved sparkle). Wildwood, hedgerow things—those were Seth.

Nobody minded.

The Lords had brought Paul and Madeleine several professionally enlarged old photos. Julia had come across the originals in a box she'd brought down from the attic to sort through. From the Hardies' wedding, 25 years ago, framed in chased silver.

For the rest of the company, whom Julia and Peter Lord thought of as 'the young people,' the gifts were nothing like so personal—cashmere caps and scarves. Red with white snowflakes for Jack, black with white starbursts for Ben. Soft solid blue-gray for Mark, deep solid blue-green for Seth. Gwen's were periwinkle blue veering to lavender—the color of her eyes, and her mother's. Gwen's eyes had little starbursts of green around the pupils, and green swirls decorated her cap and scarf.

The Lords opened an old volume of William James and antique pearl earrings from the Hardies, Christmas ornaments—Ben's odd silver spiral, intricate and compelling, Seth's carved reindeer—from the Greenlaws, an elegant leather wallet and a pretty silk scarf from Mark and Gwen.

Proper and decorous 'thank yous.'

"That's pretty, Seth, I didn't know you were making ornaments, too," said Gwen.

"There's one on the tree." He'd made the two, and no more.

Gwen, jumped up, exclaiming, "I can't believe I didn't see it," and examined the tree. "Oh, it's not my fault, you hid it all the way back. Why would you do a thing like that?" She brought the little reindeer to a place of greater prominence. "That's more like it. Thank you, Seth. It's lovely."

Gwen turned to her second present and began to open the white package, carefully keeping the 'bow' intact. Mark offered her his penknife to cut through tape, but Gwen knew there was none—the paper was carefully folded, tightly—perfectly—wrapped and tied, without tape.

A black walnut box. A tiny brass key in a tiny keyhole in the wood; impossibly fine little brass hinges. The wood had been oiled and rubbed, over and over, again and again, to glass-sheen. Inside were compartments, hinged lids of the same shining rubbed wood. Ben had made the lock, key and hinges in metal shop. The lock had been fun to design.

Seth had made the box, rubbed up the wood. Hours upon hours upon hours. Paul thought—*that's the real gift. Time stolen, sleep robbed.*

Gwen, head bent toward her box, stroked it delicately with her fingertips. "It's so beautiful. I can't believe you two made this for me. It's wonderful, I love it. Thank you. So much. It's just so—it's beautiful." Her voice was soft.

"For jewelry," Ben said. "Merry Christmas," said Seth.

"We must get you more jewelry, Gwen, to put into it," Mark interjected. "Very fine work," directed toward Seth and Ben.

Julia Lord removed her earrings, held them out to Gwen— "Won't you take these as a start? To christen that lovely box. Liz gave them to me, and they really aren't at all my style. I'm only wearing them because she isn't with us."

Gwen demurred. "That's very kind of you, but wouldn't her feelings be hurt if you gave them away?"

"Oh, I think when she sees you wear them she won't mind a bit. They'll be charming on you. Much more suitable."

Julia Lord's powers of persuasion were more than a match for Gwen's powers of resistance.

The earrings were posts, delicate clusters of carved jade leaves with tiny pearls. "Mistletoe!" Gwen exclaimed, "How adorable is that?" She put them into her earlobes. The green of the jade made the green in her lavender-blue eyes startling and bright.

"You see?" smiled Julia Lord.

"Well, I don't. But I want to." Gwen rose to find a mirror; Julia offered one from her purse.

Gwen inspected. "I love them. Thank you, Mrs. Lord. And please thank Liz for me, if you tell her."

"But they're for this." She removed the earrings. Brought the box toward her. Paul noted her tender handling. Gwen opened the lid, gently, and a smaller lid inside. Set the earrings carefully in the compartment, lined with a scrap of velvet. With care, she closed the inner lid, the outer, fingertips caressing the wood.

A little more eggnog? Perhaps unwise, but no-one declined.

Conversation slowed, but there was no awkwardness in the silences.

Eventually, Peter Lord held his wife's coat for her, and they said goodbyes and Merry Christmases. Handshakes, embraces.

"Seth, would you come and see me this week?" asked Peter Lord, "I think we may reopen our stables, this spring or perhaps the next, and I want your opinion on one or two points. The morning of the 27th? What time would be convenient?"

"Sure. Any time. I don't have anything much going on just now."

They settled on 10:00. And the Lords left.

"Time we went, too, Ben." Gwen, as she had the night before, urged them to stay, but Seth declined, and was adamant.

"Are you all right to drive?" asked Paul.

"We'll walk, if you don't mind the truck staying."

"I'll put it in the garage; they're saying clear, but it looks like snow to me."

"I can do that."

"No need. I'll take care of it."

Gwen kissed Ben's cheek, thanking him again. Did the same with Seth, whispering, "It's the loveliest thing I ever saw, the shine on that beautiful wood, but it must have taken forever. You shouldn't have. *Please* take care of yourself."

"Merry Christmas, Gwen," and his lips light on her cheekbone, were all the reply she got.

Seth and Ben set off toward home, and the Hardies and Sinclairs, Gwen putting leftover eggnog into the refrigerator and Paul garaging Seth's pickup, left further clean-up for the morning and went to bed.

* * *

Christmas Day was a leisurely one for almost everyone but Gwen, who spent much of it in the kitchen.

Paul had been right; the ground was white with a thin blanket of snow when the house began to wake. Trees sparkled icily in thin morning rays.

Seth and Ben Greenlaw arrived in time for breakfast, though less early than Gwen would have liked; after the dishes were cleared, everyone opened presents.

Despite Madeleine's mild disapproval, Paul had bought guitars—decent ones—for both Seth and Jack, whom Seth had taught to play years ago. Jack had never been remarkable on the instrument, would certainly never play as well as Seth, but he was passable, and enjoyed playing.

Seth flushed, said Paul shouldn't have, he couldn't accept it.

"Don't do that, son," said Paul, "indulge me—it's Christmas."

"I'd love to hear some Christmas music," said Gwen.

So, Seth took up the guitar, and he and Jack, having tuned up, picked out a few carols. Gwen asked for "The Holly and the Ivy."

The solid wood resonance was downright luxurious in Seth's ears, in his hands; Paul noted his small, private smile with pleasure.

Mark had got Gwen a gold pendant on a chain—a flat disk, asymmetrically studded with small rough-cut amethysts and one larger emerald, with earrings to match.

"Oh, Mark! They're gorgeous! Thank you, darling." She tried them on, took them off again. "I'll just run upstairs and put them in my box." Gwen smiled at Seth and Ben.

Seth picked up her present to him while she was gone. Six record albums—she'd remembered to get vinyl, not CDs. All wrapped together in shiny green with red curled ribbon; underneath each was wrapped individually in alternating gold and silver tissue. A single artist, and one whose work spoke to Seth; he'd had one or two CDs, but the player he'd had died.

It hadn't been replaced until Ben built them a sound system this past spring and summer out of bits and pieces he picked up at yard sales and tinkered magically with. Seth had cut a base for the workings of an old turntable. When Ben was done, the result was ugly to look at, but produced better sound than many summer people could boast.

Seth looked at the titles, and the songs. Missing was one of the CDs he'd had. That album had the song he'd been playing— to, for himself, he'd thought—the night before Gwen married Mark Sinclair. Did she remember? Was that particular album left out on purpose or by coincidence?

He picked up his new guitar on impulse as Gwen appeared in the doorway, stopping as she saw the records around him. Seth looked the question at her, played the opening notes. She flinched, sharply, visibly; he stopped. She remembered. And it still troubled her.

"These are great, Gwen. Thanks."

"Merry Christmas, Seth. Play one of the happy—happier— ones for me, sometime." Very soft.

Gwen, Paul and Jack brought dinner to the table—a big standing rib-roast, well crusted and smelling irresistible. Little Yorkshire puddings, a huge bowl of mashed potatoes, horseradish cream, caramelized brussels sprouts. Paul ceremoniously carved the meat, asked the blessing, and everyone dug in. No-one made the mistake of salting before tasting.

"*What* do you put in these?" Mark asked, gesturing with a forkful of potatoes. "I've never had mashed potatoes like

Gwen's," to the rest. "But she always says she'll never tell," and—

"I'll never tell," came out at the same time, Mark and Gwen both laughing.

"It's just six ingredients, if you don't count the water for boiling. And if you can't figure out six ingredients, that's not my fault."

"Potatoes, garlic, salt, butter, sour cream. No milk, right? I assume everyone knows those are chives," said Ben suddenly.

"Gold star for you, Ben," Gwen smiled, reaching to clink her wine glass to his. "Dead on. You're the first to even figure out I don't use milk."

She'd baked three pies—cranberry maple walnut, mincemeat (she'd been aging it in her fridge in Boston, and brought it with her), and sweet potato.

There wasn't a scrap of crust left when they were done.

Madeleine rose. "You sit, Gwen. Jack, help me clear." To Gwen again, "You're done for the day."

"About time somebody pitched in," Gwen said. "I've been working my rear end off."

"Now, Gwen," said Mark, "you know you hate anyone in your kitchen while you're cooking," and—

"That isn't fair, dear—I offered to help more than once," said Madeleine.

"Quality control, Mom. I'll leave acting to you, you leave cooking to me. I *know* how you cook."

The company moved to the parlor. When Jack and Madeleine had put the dishes to soak, Madeleine brought the leftover Christmas Eve eggnog, and everyone had half a cup to finish it off, except Gwen, who stuck with the wine in her glass. She was very tired, now that Christmas was all but over.

Tomorrow would begin the inevitable downturn in spirits.

New Year's would pick things up for a day, but, Gwen thought, to heck with 'seasonal affective disorder,' Lucy Van Pelt from 'Peanuts' had it right—what it was, was 'post-Christmas let-down.'

Still, it would be a let-down from a very high high. She hadn't been so happy, so deeply *content*, in quite some time. Everyone, all her family, all those she loved, all together. And she was home.

Tired or not, Gwen didn't want the day to end.

* * *

December 26, Boxing Day, was quiet for almost everyone. The Hardies, Lords, Grays, and quite a few other families took Christmas leftovers to St. Aidan's food pantry. This, too, was a long-standing Haven Point tradition.

Gwen walked over and rode with Seth again; Ben was upstairs, studying. The horses were saddled when she got there, and Seth didn't invite her into the house afterward.

Ben planned to take as many advanced placement tests as he was allowed. In his mind, the benefit would be two-fold. He'd be less bored when he finally got to college—with mathematics classes and labs on material he'd already mastered and beyond—Ben had been picking up second-hand college math textbooks at yard sales since he was 10. With other subjects in which he had little interest. And credits built up beforehand would reduce the number of credits to be paid for, and therefore the burden he was on his brother.

Ben helped Seth as much as he could, mostly with the farming –they grew produce for their table, and for sale at the local farmer's market in summer months. He manned the market table, bored right out of boredom into distraction that segued into near-fury. He'd designed and put together a drip irrigation system, which saved a surprising amount of time. Ben felt, keenly, what his brother had sacrificed, was sacrificing, for his future. And that future was going to pay Seth back, with a truckload of interest. As soon as he could work it. Seth wasn't the only proud Greenlaw.

Paul and Madeleine sat together on the comfortable old living room couch (this room was in the first wing added to the old house), watching old Christmas films, warm and contented.

Jack took a long, solitary walk, missing Buddy at his side. Wondered whether it was time to get another dog. Decided it wasn't—he still missed Buddy too much, might not be fair to a new puppy.

Mark Sinclair read, wrote. And thought, also, about things he had not read and did not write about.

* * *

On the 27th, Mark and Gwen drove off back to Boston, early. Gwen had to be back at work that afternoon, to prep for the dinner shift.

Seth and Ben were there to see them off. Both shook hands with Mark, who turned then to his in-laws.

Gwen said, "It's been so good to spend time with you. Both," as her gaze flicked across to include Ben. "You don't know how much I miss you." *Don't I?*

"I'll call you. And you call me, once in a while, please? You, too, Ben, I want to hear whatever crazy thing you're making." She kissed Seth's cheek, up on tiptoe. "Take care of yourself. Please do that."

"You, too, Gwen."

Ben said, "Be good." She laughed a little, kissed him, too.

"When do you fly back, Mom?"

"Early tomorrow afternoon, I'm afraid. I'll have to miss the Lords on New Year's Eve."

"I'm sorry. Take care, Mom." Gwen kissed her mother's cheek, told her brother to take care of their father, hugged and kissed him.

"Daddy." She held her father close, whispered, "I wish we could live here, with you. All my family. This felt so good."

"I miss you, too, Gwen, dear. It was a good Christmas." Paul's eyes misted. "Drive safely, Mark."

"I will. Gwen?"

"I'm coming." They got into the car; Gwen looked out the window, blew her family a kiss. "Let's go, or I'll start crying."

* * *

Later that morning, Seth Greenlaw kept his appointment with Peter Lord; gave suggestions on expanding the narrow old stalls, efficient set-ups for tack and feed rooms (his barn was not so set up, but would be when he'd finished work on it), corral and paddock placement and fencing. Offered the names of several breeders and dealers he'd found reliable.

Peter asked what his fee was for the consultation.

"I don't take money for talking with a neighbor," Seth said. And would not budge.

* * *

Mark and Gwen Sinclair drove south and west, in silence. Both were thinking of Seth Greenlaw.

Gwen's heart ached. What was it, that haunted and hurt him? Had these years of grinding work marked him with that sadness? God knew, it might be enough. She thought there was something else, though. Hoped so, because then it might be fixable. If he'd just—let her in. The way he used to.

Mark's questions had no resolution. But he'd seen enough to wonder with greater concern.

He'd made love to Gwen, testing. She, and the act, had been as ever—sweet, lovingly responsive, very tender. She came with him, as she always did; he felt the gentle waves of her pleasure, the breath of her soft sigh.

But—the speaking glances she directed at Seth Greenlaw. Whispering to him, intimate. A meaning between them he couldn't have known was in those record albums she'd hunted down.

He couldn't remember much about the song that had caught her, coming from the radio. The same artist as the albums— Mark had recognized the sound, the voice, when she played a few songs on her computer.

He'd been reading. But the power in that song had drawn his attention—and Gwen, transfixed and white as she listened, had held it. It had been a disquieting—a disturbing—song. She'd written something on a piece of paper.

Smiled at him, tucking the paper into her pocket.

She never spoke of it. Gwen didn't keep secrets from him; she had as open a nature as he'd ever encountered. Except, apparently, where Seth Greenlaw was concerned. *The secret sympathy.* Sir Walter Scott's line. Describing, expressly, true love.

Mark Sinclair could find no comfort in his thoughts.

CHAPTER 5

Early November, the Following Year

"Seth." A hand on his shoulder; he shook it off. Red mist clearing a little, the roar in his head subsiding.

Breathing hard, he looked at Amos Boyd, groaning on the floor. Amos' face was a bloody mess, and he'd piss red for a day or two, but no broken bones, Seth thought. Looked at his own hands. One little cut, knuckle of his right ring finger.

"Seth," Sheriff Ken Pelletier's deep voice, and the hand again, heavier this time. A big man, taller than Seth and sturdy-built.

The sheriff was Madeleine Hardie's cousin, family semblance showing in chestnut hair and the lavender-blue eyes Seth had never seen on anyone without Pelletier blood.

"Now, Seth, don't make me put cuffs on you. I gotta take you in, you threw first." Lower, "And you had to do it right in front of me."

He had thrown first. When he'd realized the woman Amos Boyd was speaking of—"gold-digging little tight-ass bitch, at least she got a good price for it," was Gwen Hardie Sinclair.

Something had cracked in his head.

And he'd dragged Amos off his barstool and beat the holy hell out of him. Seth knew there had been a lot of hands, pulling him off. It had felt good. It still felt good, and that was a fact.

Ken Pelletier settled his small tab (he'd just begun his second beer); Seth had paid for his sole half-drunk glass when it was brought.

It was very early November; it had been a good season, almost twice as much business as the year before. Seth had had to hire a hand for the summer. His barn held 20 stalls in working order, eight of them held horses boarded for the winter. An old riding stable about 100 miles inland had been slated for burning. Seth didn't like old wood, often in excellent condition, burned. He'd slipped the contractor a roll of bills, and carted away solid, well-built old stall dividers, sliding doors, plenty of barn boards. Hell of a lot of time and money saved, and he liked the result, the old wood mellow, not raw like new planks would have been.

Ben had applied to at least a dozen colleges in and out of state. *Scatter-shot*, thought Seth. *Like hunting game birds.* Most had not accepted him. No question of his brilliance, but Ben interviewed badly. Seth had been afraid he would.

Ben had come across as arrogant and abrasive. In most company, he was bored enough to be silent. When he was with 'family,' which meant his brother and the Hardies, affection for them and lack of interest in their conversation combined to keep these qualities hidden. But when he discussed his work, impatience with slower minds dragging on his flared. This did him no favors with college interviewers, who did not, generally, possess minds the equal of Ben Greenlaw's.

He *had* been accepted at South Maine Tech, which offered reduced tuition to Maine residents, and had one professor whose work Ben respected. Ben had passed the advanced placement tests he'd taken with top marks, and Seth had moved him downstate at the end of August with three semesters' worth of credits already on his record, one semester paid for, and the next two in the bank.

This was all good. He was thankful for it. But Seth Greenlaw looked out of a dark place onto a dark world. It wasn't just that Gwen hadn't been home but once all year, very briefly, and would not be again until next. He'd heard the tears in her voice when she'd told him. Calling to wish him 'Happy Birthday.' Seth missed her, painfully, but maybe it was better she wasn't there too much. Maybe. Her smile, her eyes, cut him open, sharp as one of her own knives—all that love, every way but the—final, ultimate—one.

The sun went down on his life when she was gone.

He missed Ben, too. He was lonely.

He was restless. He was tired. Work and hurt. That was his life.

He was 24 years old.

"Get in front. I want to talk to you some, son, and I don't want to throw my neck out doing it."

"You're not old enough to call me 'son.'" Seth was proud to be called 'son' by Paul Hardie, but the sheriff was only ten years older than he was. He got in the front passenger seat.

Ken Pelletier started the motor, backed out of his parking space, and drove them away from the Main Street Tavern. The 'nice' place. If you wanted not-so-nice, there was another up 226, past the Haven Point town line, and the next.

Seth went to the in-town tavern for a beer now and then. To the other place when he needed a woman. There wasn't anything he could offer a nice girl. But there were women who were glad enough to take the little—he never lied to them—he did offer. A surprising number of them.

He never took a woman twice. No redheads. He never brought them to his home. He'd never actually *slept* with a woman.

"Here's this thing from my lookout," the sheriff was saying. "I'm having a peaceful beer or two on my way home, and that no-account starts bad-mouthing a nice girl. You take issue with that—more power to you. But you can't just jump on a man and beat the daylights out of him, provocation or no. Not when the sheriff's sitting right there, anyway. That wasn't smart, Seth, and you're a smart man. So, now, I got to take you in, book you, do the paperwork, make the phone calls, when I should be heading home to my boys and my supper."

"Didn't do any real damage. No bones broken. I'm pretty sure."

"One or two cracked ribs, I'd say."

"Cracked ribs don't count."

"Well, you didn't break his arm. Good thing, too."

"Could've."

"Don't doubt it. Did quite a job on Amos, and not a mark on you. But, next time you find yourself in a similar situation, and the sheriff's present—that's me—make the other guy throw the first punch. That way, you save me all this trouble."

"I gotta let him land one, then I can take him out?"

"Didn't say you had to let it land."

Ken Pelletier booked Seth for disorderly conduct. "Amos wants to press assault, we'll have to deal with that, but I think I can get him to drop it."

Amos Boyd was not a drop-it sort. "How're you gonna work that?"

"You know that little weed patch he's got out back of his place? Long as people are peaceable, and don't bring in bad elements, I let 'em go their way, but I can cut it down and charge him anytime I want to.

"Circuit judge'll be in Friday. I'm releasing you, but you show up 9:00 a.m. I'll talk to the judge—we can probably see you get a waived fine and no time."

"You're being real nice about this. How come?"

"Well, Seth, I kinda like you, and I don't like Amos Boyd. And he *was* saying things he'd no call to about a real nice girl. Who happens to be my cousin.

"You still play guitar any?"

Seth switched mental gears. "Some. Not as much as I'd like, but I keep it up."

"I'm pretty fair on a fiddle. And I got no-one to play with. Wanna come over some evening, see about making a little music?"

Well, hell. "Yeah, I would. Thanks—Sheriff."

"Ken. How's Thursday work for you?"

CHAPTER 6

Late March, the Following Year

Crocuses pushed through late unmelted snow, green shoots poked first points from branches. Haven Point might get five seasons this year. Spring did not always come; the four you could count on were summer, fall, winter, and mud.

After evening stables, Seth drove down to the end of Gray Way, where the Gray, Hardie, and Greenlaw mailboxes sat, picked up the day's mail.

Back at his house, he made a pot of coffee, measuring twice what the can said. Thinking of Gwen, as he did every time he made coffee. Poured himself a cup, and looked over what the postman had brought. Circulars, only two bills for a change. A letter-sized envelope. Stiff, heavy paper. The Lords' Haven Point address on the back flap.

Seth slit the envelope with his knife, unfolded the enclosed sheet of paper. It was addressed to Ben, the dorm in Portland. Seth checked the envelope—that was addressed to him, of course, or it wouldn't have got here. He scanned the paper; at the bottom, under the signature and the word "attachments," was a line reading "cc: S.D. Greenlaw w/o att."

He read the letter, read it again. Couldn't make sense of it. Long formal words swam in twisting indicators; he kept losing the line. Seemed like someone wanted to give Ben a job . . . but Ben wasn't through his first year in college. Not even 19, for a couple of weeks yet.

Seth picked up the phone, dialed Ben's dorm room. No answer. Tried the cell number Ben had given him. Left a message.

Thought, and tried the Lords' local phone.

Half an hour later, he sat across from Peter Lord, massive wood desk between them, as Peter tried a second time to explain. A special facility, in Arlington, Virginia. For brilliant young minds to learn and work. It was Department of Defense work; and yes, that meant weapons. Seth did not like the idea of scores of Bens, working at weapons design. That could produce a lot of damage.

It would give Ben more advanced learning, immediately, than the program he was in, and would pay him a damn good salary. More than Seth netted, and Ben would have housing and meals provided.

Different viewpoints. "The pay isn't very much, but it will be a start, and the bonus is, these young people have the use of the labs for their own projects, though any patents will be Defense property."

How had they found Ben? There were high-level grapevines. Sort of like the local gossips' telephones, it seemed to Seth, but in rarified air. One of the instructors was sister-in-law to one of Peter Lord's cousins. Peter Lord had bumped into Ben in Portland (truer to say Ben had bumped into Peter Lord; Ben had been working out an equation in his head, and not paying attention), and taken him to lunch. Asked about his work.

"I can't say I understood it. But I can tell when a man knows what he's talking about. And when he spoke about having taken out over a dozen patents already . . ."

"Wait—*patents?*"

"Hasn't he told you? Copyrights, as well, I understand." Seth shook his head. "In any event, I suggested that Emily take a look at them. *Et, voila.*"

Seth knew that much French. He thanked Peter Lord, who waved thanks away. "Good for everyone—and the nation. Ben's mind will be a great asset."

Seth still wasn't happy with the idea of Ben designing weapons of mass destruction. He might—likely would—see it as a game. Keep score with hypothetical body counts.

The message light was flashing on the phone when he got home. Ben. "Call me." Click.

Seth dialed.

Ben had signed the three-year contract and sent it back via overnight mail before Seth had opened his carbon copy.

"But they screwed themselves. They only get actual patents. I took it to one of the law professors to be sure. Anything I come up with on my own and *don't* put in line for patent while I'm there, I can patent when the contract's up, and it's mine. Assuming I haven't come up with something better in the meantime, which I will," Ben laughed. "I guess that's government for you. No wonder they have to hunt for decent brains.

"It means you're off the hook, brother. For good. Enjoy yourself. Take things *easy*, for a change."

And wasn't *that* something to wrap his head around.

* * *

Seth was, in fact, enjoying himself, more or less. He spent several evenings a week over music with Ken Pelletier, who was better than 'pretty fair' on the violin. The two listened to CDs or Seth's vinyl records, chose songs, worked up arrangements, played them until the music flowed like silk through fingers, rippled like water over stone.

Sometimes Seth sang; it was a shame, he thought, that Ken's rich, deep baritone couldn't carry a tune. His own baritone was light, a little husky, but he could put a song over. And hit the damn notes.

He and Ken pushed each other. Seth had started playing around with a bottleneck slide on a few tunes.

It was excitement. It was comfort.

And he'd be *damned* if it wasn't pleasure.

* * *

Gwen had learned the difference between school-days and the world of full-time work. This was a structure without the measured and scheduled breaks that had allowed her to go home so often (*so often? Sometimes fewer than four times a year!*).

Gail pushed her hard; she loved what she was learning. Loved her work—exquisite plates, decorated with flowers, herb sprigs, tweezed into place. Gold leaf sparkling. Looking too pretty to eat, tasting even better than they looked. One Friday and Saturday each month, Gwen prepared a special tasting menu for select guest-customers; that was pressure, excitement, and the glow of a job well done. Yes, Gwen loved her work.

Kitchen noises—these she knew, these were comfortable— drowned out the ever-present city buzzing that had begun to get inside her head, that she hated. But she wished she could take longer breaks, *go home*, spend time with her family. *Recharge*, in the quiet.

There was *never* quiet in the city.

One day in the seven off per week. Fifteen hours' drive, round-trip, to home.

Her last semester, Mark had tailored his reading to her own assignments, so they could discuss their work together. The way he had the first year or so of their marriage. They'd even watched filmed adaptations of her beloved Jane Austen, discussed the relative merits. That had been so much fun.

Gwen was fairly certain neither of them had fully understood James Joyce's 'Ulysses.'

Now, she didn't have time to crack a book for pleasure. Let alone hide in a quiet library to read one.

* * *

Mark saw everything. He was selfish, keeping her in Boston. Gwen might love her work, but she was in Boston for him. He knew that. Knew she did not like city life.

He was not ready to leave it. The quiet of the old libraries, college and public, spurred his mind; and he was not where he needed to be. Yet.

But he heard her cry, sometimes, when she called her father. Heard her try not to, when she spoke with Seth Greenlaw.

She wasn't really unhappy, he thought. Hoped. But he would have to make plans. For change. Soon.

Mark had believed the words Seth Greenlaw said to him at their wedding reception. He still believed, enough not to want to test Seth on them.

Gwen deserved to be happy. Mark believed that, too. And for

Gwen, he'd learned, 'happy' meant 'home.' Which meant Haven Point.

He worked harder. Pruned his reading list, with difficulty and regret.

She'd asked no sacrifice from him. Simply, in love and trust, offered hers.

He would do right by her. He must.

CHAPTER 7

Mid-September

Seth had been following the crimson Mercedes since they'd both turned east off I-95. Definition of 'flash.' Who drove something like that?

Turned his mind back to the road, kept his eye out. Almost missed the hand-lettered sign (raw-looking wood, fresh-looking paint), "Ouellette Stables," but made his turn.

Everything went slow-motion as the Mercedes reversed sharply, swung hard and too fast into the lane at an angle. Skidded in the dirt, and slammed into the back-left corner of his pickup, jolting it forward.

Hell. He pulled further forward, reversed a little way. Smooth, no off-noise. Got out of the truck.

Big new dent, but it was one of many. Axle looked fine. Seth had kept the old pickup running long after it should have been put to pasture. He'd been putting off replacing it; he would, now.

The Mercedes' driver was attempting to move the vehicle. Seth could hear grinding; the car didn't budge. *Serve you right.*

She—the driver was female—got out. "Sorry. Are you all

right?"

"I'm fine, Miss Lord." The notorious Elizabeth Lord. Famously beautiful, with her father's china-blue eyes, her mother's elegant bones and thick, fine dark hair. The full mouth was her own.

"You?"

"Just embarrassed. And without wheels, apparently." She knew she should know this man.

He smiled at her, and she recognized wide dark-slate eyes.

"Seth Greenlaw, how are you?" She offered a hand, he took it. "How long has it been? You *have* changed." He certainly had. Liz Lord remembered a worn scarecrow of a boy; not the good-looking man in front of her. Seth was five years younger than she, which would make him 25, give or take a couple of months. He looked older than that, capable, confident. The long-ish, untidy dark hair was familiar; the beard, close-trimmed, was new and suited him.

"Of course, I'll cover the damage."

"Don't worry about it, she's running, past time for a new one, anyway. I've got chains, you want me to tow you somewhere."

She shook her head. "Thanks, I'll call for one. But if you could give me a lift to Haven Point? After I look at some horses—I'm assuming that's what you're here for, too?"

"Sure."

She called triple-A on her cell and, arrangements made, they drove off down the lane.

Seth was here to look at a sorrel mare; Liz was just scoping, at her father's request. Her plane had touched down in Bangor an hour back. Half an hour late.

Ouellette Stables was new; Seth hadn't dealt with the man before.

The sorrel was pretty. Liz watched Seth go over her, soft-talking, hands almost *listening* over the reddish flanks, legs. He took his time. Liz wondered whether he paid that kind of attention in bed. Probably not—so few men did. Was it worth finding out? What those hands would feel like, how they'd touch her?

He said something to the dealer she didn't catch. Patted the sorrel, scratched her forelock.

"Let's go."

"But —"

Seth shook his head. Horses were his business; Liz shrugged, and got in the pickup.

When they were out of the lane (Liz's Mercedes was nowhere to be seen—fast service), heading back to I-95, Seth said, "You don't want a horse from that yard. Sorrel's got bad wind. He didn't say a word."

"Could it be he didn't know? Maybe he just bought her?"

"His business to know. Stupid or dishonest, it's the same in the end. I don't do business with either one, if I can help it."

Liz laughed. "That's a sound philosophy. I don't, either. Thanks."

"Don't mention it. I *owe* your family, Miss Lord."

"Call me Liz."

She looked out the window. Liz hadn't spent much time up here in recent years; the September trees flamed red, gold, orange.

The colors reminded Seth of Gwen. Her hair. Every Maine autumn. "Beautiful, isn't it?" he said.

"It is. I forget, sometimes." On impulse, "Listen. My parents are down in Boston this weekend. I hate to eat alone—can I buy you dinner?"

"No, you can't. But if you want company, I'll buy yours. I

told you, I owe your family."

"Suit yourself. You can pick me up at seven."

* * *

At one minute to seven, Seth pulled into the Lords' driveway. He'd found jeans with no holes in them, and put on his newest shirt. Nothing to be done about his old boots and leather jacket.

Liz Lord opened the door before he could knock. Tall girl, only a couple of inches shorter than he in her Western bootheels. Slim, strong-looking. She, too, wore jeans and a leather jacket, from a different world than his own. She was from that different world.

He took her to the Main Street Tavern, the 'nice' one; they served decent food. There was one summer-seasonal restaurant still open, but Seth had been there once and found the food no better than the tavern's, just more expensive and fancier. Gwen had agreed with him. If she ever moved back home, maybe Gwen could take it over, turn it around. Work her magic.

Thinking about Gwen wasn't always a good idea, but Seth had a feeling he should keep her close to the surface of his mind.

"You're looking very handsome," Liz said, unzipping her jacket, draping it over the back of her chair.

Seth's eyebrows went up. "Thanks. You're—quite a sight yourself."

Her top—you really couldn't call it a shirt—stretched tight over high, full breasts. The low neckline exposed creamy flesh and impressive cleavage. The top clung, narrowing to a slim waist, and what her close-fitting jeans revealed matched the rest.

Can't blame a man for looking.

She made him wary. *Bait*, Seth thought. You baited a *trap*.

Elizabeth Lord was a predator. *Maneater.* Seth was a predator, too; he'd brought down his first buck at age nine. This wasn't his hunt, though, women weren't—and she wasn't—his game.

Game, you hunted. And you *played* games. He didn't like feeling he was prey. Or a toy.

There was no denying the bait was tempting as hell.

They ordered ribeye steaks, fries, salads. Liz looked at the wine list, suggested a mid-priced bottle. It was pleasant, having money enough to order it. Life was one hell of a lot easier, now that Ben didn't need college tuition, dorm rent, living expenses.

Liz asked about horses. Questions about his own stock, the new foals (her father had contracted for two). Since Ouellette Stables were to be avoided, were there any other new dealers who might be worth looking at? He didn't know of any.

The wine came, followed shortly by their plates. Liz commented, favorably, on the blueberry salad dressing. The steaks were a nearly perfect medium-rare, well crusted on the grill and smoky-tasting. The fries were crisp and brown.

"Not like eating Gwen Sinclair's food, but it's *very* good," she added.

Seth knew she and Gwen had got friendly in Boston. *That,* too, was something to keep in mind. A handhold to grip.

"How's she doing? Been a while since she was home."

"She's the same, Gwen never changes, does she? Very busy, very stressed, but happy enough. I think. Of course, she doesn't like Boston, but if she wants to cook that sort of food, big cities are the place."

Seth didn't think Gwen was happy; her voice was sad, lately, when she called. Asking him to tell her what he'd done that day. Leave out no details. Said it made her almost feel like she was home, hearing him talk. Horses, crops. Riding, hunting. Music with Ken Pelletier—when he spoke of that, he heard real pleasure in her brief comments. Always, she thanked him.

Damn Mark Sinclair. Not keeping her happy, as he'd promised. But Gwen still seemed glad to be Mark's wife. While that was the case, Seth couldn't see his way to killing him.

He'd officially closed his mechanic's business, though he still took an occasional job—the old equipment he understood so well, mostly. Sometimes an auto, if it were interesting enough.

Horses paid better. Even if they hadn't, he needed less, now, and loved working with them. He'd never felt the same about machinery. Horses were alive.

Liz was at the jukebox. Seemed like she scanned the entire list. Seth watched her. Shifting her stance a little, now and again as she read song titles, showing herself off. Subtly, but with too deliberate a grace not to know exactly what she was doing. She was so damned beautiful, those fine bones, like a painting of some saint, except for her ripe mouth. That body. *Dangerous* curves.

A man would have to be dead not to want her, turning it on like this. Even that might not be enough. Seth was a long way from dead.

But she set off warning bells. Loud ones.

Her glass was empty. The bottle, and Seth's glass, were half full; he didn't pour more.

Finally, Liz put money in the machine, punched buttons, and came back to fill her glass. She gestured toward Seth's; he shook his head.

A slow song; her head lifted. Old. Marvin Gaye. Sensuous,

sexual. Liz looked at him, smiling. He smiled back, said nothing.

"Aren't you going to ask me to dance?"

"We can, if you want."

Seth held her lightly; she pressed closer. Just enough to make him feel her breasts against him. *Bitch*, he thought, and eased back. This was public.

"Behave yourself, Elizabeth. I live here, I've got a reputation to protect; you don't."

"What makes you think I don't want to protect my reputation, *exactly* as it is?" Low, throaty, inviting.

"Behave yourself, or I'm leaving the floor."

"Oh, all *right*." And she let him keep a respectable distance. The song finished; Seth wouldn't dance the next.

"What's your game here, Elizabeth?" *Make her say it.*

"It's exactly what it looks like, Seth Greenlaw. Give it some thought, if you need to." Better not to look at, best not to *think* about, how her easy breath made her breasts move in that revealing garment. He wanted her, wanted to make her pay for teasing him. Knew she was counting on just that.

He'd thought enough, anyway. "I appreciate the offer, but it'd upset my little sister."

"You don't have—oh. Right." Gwen Sinclair did call Seth Greenlaw her 'favorite brother.'

"Would she have to know?"

"She'd know. Everybody would. This is a small town, Elizabeth.

"I'm going to regret 'yes,' I'm going to regret 'no.' I have to pick what regrets I can live with. And—no. Thanks, though. Won't say it's not a pleasure to be asked."

He'd thought of Paul Hardie, Gwen, Jack, knowing. Peter and Julia Lord, knowing. It would shame him. He would not live with that.

Something Gwen had said to him, long ago, a decade, had flashed bright in his mind. After she'd taken his .22, shot that pretty, slow-dying vixen. He'd been out riding; she'd got his gun from the house. "It's what you'd have done, Seth, you *always* do the right thing." He held to the lifeline—he had held to it before this. *Thank you, sweet Gwen.* His true north.

He let Liz pour him another half glass, let her try to persuade him. She could make this harder, and was doing her best. She couldn't change his mind.

Seth's life had been full of hard choices.

* * *

Before the tavern door closed behind them, the bartender was on the telephone. Drinkers and diners paid tabs, and went home to theirs.

A good many minutes before Seth's pickup turned down the Van Leyden road, half the locals knew—the consensus of eyewitnesses was that Liz Lord had been selling hard. Seth Greenlaw had appeared to enjoy the pitch, but it didn't look like he was buying.

By mid-morning the next day, it had been verified by the Lord servants that Seth had taken Liz straight home (given their arrival time), and driven away without entering the house.

Obviously, Seth Greenlaw was crazy. But withstanding Liz Lord—that was impressive. 'Crazy but impressive' was not too far from what they already thought of him, after the incident with Amos Boyd (who had been persuaded by the Sheriff not to press assault charges).

Seth's reputation remained unscathed.

He'd stood a long time under a cold shower, and slept very badly. But he knew he'd chosen right.

CHAPTER 8

October

"I must be getting old—either that, or I'm losing my touch. Twice. In a *month*." Liz complained.

Gwen laughed. "I wouldn't know about the second part, Liz. But you're the most beautiful woman I ever saw, except maybe your mother, and you're certainly not old. Still, nobody is everybody's cup of tea. And no-one ever bats a thousand, do they?"

She'd joined Liz for a drink and bar food at Volution, after Farmhouse Table was closed and cleaned. A trendy late-night spot, overlooking the Charles. Plate glass windows showed dark water, city lights glinting on ripples. Boats. It wasn't home, but it was a reminder, Gwen thought. Water, boats. Of course, you couldn't see the far shore of the Atlantic Ocean as you could see across the river. Nature—what there was of it—was so much *smaller*, in the city.

"Tell me about these men who don't want a fling with Elizabeth Lord? They must be unusual."

"Well, one of them was in Haven Point. A friend of yours—Seth Greenlaw."

Gwen went stark white. *Livid.* "Oh, my God. Liz Lord, you *didn't.* My *God,* Liz, he's my *family.* I thought we were friends. He's not the sort of person you—I could absolutely *kill* you."

"Oh, Gwen, not you too. My father read me the riot act."

He'd called her on the carpet like a badly-behaving child. She'd embarrassed him, made a public spectacle of herself. Her poor mother felt positively humiliated. She'd put a friend of theirs, a man they'd known since he was born, someone they exchanged Christmas gifts with, in an awkward position.

Of course, Seth hadn't said anything. He wouldn't. She must know the way gossip worked in a town like Haven Point.

If she could not behave respectfully toward their friends and neighbors, perhaps she should stay away for a while.

Liz had been made to feel very small. *Shabby.* Had flown— fled—to New York, before returning to Boston.

And her lab. One last formulation to get right, and it resisted her. Like Seth Greenlaw. Like Patrick Riordan.

"Good for him. Seriously, *Liz.* What is *wrong* with you? You can't play those games with Haven Point people. It's *trifling.* We're just not *like* that. You should know that by this time. People get *hurt,* playing your games. People who aren't *you.* Honestly, I could *kill* you."

"I didn't do him any harm. It was strange. I got to him, I know I did. He just wasn't going to do anything about it."

Gwen's face softened. A little, private smile, as she said, "When Seth Greenlaw decides he's going to do something, nothing stops him. And when he decides he isn't going to, nothing makes him. Maybe some glory-hallelujah-road-to-Damascus lightning bolt thing might work, but I wouldn't bet on it.

"I'll probably forgive you sooner or later. As long as Seth's really okay. I'll call him. Then I'll know.

"Tell me about the other. I was right about one thing—Seth is *definitely* unusual."

"That's why I was interested. The other's a writer—a mystery novelist, in New York. He was even worse—he just laughed at me and flat out said I wasn't what he was looking for."

Gwen laughed, and Liz shut her mouth. Because, speak of the devil. What on earth was he doing in Boston?

"Good Heavens, Elizabeth. I didn't expect to run into you—won't you introduce me?"

Black-Irish handsome. Even Gwen, accustomed to Mark Sinclair's beautiful face, was impressed. Crackling energy. Wickedly sweet smile.

"Patrick Riordan, Gwen Sinclair. Patrick's the writer I was talking about. Gwen's a chef at Farmhouse Table."

"A pleasure, Ms. Sinclair. I must give your restaurant a visit while I'm here—I have a couple of book signings. I hope Elizabeth hasn't been telling you terrible tales about me. Not that they aren't there to tell."

"Nothing the least bit bad, as far as I'm concerned. Please come—I'm doing a tasting menu this Friday and Saturday—and the regular menu is terrific.

"But I have to get home. If I want to be awake enough to actually *see* my husband before he leaves in the morning. And I do."

"Please, stay just a little longer," said Patrick Riordan. "Let me buy you one drink."

"Thank you, but I really mustn't. Nice meeting you, Mr. Riordan, I hope we'll see you at Farmhouse Table. Thanks, Liz. I'll call you. Good night." And she was gone.

Liz heard the *don't-call-me-first* undertone. Gwen was not pleased with her.

Gwen was right, her father was right. She had been emotionally tone-deaf. Seth Greenlaw attracted her because he paid attention to what he did. But *she* hadn't been paying attention. Liz would have to take a hard look at herself. And maybe pay some attention to Haven Point, and to her parents, as well.

As soon as she cracked that last formula. Maybe *that* needed a different sort of attention.

"*Who*," asked Patrick Riordan, "is that enchanting creature? I've never seen such eyes. She looks like something out of a fairytale."

Well, well. Liz had wondered what he *was* looking for, since it wasn't her.

"Don't even go there, Patrick, she's *very* married. They adore each other."

"A pity. She *is* exquisite."

Gwen Sinclair looked like something he might have dreamt. Exquisite, unique—those *marvelous* eyes—and almost virginal, which was odd in a girl with a husband.

Many writers have a romantic streak; Patrick Riordan's was wide and deep.

CHAPTER 9

The Following May

Haven Point readied itself for another summer season. Those Main Street shop doors which shut after Labor Day were unlocked, shelves restocked.

Melody Gray looked at the 'Grand Opening' sign above the storefront next to her mother's shop. She'd been saving, searching, collecting for this dreamt-of day. Melody had replaced her sister in their mother's second-hand clothing and tailoring shop when Joanna went off to Portland and a nursing career. Melody's needle was even swifter and surer than Ann's, whose skill was close to being a local legend. But she had wanted something more.

The Dress-Up Box would offer vintage and high-end slightly used clothes, jewelry, and accessories. She'd been clever, advertising that ten percent of all proceeds would be donated to St. Aidan's food pantry and outreach ministry. Summer people—and a few locals—donated clothes for the small tax break.

Melody had spent weeks arranging and rearranging the interior; tomorrow would see her neighbors'—her customers'—reactions. *Please, God, make them like it.* But she thought they would—in her heart, she knew it was beautiful.

* * *

Seth Greenlaw's stables had grown as far as he could take them, without changes he didn't want to make. His stalls were filled in winter with boarders. Seth paid two hands year-round, two more in summer, and had delegated most of the riding lessons. He took in no more horses than he could train himself; he hadn't found anyone else with the gift for it.

That might change. in time; Caleb Pelletier, the sheriff's elder boy, not only rode well, but had good, sensitive hands. With Ken Pelletier's approval, Seth had let Caleb hang around the previous summer. He'd done a few odd jobs, and been paid for them. Caleb, who had turned 15 in February, watched with intent eyes as Seth trained; Seth had begun telling—showing—him how to evaluate a horse, what to look for, what to listen for, what to feel for. How to *listen* with your hands. How to soft-talk the horses, reassure them—it didn't matter what words you used, non-stop obscenities if you wanted. What mattered was the tone, and the inner calm. The *tenor*, Madeleine Hardie would have said, but Seth didn't know that usage. He knew the living reality; that was enough.

At the end of the day, Seth put the boy's bike in the back of his pickup and drove him home, answering each fresh barrage of questions. Both Caleb and his younger brother, Kyle, 12, were clever boys, and kind. Ken Pelletier might be raising them alone, but he was doing a fine job.

As often as not, Seth stayed for supper, and played music with Ken after. He'd persuaded Ken to let Jack Hardie join them. Not on evenings when they chose songs, worked out arrangements; just for playing. The sheriff had admitted an extra guitar rounded the sound out. And Jack's tenor was clear and tuneful, his ear good. His playing improved with regular practice and Seth's careful arrangements for him.

Ken and Seth began, between themselves, to speak, tentatively, of performing. 'Down the road, sometime, maybe,' terms.

* * *

Jack Hardie was still considered a good boy. An excellent seaman and captain, a thorough workman, and a more than fair boss. Surprisingly good on the business end, which he was more and more taking over from Paul, who no longer went out with the boats. But the (usually unspoken) label "boy," he could not shake out of their minds. Or his own.

He'd felt, for as long as he could remember, a little inferior in his family. His mother was a great actress; his sister a great cook—chef, he corrected himself. His father read literature, could discuss it with Madeleine and Gwen, who were also readers. They all had imagination, was what it was. Jack didn't imagine the world out, as they did. To make up for this failing, Jack worked as diligently, as *earnestly*, as he could. He ought to be earnest, after all; it was his name: Ernest John Hardie.

* * *

Another 'Opening' sign, up past the unpaved end of Gray Way on 226 South.

Althea Jones breathed her own "please, God." She was almost tapped dry, everything she'd saved, worked for, done things she hated for, sunk here.

The old, small house had been perfect—already set up as a

restaurant downstairs, with living space above. Althea had worked up a menu of her mother's down-home Louisiana recipes; Downeast Bayou would offer breakfast and lunch six days a week.

She'd brought Nerise, her then-ten-year-old daughter, up at the end of last summer so she could start the school year in Haven Point. The house had needed little work, thankfully; Althea's energy had gone toward getting acquainted, making contacts. She scoped out food artisans who packaged their wares for sale in local shops—Althea had shelf space, and enticing, locally-made products would be welcome.

It helped to have a girl in school. Althea baked cookies and cupcakes, little crawfish pies, for class events and bake sales. She hated having to use frozen crawfish, even if no-one but she (and Nerise, maybe) would know the difference. Maybe one day she'd be able to raise them live, but licensing and permitting for aquaculture was far beyond her budget for now. Not to mention the expense of setting it all up—tanks, plants, pumps, heating. Might be cheaper to have them shipped, but even that was beyond her means at present.

Nerise was the fastest girl on the track team. Faster than the fastest boy two years ahead of her. Althea burst with pride, watching her daughter's dark legs flying down the stretch, lead widening with each footfall, thin body breaking the tape. Her first year here, and with a new coach, in a new environment, she'd broken state records for her age group at 100, 200, *and* 400 meters.

Althea had braced herself for small-town prejudice in a hugely white state, but had found surprisingly little of it. A fishing town, a quarry town, Haven Point historically had a more diverse population than many small Maine localities. There were two other black families, several Mexicans, a little group of Vietnamese (Althea's Louisiana days made their culture familiar to her, though these families did not feel the same about her). Italian, Polish surnames. Others. A little too much diversity, among so tiny a population, to squabble yourself out of charity with your neighbors. Small communities in hard climates need at least a loose social cohesion.

No-one had to say this; they knew it in their Mainer bones.

Haven Point folk mostly took Althea Jones and her daughter at face value, and didn't count the color of those faces.

* * *

On his way to Ken Pelletier's one early evening, Jack Hardie stopped along Main Street for coffee. Fine Grind had the best in town; Jack missed his sister's. She'd told—shown—both him and their father, multiple times. It never came out like hers.

Paper cup in hand, he looked at the shops. He hadn't been in Melody Gray's new place yet; he ought to, for courtesy. Even if it was a women's clothing store, even if he couldn't expect to be interested.

Melody was his neighbor, and a very nice young lady.

He opened the door, and his life changed.

It was a riot of color, fabric, richness. Silks, velvets, lace everywhere. Beautiful, magical arrangements, gowns spread on walls, skirts pinned out, embroidered shawls, dripping fringe, spread on the pitched ceiling. Racks and racks of dresses; the frocks on the walls tempted you to discover hidden beauties. Soft light from old lamps, mirrors reflecting and multiplying the magic.

Billie Holiday's voice sang a sweet-sad, nostalgic soundtrack.

It was Ali Baba's cave, it was Arabian Nights tales. A door he hadn't known was inside him opened on strange, lovely vistas.

And little Melody Gray had made this.

"Jack! How nice of you to stop in. I've been hoping to see you. I was just about to close, but look around, I'm not in a rush."

"I am looking. It's—it's *fantastic*, Melody. I never saw anything like it.

"It's like—it makes things—I don't even know what—look like they're—I mean—*possible*. That weren't, before."

Melody Gray was small, shorter than his sister by an inch, and tended toward a pleasing plumpness. Flax-blonde curls, eyes gray as her name.

She'd always been fond of Jack Hardie, but she'd been laser-focused on this dream since high-school.

Which he *got*. Melody saw his wonder, and began to wonder, herself. His semi-coherent words pointed at what her shop meant to *her*. And he was only inarticulate because he was impressed. Maybe even moved.

Lots of people, these first few days, had said her shop was beautiful. None of them had said anything like Jack had.

Jack, like his father, was of middle height, fair and stocky, pleasant-featured and blue-eyed.

He had to find out just what these now-possible things were. He thought maybe he could even imagine them out. Maybe. With practice.

And she made this. I've known Melody all her life, and I didn't know anything about her. He wanted to know who she *was*, who she *really* was, when she made this mind-bending beauty.

Jack asked Melody if he could take her to dinner, the following night. Melody said yes.

Jack arrived at Ken Pelletier's house wreathed in smiles, and played better music than he had in his life.

CHAPTER 10

Christmas

Gwen was dressed, pacing, when Mark arose on Christmas Eve. She kissed him, said "Merry Christmas," poured him coffee, gave him bacon, toast.

Her suitcase was out, packed, her coat and boots ready. She said nothing to rush him, but Mark ate quickly, dressed without showering, and took their suitcases down to the car.

She was—almost, and quietly—distraught, these days, and had actually demanded that Gail give her Christmas Eve off. Gwen was not a demanding person.

It would be a brief visit, but she *would* be home this Christmas.

Gwen felt Boston was winning. The picture of her life was changing, warping. Colors muddied, faded, outlines morphed, blurred and sharpened. *Distortions.* Draining life and blood out of her life and blood. Filling her with empty noise.

She hated it. She *needed* her family, her father, her brothers. She *needed* the soul-quiet of the night sky in Haven Point. And she would have it—at least, a very little.

Gwen was afraid it would not be enough, that something important to her—something *of* her—was gone forever, and that fear terrified her.

* * *

They had not stopped to eat. Mark, hungry, had looked at Gwen's tense face and had refrained from suggesting it; both were starving when they pulled into the Hardie driveway.

Gwen, unlike her husband, was starved for more than food.

The front door, rarely used except during holiday season, sported a balsam wreath, red-bowed and decorated with mussel shells. She touched one of the shells, Maine things, *home* things, before opening the door.

"Daddy? Oh, *God*, I've missed you *so much*," and she wept in her father's arms. Sniffled, stopped, as she hugged Jack. Even embraced her mother—"Mom. It's *good* to see you."

Mark, ashamed of his selfishness, brought in suitcases. He should have insisted Gwen take a vacation, that they bring her home, long ago.

It wasn't many minutes before the Greenlaws arrived.

"*Seth!*" and her arms locked around him; his embraced her. Gwen looked up at him, fresh tears in her eyes. "My brother. My *best* friend. It's been *awful*, not seeing you for so long." She leaned her cheek against his chest, didn't let go of him; it was as if his body gave hers the quiet she needed so desperately to feel.

Over her head, Seth Greenlaw's eyes met Mark Sinclair's with a look so black Mark's blood ran cold. He felt the chill in his veins.

Gwen breathed deep, and, at last, stepped out of Seth's arms. Held his hands, smiled at him—a ghost of her happy grin, but loving. *And brave*, Seth thought. Her lips formed "thank you." He smiled back.

Gwen turned to Ben—"I hear you're planning how best to eliminate the species. How's that working out?"

Ben laughed, Gwen smiled a little. They hugged.

"Well, I am *starving*. Anyone else? Sorry about the short lead time, Mom. How did you do? We can work around whatever, just let me know."

Trying so hard. To be her old self. For us. For him. Seth's heart ached.

"I think I got everything, Gwen, dear. Don't do too much today, you've just arrived."

"Thanks, Mom, I won't now, just a snack or something. But I have to put on a good show for the Lords."

Mark felt a hand on his shoulder.

"Let's take a walk," said Seth.

Heart thudding, Mark put on his coat. He'd seen Seth Greenlaw's eyes.

* * *

"I warned you." They'd walked halfway to the woods before Seth stopped, turned, and spoke.

"Do I get a last meal?"

"You think her being this miserable is a *joke?*"

"No. No, of course not."

"Then *fix this*. It's your job, you took it on."

"It isn't only me, you know, it's really more the restaurant—I brought her home much more often when she was in college."

"She's there because you are."

"And I *will* bring her home. For good. It won't be long. We'll live here; I hope it will make her happy."

"When? Does she know?"

"I don't want to tell her until I can make it happen. Soon."

"What do you think another year will do to her? We can all

see what the last three did."

"Not a year. Six months, perhaps. By the end of the summer. I *promise* that."

"You *promised* you'd keep her happy."

"She's never had a harsh word from me, not in five years."

"You think that's *enough*? Not even close."

"No, I know that."

Seth looked at Mark. Something clicked. "You don't love her. You *couldn't*, and put her through this."

"Of course I love her. Do you think anyone could live with Gwen, and not?" Daring despite fear, "It's possible I don't love her as much as you do."

Seth looked daggers at him. Said nothing.

"What's my sentence? Are you going to shoot me? I don't see a gun."

Seth shook his head, "For her sake. Not for yours. And I wouldn't need a gun.

"*Fix this*, or get out of her life and let her come home to— the people who love her best."

"I don't want to break her heart."

"You're breaking it now. Fix this. One way or the other. Before the end of summer." *Or I will.*

Mark heard the unspoken words.

Seth turned on his heel, stalked back to the house. Mark walked.

* * *

Mark Sinclair felt he'd scraped through a very tricky situation. He hadn't handled it badly, he thought. Not shown his fear, not too much at least.

It had disturbed, as well as frightened, him.

Mark Sinclair valued dispassion, clarity, *civilization*. He understood the angel-demon dichotomy of human nature; he was less comfortable with his species as part of the animal kingdom, predators in the natural world. Which was so immediate, here, and so beautifully *removed*, in Boston.

He had no doubt that Seth Greenlaw, hunter, *predator*, could kill him with his bare hands. And enjoy doing it.

It was hard—in more than one way—to visualize him with Gwen. The juxtaposition seemed like violation. Gwen was small, and so delicate. Meant for a *civilized* world, not a primitive one. How could he even think of her in the hands of so dangerous a man without recoiling?

Mark hated anything suggestive of roughness, violence. For him, love must be tender, kind. And so Gwen was—in everything. He loved their gentle lovemaking—they were, surely, well-matched in that.

But Gwen wanted 'home,' which *was* the natural world. She had her own animal, sensual side. Her pleasure, her comfort, in physical contact—hugging those she loved close and often, snuggling like a kitten in a litter.

Gwen was also flexible, adaptable—except about her need for her home, and she'd done her best there, too. She loved to please.

In Mark's bed, she rendered gentleness for gentleness.

Would she render passion for passion, in Seth Greenlaw's?

CHAPTER 11

The Following Spring

Mark Sinclair was still thinking of Christmas as calendars flipped to March. He'd put out feelers with real estate agents, let them know the condo would be available—soon, but he'd given no specific date. His parents had given them a significant down payment; the unspent portion of Gwen's college fund had been added to that. Madeleine Hardie had invested after-tax dollars, so there was no stricture on how the money could be spent. The return on their equity would be more than enough to purchase a small Haven Point house.

Still putting it off, and he couldn't do that much longer. Moving would be relatively simple—they had little enough.

He read, he wrote.

Farmhouse Table was closing its doors. Gail Winthrop's grandmother was very ill, and Gail was returning to California to spend what looked like last months with the woman who'd taught her to cook. She'd already been approached about opening a new place in San Francisco.

Gail had shelled out severance, back vacation pay, and bonuses. Gwen's, combined, represented more than Mark's trust fund distributions for a year.

* * *

Late, the early-April night Farmhouse Table served its last dinner, Mark was working, trying to get through one more book. How many 'one more books' had he indulged in? He must have written enough to determine whether he had the makings of a book himself. But the process itself was what compelled, drove him, not the result.

A knock on the door of his study—a tiny second bedroom; it was piled and packed with boxes and boxes of the notebooks he'd filled.

Gwen opened the door without waiting for a response. She had never done that.

"Mark. Listen. I've got to go home for a while. I know you're busy, I understand if you don't want to take the time. You don't have to come. But there's a flight at 7:00 tomorrow morning, and I want to be on it."

Mark closed his notebook, set down his pen. "How long were you thinking?"

"I don't know. A month, two maybe. Maybe longer. I don't know. I just—I need to get away, get back home for a while. I need to breathe, recharge. Get some *quiet* back into me."

Mark did not like the idea of Gwen in Haven Point, for a month or more, without him. Bad enough she was content to be apart at all. But what would happen if she were happy, with her father, her 'family,' without Mark? *With* Seth Greenlaw's daily presence?

Mark did not want to lose her. His fine words to Paul Hardie were hard to live up to. He liked having Gwen for a wife.

Over Christmas, she'd ridden with Seth twice, alone. Played

cribbage with him after the Lords left on Christmas Eve, and after Christmas dinner. Sitting on the floor by the hearth, laughing over the peg-board and cards. Fifteen-two, fifteen-four, and six makes ten.

Mark could see ghosts, hear echoes, of the children they'd been, playing together. Gwen had looked happier than Mark had seen her in well over two years. Certainly since before the last two Christmases, when they had not gone to Haven Point.

Worse, she'd welcomed—*asked*—Seth, not he, into the kitchen while she cooked. Mark, getting coffee, had seen her teaching Seth how to slice vegetables on a mandoline. More laughter; with Seth Greenlaw, in the kitchen which had been hers for so long, Gwen had relaxed further.

Mark realized that he had, in the immediate aftershock of his talk—if you could diminish it to that—with Seth, oversimplified his evaluation of the man in relation (awful thought) to Gwen.

Certainly, Seth Greenlaw was dangerous. Mark had seen the potential, at his wedding. At Christmas, he'd seen the realization of that potential. But Mark had never seen Seth offer Gwen anything but tenderness. All the love he could—decently—show her. Mark had to admit, the man had behaved with honor on that score. So far.

Seth, in fact, behaved with more honor than Mark had. He loved Gwen more, and certainly more unselfishly. Mark had broken his promise to keep her happy, and continued to break it. The only promise he knew of that Seth had broken was to kill *him*, if he broke his own promise. As Mark had done.

If he let her go on her own, Mark wasn't sure he had a better than 50/50 chance of keeping her. He did not like those odds.

"Of course, I'll come, darling. Pack a bag, I'll pack mine; in the morning you can call your father, and we'll head out first thing."

* * *

They drove away before it was light. Gwen had called her father, almost frantic with happy impatience.

She'd been a little calmer when she called Seth Greenlaw, but eagerness bubbled up in her words, her tone.

Mark's little vintage yellow convertible two-seater was the only luxury he indulged in. He'd had it for eight years, kept it in excellent order. Mark did not approve of attachment to objects, but the car was his weakness.

Having navigated their way out of the city and its traffic, Mark turned off the interstate to a quieter and prettier route.

The sun rose, and with it the temperature. It was warmer than usual, for this time of year.

"I know it will be chilly, but I'd love some wind. Could we put the top down? Would you mind?"

Mark pulled over, and did as she asked. Gwen unclipped her hair; when they got up to speed, it blew around her face wildly. She smiled through the red strands.

Now for it, he thought.

"Gwen, darling, I've so much material written, it's time I started sorting through it. Seeing if anything worthwhile has come of my efforts.

"You've indulged me more than I had any right to ask, Gwen, and I am so grateful I couldn't begin to tell you. I've loved our life together.

"Now, it's your turn, darling. I know Boston's made you unhappy—I hope you know how very sorry I am. I think it's time to get you home on a permanent basis. We'll sell the condo. Let's look at some houses, and make plans."

"Oh, Mark, do you really mean it? You don't *know* what that means to me." She paused. Shyly, "I don't suppose you'd consider moving into Daddy's house, would you? There's tons of room, and that big library you could work in."

Mark wasn't eager to be a satellite in another man's home. "Darling, I think we'll need space that's our own. Let's see what's available to us in the way of houses."

She hadn't expected him to say different. "What will I do, though? I'll need a job. And I don't think Haven Point is quite ready for gold leaf, edible flowers and tasting menus."

"You don't really need a job, I think—my income will stretch a lot farther there than in Boston."

"But I don't want to be idle! I'm no *idler*. I'll have to do *something*."

"Perhaps you can find something—or things, you can make and sell. There's a decent market for artisanal foods."

"That's not a bad idea. I can probably figure something out on those lines." *But what?*

Mark smiled at his wife, taking his eyes off the road.

Gwen saw the big pickup spin out of control. Time slowed, each moment eternity, as the huge vehicle thundered toward the little yellow car.

She felt the crashing impact. And knew nothing more.

* * *

Seth Greenlaw was reviewing the week's schedule over coffee when the phone rang for a second time. Gwen was coming home, the first call had told him, her voice fervent with relief.

"Seth." Paul Hardie's voice, frighteningly old-sounding. "There's bad news—are you sitting down?

"There was an accident. Mark's dead."

"Gwen –"

"Unconscious. They took her back to Boston, to the hospital, in a helicopter. She's—injured. They don't know if—it's bad, Seth.

"Her mother is flying from California. Jack and I are driving down. Will you come?"

"Twenty minutes." On auto-pilot, Seth threw things into a canvas bag. Locked the house, headed to the stables, spoke to Jim Marshall, the first hand he'd hired.

"I have to go to Boston. Here's the schedule, we're not training yet, you don't need me. Cancel anything you have to, there isn't much. House keys—stay here if you want. I'll make some arrangement with the bank, in case you need anything,"

"What happened? How long you think you'll be gone?"

"Family emergency. Don't know. I'll call."

Seth pulled into the Hardie driveway less than 15 minutes after disconnecting with Paul.

Paul's big station wagon was out, hatch open. Seth threw his bag beside the others, slammed the hatch.

Paul and Jack Hardie, coats buttoned, were out, too, waiting for him. Jack looked stunned, shocked. Paul looked ten years older than he had yesterday; he looked made of sadness.

"I can't drive, Seth—you or Jack—"

"I'll get us there faster." Jack drove at speed-limit, or at least within 5 miles per hour. Seth didn't.

CHAPTER 12

April to May

Outside Boston, they bought a street map, found where the hospital was. Plotted a tentative route, though Paul noted the map didn't say if a street were one-way. There were two such in all Haven Point. In-town.

They'd stopped, briefly as possible, when necessary. No-one mentioned food.

Even so, and Seth doing 85 or faster when the coast was clear, it was 2:00 p.m. by the time they hit Boston's city limits. It was 3:00 when they'd navigated the maze of streets, detouring around construction, circling round one-way streets. Seth got angry—angrier—but not lost.

Seth took the parking ticket the little machine thrust at him, and pulled into the hospital's garage. Paul demanded the ticket; Seth handed it over, distracted.

Gwen was out of surgery, at least for now. There might be another, to drain her subdural hematoma, if it did not respond to non-surgical efforts.

Mark Sinclair was no more. After being tossed down the hill, the car had burned and exploded. The little left of him would barely make a tablespoon of ashes.

Gwen had been thrown clear, and landed on grass. Her request that Mark put the top down had saved her life, though no-one living knew, or would know. Gwen would remember little of the drive. She was concussed, not as badly as originally feared, but she had not regained consciousness. Mercifully, her skull was intact.

Her right arm, broken in two places, had been pinned. Three broken right ribs; two of them had shattered pieces which had been repaired via surgery.

She was lucky she breathed on her own, lucky to be alive at all. Or so the doctor told Paul Hardie, whose eyes swam with tears. *Lucky?*

But they did say Gwen would, likely, recover. To what extent, given her head injury, they could not say. But the chance of her returning to at least a relative normalcy was 60%, maybe a little better. Which the doctors said was encouraging. Paul could not quite feel a four-out-of-ten chance his daughter would never be herself again was cause for optimism.

Like many, the hospital had a liberal visitation policy for patients in their Intensive Care Unit. When Gwen regained consciousness (still a question, but they had to think 'when,' not 'if'), she could choose what visitors she'd see, and when. Until then, the hospital would proceed according to her father's wishes.

Jack Hardie had stood with his father as the doctors spoke. Seth stood by Gwen's high ICU bed, looking down at her.

It was not a large bed. But she looked so small in it. Hair matted, a messy red tangle. Right arm bent and cast, shoulder to fingers. She was *broken*.

He'd thought, years ago, that facing her marriage was the worst he could go through. Hearing her unhappy voice over the miles of wire—that had been worse; seeing her miserable at

Christmas worse still. At least he had the comfort of knowing he gave her something she needed.

A world without Gwen, her bright energy gone out of it. Not much frightened Seth Greenlaw, but that did.

Stay with me, Gwen. With all of us. We love you, we need you. I need you, love you. You have the strength. And if you don't, take mine.

He wanted to hold her hand, *will* strength into her, palm to palm, but was afraid to touch her.

Hoped, savagely, that Mark Sinclair had been alive as he burned up. Made her unhappy, almost—maybe had—killed her. Let him burn, here and hereafter.

* * *

Madeleine Hardie arrived two hours and a bit after her husband. She was relieved Gwen's prognosis was better than initially feared, but broke with tears at the sight of her daughter. Paul held her, weeping quietly himself.

Jack did not weep; silently, he prayed for his sister. Her life, her return to full health.

They all prayed, each of them. Even Seth, whose prayers were infrequent and whose attendance at St. Aidan's had become lax in recent years.

The hospital requested their departure at 8:00 that evening. Jack had found a hotel, booked three rooms. It had been recommended as 'reasonable,' but Paul's eyebrows shot up as he paid two nights for everyone.

Seth didn't use plastic; in Haven Point and through much of Maine, it was not necessary. He told Paul he'd reimburse him when they got back; he'd taken all the cash he had, but had not brought his checkbook; he'd thought Jim Marshall might need it, and had not thought out expenses in Boston.

Paul waved this away; they could talk about it later. He had no intention of allowing Seth to be put to expense. This was for Gwen, Gwen was Paul's daughter. And he did love Seth—a son any father would be proud of.

Paul Hardie wished, sadly, that Mark Sinclair had not been born. He'd genuinely liked his son-in-law. But—this ending? Possibly Gwen's?

To be sensible, they tried to eat. Managed to force down a few tasteless mouthfuls. It was a dispiriting meal, everyone battered with grief and anxiety.

The precarious hope was almost worse.

None of them slept.

* * *

There had been a late snow overnight; six inches, give or take. By a little before 8:00 a.m., when Seth took the ticket and parked them, it was already blackening with city soot, city dirt. Seth remembered Gwen's voice, *I miss snow that isn't black in a day.*

They'd eaten a little breakfast, more than at dinner; they'd all been without food long enough for the body to make demands.

Talk was difficult, and mostly they didn't try. Non-verbal was easier, and worked fairly well. They didn't need more than eye contact to agree it was time to get to the hospital.

Gwen had not regained consciousness, but the doctors said her hematoma appeared to be responding to the drug cocktail. Surgery might still be necessary; for now, they'd continue the medications, monitor her.

Gwen was young; she was healthy. These would work in her favor, Paul and Madeleine were told.

Seth asked a nurse if would be safe to hold Gwen's hand—the left one, and was cautioned not to disturb her intra-venous drips.

He pulled a rolling stool by her bed, and, carefully, took the limp little hand in both his own. Talked soft, hardly knowing what he said. Her name. Words of love, prayers. The 23rd Psalm, more than once, he thought he remembered, later. *Valley of the shadow of death. Come through, Gwen.*

Seth didn't know about God, but *he* was with her.

* * *

A regular cell phone was a waste in Haven Point. The town was a virtual dead zone. There were a few spots where you might get signal, but you'd likely lose it before five minutes were up.

Seth had a cheap pre-paid phone, for travel out of town; he kept several refill cards on hand.

When they were shooed out of Gwen's room for a few afternoon hours, he checked in with Jim Marshall; all quiet, all correct, at the stables. Jim didn't need anything; Seth could skip calling his bank, for now.

The Hardies had stayed in the building, deciding to have coffee in the cafeteria while they waited.

Seth wanted to see a little of the city that had made Gwen so unhappy. He walked, noting without thinking where the sun hit, where he changed direction, how many paces. He'd find his way back.

The remaining snow was covered in soot. Litter sodden in the gutters. Traffic noise everywhere, car horns, raised voices, music coming from one shop clashing with what came from the next.

How could anyone live in this? No wonder Gwen wept for quiet.

Seth was back at the hospital by the time visiting hours opened again. Rejoined the three Hardies at Gwen's bedside; they took turns sitting, holding her hand.

A little over an hour later, Gwen's eyelids fluttered. Seth felt her hand, weakly, return pressure. "Gwen—we're here." And her eyes opened.

"You're here," so soft a whisper. "Seth." Her eyes moved, taking her family in. "Daddy, Jack. Mom." She looked past them, to the window. Tears started in her eyes.

"No. *No, no.* I'm still—in—in—*here.*" The doctors had warned she might have trouble finding words. Hopefully, that would get better.

"This—city. I just can't get out, can I? I was going to fly home . . ." Gwen remembered that, but nothing beyond.

No one corrected her, this was not the time.

Paul Hardie looked at Seth, who ceded place to him. Held his daughter's hand, "Gwen, my darling daughter, as soon as you're well enough we'll take you home. I promise."

"Home." Gwen sighed, and closed her eyes.

Was it odd she hadn't asked for Mark?

* * *

She asked the next morning, when Mark would be able to come to see her. "He's so busy all the time, now."

"Gwen. Mark—you had a very bad accident. He—Mark—he didn't make it." The hardest words Paul Hardie had ever had to say to his daughter.

"Mark is—Mark's—dead? No. No, he *can't* be. He's going to turn 30 next month. I already got him a—a—a *present. He can't be dead!"*

Nurses shooed them all out, and sedated Gwen.

* * *

They stayed in Boston another day. Madeleine's manager was fielding frantic calls from her showrunner and producers. Jim Marshall was beginning to gripe, though it sounded as if he had everything in hand. Jack was uneasy being away from his business so long.

Paul would have stayed longer; Seth would like to have stayed, too, but was conscious of the mounting total he'd have to repay Paul (he thought) for hotel bills. It was probably a good idea to get back, anyway. An owner's presence was good for quality control, and Seth liked both quality and control.

Gwen was out of danger. The hematoma was responding to the drugs, her arm was mending, and her ribs. She'd be two more weeks in the hospital. But she lived and would live, and would, the doctors thought, make a complete recovery, or nearly so.

They left; they'd be back. On the drive home, they worked out tentative scheduling—who'd go, and when.

* * *

Seth drove down again the following weekend, starting out as early as possible on Friday afternoon, leaving evening stables to the hands. He had one or two new horses in training, but was not busy—the summer people who made up so large a portion of his customer base would not arrive for some weeks.

Gwen had accepted Mark Sinclair's death; she wept often, but was no longer distraught. She remembered her decision—

her determination—to get home, remembered finding a flight. Nothing after. She knew she and Mark had been driving, but that was a bleak blank in her mind. Gwen hoped her memory would return—she felt *horribly* robbed of their last hours. But Mark was dead, and that would not change.

She thought she'd never again love as she'd loved him.

It was the right answer, but she was asking herself the wrong question.

Saturday morning, she woke to Seth holding her hand. She squeezed his, less weakly than before. "You bring the quiet with you. What I need. The best medicine. Thank you."

* * *

Elizabeth Lord had cracked her last formula; it was in final testing. The dream she'd been working to make reality since before she was 16 was so close that, if she stretched out her hand, she could feel the imminent reality in her fingertips.

She'd kept a low profile, as far as the tabloids were concerned, and her father (Peter Lord, unlike his wife, admitted these publications' existence) had restored her Maine privileges. Liz found herself taking advantage more than she had prior to being warned off.

Liz hoped she'd run into Seth Greenlaw; she meant to apologize. But that had not happened; and one day, she drove across 226 and up Gray Way.

Seth and the hands were wrapping up morning exercise when the Mercedes pulled in. Red as a fire alarm; but the hands were chaperone / witness, Seth figured.

He went to greet his visitor, warily. Liz Lord was, along with everything else, the daughter of a neighbor and a customer.

"I owe you an apology. I misbehaved, I know it. I'm sorry."

Well. "No need. Write it off, incomplete pass."

"Yes, there is. It was a very *forward* pass."

Seth laughed at that. *Good.*

"And I *am* sorry. It was stupid. I don't like being stupid. I misread, badly. I should have been straight up. Just told you I wanted to get into bed with you."

One thing you can say for her, she's full of surprises. That would have made saying "no" even harder.

"You'd have got the same answer, but I'd have liked you better."

Liz held out a hand. "I hope you *will* like me better, going forward."

They shook on it.

One day, maybe, he'd ask her what he still couldn't figure. *Why him?*

* * *

Seth missed his next visit to Gwen; Jack drove down in his stead. Colicky horse. If it had been one of his own, he'd have let Jim and the hands deal with it, but not a customer's property. Colic in horses could have serious complications.

When that was dealt with, he found a space during the week, and drove down to Boston. Paul had told him that the doctors worried Gwen's hematoma was returning. Or a new one forming—Paul wasn't quite clear.

He ran into traffic held up by (*another!*) bad accident. Multiple vehicles, this one. Seth sat stalled for two frustrating hours, and arrived at the hospital almost at the end of visitation.

Gwen was no longer in ICU, she'd been moved to a semi-private room. Mercifully, the other bed was empty, but the hospital battered her ears with so many noises, in such variety, she actually missed normal life in the city. By comparison.

She was off morphine; this was good and bad. The alternative painkillers often made her vomit, and were less effective against pain. But they did not make her skin itch unbearably, as morphine had.

All of them fuzzed her mind; she had kept the drip turned as far down as she could stand, and now took few pills. Up to a certain point, she'd take the pain. But the headaches took it past that point, too often. Pain almost *visible*, blinding her to anything else.

Her eyes lit up when Seth came in. She got out of bed.

The cast on her arm made embrace awkward, but she leaned her head against him, felt his heart beat quiet into the rhythm of hers. Seth *restored* her, as drugs could not begin to do.

She laughed when he gave her the earplugs he'd picked up at a stop for gas. "*These*, I can use. Thanks."

Getting thinner. She looked as if she'd lost ten pounds. And was losing more. She hadn't had the pounds to lose. The delicate bones of her face looked scraped of flesh. Skin almost transparent; he could see every vein in her too-thin hands.

"It's the food. I swear, it's cruel and unusual punishment. I wouldn't wish it on a—a rabid . . . *damn it*—a rabid . . . animal."

A nurse came in, to announce the end of visits. Gwen rounded on her.

"One hour. He just got here. This is my brother, my best friend in the world. He does me more good than any bed or drugs you've got. Damn it, I had more time with my family when I was unconscious. When I didn't even know they were there."

A week ago, she'd have wept, and accepted the stricture.

Nurse Cabot said, again, that visiting was over for the day.

"*One hour.* If you don't I swear to God I'll make such a—a—such a *ruckus,*" (the word she'd been groping for was simpler), "you'll wish you'd shut up and let it alone, I promise you."

Other nurses were called, and a doctor; in the end, Gwen got half an hour with Seth.

It was good to see her high-handedness coming back. *In spades,* Seth smiled to himself. If his presence was comfort to Gwen, glints of her old, whole self were *enormous* comfort to Seth.

Bad food. How she *would* hate that.

Seth didn't like the hospital any better than Gwen did. An old building cut into inharmonious, inorganic spaces. Jangling energy from too many conflicted presences. Constant noises of different busynesses. He didn't trust it. Or the doctors, who were people he didn't know.

Gwen's voice getting stronger, *will* coming back to her, those were real. *Those,* he trusted.

* * *

Her family were not Gwen's only visitors. Once Jack brought Melody Gray; she'd known they were dating, and Gwen thought they looked serious.

High time Jack had a girl. Gwen had always liked Melody, they'd worked together on a couple of science projects in school, and enjoyed it. If she hadn't been such a tomboy, always running around, or riding, with Seth and Jack, Gwen and Melody might have become closer friends.

The most interesting thing, though, was Jack's description of Melody's new shop.

"You wouldn't believe it Gwen, it just blew my mind clear into another world. It's like Ala Baba's cave, only it's beautiful fabrics, not gold and silver and stuff. I don't know, I mean, I don't even care about clothes, but that store . . . It makes me look at—everything—I don't know, different, somehow."

What had Melody *done* to Jack? He just didn't *talk* like that.

Well, well. Good for Melody. Good for you, too Jack. I think I'm going to like this. A lot.

"It sounds gorgeous, Melody. I'll stop in soon as I can, when I get home."

Ken Pelletier brought Caleb and Kyle to visit; Ben Greenlaw had flown from Arlington. Her in-laws, Charles and Margery Sinclair, came. Mark's two elder brothers, Charlie and Geoff, brought their wives. His younger, unmarried sisters, Isobel and Mary.

The Sinclairs only upset Gwen; she tried to hide this. Did not, quite, succeed, and their visits became infrequent.

Liz Lord checked in on her several times.

Once, with that New York writer with the nice smile in tow —she didn't rummage in her brain for his name—but it was not a good day, and Gwen had not felt up to company. Especially someone she barely knew.

* * *

A day or two later, Gwen was released. Paul had promised to bring her home immediately, but reality set its own rules.

The doctors wanted her to stick close for a few weeks, in case the hematoma returned. She was not to drive or to fly, not for at least a month.

I can't get out of here. 'Boston' was a word that eluded her often.

She went back to the condo. It would have to be sold, belongings packed up. Mark was all over it. Every corner, every shelf.

He had been buried, what little was left of him, while she was in the hospital. Charles and Margery Sinclair took her to his grave. They were even more hollowed out by loss than she was; all of them wept.

It was setting in—she'd never hear his beautiful voice again. See his beautiful face. Nestle against him, curled up on the sofa. Mark was dead. Gone.

Her life here was over. Her heart had a hole in it. Gwen wasn't sure she could bring herself to hope it might close.

Gwen would be grateful to put the city behind her. Put it in a box, set it up on a shelf in the very back of her mind.

But Mark's ghost danced beside her everywhere.

She slept most of her days. Her parents-in-law brought her a good deal of paperwork; they explained, or tried to, but information didn't filter well through Gwen's cocktail of pain, loss and exhaustion. She signed what they put in front of her.

The Sinclairs urged her to leave all thought of condo sales and moving arrangements to them. Gwen should rest now, and go home when she was ready. They would have everything shipped to Haven Point, put the condo up for sale, send her the proceeds.

One of the documents she signed was a power of attorney, limited to the sale.

"Sign there, dear."

Charles and Margery Sinclair were as kind as could be. It was good of them; especially since they'd always thought Mark married a little beneath him. They'd done their best not to show it, maybe even tried not to feel it—they were decent people, really.

But Gwen knew. Suspected they'd be more than a little relieved when she went home. She wished them nothing but well, but she wouldn't miss them, either.

CHAPTER 13

Early June

Six weeks out of the hospital, the doctors gave her the go-ahead to travel. Gwen packed a few things and booked a flight to Bangor.

Paul Hardie spoke with Gwen's doctors, too, and bought a round-trip ticket to Boston for himself, his return the same Sunday flight as Gwen's. She shouldn't be traveling alone. And she would not be.

Seth Greenlaw discussed logistics with Jack Hardie.

"We should take two vehicles. Two flights, you never know."

Madeleine Hardie was flying back east, to spend Gwen's first days at home with her; the flight from California was scheduled to arrive within half an hour of the plane from Boston.

Seth's distrust had been prophetic. The flight from Boston landed 20 minutes ahead of schedule; Madeleine's flight had been delayed, the Minneapolis connection missed. Her arrival was projected at two hours and some later.

"Seth, you drive Dad and Gwen when they get here; I'll wait

with Melody for Mom." Melody Gray had come in Jack's truck, to be support and company. They had not spoken yet of marriage, but they were both comfortable that was coming. Best to wait—the Hardies had enough to deal with, for now.

Seth had driven Paul's station wagon, at his direction. For the extra passenger space. Jack's pickup had a small space for passengers; Seth's did not.

Bangor Airport is very small, and easy to navigate. Paul Hardie had had a quiet word with one of the flight attendants; he and Gwen were first off the plane. Paul took both of their carry-on bags; Gwen had no checked luggage.

"Give me those." Seth took the bags out of Paul Hardie's hands, set them down, and turned to Gwen, who moved, a little hesitantly, into his arms. She didn't sob, but he felt wet tears through his shirt.

So thin—she'd put back a few of the pounds lost in hospital, with better food available. Not enough, not yet. She'd braided her hair—it was getting quite long. The end of the braid came six inches below her shoulders. She'd had a longer braid, when she was 12. The summer Seth had known he loved her, wanted her for his. When it came time.

Paul had spoken to his own thoughts, a couple of weeks past.

"When she's ready –"

"Be a while, I'd think. It's a lot to get past."

"It is. I wouldn't leave it too long, though, son. She thinks she won't, but she *will* get past this. Haven Point's a hard place for a woman alone. She'll need a man—and she couldn't do better."

Gwen stopped her tears. Stood back a step, holding Seth's hands, best smile she could conjure. She had to be brave, strong. And with her family, *these dearest*, she could—she *would*—

manage it.

She hugged both Jack and Melody Gray. "I'm really touched, Melody—thank you for coming."

Melody shook her head, waved thanks away. "It's good you're home, Gwen. Now we can all look after you, 'til you get strong again."

Gwen hugged her again, whispering, "I'm so happy for Jack he found you. Welcome to the—the," *no. This was a word she would not, NOT lose,* "family. From me, anyway."

"Thanks, Gwen. It's a super family," Melody whispered back.

Gwen's head ached; the sun outside the window looked hot, too bright. She'd need the dark sunglasses the doctors had instructed her to buy. Almost no-one wore them in Haven Point, and Gwen had never before owned a pair.

"Dad, Mom won't be here for a couple of hours. Seth'll drive you and Gwen down now, Melody and me will wait and bring Mom when she gets here."

Seth helped Gwen into the back seat; went round and assisted Paul in beside his daughter. Got behind the wheel. They all waved to Jack and Melody.

"See you soon," Gwen called.

"What's up with those two?" asked Melody. "I mean, you guys have always been close, I know about the 'brother' thing, but if that's all there is to it, I'm a monkey's auntie."

Jack, with new eyes courtesy of Melody-created beauty, had been wondering, himself. Ever since the accident. Looking back with those new perceptions confirmed it. He wasn't sure, yet what it was.

But there was more to Gwen and Seth than brother-and-sister.

He thought.

"It's kind of complicated, I guess. You know, Seth's mother died when he was seven. She had a bad time, carrying Ben, and there were complications. She never really got over it."

Jack wondered whether Gwen would fully get over her concussion. It made him so sad that she might not.

"Then she came down with something—I don't remember what, flu, pneumonia maybe. Ben was about one-and-a-half, then. One morning she didn't wake up. Her name was Abigail.

"I don't think Ben even remembers her. I don't know what Seth felt, he never talked about her, later."

"I think I remember the funeral. We never were as close with them as you guys were. It got easier, after their Dad died. Daddy didn't like Hank Greenlaw."

"He wasn't easy to like. But we were close with Seth since I can remember. I guess him and me were what people call 'best friends,' except by the time Ben was old enough to tag along, Seth and Gwen were even closer.

"Seth was always the leader. He was the biggest, even though I'm a little older. Much stronger personality than me, too."

"Don't you go putting yourself down, Jack Hardie. You don't lack any strength, it's just you're kind and easy-going. Seth's— he's got a lot of—dark. He seems laid-back, on the surface, but there's no way he's easy-going. Not deep down, not for real."

"His life hasn't let him be," Jack surprised himself by saying. He hadn't really thought of it before. *Life does things. Good and bad. To all of us.*

"Anyway, with Ben being so much younger, and Gwen being the only girl . . . I don't know, it made her and Seth sort of . . ."

"I get it—they were the parents."

Jack had never looked at it like that, but it made sense. In a weird way. "Yeah. Kind of."

Melody—she *got* things. Was opening them up to him, inside him, so that he could begin to *get* them, too.

But there was definitely something he *didn't* get about Seth Greenlaw and his sister. Now he thought about it, it didn't look as if *they* did, either.

* * *

Seth drove Paul and Gwen the hour-plus south by southeast, in silence.

Crippling headaches that made Gwen vomit. Sunlight intolerable to her eyes. Words she couldn't find. Her quick, darting grace gone, the bodily confidence which had been its bedrock shattered.

This was what the doctors congratulated them on. An excellent outcome. Almost-full recovery. She might get better than this, she might not. His sweet girl. Paul bled inside as from an open wound.

Gwen, behind her dark glasses, beneath the pain she floated in, felt 'home' in her heartbeat. Closed in the car, *Seth and Daddy and quiet. No place like home.* Sweetness wrapped her sorrow.

Seth, ripped by pain for her, and his own sharpening hope. For down the road, *wait, wait, no rush.* It would take however long it took.

He knew how to wait. He'd been on this road a long time.

* * *

Seth's pickup stood in the Hardie driveway; he stopped the station wagon short of it, helped Gwen out; Paul got out unassisted, clicked the garage open.

Seth pulled around his truck, parked in line with it, leaving

Jack a clear path straight in.

What an unholy mess of a shape, Gwen thought, looking at her father's house with love.

They went in by the kitchen door. Gwen, smiling a little, touched stovetop, sink, surfaces. Her *place. Home, home.* She was home.

It was the same, but she was not.

"Excuse me a minute."

She went to the little half bathroom closest, and threw up. Cleaned her teeth (she'd always kept the bathrooms stocked with fresh toothbrushes and paste, and here they still were, thanks be to God).

Seth had put on a pot of coffee. "I measured twice what it said—?"

A tiny part of her wanted to pour it out and make her own. And thank God for that—good to know it wasn't gone, with so much else of her.

Gwen had to put herself back together, and she didn't know what the pieces would even *be.*

She accepted the cup Seth handed her. Milk-no-sugar. Sipped. Not like hers, but not bad. "Thanks, Seth, it's good. And caffeine helps with the headaches. They say."

They moved to the big living room; Seth and Gwen on the deep-cushioned sofa.

"If there's a—ball game, you can put it on. It won't bother me."

Paul switched on the Red Sox, turning the sound low. Both Seth and Gwen liked baseball, as did he. A pastoral sport.

"I'll just call the airport, see about your mother's plane." Paul left the room.

"I won't always be so useless. I promise."

"Couldn't be useless if you tried, Gwen. Not to me."

"I've missed you so much. Such a hole in my life, not having your company. You don't *know*."

Carefully, gently, he put an arm around her, drew her close. "What makes you think I don't? I missed you, too." *Every bit as much, maybe more.* "It's good, though—you're as silly as ever. Glad that hasn't changed." He kissed her forehead; she smiled up at him, nestled closer.

Her head throbbed much less, now. Receding pain took her last energy with it.

Gwen slid down on the couch, kicked off shoes. Drew her feet up, her head resting on Seth's thigh.

"I'm not the best pillow. Here—" he pulled a cushion from the corner. Lifted her, slid it under her head. "This'll be more comfortable."

It was certainly *softer* . . .

"I'll wake up when Mom comes."

"I'll be here." He stroked her bright, braided hair, very lightly. *Too close to happiness, this.*

Gwen sighed.

This was home. This was peace.

Sleep took her; she yielded.

CHAPTER 14

Summer

June turned to July. For those first weeks, Gwen did little. Her mother had come and was gone; Gwen didn't miss her much. At all, really. Mom didn't represent *home* to her. And home—and all that went with it—was her comfort. Her only comfort.

Mark was dead.

Meals were takeout. Not one of the men in her life had ever been even a decent cook. Paul bought large orders—big containers, not single portions—from that new place, up the other side of 226. With the funny—but catchy—name. Gwen insisted on supervising the heating up, from the beginning.

Men would just use the microwave, God bless them. Use it wrong, at that.

Even reheated, the food was good. At least as good as Amy Mason's catering. Fresh, it would be better than that. Shrimp and grits (Gwen knew a couple of tricks to make the grits 'come back'). The seasoning in those crawfish pies . . . the lady knew her stuff. Gwen would have to meet her. Sometime soon.

Melody Gray never dined with them; she was a good cook, and was counted on by her parents, who were both years older than Paul Hardie. Still, not a day but she was at the house, for Gwen as well as Jack.

The two girls liked many of the same movies, and watched more than a few over together. Found some new ones. *She's the best sort of Maine woman,* Gwen thought, *down to earth, but with an artist's soul.* Jack was very lucky. They all were. Melody was good as the gold of her hair.

Seth joined the Hardies for dinner, most days. Gwen wished he just lived with them. Everything was better when Seth was there. Always had been.

Within a month, she asked her father to take her food-shopping. She was afraid to drive; she would have to address this—it would be crippling, here. Driving was part of home.

It took most of the day, and exhausted her; one last night, they dined on Althea Jones' cooking.

Gwen was in her kitchen the next morning.

I'm back.

*   *   *

After breakfast, she got behind the wheel of the station wagon, drove up and down Gray Way. Slowly, faster. Up and down, up and down. Day after day. After day.

Until, one morning, she drove down, and turned onto Route 226. Up a way, down a way, at 75 miles per hour. Up again, down again. Her stomach churned a little, but she drove steady.

And down to town, for the first time.

"Hi, Melody—*oh, my God!*" As fabulous—literally, something out of a fable—as Jack had tried to tell her. It didn't blow her mind as it had his, but—still. "*Wow. Melody—just, wow."*

Melody chuckled. "Thanks, Gwen. Good to see you getting out. Friendly visit, or do you need anything? Look around, either way; let me know if I can help."

Gwen hadn't planned on new clothes, and the ones in front, on the walls, were nothing she needed. Too fancy, really, for Haven Point. Except maybe summer-people parties, and few even of those would require evening wear. Who did Melody sell them to?

"You'd be surprised. Your mother's bought a dozen, for one. And I think sometimes women just buy them to have, to look at."

Gwen could almost see that. Those gowns were things you could dream on. People needed dreams.

But the back room, that had pretty, more casual dresses.

"Look at this." Melody held up a long-ish, short-sleeved dress of dark green knit linen, with a print of tiny fish in turquoise, orange, pink. "This should fit you; I have a couple of others I think might be tiny enough." It buttoned the whole way down the front.

A modest sort of sundress, Crisp, striped cotton in aqua, violet and white. Also buttoned.

One a bit dressier—heavy, solid peacock-colored silk jersey, shimmering subtly. Princess lines, sleeves just above the elbow, a fine zipper up one side.

"Oh, look at that color on you. It makes your hair turn to fire."

Melody wanted her to accept them as a 'coming out' gift. Gwen didn't think it right.

Eventually, they agreed to a 50% 'family' discount. "One time only," Gwen said.

"We'll see. Have fun—I'll see you later at the house."

Jake and Ann Gray were off for vacation, and Melody was dining with the Hardies tonight.

* * *

Gwen's next stop was the library, but they'd changed their infrequent hours. She'd have to come back—carefully noted the new days, times. Not tomorrow, either.

There had been a fine development for the local and area food producers. A newcomer, Angela Bianchi, retiree from New York, had organized, and space had been donated for, a centralized marketplace for their wares. A small markup paid assistants, electricity, incidental expenses.

Produce, meat, fish. Jams, pickles, popcorn. Baked goods— bread, pies, cookies. Plants, flowers.

Gwen bought several flats of herb plants. Low-bush blueberries—the ones Maine was famous for—tiny berries bursting with deep flavor that put the big balls you found elsewhere to shame.

Twenty pounds of ripe heirloom tomatoes. A great big bunch of basil, in addition to the little plants.

Sixteen quarts of strawberries, from one blessed soul several towns away, she was told, who grew late-bearing plants.

Some stuff for the next few days' dinner.

There were quite a few unfamiliar faces, at the marketplace and in town, Gwen had noticed, and they couldn't all be tourists and summer people.

Even Haven Point changed.

At the local food co-op pickup place, she placed an order for champagne, cabernet sauvignon, and white balsamic vinegars, extra-virgin olive oil, in bulk.

At the craft shop, small bottles with screwcaps, a few larger ones with corks. Wax. Mason jars. Cheesecloth, string.

She had to do something, *work* at something, and she'd had an idea.

* * *

At home, Gwen mixed up lemon cake, set it to bake.

Put aside a few of the tomatoes, a quart each of strawberries and blueberries. Pureed the rest, filling freezable quart containers.

As soon as her oil and vinegars came in, she'd be ready to start.

Now, it was time to start—dinner. Seth would be here—Gwen glanced at the clock—any minute, in fact.

Where had the day gone? She was tired, a little shaky, but not exhausted. A good day, not one headache. She'd only had to search for a few words, and had found the right ones, mostly.

And she had a plan, *purpose*, beyond just being home.

Something quick—she'd planned shrimp, and had peeled three pounds right after breakfast. Carbonara? Fresh duck eggs. Good, local bacon (you couldn't get guanciale in Haven Point). Gwen microplaned a big bowl of parmesan, put salted water on to boil. Shaved some thick asparagus, not local, but organic. Pulled a box of fettucine off the shelf, chopped the bacon, fried it halfway, and turned the flame off.

Tossed some greens in a big bowl—she'd salt and dress them at the last minute.

Her cake was done. She'd cut it into wedges, serve it with strawberries and a little of the lemon curd she'd made a few days back.

Seth liked desserts not too sweet, just as she did.

* * *

On the sixth day after picking up her oil and vinegars, Gwen carefully strained the eight sample fruit-infused batches that were ready. The herb vinegar infusions would take a few more days, the oils—herbs packed tight and weighted down to prevent spoilage—another five weeks.

But the most ambitious vinegars, paradoxically, were ready. Strawberries, blueberries, tomatoes.

She'd tried infusing the strawberries and tomatoes into all three vinegars—champagne, white balsamic, cabernet sauvignon. A fourth tomato variation, including basil in the cab sav. Two blueberry batches, cab sav and white balsamic.

She filtered the results into little screwcap bottles, tasted. All three of the strawberry batches were good, interesting variants, full of strawberries and light acid bite. The champagne batch had the clearest flavor of strawberry; the white balsamic and cabernet you could pour on ice cream.

Gwen wasn't sure about the basic tomato-cab batch, the wine flavor masked a little of the tomato, but the other two were fine, and the cab sav with tomato *and basil* worked like gangbusters—to her palate, anyway.

The blueberry-cab was wonderful and deep-flavored. She'd added a tiny bit of fresh-grated nutmeg—it brought out extra richness in the berry flavor.

She'd had the idea as she'd unpacked her freighted stuff. Gwen had brought her own bottles of Gail Winthrop's signature flavored vinegars, and thought, sadly, that when they were gone, there would be no more.

Unless she made them herself. *And why not?*

Gail used white vinegar as a base; Gwen had wanted to get racier.

It was too late to hope for a good return this season, but she could make a start. And there would be the next summer, and the next.

Mark's notebooks went directly into the attic. Gwen couldn't even think about dealing with them.

Not yet. *When, then? I don't know, maybe never. He's gone.* Gone.

The headaches were fewer and fewer, she'd gone three or more days at a stretch without.

She'd got strong enough to ride out with Seth and his hands, exercising the horses, twice a week. In a good week, three times. Usually, he put her on Belle, who was a smooth ride.

All things considered, Gwen was content—enough. Mark receded a little, in Haven Point. He hadn't ever been part of her life, here, not really—their life had been all Boston.

Now she had her home, her family—which Boston, and Mark, had kept her from.

Romantic love, she could not think of without weeping, as several local young men had discovered when she turned down 'date' requests. She kept Mark's place in her heart empty. It was still his.

But love she had in abundance, to give and to take. She concentrated on those filled heart-spaces, and was grateful to her marrow.

* * *

Half an hour before Downeast Bayou's closing time, the red-haired young woman took one of the little tables. Althea hadn't seen her before, but gossip had told her enough to make a guess she'd bet on.

Went to greet the new customer. "You're Paul Hardie's girl,

aren't you? Real sorry for what happened, and your loss. Glad you're getting up and about."

"I am. Gwen Sinclair. Thank you." She scanned the menu, quickly. Something she hadn't tried.

"What can I get you?"

"Um, I think I'll try the half oyster po-boy." It had bacon, mornay sauce, and tomatoes. "Good move, offering the halves."

"Learned that fast. Saves food, and more people buy. Fries?"

"Please. And a side of coleslaw. Would you have a minute to talk, when you close? I'll help you clean up, after, so you don't lose time."

"Sure. 'Preciate it."

Althea Jones brought her food. It was simple stuff, of course, but perfectly executed. Oysters and fries crisp, smoking hot. Ripe local tomatoes. The mornay was just right. Coleslaw sweet with a good cider-vinegar bite, and an undernote she couldn't quite identify.

Flavors balanced, seasoning that brought them together and piqued the palate. *Damn, Althea Jones. You can cook.*

Gwen looked at the local products on the shelves. She'd have to design labels. Pretty ones, clever ones. She hadn't thought.

Maybe Liz could give her a pointer or two—she'd been working like a demon on the marketing campaign that would hit print and television next month.

Diners finished and departed. Gwen waited while Althea closed out her register.

As beautiful as Liz Lord, Gwen thought. *Even better, if you like exotic.*

Brown-gold skin with a sort of coppery shimmer under, or over it. Gold-brown eyes, iris ringed in dark grayish-green, large, wide, deep. Fine profile—nose as elegant as Liz's, mouth even fuller.

She couldn't be sure about Althea's figure in her working clothes, jacket, apron. Robust, strong, anyway.

Althea, receipts balanced, joined her.

"I guess you're glad to be back in your kitchen."

"Oh, yeah. *Very.* Sorry about the lost business."

"Can't say I don't miss it, but you're entitled. Now, what can I do for you?"

Gwen pulled out the sample bottles.

"Would you taste these? See what you think?"

Althea got tasting spoons from the kitchen. Opened tomato-basil cabernet sauvignon vinegar, poured a few drops, sipped. Her eyebrows shot up.

"Girl." Pleasure and respect in her voice. She poured more, sipped again, rolling the flavors in her mouth. *"Girl. Damn.* I'd serve this by itself on a salad. This is *fine.*"

Gwen had not thought of Althea's putting them on her menu, said so. "I was really thinking of offering it retail, but I'll be glad to give you a good wholesale price. If it goes on the menu, though, so does my name."

"I wasn't born *last* night, girl. You'll get credit. Won't hurt me any, having *the* local-girl Michelin chef on my menu."

"Make it specials only, at first, to test them out. I'll give you one free pint each—pick what you want for now—and we can work out pricing if they're popular."

"I'll take some for retail too—but it's consignment only."

"I never thought different."

They shook hands on the bargain, and went to clean the kitchen. The two women worked comfortably and effectively.

Skinny, but pretty. Where do you get eyes like that from? Althea thought. And Gwen Sinclair had undeniable *presence.* About her own age, Althea, who was 28, guessed. *Maybe a couple of years younger.* As it happened, Gwen was not quite 25; Althea wasn't too far off.

"I'm going to pry, now, sorry. Small town, and you can tell me to mind my business. But—what brings you to Haven Point? Long way from your roots, from what I hear. Not that you aren't a great addition, with this place. Bet you're busier than you expected."

Althea told her a much-simplified version. Left out a lot, but spoke only truths—selected ones.

"I took Nerise away from New Orleans because of the violence. People I knew got shot, killed. Over nothing. That was a while ago. And before you ask, Nerise's father—he ain't in the picture, good reasons and plenty of 'em.

"Been working ever since to get her somewhere safe, saw this article about Haven Point in some paper. It sort of struck me it might be a good place for us. I go on impulse when I know it's right."

Gwen *liked* this gorgeous, impulsive, talented creature.

And could be impulsive, herself. "I'd love it if you'd come to dinner some night, bring Nerise—I'd like to meet her. Fastest thing in school, I hear."

"That's real kind of you, I'd like that."

"You free tonight? It'll be chili, I made it yesterday, so it's had time to develop."

'That'd be great. 'Preciate it. What time?"

"I serve around seven, but come anytime. We can talk food."

"I'll need to get Nerise cleaned up. I don't know how that child gets so damn' *dirty.* Maybe six, six-thirty?"

"Any time," Gwen repeated. They shook hands, Gwen left Althea to lock up.

Gwen wondered who Althea was dating. There had to be someone, or there soon would be. Althea was too gorgeous, too rare in Haven Point, not to have generated quite some interest.

Who was there? Not many impressive enough to match her.

Gwen's cousin, Sheriff Ken Pelletier, was also a single parent. But he hadn't dated anyone seriously since he'd come home from Portland six years back, or so she'd heard. After his wife left him and the boys. She didn't think he'd even divorced her, yet.

She hadn't heard enough, or seen enough, of Haven Point as it was now, to know too many others. Most men the right age she knew of were married, or dating seriously. People married young, here, mostly.

Of course, there was Seth. Certainly, he was impressive enough to match Althea Jones, or any woman.

Gwen didn't really like that idea. Althea was impressive, gorgeous, and Gwen got a very good feeling from her. But she couldn't know, yet, if Althea were good enough for Seth. In her heart, Gwen didn't believe anyone was.

And, if she were honest, she loved coming first with him. Which was unforgivably selfish. If Seth found—that sort of love—with Althea, with anyone, she should be happy for him.

Gwen, unused to questioning her heart too deeply, stopped there.

Jack wouldn't be with them tonight, he was dining at the Grays'. Seth would be, though; she'd watch and see.

*　*　*

Gwen was almost wrong about her cousin. Ken Pelletier had, in fact, filed for divorce, having jumped through the hoops making it difficult to divorce a spouse you couldn't find. Not in Portland, where they'd lived, not in Manchester, New Hampshire, where her note had said she was headed. Not in

Boston, not in New York. He'd had notices published in Haven Point, Portland, and Manchester, and they'd called it good enough. The divorce would be final in a few weeks.

Ken had been in law enforcement in Portland; he'd brought his boys home to Haven Point as soon as he could. A deputy sheriff position had opened up, his application was accepted.

Sheriff Mike Mallar had announced his retirement two years later; predictably, Ken and Deputy Cole Jennings had vied to replace him.

Ken was a local boy, with big-city (in Haven Point, Portland qualified) and small-town knowledge. Cole Jennings had come from Ellsworth, a small city, and was ambitious.

Sheriff Mallar had declined to pick sides, officially. But he was occasionally seen having a beer with Ken. Not with Cole Jennings. This was noted.

Cole Jennings had wanted a public debate. Ken had been amused, but agreed. Didn't think it would hurt his chances any.

Cole had outlined his platform, which included increased enforcement of traffic violations and public intoxication penalties, and a plan to put half a dozen traffic lights downtown.

When it was Ken's turn, he spoke from his heart.

"Didn't rightly study about a platform. Figure I'll keep the peace as best I can, and not arrest anybody I don't got to.

"Might be a traffic light or two'd be a good idea. Wouldn't need 'em but in summer, we could shut 'em down when the season ends. Maybe a couple of yellows, could be red in summer, up 226 both sides.

"We could ask the town council to look at that—their business, not mine, I reckon."

Ken had won in a landslide, and had to hire two new deputies. Chris Appleton and Joe Russell were good, hardworking farm-raised boys. Took their jobs serious, but kept a light hand.

As it should be, in Haven Point.

* * *

Althea and Nerise Jones presented themselves at the Hardie home at 6:18 that evening. Taken down from the tight, scraped-back style she hid under her chef's hat, Althea's hair fell shoulder-length in loose, glossy black curls.

Nerise was quite cleaned up, and excited—there had been few invitations to dinner, as yet. This was due principally to the Jones ladies' newness in—and remoteness from—town.

Most of the non-school socializing they'd done was with those kind folk who showed up to help Althea shovel snow the previous winter; Althea cooked breakfast for them after the snow was cleared from her driveway and steps.

Mostly these people were the Sheriff and his two sons. They had been the first, and were the most frequent. The two times there had been over two feet of snowfall, Seth Greenlaw and two hands joined the Pelletiers. Seth had refused breakfast, for all three of them, with thanks. Ken Pelletier and his sons never declined, and Althea thought them good boys with a real decent man for a father.

The sheriff drove his patrol car by the café most evenings in all seasons, making sure all was well. He thought Ms. Jones a fine woman, doing right by her daughter. As well as being the most beautiful woman he'd ever seen. And one hell of a cook, to boot.

Haven Point was difficult for women on their own, especially in winter; Ken was glad to bring his boys to help out. Their remote location concerned him. Haven Point folk were, for the most part, a law-abiding bunch, but bad elements occasionally drifted south from the cities inland.

Paul Hardie was glad to see Gwen getting out, making possible friends, feeling up to new company.

Back in her kitchen.

She was improving greatly; he'd been afraid to hope for so much so soon. Perhaps, as the doctors said, youth and health made the difference. Perhaps, as Gwen said, home and family were the best remedy.

Seth Greenlaw arrived shortly after the Jones ladies. To Gwen's surprise, Nerise yelled, "Seth!," and ran to give him a hug. Reminded her of herself. She wasn't as fast, certainly not now, as a track star—even a 12-year old. Nerise, for a fact, was an inch taller than Gwen. It appeared she took riding lessons in summer.

But Gwen got her turn, and was embraced. "Good day?"

"So far."

"Headache?"

Gwen shook her head. "Not today."

"Bet that's a word you wouldn't mind forgetting."

"Not so much, no."

Seth shook hands with Althea. Gwen, watching narrowly, neither saw nor felt a hint of romantic attraction. Not one spark. On either side. Which was fine by her.

"Okay, guys, everyone but Althea out of the kitchen. I'm going to whip up a couple of pans of—of—cornbread, and I want to know how they make it in Louisiana."

"Depends. You're white, maybe no sugar. Us black folk, we like it sweeter."

Gwen herself was in the no-sugar camp, but she followed Althea's direction. Almost. She almost invariably cut the sugar in any recipe by half or more, and did so now.

"Sorry. I have sort of the reverse of a sweet tooth."

"Your kitchen, do what you want. That's white cornmeal, anyway. Sweeter than yellow."

Gwen cherished two ancient cast iron skillets, handed down through generations of women Hardie-born and Hardie-married.

Madeleine, in the days when she was a Haven Point wife with a hobby, rather than a famous Hollywood actress with a Haven Point family, had been afraid to use them.

As a result, they had not been ruined. Gwen had kept them well-seasoned, since she was a little girl; they went unused while she was in Boston. She had missed them in the city, but they belonged in Haven Point. In what was again her kitchen.

As cornbread baked, Gwen took her big pot of chili from the refrigerator, set it over flame.

Put on water to boil for rice. Chili should *not* be served with rice, in Gwen's opinion, but she knew her menfolk would want it. And extra carbs wouldn't hurt Nerise—she looked like a beanstalk. Darker, much thinner, curls not *quite* kinky. Nowhere near as beautiful as her striking mother.

Althea's t-shirt and jeans revealed a fine figure. Not slimly elegant with deep curve, like Liz Lord, but lush everywhere.

Gwen thought, a little wistfully, of her own meagre, diminished flesh. Maybe she could put back the needed pounds, at least to get to where she'd been.

She'd made coleslaw, taking it from the fridge reminded her.

"What *is* that extra seasoning you put in your coleslaw? I've been wondering all afternoon. I can't place it, and I know I should."

Althea shook her head. "I bet you got some secrets you don't tell."

"Oh, one or three. Fair enough. I warn you, I'll be in again.

And I'll figure it out sooner or later."

"Fair enough," Althea echoed, and they both laughed.

"I didn't know you two came up Gray Way regularly. How does Nerise like riding?"

"Loves it. Not as much as track, but it's good for her—helps her keep in with the town kids in summer, group lessons."

Seth gave locals a discount—a substantial one—on kids' lessons.

"We're practically a mini-community on this road. Have been for over 200 years. Of course, the Greenlaws came later, about a century after the Grays and us."

Althea was at the window. "What's that big building, out back aways, over near the woods?"

"Oh, Lord. That's one of Martin Hardie's follies. He wanted to start a fish-canning plant. It did *not* work out. Never got off the ground. That awful, wannabe-grand wing, that was another of his projects. He had to sell 40 acres to the first Greenlaws here, in the end."

"What's it like, inside?"

"In need of a lot of repair, is what. Not super-safe, I'd guess, by this time. A lot of tile—it was—*ceramic* tile, that's probably in fair condition, it never was used. I haven't been in there for years and years."

"You fixed it up, might make a real decent commercial kitchen, if you wanted to get ambitious."

"Hmm. It might, at that. If I did. It's a thought."

"*Smells* real good." The warmed chili gave off an inviting aroma.

Gwen tasted it, dropped the spoon in the sink, handed Althea a clean one.

"See what you think."

Althea took a small spoonful. "*Girl*," like that afternoon.

"Damn. *Damn.* This is *perfect.*"

"Nothing's ever perfect. I hope everyone likes it."

"Just us here. No false modesty, please, ma'am. It's— a'right, *nearly* perfect. I don't even miss the beans—and that's from a Louisiana girl. I do love me some red beans."

Gwen laughed. "Okay, I'm pretty pleased, I admit it."

Nerise darted in. *Oh, God, to have that in-body—certainty— back.* One thing being almost killed taught you—you were breakable. One day, you would die. It shook you.

"Mama, when do we eat? I'm hungry."

"Nerise! Where are your manners, child? We don't ask that in other people's homes. We're guests here. Now, you tell Miss Gwen you're sorry."

Nerise hung her head, squirmed. Dutifully repeated, "I'm sorry, Miss Gwen."

"Okay, Nerise. We'll serve in a minute. Would you go and tell the others, please? And take a seat."

Darting out again. A dark, nostalgic ghost of Gwen-past. Like God reminding her what he'd taken away.

The two women brought out serving bowls of chili, rice, coleslaw. Crumbled cheese. The skillets of cornbread, sliced into wedges.

All seated, Paul Hardie asked the blessing. Bowls passed round, plates filled.

Nerise reached for salt.

"Taste first." Althea Jones' deep, rich alto chorused with Gwen's light contralto. Everyone laughed.

And dug in.

"*Wicked* good, Gwen," said Seth, "*Damn.* It's just about perfect."

Althea, seated beside Gwen, murmured, "Told you."

"And I'll say it again, nothing's perfect. Thanks," to Seth, "glad you like it."

"It's real good, Miss Gwen, but where's the beans?"

The two women spoke together.

"Nerise! I swear, your manners. I apologize, Gwen. Nerise."

"This recipe doesn't have them. Texas chili doesn't, if it's authentic."

"I'm sorry, Miss Gwen. It *is* real good. But I still think it'd be better with beans."

"Nerise! You just hold your tongue or I'm taking you home right this minute."

"Don't worry about it," Gwen murmured very low, so Nerise couldn't hear. It didn't do to interfere with parental choices.

"Sorry, Miss Gwen." *Willful kid. But no harm in her.* Gwen smiled at Nerise. She'd always been on the willful side, herself.

* * *

Seth stayed, after the Jones ladies left. After Paul Hardie went up to bed. Jack had not yet returned from the Grays'.

Playing cribbage, sitting on the floor with Gwen.

"How's Nerise's riding?"

"Fair. She'd be better if she paid attention. It's just like with her mother tonight, I tell her and tell her, and it doesn't sink in."

"Kind of like you, at that age."

"I was *way* better than *fair* at 12. And you're *quite* wrong. I paid attention, all right. I *always* paid attention. I just didn't— I didn't—*mind*."

"Fair points. Got you thrown off, though, not minding me, remember?"

"Of course I do. You were *so* mad at me. Shook me 'til my

teeth rattled."

She'd laughed off persuasion. Everything else he'd said, admonishment to downright order.

Turned her mount to that damn' fence and taken off. Barefoot and bareback. Worse than silly, it was stupid-dangerous.

They did clear the fence. But the horse took a tiny stumble with its next pace, and Gwen had come off-balance during the jump. She came off entirely.

At least she knew how to fall. Not injured, and the horse was fine.

Seth had breathed a prayer of thanks, and been furious with her.

Could have smacked her, but he didn't hit girls, and settled for a good shaking. Yelling at her for being so reckless, risking her neck like that.

And still, she'd laughed.

Until he'd calmed down a—*very*—little. Said, still holding her shoulders, "How do think I'd *feel*, if you went and killed yourself? You think I could *live* with that?"

She hadn't laughed, then. Said, simply, "I'm sorry, Seth. I didn't think of that. I wouldn't have you hurt for the world. I'll mind from now on." She'd put her arms around him, kissed his cheek. Up on tiptoe.

He knew, in that moment, just *how* he loved her.

She'd been good as her word.

CHAPTER 15

August—September

"Next week, they'll be in magazines and on TV screens across the world's best markets. You've heard the process the last six years, I thought you'd like to see the finished product."

Gwen had never seen Liz Lord so *excited.* Always above things. Not now, not above *this*—this was what she'd worked for. Cheeks pinked with it. Eyes all shiny—she looked like a woman in love.

The print ad proofs—she'd brought quite a few—showed the faces of famous women. A senator, the CEO of a Fortune 500 company. Reigning Olympic champions—figure skating, gymnastics, a skier from Norway, a runner from Nigeria. An opera singer, a prima ballerina. Julia Lord, listed as "philanthropist"—and Madeleine Hardie.

Women of accomplishment. Their faces looked proudly from the proofs.

Gwen had noticed her mother's makeup had changed a little, on her last visit, and thought it an improvement.

The copy—"Don't conceal—reveal *who you are.* Be Yourself." The cosmetic line did, of course, offer vivid colors for those that would want them, but each of the ad-faces was made up in Liz's own personal style—understated, natural colors. The women looked both undisguised and perfected.

Even Gwen, who didn't wear makeup, wondered how she would look, done up like that. She could have found out—Liz had asked her to model. She'd laughed, "No, thanks, but really, no."

"Madeleine Hardie (signatures across the bottom of the images). Makeup by Elizabeth Lord." Liz's own signature below. "New York—London—Paris—Los Angeles."

The video of the television ad was cleverer still—the makeup sessions had been taped, screens filled with one closeup after another. Mouth, cheekbone, eyelid, brow; bits of hands brushing on, fingers gently rubbing in, the products. Each receding into a tiny image as the next appeared large. Not enough in any to identify the subject, as Liz's voice spoke the lines; the full image of the transformed woman dissolving in as one heard, "Be Yourself. Senator Jeanette Forrest. Makeup by Elizabeth Lord."

You saw the signatures being scrawled. Liz's own perfect face, repeating "Be Yourself." Which was the brand-name. Fadeout, on her signed name running across the screen.

"There'll be more venues, soon. Four's enough to start. You wouldn't believe the Rodeo Drive space I lucked into."

Gwen thought plenty of women would spend money on this. Some—too many, most likely—would spend more than they ought. She didn't know the prices, but they would be way out of her reach.

"I've got a sample case for you, but you have to let me show you how they work before I give it to you."

Liz had presented a personalized case of the products she'd used to each of her models. And she knew Gwen's face well enough to have a pretty good idea what she'd have used. Nothing outside of the basic—Gwen was young and so pretty, she didn't need much enhancement.

"Come up to the house. I've got good light there, mirrors. Do you have some time tomorrow?"

Gwen agreed to the session. It would probably be fun . . . and she'd get to see the face of Gwen Hardie Sinclair, makeup by Elizabeth Lord.

"I honestly don't think I've slept two hours at a stretch the past month. Mother told me I sounded absolutely hectic, and ordered me up here for a rest. As if I could. I'm trying . . ."

"Liz, they're beautiful. I don't know *anything* about makeup *or* marketing, but they make me want to try your stuff out, and I've never felt that way about cosmetics, not ever. That must mean something."

"My idea, my concept. From the first, I knew what I wanted. It's changed a bit, but only tiny details, not the—the—"

"Story-arc?" suggested Gwen, familiar with the term courtesy of her mother. Nice to be *supplying* a word. For once.

"Yes. Story-arc. They tell a story. Thanks. You wouldn't *believe* how hard I had to argue with the Mad Ave people. Watch, though, it'll work, and they'll all be congratulating themselves for coming up with it. People are so dumb, sometimes."

"We sure can be."

* * *

Liz's fine strong fingers massaged in brushed on colors, cool voice—with hot excitement under—explaining the process, the way the warmth of hand activated powder-cream.

It was an odd sensation, sensuous and—and—*clinical,* at the same time.

"They don't smudge. Kiss as much as you want, your lip-color won't smear." *Kisses. Mark.* Gwen made herself not cry.

"There. See?" Liz put a large mirror in front of her.

Gwen looked at her cosmeticked face. You could barely tell it wasn't her own skin. But—the stuff worked. She had never looked this pretty, and she knew it. Maybe on her wedding day—because it was her wedding day, and to Mark. *Mark.* But her makeup, done by her mother, hadn't been this—*perfect.*

Not that she'd ever wear makeup on a daily basis. Or ever apply it as well as Liz did, if she tried every day 'til she was 100.

"Oh, I almost forgot—Patrick's coming up. You remember him, Patrick Riordan—he's that writer who turned me down a couple of years back. God, that was a bad September for my self-esteem. From all sides.

"I like Patrick, though, he's very fun company. He's been pestering me for an invite, and I finally gave in and asked Mother.

"He'll want to see you."

* * *

Gwen's infused vinegars and oils sold well, at Downeast Bayou and elsewhere.

The tomato, strawberry and blueberry varieties practically vanished overnight. The herb vinegars and oils were less wildly popular, but sold about as she'd expected.

It was a good thing she'd pureed and frozen so much, but she'd had to buy more of each fruit already.

Gwen was grateful they took so little time to infuse; she'd sold two large production runs, and had a third steeping in the refrigerator, of each of the eight fruit varieties.

She ran cases down to town, and up to Althea. Salads

dressed with Gwen's vinegars—two of these were regular menu items, and Althea used them for salad specials. Gwen's favorite was a chilled beef salad over mixed greens, with fresh parsley and dressed with the tomato-basil cabernet vinegar. Her name was printed with each item on the menu.

The Jones ladies came often to dinner; Gwen liked—felt comfortable—with them both. She'd been a little family-insular all her life, and had rarely made close friends with those she hadn't grown up knowing; her relationship with Mark Sinclair had been singular.

Sometimes Gwen dined with them. Althea Jones' Southern manners required reciprocal invitations; Gwen accepted many. Brought wine.

One such evening, Nerise doing after-dinner homework in her room, Althea looked at her, speculative, frowning.

"Can I ask you something, and you won't be offended?"

"I'd think so, what?"

"It's—Nerise came home the other day, she was upset, said Mr. Harvey at school had said bad things about Seth Greenlaw. Nerise didn't believe what he said, but it bothered her. Me, too, and I don't know if she's right to discount it.

"Seems some boys were fighting, and Mr. Harvey sent them to detention. When he dressed them down, he used some names of what he called "incorrigibly violent" boys from past classes. Seth Greenlaw was one of the names. So—is there any truth to it?"

Gwen's face darkened. "He's such a *bastard*. Always was. That is *so* damned *unfair* it's not even funny.

"Okay, here's the truth of it. Seth never started a fight, ever. But there were—the bastard was right about that—a few bullies. They were bigger, at least two had been left back once or twice. They picked on people, including my brother. Jack was always such a *gentle* boy, and he came in for a good bit of their nastiness. If it got bad, Seth *did* step in to protect him. And good for him, I said it then and I'll say it now.

"Idiots like Mr. Harvey got this 'zero-tolerance' policy put in. Which meant anybody fighting got detention, the reasons didn't matter; when they got caught, that meant Seth as well as the ones who were at fault.

"Yes, it happened a lot. At first, Jack and I went with him and stayed 'til they let him go. He told us not to, and we stopped." Gwen smiled to herself.

"And another thing—I never saw him get angry on—on—for his own sake. Always protecting someone else."

"That's the way it was, for real?"

"Cross my heart and hope to die. He's got it in him, it's true, but it's never master. Seth is, and he's a *good* man, Althea. The *best*. Hand to God. My Dad'd tell you the same. Hell, Althea, ask the *sheriff*—Seth and Ken are *very* thick.

"Why would you *believe* such a thing?"

"Gwen, I don't know Seth. Not well. He has charge of my daughter, in summer. Had to ask.

"True or not, he—I know he's your friend, but—lot of dark, that man has in him."

"Dark isn't *bad*, Althea. He's like the night sky. Sometimes I think he could hold the whole world safe in that quiet dark."

That was the most romantic thing Althea had ever heard. *In love with him, and doesn't know it?* Gwen spoke, once in a while, of her late husband. Wistfully, sadly. The white-gold band still shone where Mark Sinclair had placed it. Puzzling.

Even if Gwen were over-partial, Nerise didn't trust, or warm to, everyone. On balance, Althea decided, she'd trust that.

The ability to command loyalty was something she respected.

* * *

Patrick Riordan arrived at the Lords' early one September evening, a case of wine for his hosts' in the trunk of his converted Jaguar, a brilliant smile on his face.

A beautiful setting, Haven Point. So *quiet*. A nice change from the constant racket of Manhattan. If things went well, perhaps he'd rent a house here himself, for a while.

He'd never shaken his first, enchanting impression of Gwen Sinclair. Perhaps he might have, if he'd tried, but he hadn't. He'd gone to Farmhouse Table, dined at the tasting bar, which opened to the kitchen. Patrick had found watching her delightful. Neat, quick, sure. And the food. Which no server, but she herself, placed in front of these favored customers. Beautiful, aromatic, complex flavors resolving into deliciousness. *As delectable as she is.*

Patrick had found reasons—excuses—to visit Boston, and Farmhouse Kitchen. As often as he could arrange it. Managed to exchange a few words with Gwen at each visit.

Until the restaurant closed, and that dreadful accident. He'd only tried to visit her once, and been turned away. Liz told him Gwen had plenty of visitors.

People much closer to her. *For now.* He'd get lost among them. He stayed away.

But she was here, she was recovered. And she was no longer a married woman.

He should, really, look into rentals. He couldn't burden the Lords over a long siege, and he was afraid this would be just that. But worth it, if he succeeded. *That fairytale princess of a girl, with eyes like no one else's.*

Patrick Riordan was determined to succeed with Gwen Sinclair. She stirred his imagination, captivated it. Gwen was a princess—he wanted to be the lucky man she chose as her prince.

CHAPTER 16

September—October

"Your parents are charming, Elizabeth."

"It's practically Mother's profession. Oh!" Liz watch beeped an alarm. She switched on the big television, clicked the channel button.

"Watch this, Patrick."

The first 'Be Yourself' ad, in prime time. The closeups, her voice, the slogan. Madeleine Hardie's beautiful face. Her own face, her voice speaking, "Be Yourself."

It was neat, spare, and full of glamour. In the old sense—it was magical. *Just what I wanted.*

Patrick laughed, appreciatively. "I'll never say you aren't clever, Elizabeth. Very effective.

"How did you prevail on Madeleine Hardie to model for you? I don't think she's done product endorsement her entire career. I've met her, once or twice, in New York. An admirable actress. I saw that "Much Ado" she won the Tony for. She was marvelous."

"Didn't you know? She's married to a local, here. I've

known her all my life. Madeleine's a semi-local herself—there were Pelletiers here, but the last ones died, left a decent bit of property to a couple of Georgia cousins, and they moved up here.

"I think she was about 15, and her cousin—he's the sheriff here, was maybe 5-ish."

"Aha! Was this her secret family, the one she never spoke of?"

"Yes. Paul Hardie—lives down across the road from us— old, *old* friends with Mother and Dad. Long story, but that family friendship's part of—well, we inherit it."

"Children? A son or daughter she's been secretly grooming to follow in her starry footsteps?"

Liz laughed at him. "Her son's following in his father's. Lobstering—very successful. You've met the daughter."

"Never tell me—Gwen Sinclair? Madeleine Hardie's daughter? Ah—I see it—the hair, the eyes—a little. Madeleine hasn't that startling green at the center."

"You've got it. Gwen Sinclair was born a Hardie."

"Wonders never cease. Congratulations on the ad, Elizabeth. You must let me take you somewhere to celebrate. Bring your pretty friend, if she'll come."

"I'll ask her. But it will be my party—you're a guest. You want to treat someone, take Mother and Dad out sometime."

They squabbled amicably over the host role for a minute or two, but Patrick ceded the field.

Three was an awkward number. Liz was not thrilled at the prospect of sitting by while Patrick Riordan talked to Gwen. Patrick was ridiculously transparent.

Since it *was* Liz's party, she would invite a fourth.

"Casual dress, Patrick. The best place around here is the local tavern. They have a decent wine list, and the food's good."

"Ye gods. A small-town local tavern. It's either absurd or charming. I'll know which when I've eaten and drunk."

Liz suggested she and Patrick take one car.

"I'd rather start getting to know the roads, thanks. I'll follow you."

They drove south on Route 226.

Patrick admired the rural scenery, the fall leaf-colors. More evergreens than hardwoods, though.

Rural segued to not-quite-in-town, smaller plots around neat houses.

Into town, old granite and brick buildings, storefronts, art galleries. Churches, official buildings.

When they'd parked, "There was a nice-looking restaurant back a bit—is that not a place to go?"

"It isn't bad—just not as good as they think, and over-priced. The tavern's better—really."

Paul Hardie's station wagon was already in the parking lot. Gwen was inside, making a temporary fourth at her cousins' table—Ken Pelletier and his sons, enjoying a dinner out.

Liz introduced Patrick to Ken, Caleb and Kyle Pelletier, Gwen took leave of her cousins, and the three took their own table. Liz looked over the wine list. Ordered a bottle of champagne to be iced pronto.

A good wine, one she knew. It was what Madeleine Hardie poured, and Liz preferred it to the much more expensive brand her mother served. Mother liked a pure Chardonnay champagne. Liz preferred a mix with Pinot Noir grapes, as did Madeleine.

Liz's chair faced the door; she was, therefore, the first to notice her third guest. She rose and waved. Gwen, facing her, looked around—her face lit up and she, too, jumped from her chair.

"Seth! I didn't know Liz had invited you, too!"

Minding his manners, Seth shook hands with Liz, thanked her. Hugged Gwen, kissing her cheek as she kissed his.

Liz introduced Seth Greenlaw to Patrick Riordan (younger presented to elder—Patrick was 38); they sat.

"Belinda missed you this morning, Gwen. You two need to get better acquainted."

"I know. I'm sorry, I had to get another production run going, and make some extra deliveries. Everyone's running out faster than I can make the stuff."

"Maybe you need to hire some help."

"Not yet, but if business gets any *better*, I really might. It'll slow down soon, anyway, for winter. *Not* the right time to hire—you know that as well as anyone."

"Who's Belinda, Seth?" asked Liz. "Lady friend? You could have told me, she'd have been welcome to join us."

Seth laughed, Gwen giggled.

"She's my birthday present, I turned 25 a week ago," said Gwen. "Seth always gives the best presents," turning to him, "but this beats everything. Really Seth, it's so—too, *really—extravagant* of you."

Extravagant was not, normally, a word one associated with Seth Greenlaw.

"She's a filly foal. Red roan, maybe, can't tell yet. The dam's my strawberry roan, Belle, sire's Minister—you know them, Elizabeth. Wicked pretty little thing."

Liz had been to the stables on her father's business a number of times. The first commission, after she'd reported her successful apology, she took as a sign she was forgiven—and trusted.

"Gwen. I thought you'd like having Belle's first."

"I didn't say no, did I? Of course, I love her. But it *is*

extravagant. And I still think you ought to let me pay her board and training fees."

Seth shook his head. "Package deal. I'll barely notice it." *Not quite a lie.* And how much board had he had, at the Hardie table? Plenty, that was sure.

Icy champagne was presented, poured. Gwen smiled in recognition at the bottle.

"Nice pick, Liz. Thanks."

Patrick raised his glass, "Here's to you, Elizabeth, and thundering success to your venture."

"Hear, hear!" exclaimed Gwen.

"Elizabeth," Seth echoed. "I saw one of those TV things. Don't care for makeup, but it looked like smart work to me."

They drank to Liz.

Liz, her own glass on the table, smiled. "Thanks, all." To Seth, "I'm pleased. Glad it impressed you favorably.

"I'll give you one, now—to Haven Point, and all who sail in her. Or on her. Whatever."

Seth and Gwen laughed, glancing at each other; all drank.

Another glass for each, and an empty bottle turned down in its ice bucket.

"Gwen, you're the expert—what's the best thing on the menu?" asked Liz.

"I'd stick with the ribeye. They go to the same farm I do; the meat's good, it's even aged a little. Seasoning's right on, and they fry the potatoes in duck fat. They're even using my blueberry vinegar in the salad dressing, now—see?"

Her name was on the menu; Gwen liked seeing that—it made her feel she still had a hand in.

She turned—"Seth, you agree, don't you?" He did.

Liz said, looking at Patrick only, "I've had the ribeye; it was very good." Seth smiled a little, not looking at her, either.

"What would you all like to drink with it? There's a good red, Cab Sav. That suit everyone?

General assent. Seth liked beer better, but Gwen was acclimating him to wine, and he didn't want to stick out. At least, not that way.

Liz ordered two bottles, and four steaks.

Seth didn't like the way this Riordan guy looked at Gwen. Like he could just eat her up. At least, she appeared not to notice.

He'd worked so hard, himself, to keep from showing anything she'd see, and know. Perhaps he'd got too good at it.

"The fries are even better than they used to be," commented Liz.

"It's the duck fat," said Gwen. "They just started using it. The match is *totally* made in Heaven. Never fry a potato without. Good for authentic Louisiana roux, too, Althea Jones tells me."

After they'd finished, Patrick said, "Ms. Sinclair—may I call you Gwen?"

"I'll answer to it." She smiled.

"Help me pick some dancing music, if you will be so kind."

Gwen looked first at Seth, shrugging.

They picked a few, Patrick dropping coins in the machine.

"Fly Me to the Moon." He'd hoped one or another of the others would come first. *Ah, well.*

"May I have this dance?"

Patrick Riordan took Gwen Sinclair in his arms. *The first step.*

At the table, Liz Lord cocked an eyebrow at Seth, who nodded, and took her hand. He could keep a better eye on Gwen if he were dancing, too.

"A belated happy birthday, Gwen. This is a lovely little town. Almost idyllic."

"What do you mean, *almost?* I never want to live anywhere

else. Right now, I don't want to *go* anywhere else. Not for a day."

"You've been badly hurt. No wonder you want home and loved ones around you now.

"I'm so sorry, Gwen, for your loss. It must be hard."

"You learn to live with it. He's not coming back. People never do." She sounded like a wistful child, he thought, and was charmed.

He'd been so taken with what looked like eternal youth in her. A lovely girl, forever.

She looked older now. No longer untouched. *And why should she be? Death, pain, had touched her. Manhandled her, poor lass.*

Liz and Seth danced, respectably and quietly. She was wearing a plain white shirt, buttoned up enough, jeans a size or two larger than the painted-on ones she'd worn that night, Seth thought. He was wrong, of course, but Seth knew nothing of differences in cut and fit within the same size.

He did like her better, like this.

The song finished; the couples changed partners. *Blast,* thought Patrick, as Van Morrison's "Crazy Love" played, Gwen smiling up at Seth Greenlaw, in his arms.

"I don't think we've danced since high school," Gwen murmured.

"No."

"I'm really not tall enough for you. I should get some high heels. For next time."

"Still rather dance with you than anyone."

"Me, too." They smiled at each other. Danced.

"Would that be my to-be-hated rival, Elizabeth? I suppose there must be one. Do tell me."

"I don't know." *Not lovers. But—something.* Seth Greenlaw's hard eyes softened on Gwen. More tenderness than amusement in his smile. Protective. *Favorite brother. More than that.*

"Anyway, wouldn't that make you *his* rival? If he's already in the field, you're the newcomer. Don't discount that advantage on his side. Especially here. Especially with Gwen. You *must* see how she loves him."

"That can be managed, surely. A man always takes a girl from some relationship or other."

"You won't manage *that*, Patrick, don't even try. They've been super-close their whole lives. Her marriage didn't shake it, and Gwen thought Mark Sinclair was Prince Charming come to life. She still called Seth. Often.

"In fact, the fiercest I ever saw her—it was about him. She was really passionate over it. It sort of cute—she was being protective."

"She is adorable."

"Be warned, Patrick. I mean it. Even if you do succeed with her, Seth Greenlaw comes as part of the deal."

* * *

Gwen was at Seth's stable bright and early, before the hands showed up. He was waiting for her.

Seth had stopped farming—he'd had ten more acres cleared, but it all went for pasture, corrals, hayfields, and the foaling barn, with a small turn-out area, until they could join the rest of the herd.

Too little woodland left; barely enough deadfall to heat the house and barns. *Cramped*, for hunting. Maybe Paul Hardie would sell him some. Seth did still hunt. In all seasons.

Belle contentedly ate hay from her net, her (and Gwen's) foal nursed. Knobby little legs.

'Getting acquainted' meant 'getting acclimated.' You did

not interfere with foal-mare bonding. Seth made Gwen stay outside the stall, nor went in himself. Not just now.

They watched. Belle whickered to the little one, nuzzled her gently.

"Aren't they sweet? She's absolutely adorable, Seth. I can't thank you enough."

"Already have."

"I should get back. You don't need me getting in the way," as Jim Marshall's truck turned into the driveway. She wasn't riding today.

Seth told her she wasn't in the way, but walked back with Gwen, as far as the wood.

"How're you doing, really, Gwen? How's the arm?"

"Almost 100%. A little stiff, but I keep doing the exercises. I mean, it's quite functional."

"Headaches?"

"Hardly any. One or two, this month. Okay, three, maybe. But not as bad, and not as many.

"I'm getting there. Five months."

It seemed a much longer time, to Gwen, since the accident that had left her broken and a widow. Her body was healing.

As for her heart, she'd boarded over the hole that Mark left. Not broken. Closed.

She was happy enough. Gwen had made a new friend in Althea Jones. She'd made friends, too, with Melody Gray (*what were she and Jack waiting for?*). She was getting to know her cousins, Ken Pelletier and his boys, better.

She'd found—made—work for herself, and it seemed to be a success, so far as you could gauge at this point.

She was home. Her family loved her, she loved her family, they were together. It was more love than anyone could need. Gwen was profoundly grateful.

She had what had been so painfully missing from her Boston life.

What had been lovely—the one thing—in that life was gone.

Life played games with you. It played rough. And death was always waiting.

* * *

Gwen walked back through the woods. Crisp smell of pine, dead leaves and needles rustled under her feet. Not as magical as they were at night. Not so dangerous, either.

She checked the progress on her infusions; made breakfast for herself and her father; Jack was out with his boats.

It's enough, thank you, God, it's enough. I won't ask for more. She didn't dare.

Mid-morning, Margery Sinclair telephoned.

"Mother Sinclair. How are you both?"

"As well as we can hope to be, thanks, dear. And you?"

Gwen murmured she was doing well. Thanked her mother-in-law for selling the condo. She hadn't done anything with the check; she'd put it with all the other paperwork she hadn't dealt with.

"That lawsuit, Gwen—"

The truck which had struck Mark's car had been corporate-owned. It had been slated for repair and put on the road by mistake. Stiff fines had been imposed; the Sinclairs, who were named executors in Mark's will, had sued.

Gwen had signed on, reluctantly. The lawyers had made it clear she was key—the crash, with photos and video of the scene, Gwen's removal to hospital, had been all over the Boston news.

Jumped on, by the media talking heads. Good-looking

young couple, tragedy, uncertainty of outcome. Red journalistic meat.

Reckless disregard of human life. Pain and suffering. Loss of consortium. And so on.

"They didn't want a trial, dear, they knew it would be a public relations disaster. Quite a good settlement." She named the amount, which was comfortably into seven figures. Legally, Gwen was the sole beneficiary.

Gwen whistled. "I'm glad they have to pay. But it won't bring him back."

"No, dear, of course it can't."

Money couldn't make it all not have happened. The Sinclairs should take two-thirds.

She argued, for a while. Arguing about money. What a *waste*. Time, energy.

Gwen should, though she hadn't done so yet, take those stacks of papers to Tim Douglass, her father's accountant. Tim also provided informal financial advice. She really must make an appointment.

Tired of the battle, Gwen agreed to take half of whatever was left after the lawyers were paid.

She wondered about the cost of restoring the old canning building. It would be nice to separate her professional work from the family kitchen. And a certified commercial kitchen would allow her more leeway in what she produced. Expansion into other jarred and bottled things, not shelf-stable. Maybe beyond that. If she wanted to.

And Christmas was coming. Well, it was—three months plus, but still. She owed Seth something *very* special. And he wouldn't like being singled out that way. Not *too* much, anyway—he'd have to acknowledge he owed her a return acceptance, after giving her a *horse*, for goodness' sake.

With the check, Gwen could provide camouflage. And it would be fun, picking something extra-special for everyone on her list.

There'd been a mildew problem in the library, which was in the newer wing; problems seemed to concentrate there. It was fixed, now, but some of her father's favorite volumes had been among the casualties. She could replace them all for him, too, and not as a Christmas present.

She was lucky in the men she knew. They were *good* men. Daddy, Seth, Jack. Good as they came. Ken Pelletier, her cousin, another such.

What could she give Althea, for Christmas?

Gwen had a pretty good idea—generally—what she wanted to give Seth, and where to start on particulars.

And won't he be surprised?

CHAPTER 17

Late September—October

Without having discussed it, Gwen, Jack, and Seth Greenlaw were worried about Paul Hardie. He'd looked 10 years older after hearing of Gwen's accident, and the years had not left his face. His hair, over the following weeks, had turned white from its gray.

Paul wasn't old, not really—he was in his mid-60s. He felt much older.

Gwen had recovered better than he. And so she should. Young, strong, healthy. It gladdened him; he was grateful.

But Paul was not young. And he was tired all the time.

He sat down, with Madeleine—via telephone—and with Jack, separately. He did not consult Gwen. She was likely to argue with him, and he had no heart for arguing over this.

It would be a wrench. First time in family history.

Madeleine, though she did not argue with Paul's plans, was more concerned with the break from tradition than Jack.

"No, I understand, Dad. I think it's right. I'm fine with that." He and Melody planned to announce their engagement at Thanksgiving; they hoped to be married in late September the following year.

Jack told Paul. "And you know she won't live here." Paul did know, because Jack had told him the problem, had seen it on the horizon. And made his own plans.

In the past, it was by no means unknown for more than one family in a single Hardie generation to occupy the big house, after Martin Hardie's wing had been built. There were 12 bedrooms, all told, most of them dust-sheeted for decades upon decades now. Paul Hardie, like his father, George, had been an only child.

But Melody was a good cook, and proud of her cooking. Gwen was a far better one, a bona fide chef. Who would not tolerate a lesser having say—*any* say—in *her* kitchen.

Put them together, it would spoil their growing friendship, and make for a very discordant household.

Much wiser to let each have her own domain. Which meant Jack would need his own house. He'd bought 10 acres a little way north on 226, cleared a house lot, dug a well, set up septic.

The plan was to lay the foundation, frame and Tyvek it before snowfall. Finish it in spring and summer.

Jack had always been *bothered* by the ungainly outlines of the Hardie home, the inconsistencies of room sizes. Unlike Paul or Gwen. Had never loved it half as much as they.

Paul found the stairs were getting a bit much for him; he converted his study into his bedroom, and the small half-bath adjacent would be enlarged and renovated over October and into November.

* * *

Gwen and Seth explored the old cannery. Seth made Gwen stay outside until he told her it was safe.

Better than she'd expected. Only a few small roof leaks. One wall needed shoring up a bit, and the tile there would need replacing. So would the cement floor, which was badly cracked.

Any equipment had long been sold or scrapped. A few built-in counters remained, which would have to be torn out.

The biggest issue would be replacing the pipeline to the well. Seth, who'd already been through running pipe to his barns, told her to call Charlie Eaton, *not* Mitch Rice. Mitch—he'd failed to show up three days running, and hadn't returned calls. The third message Seth left was to fire him.

Charlie showed up when he said he would, on time and with all his ducks in a row, and got the job done.

Electric would have to be checked out, upgraded.

Gwen would need a stove, a dishwasher, stainless tables and shelving, a big refrigerator. She could clean by hand for a while, but she'd price a pressurized system. A big double sink, another washing sink, and one for hand-washing.

And all the tests and inspections. The facility. Water quality. Septic system. The floor drain might need replacing.

What was she letting herself in for?

Gwen had the license she needed for shelf-stable goods. Did she really want to take this on?

Yes. Yes, she thought she did.

She didn't need Seth to tell her Tommy Hutchinson was the best general contractor Haven Point boasted. Her father had engaged Tommy for his bathroom expansion.

He'd laid in the radiant heat system Paul had had installed in the older two portions of the house, more than a decade past. It had taken the better part of two years, and gone slowly, causing as little disruption as could be managed. Gwen remembered—it had been quite an upheaval, as it was. Ancient dust, new sawdust, everywhere.

Radiant heat changed everything, though—she and Jack

went barefoot in the house year-round. Except when they had company, and Paul insisted they dress properly. It kept moisture in the air—a problem in Maine winters.

Gwen thought about installing radiant here. If she had to replace the floor, anyway . . .

That meant a new wood boiler. Well, it wasn't as if they hadn't deadfall enough to keep it running.

How busy will I be, realistically, in winter, anyway?

Maybe she could lay in the piping for the system, leave the connectors open, and put off buying the boiler for a couple of years.

And what about food supplies, in winter? There wouldn't be ripe tomatoes much longer. Not good ones. Strawberries were gone, and she'd soon be out of the puree she'd already frozen.

Blueberries, local and organic, were available frozen year-round, so no problem there. Some frozen strawberries, at the central marketplace, but what kind of bulk she could count on, Gwen didn't know.

If she wanted tomatoes and maybe strawberries year-round, that meant greenhouses. Radiant heat, with the sun, could keep her stocked.

Seth thought she was maybe getting over-ambitious. *He might be right.*

No harm in pricing out her options, though.

For this autumn, fix the roof, the wall. Run the pipe to the well.

That would do until snow-melt, and give her time to think.

* * *

October saw a big drop off from Gwen's August-September sales. She'd expected it. The marketplace was steady, but reduced to a much smaller stream with summer-people and tourists almost gone. The last leaf-peepers dropped off, too, as the brightness fell from the trees.

All the seasonal shops which carried her wares would close by the end of the month, if they hadn't already. Downeast Bayou closed the week before Hallowe'en.

Which was the week Seth Greenlaw turned 27. Ben called from Arlington. His contract would be up at the end of spring; he'd been offered a substantial increase in salary to stay another two years. Hadn't decided whether he would, leaning 'no.'

"The thing is, the money's really good," Ben didn't say how much, "but a couple of the guys here—they kind of want to make the same sort of things I do; they've got their own skillsets, I've got mine, we mesh. I've saved some, they've saved some. I have a sort of idea . . . they want to do it. By spring, we might have enough for prototypes of some other stuff we've come up with, maybe get funding or a loan."

"Loan" was an alarm-word for Seth, who hated debt. He hadn't let Ben take out student loans, and had refused to mortgage their property. Which hadn't mattered, as things had turned out.

Ben was 21, though—his life, his choices.

Gwen threw Seth a little birthday party. Beef Wellington, accompanied by her mashed potatoes, roasted carrots with thyme-butter, green salad with tomato-basil vinaigrette. More people were planting in greenhouses—the lettuce was local, tender, very fresh.

Lemon cake with tart lemon-curd filling alternating with raspberry. Lemon-cream cheese icing. Lots of tartness, tang, sharp flavors. Seth had even less of a sweet tooth than she, *but what's a birthday without cake?*

The party was just family. It did not include Madeleine Hardie, who was, of course, filming in California. It did include Melody, as well as Ken Pelletier and his boys.

Seth found birthdays embarrassing. It was one thing opening presents at Christmas, when everybody else was. Having everyone giving *him* things, the only one, and watching him, that was another.

A new saddle and bridle, from Gwen. Gleaming leather, handmade. Not a lot of tooling, the leather was beautiful without it. And she'd checked the saddle size—just right for Minister's back.

"Thanks, Gwen," he couldn't really say she shouldn't have—no credibility, after giving her Belinda.

"Happy birthday, dearest Seth. Many, many happy returns of the day."

A fine old rifle from Paul.

Ken gave him a well-made hunting knife, hair-split sharp.

From Melody, a large, leather-bound diary for appointments. It really was time he did better than scribbles on innumerable scraps of paper. But he always kept appointments, and promptly.

Useful stuff. Useful is good.

Jack's gift, though—that was the inspired one, Gwen thought.

Seth's old hunting dog, Bonnie, had died, at 17, while Gwen was in the hospital. He'd had her since she was a puppy, and he a boy of nine.

Couldn't bear to replace her since.

Jack brought in the three-month-old redbone puppy with a 'ta-da' flourish. He figured six months plus was long enough to be without a dog. Jack had not replaced Buddy, long gone, but Seth had no other company at home.

"She doesn't have a name yet, but she's house-trained."

He handed her to Seth, who cradled her. Smiled down, "Hey, little girl, what *is* your name?" To the others, "I figure she'll let me know, sooner or later.

"Jack. Thanks. I wouldn't have, not yet. But you're right. It's time. Thanks. She's great." The puppy—*Rosie?*—licked his nose, nipped at his fingers. He laughed.

"Thanks again, everybody."

And everyone, once more, wished Seth a happy birthday.

Not a bad one, at that.

* * *

Soon after, Gwen drove up to Brewer, to check prices on second-hand restaurant equipment.

The supply house had very little, and nothing of what she needed. Used equipment came in and went out rapidly. Which was fine, for now. She left a list of what she wanted, her name and phone number. They'd call her, they said, when anything came in.

She drove further, into Bangor.

Gwen had first spoken with Jack, taken him into her confidence—to a point. She'd visited the Haven Point library, which kept subscriptions to several helpful periodicals, and read up, a little. Enough to focus an idea or two.

She found the store she wanted. Spoke with the clerk, who turned out, happily, to be the owner. Told him enough to convince him she wasn't playing games, despite her general ignorance.

He didn't have what she was looking for, any more than the guy in Brewer, but made several calls. Gwen might try a place in Portland. They had a selection or six which might suit.

Portland was another two hours, which meant three-plus back. She hadn't planned on so long a trip. Gwen hadn't before driven as far as Ellsworth, let alone Bangor, since the accident.

It was only 10:00 a.m., though. *Just do it.* Wasn't that what the commercials said?

I-95 South. The interstate wasn't crowded, but merging into what traffic there was made Gwen's heart pound. She kept her hands and her driving steady; fear subsided.

Outside Portland, she stopped to fill her tank. Her father's tank. She ought to get her own car. Bought a city street map, marked the address she'd been given on it, mapped a route.

The store was downtown; Gwen circled it a few times before finding the right path through one-way streets.

The man behind the counter couldn't be much older than she, if that. Curly dark hair, glasses, and an enthusiastic smile when she told him what she was doing. What she wanted.

He was knowledgeable, too, on the lesser, but important, issue, and she committed on that score.

For the other, the big, question, "You might just have got lucky. As it happens, I think we may have what you're looking for. You know this'll cost you?"

She did. In the end, spent *quite* a bit more than she'd earmarked, and bought things she hadn't known would be needed.

Gwen drove home with a full station wagon. And a warmly happy heart.

She'd have to smuggle all this into the house, without Jack seeing.

But Jack's pickup was nowhere in sight, and it was easy.

Sentimentally, she set things up in the old bedroom next to hers, which Seth and Ben had slept in more times than Gwen had fingers and toes. She'd tell Daddy. Some of it. *Not* what it had cost.

Locked the door behind her, and taped onto it a piece of paper.

Do not open before Christmas.

CHAPTER 18

November

The first thing she'd had done on the old canning-plant-kitchen was to fumigate. Neither Gwen nor Seth had actually *seen* rats, but there'd been evidence.

Tommy Hutchinson and his crew patched the leaks in the old building's roof, and several weak places which hadn't leaked yet. Tore out and replaced the bad wall. He'd had time to re-tile it, and Gwen had greenlighted that. It would need doing, anyway.

Charlie Eaton was careful, taking up sod before he dug the pipeline. Deep—below frost-level. When he was done, you had to look close to see where the line lay.

Gwen wrote checks.

Paul had written checks, too.

The new bathroom had been more disruptive, and taken longer than planned, but Tommy got it completed during November, before Thanksgiving.

Gwen set her stack of papers on the desk of Tim Douglass, CPA.

Tim was a small, neat, sandy-haired man, with a kind face which tended to worry in repose.

"I don't know what it all means, my father-in-law did *try* to tell me, but I wasn't in any shape to take it in."

Tim put on his half-glasses. "Gwen, if you get any more papers to sign, please bring them to me first."

She promised. *But what more could there be?*

Tim Douglass pored over the papers so long Gwen wished she'd brought a book.

"You're too generous, Gwen. Half? That's a lot of money to forego."

"Money's not that important. I think their hearts were brokener than mine."

Only those who'd lived wanting nothing said things like that.

Paul Hardie's daughter had been—*was*—regarded as quite a catch, and rightly. Leaving her good looks, kind heart, and cooking skills entirely out of the equation.

Not to mention whatever she'd inherit from her mother. Which, from conversations with Paul, Tim Douglass thought would be substantial. *Very* substantial.

And if Gwen had been generous with the Sinclairs, they'd matched her well enough. Charles Sinclair had a family medical insurance policy, an excellent one, which would now cover Gwen for her lifetime. If she married again, had children, she could sign her new family onto it, although those premiums would be at her charge.

With the proceeds of Mark's small life insurance policy and the sale of their condo, as well as Gwen's inheritance—also for her lifetime—of his portion of the trust income, half the settlement brought her into quite a comfortable position.

She'd also brought her rather informal business records. At least they were kept in a spreadsheet. Mary Beth Ruggiero, Tim's bookkeeper, lamented over handwritten accounts every quarter; Seth Greenlaw was one, but by no means the only, such offender.

Impressive sales, for about a month and a half of the season. Too soon to tell how well she'd perform over the course of a year or two.

"Gwen, your margin is lower than it could be. Not bad, but think about raising your prices a little, next summer."

He "tsk'd" over the contracting bills, and was alarmed at her projected expenditures, both business *and* personal. But even if she ended having spent half again as much as she'd anticipated, it was a fine nest egg. Into which nest other eggs would be laid, in the future.

Tim Douglass wondered when she'd marry again. Not whether. He knew, gossip traveling everywhere, that Gwen did not, would not, date. But it was only a matter of time. Of that, Tim had no doubt.

He'd be one lucky man, whoever he was.

* * *

Patrick Riordan returned from two long weeks in New York. To the Haven Point house he'd rented. Month-to-month, open-ended. An old house, on the 'old' side, south of the Lords. Small, but insulated, habitable year-round. Most of the rental properties were not.

Gwen Sinclair was very busy, and he'd been away more than once since Liz's little party.

He'd asked her to dinner twice, and been refused.

She was, however, quite willing to talk with him when she ran into him at the Lords'. Which he tried to make happen as often as possible.

They talked literature, mostly. Gwen was surprisingly well-read, had definite, intelligent opinions. Sometimes out of left field, such as her views on Kafka's 'In the Penal Colony,' which she hated. She had a quite novel take on the narrator, however, which she supported eloquently. Patrick told her, with perfect sincerity, that he would now need to re-read it.

She'd read a couple of his mystery novels, out of curiosity.

"I like the style, it's clever, it's fun and very—readable. But—kind of a lot of—sex. And violence. A little graphic, for me."

"The insistence of my publisher on the conventions of the genre, I'm afraid."

"I'm kind of more the Jane Austen-leaning sort. I like Henry James, too, especially those great last three."

"Ah, 'The Wings of the Dove,' 'The Ambassadors,' 'The Golden Bowl.'"

"I *love* those, that dense, brilliant-cut prose. So many facets to *everything*. That *deep* sense of mystery. A few others, too. "The Tragic Muse" is sort of hilarious, in a weird way. If your mother is an actress."

"Your mother is a *great* actress. I saw her, how many years ago, in "Much Ado About Nothing," in Central Park. I saw it again when it opened on Broadway. After that, I saw every New York play she appeared in, which were sadly few."

"Were you really at the Broadway *opening*?"

"I was."

"So were we!"

Patrick wished she had said—had thought—*so was I*, but it was a happy coincidence, nonetheless, if predictable. Of course, her family would come to Madeleine Hardie's Broadway opening nights.

"We saw it twice, too—in the Park the first time, as you did. I liked that better. Before, we had a picnic, my father and Jack and I." *Funny.* Her grammar was better in Patrick Riordan's company.

Because they talked about books, great books, which used grammar impeccably, nudging hers. It did not occur to Gwen that Patrick's own perfectly grammatical conversation might be an influence.

"I do need new authors, though. I'm in a rut, just re-reading. I went back to Jane Austen after—after—it made things easier to deal with, that cool, funny, perceptive perspective. I got stuck there."

Perceptive perspective. Charming.

He was delighted, and a little relieved, to find a common interest.

"Do you know Robertson Davies?"

Gwen didn't.

"May I send you some books?"

He sent her all eleven novels in hardcover.

* * *

One cold, bright November morning, Seth and Gwen drove up to Ellsworth, to look at cars.

Good girl, he'd thought, when she asked him to look them over with her. If Gwen were going to buy a car, he wanted to be sure it was sound.

There were three reliable—relatively speaking—used car dealers. Seth didn't like any of the stock at the first.

At the second, they found what he wanted for Gwen. *If it checks out.*

Bottle-green Volvo sedan. Five years old. Turbo, diesel.

"Why diesel, Seth? God-awful pollution."

"Stabler than gas. Harder to ignite."

Harsh, but she'd asked. *To hell with pollution, if it makes her safer.*

"Engine'll last longer. Give you better torque, too."

Gwen sat down with Seth and the dealer, while Seth spent half an hour poring over service records, the vehicle history report.

Stood by for an hour and a half, while Seth inspected the car itself.

No oil or fluid leaks. Frame good, axles straight. No rust underneath, which confirmed the dealer's claim it had been cleaned regularly, and kept garaged. Timing belt in good condition. He saw nothing to indicate the record and report were inaccurate.

Seth test-drove the Volvo first, alone. Another three-quarters of an hour, before he brought it back. He knew the roads around here, and had driven over bumps, potholes, unrepaired frost-heave cracks. Good suspension. The wheels tracked. No off-noises, no red flags.

He got out, leaving the door open, key in the ignition. "Your turn," he said, and got into the passenger seat.

Gwen took the driver's seat, pulling it forward. Buckled her seatbelt, and turned the key. "Where to?" Smiling.

"Brewer and back."

"Seth, have I *ever* driven you before? I don't think I have—not since I got my license, anyway." He had given her a few lessons, though her father had done most.

"Probably not." For preference, no-one drove him.

Gwen liked the car. It felt *right*. Like it *fit*. It handled *very* well.

"Volvos are good cars, Gwen. Take a lot of impact. She won't crush easy."

She drove further than he'd said, "I want to let her out on I-95. See what she's got." *See how safe I feel then.*

Nothing wrong with that, Seth thought. He knew how she'd worked to get over her fear of driving. Part of him had—almost—wished she wouldn't. It was still hard to think of "Gwen" and "car" without adding "crash."

But not driving wasn't an option. And he respected her determination.

Not that she'd ever lacked *that*. If she *was* ready to hit the interstate . . .

Of course, Seth knew nothing of her trip to Portland.

North of Bangor, there was little traffic, and Gwen pressed her foot down on the accelerator. Hit 85 miles per hour, 90, and laughed for pleasure. She wasn't afraid, now.

"Please tell me it's okay to buy her."

"If you're comfortable. He'll take a little less—try to get him to drop $500. Or I will, if you want."

"Thanks, but I think I can handle that. You've done your part. *Very* thoroughly, thank you.

"Do you know, this will be the first car I've ever owned? Mark had that little roadster, and Daddy used to keep three so Jack and I had wheels, but none of them was ever mine, before this."

"Gonna christen her with champagne, you think?" Seth laughed.

"I just might, at that."

Gwen asked for a $750 reduction in price, and got the $500 off Seth had suggested.

Always give people room to dicker.

* * *

Gwen took Althea and Nerise to the tavern for dinner. When cooking was your profession, sometimes you needed a break.

No matter how much you loved it.

"I'd love it if you and Nerise would come for Thanksgiving dinner—and Christmas, too. Please say yes."

"Oh, can we, Mama! I love your house, Miss Gwen."

Nerise had been in the ladies' room; Gwen hadn't noticed her returning. Had not meant to put Althea on the spot. Mouthed, "Sorry," at her.

"That's real kind, Gwen. If you let me help in the kitchen, I *will* say yes."

"Of course! I'm counting on it." Althea was one person she didn't mind cooking alongside. "You have no idea. My family—I love them all to pieces, but I don't know how they kept from starving to death when I was gone. My menfolk can barely boil water, and my mother isn't much better."

"Your Dad was a regular from when I opened, with the takeout for dinner. Came in for breakfast, or lunch, too, sometimes. And your brother came pretty often."

"Well, thank God for that. And I know what Seth Greenlaw did, and Ben, until he left. They just cooked badly and ate it anyway.

"Last few times I saw Ben, he was getting almost as stubborn as his brother. Who is probably the most *pig-headed* man ever born. When he sets his mind on something."

Nerise, who was working on her third glass of lemonade, announced she had to go to the ladies' room again.

"Nerise –" Poor Althea. She sounded weary.

"Sorry, Mama. May I please be excused?"

Althea nodded, and Gwen took advantage of the girl's absence.

"Look, Althea, I'm sorry Nerise heard the invitation. I really didn't mean to put you on the spot, with her there. Thanks for accepting.

"There'll be people you know at Thanksgiving—the family, of course—I don't know how Jack is going to handle *two* Thanksgiving dinners. We'll have to stagger them. Seth, and my cousins Ken and Caleb and Kyle.

"A couple of new faces—to you—at Christmas—Ben Greenlaw, I hope, and my Mom.

"And I need to talk with you, not with Nerise around. It's—it's sort of delicate—no, no, nothing to worry about. Not like that."

When Nerise returned, her mother handed her a bunch of quarters.

"Honey, you just go play some video pinball, or whatever, for a bit. Your mama needs to talk with Miss Gwen a minute."

Nerise flew to the bank of machines, dropped a coin in.

"She gets playing, that's all the world in her head. Say your piece."

Gwen, hesitantly, said, "You've maybe heard, I just got a pretty big settlement from a lawsuit." Althea nodded. "Well, it doesn't seem real to me. Like Monopoly money.

"Anyway, I'm kind of splurging on Christmas presents, to at least spread it around some. I'd like to get you and Nerise something *super*. But I wouldn't do that without checking."

Althea looked down. Then up. "Gwen, you got to be about *the* most generous person. But even by Christmas, we won't have known each other six months. I just wouldn't feel right."

Gwen nodded. "I was afraid you might see it that way. What *can* I get you two, then?"

"Maybe I could get Nerise a pair of really good running shoes? Maybe two—one to grow into? Would that be okay?"

"One pair—her size 7s should be getting tight round then . . . You know what I need? A new mandoline. One I had broke just before we closed for the season."

"Can I get professional-grade? Something that'll stand up to what you need?"

"A'right. If you got to." Gwen offered her hand, and the ladies shook on it.

CHAPTER 19

Thanksgiving

The Tuesday before Thanksgiving, Gwen woke to blinding pain. Worst headache she'd had in months. She took one of the pills—she still had plenty. Threw it up immediately.

She sipped warm ginger ale, tried another pill. Which came up fouly gingery.

It was three hours before she managed to keep one down. It didn't help. Gwen drank water, threw it up. Kept drinking—it was better than dry-heaves.

Paul called Dr. Oliver, who arrived at the Hardie home within 20 minutes.

Dr. Nora Oliver was in her late 40s, a square, stocky woman with brown hair and hazel eyes behind tortoise-shell glasses,

She examined Gwen, shone a little light into her eyes. Which hurt, it *located* the pain. Gwen wept a little, weakly.

Dr. Oliver checked the pill bottle; it was what she'd prescribe.

"Gwen, I don't like that it isn't responding to these—it ought to be. I want you to have a CT scan."

The nearest machine was in the Ellsworth hospital. Dr.

Oliver called them, made arrangements.

"Can I drive her?" Asked Paul.

"Better she goes in the ambulance. I can monitor her, and we'll get her rehydrated. You follow."

"Daddy, Althea. Turkeys—need brining," Gwen whispered.

Paul wanted to laugh and weep. His Gwen—thinking of cooking. Thanksgiving dinner. Through pain. Which was nothing to be thankful for.

Dr. Oliver called the ambulance; Paul called Madeleine in California, left a message.

Next, Althea Jones.

"I'm real sorry, Paul. Tell Gwen I'll take care of it, tell her anything she needs me to do—I've got it covered."

"I'll leave the kitchen door unlocked."

"You call me when you know anything, now. I'll either be here or at your place."

Paul promised to do so. Hung up, and called Seth Greenlaw—who should, in Paul's opinion, be told.

"Meet you at the hospital."

Paul dissuaded him—there was nothing Seth could do, too much commotion for Gwen already.

"I'll call when we know anything."

The ambulance arrived and took Gwen away. Paul followed it to Ellsworth and the hospital, praying they'd find nothing but a bad headache, residual from prior trauma, not a new complication.

Despite some beautiful houses and a quaint Main Street, Ellsworth was an unlovely city, strip malls lining the road to downtown.

The hospital was past Main Street. Gwen was removed from the ambulance, transferred from one stretcher to another, and taken away to have images of her brain recorded.

Paul sat in a waiting room, tried to read, gave it up. And prayed.

Waited for what seemed like days, but was only a little over an hour.

His prayers had not hurt, at least. There was no new hematoma, no bleeding in Gwen's brain.

She'd been given a shot of something. No need for an ambulance back.

Dr. Oliver wrote a prescription, which Paul had filled.

"I want her to try these, when the shot wears off, if her head isn't better. If they don't work, call me."

Paul found a public telephone, left another message for Madeleine.

Called his own number.

"Paul?" Althea Jones' rich alto. "What'd they say?"

He reassured her, said they'd be home soon. Althea's intuition signaled—leave Gwen be just now. Said she'd be gone by the time they arrived.

"Tell Gwen the turkeys are brining. Nice birds. Haven't had wild turkey in quite a spell."

Paul dropped more coins, dialed Seth, who answered on the first ring.

"She's all right, Seth. False alarm, thank God."

He heard the sharp exhale. "*Okay.*" Very low; it sounded like "amen."

Gwen was wheeled out. Dazed with pain and painkillers. But safe, for now.

An attendant helped Paul get Gwen into the station wagon's back seat, and they made for home.

Within minutes, Gwen was asleep. Dreaming of pain.

Seth had gauged their driving time well; he'd only been waiting a few minutes when Paul's station wagon pulled in.

Gwen was *out*, didn't stir as the two men, carefully and not easily, got her bundled into Seth's arms. Didn't stir, as Seth carried her into the house and upstairs. She weighed nothing.

He laid her on her bed. A travesty, a mockery, of his desire.

Seth smoothed Gwen's hair, kissed her forehead, and left her.

* * *

Gwen woke around 8:00 that night. Into pain. Her father, she saw through bright, hurtful stars, in a chair with a book.

"Daddy?" She sat up, slowly, half-way.

He was by her side. "Gwen, darling. How do you feel?"

"It hurts. It's not better."

Paul took up the bottle of pills Gwen was to try. Two every four hours. It was well past the hour she could begin after the shot. He shook out two very small white convex discs. Poured a little water from the pitcher he'd filled, and gave them to her.

She took the pills, sipped the water. Carefully, Gwen got out of bed.

"Give them a chance to work, Gwen."

"I'm tired of being in bed. And I need to check on the turkeys."

The two went downstairs, found Seth and Jack playing cribbage in the parlor.

"Hey, guys," Gwen smiled. "Who's winning?" She couldn't focus on the board.

"Me, for a change," said Jack.

"How's the head?" Seth asked.

"It hurts. I took something just now; hopefully it'll help."

There was nothing he could do that would help her. Seth hated feeling helpless; he'd had too much of that, this year.

Over her, over her pain.

Gwen checked on the turkeys, smelled the brine closely. Not safe to taste, of course, with raw bird in it.

As far as she could tell, Althea had done what she'd have. *Good girl. Thanks, Althea.*

The pills were working, and fast. Pain diminished to a tiny pinpointable ache, no longer an enveloping world.

Gwen went back to the parlor, curled up on the old settee, and watched her brothers play, pegboard and cards, in front of the fire.

As usual, when pain receded, energy followed in its wake. Her eyes closed.

She was still asleep, two hours later.

"Guess it's time I called it, Jack. You want help, getting her upstairs?"

Jack shook his head, "Thanks, I'll manage. 'Night, brother."

"'Night, Jack. Call me, she needs anything."

Jack nodded, Seth left, and Gwen's blood-tied brother carried his sister upstairs.

* * *

Over the next day, Gwen waked for no more than half an hour at a stretch. Slept three or four hours between.

Alarmed, Paul called Dr. Oliver.

"Well, if she hadn't just *had* a scan, I'd order one. But, frankly, that is a possibility with this particular medication. I'd cut the dose in half, next time.

"I wouldn't worry, unless it lasts more than a couple of days. Keep me informed. Let me know how she is tomorrow. Yes," she cut Paul off, "I know it's Thanksgiving. Call me anyway." She gave him her home number.

Paul was still uneasy, but accepted the doctor's word.

And called Althea Jones.

Thanksgiving morning, Gwen woke. It was after 10:00 a.m., late, late, for the household. Late, for the holiday.

Feeling hapless, helpless, drugged and groggy.

And starving. Which was natural, wholesome, enough. She hadn't eaten for over two days.

Feeling no trace of headache. Except the current, resultant thick fog of drug-pain-sleep hangover.

Gwen dressed, sweat pants and an oversized t-shirt—whose? Her father's, Jack's. It was there, clean or clean enough.

Took the stairs carefully—her feet felt the floor spongy under them. Senses not quite, not yet, trustable.

Didn't see her father or Jack on her path to the kitchen, but found Althea and Nerise busy there.

They spoke at once—

"Happy Thanksgiving, Miss Gwen!"

"Girl! Glad you're up and about. How you feeling? Nerise, you go and find Mr. Hardie like a good girl."

Fleet feet flew the youngster away. Gwen looked after her.

"I don't even know. Starving, and no headache, at least."

"Good to hear." Althea turned the heat up under the saucepan of water she'd been simmering, replenishing, for the past two hours.

Lowered a spoon with two eggs into it, sliced bread.

"Made the pies already—I tasted that mincemeat, Gwen—that's a real Southern recipe, or I'm damned."

"A tweak or two on a South Carolina original. Hardly any change, really, so 'yeah, you right.'" *Okay.* She could talk words.

Althea set two mugs in front of her—soft-boiled eggs over toast, the other milky-brown liquid. Gwen sipped.

"Hot cocoa? Last thing I need is more sleep, Althea."

"Your *palate's* asleep, girl. It's half strong coffee. And you *do* need calories and endorphins, that's what the cocoa's for."

"Yes, ma'am." Althea was right. And the eggs tasted phenomenal. As any decent food would, right now.

Althea watched her eat, put another two eggs on, served them up with more toast. Gwen devoured them, too, with another mug of coffee-cocoa.

"We're in good shape for dinner. Got the dressing put together, just needs stock and eggs added, cleaned up those nice green beans. Dough for rolls is on first rise. Turkeys still brining; I'll get them ready next, but wild ones don't take as long to roast."

"I rub butter under the skin, and tie bacon slices around before they go into the oven. You're an angel, Althea. I should be mad—you wouldn't let me get you something special for Christmas, but here you are, cooking Thanksgiving dinner for my family. For *me*. Doing my job."

"Ain't no thing. Cooking for mine, too, since we're gonna eat here. You just sit, now. I got you."

"Thanks, Althea. I'll help. Once I—I feel like one of those marionette puppets, with no-one holding the strings."

"Honey, you just sit there."

"Here he is, Mama!" Nerise preceded Paul Hardie on swift bare feet.

Oh, that quickness. Barefoot on the floor. Nerise—dark positive of the girl Gwen had been. She herself the pale negative.

"Darling girl. How do you feel?"

"Better, Daddy. You called Althea—thank you, smart move."

"I thought best to. You had us worried, Gwen. Dr. Oliver gave me her home number, in case."

"Me, too, Daddy. *That* was *weird*."

"Seems like it happens, that drug, sometimes. I crossed out two pills, put one, on the bottle."

"I should double the time between, too. If I ever take them again, which I might not.

"Jack at Melody's?" Gwen asked, and Paul nodded. "They eat around 1:00, don't they? Althea, what time are we serving?"

"Figure on 5:00 or 6:00, that okay?"

"Perfect. Daddy, when is Seth coming? And Ken and Caleb and Kyle?"

"Ken and the boys around 4:00. Seth, when I call."

"You could call him."

* * *

Seth arrived shortly, wishing them Happy Thanksgiving.

Hugged Gwen gently, kissed her cheek. Asked about her headache.

"Gone, thank heaven. You're better than any drugs they give me, anyway."

"Couldn't stop the headache. Glad *something* worked."

"Me, too. Quite a price, though, losing almost two days."

He nodded.

Althea poured coffee for herself and Seth, mixed up another half-cocoa for Gwen.

"Thanks, Althea," said Seth, "How's—and where's—Nerise?"

"She's fine, exploring, I guess. She does like this house. *Lot* of rooms here, Gwen."

"For a fact. Family legend says we once had *three* siblings inherit, they all brought their husbands or wives here, and had families. Three of them, all living together.

"I used to love hearing Daddy tell that tale. Now, what can

I do to help?"

"Not a thing. Hour or so, you can help with getting the rolls shaped, chop some herbs. I'm going to sit down, myself, a while."

"You're an angel," Gwen repeated. *Making sure I get to do something—a little, anyway.*

Althea Jones was one reason to be thankful. One *more* reason—Gwen had lots.

Including no headache. Not today.

* * *

Nerise might have done some exploring, but they found her in the big living room, in front of the television.

"Nerise, did you ask Mr. Hardie before turning that thing on?"

"Yes, Mama. He said it was okay."

"Gwen, how's that on your head?"

"It's fine, Althea," but the flickering light—it didn't actually hurt, but it made her brain jitter. She closed her eyes.

"We'll just turn that off now, Nerise."

"But, Mama –"

"I said *now*, child. It hurts Miss Gwen's eyes."

"Oh, Miss Gwen, I'm sorry. I wish you felt better." Nerise clicked the remote switch; black, no sound, no flickers.

"Thanks, Nerise. I feel a *lot* better than I did. And we'll all feel better yet, when we eat what your mama's cooking for us."

"Up to some cribbage, Gwen?" Seth asked.

She shook her head.

"I wish I were, Seth. I don't think I could put 'fifteen-two' together just now.

"Maybe you could teach Nerise how to play. I'd enjoy

watching that."

"Sure—Nerise, you game?"

Nerise squealed. "Sure am! Is it okay, Mama?"

Althea allowed as how it was, and Gwen watched Seth teach Nerise pegging, what card combinations scored, and how to count them.

Nerise paid attention, learned fast when she did, Gwen noted.

Althea murmured, "That's one *complicated* game."

"I know, right? I think it was made up just to keep people awake after too much heavy food and alcohol. I love it, though. Daddy taught me, we used to play. Jack wasn't as keen as I was, though he still plays, sometimes."

"Daddy taught you, too, Seth, didn't he? And Ben?"

"Sure did. Few months, Ben could beat me four times out of five, if I wasn't *real* lucky."

"And you were the only one who could beat *me* three times out of five, if *I* weren't really lucky. Forget Ben. It got so I *hated* playing him," Gwen laughed, "I'd forgotten. Thank you, Seth, for reminding me of *that* ignominy." She grinned at him, and Seth laughed back.

"Any time."

Althea watched Seth, speculatively.

* * *

Back in the kitchen, later, Althea asked, "How many secrets you think that man keeps?"

Gwen's eyes opened wide. Laughing a little, "*S*mart, Althea. Seth and his secrets. He's always been like that, as far back as I remember, anyway. Hundreds, probably. I'd guess most of them aren't his. People tend to tell him things, sooner or later.

Because he never tells.

"He likes surprises, too. When he's the one handing them out. Taking us, when we were kids, or sometimes just me, places he'd explored on his own, not telling us where 'til we got there. Or what we'd find—a new swimming hole at one of the old quarries, bird's nest of a species we hadn't seen.

"Once, way north—we had to ride our bikes—a really beautiful cove, limestone all around, the land sloped down and we could reach it without killing ourselves. I think I was about nine, then. We went there often, for a few years. A lot of times, just Seth and me. It was quiet there. So were we. Just the sea, and the gulls crying. I never knew why we stopped."

Far away. Althea looked at Gwen's eyes, dreamy in reminiscence. Her soft smile. Soft, too, her voice.

She couldn't make out this Seth-and-Gwen thing. Long history, lotta love, both sides, anyone could see that—it was out in plain sight. And maybe it wasn't erotic, you didn't see *that*, but it was romantic. In some off-beat way or other. *Off-beat.* If you made a musical metaphor of it . . .

She didn't, Althea reminded herself, know a damn thing about any of it. And wouldn't. Gwen might be transparent as crystal, or near as made no nevermind, but there were closed doors, doors *bolted*, behind Seth Greenlaw's eyes.

It was none of her business. Which she should mind. She owed Gwen that courtesy. Being nosy wasn't—delicate.

Althea turned the conversation to dinner, and Gwen came back to earth with a small thud.

* * *

Ken Pelletier, with Caleb and Kyle, arrived at the Hardie kitchen door a little after 4:00, chorusing "Happy

Thanksgiving," greeting their cousin and Miss Althea warmly.

Ken enjoyed Althea Jones' Southern-ness; he'd left Georgia at five years of age, but it was green in his memory, and he'd never shaken the early-set drawl imprinted in his speech.

The boys had brought ice skates; there was a wide depression in the field behind the house—water collected and froze there, making a smooth-ish surface. No give to the ice, no spring, as a real pond would have, but you could skate on it.

Kyle, now 14, was two-way forward on the middle-school hockey team.

The Pelletiers had several old pairs of skates, and Ken had brought a couple of them for Nerise to try on. If she were interested. And if Miss Althea approved?

Althea thought it would be okay, if the boys didn't mind. They both told her, quite sincerely, they didn't.

Both liked Nerise Jones, and both respected her speed on the track. Ken had taken them to several races, this past summer and fall.

And Caleb knew her from Seth's stables.

First, though, everyone was to be found and greeted.

"Hey, Seth. Happy Thanksgiving. You want me at the stables tomorrow?"

Caleb had been graduated to part-time assistant trainer this fall, halter- and lead-training the new foals with their dams. Now they'd be left alone until fully weaned, at which point Seth would take over, at least for the pre-sold foals. Contracts specified he'd do the early training. Some of the foals would be boarded for years, until they could be fully trained. And some were his own.

Caleb would have those years to grow into the talent he had. He was 17, now; big like his father, dark-haired, but with the Pelletier lavender-blue eyes.

For those foals, and for some of the younger horses not contracted and awaiting full training, Seth wouldn't lie, would give truthful answers if asked. But any horse he considered fit to go out of his stable was, and would be, a well-trained horse.

Seth liked Caleb, liked working with him. Boy learned fast, kept quiet unless he needed an answer *now*. Mostly held questions to the end of his day's work. Then, they broke in a deluge. Smart questions, most of them.

"Come if you want. Not much to do."

"I'll be there at 8:00." Seth's stables were just about Caleb's favorite place to be. He loved each and every horse there—and they were all different—they were almost *people*.

Nerise was beyond *interested* in trying out ice skating— "Mama? Can I? Please?" Kyle's old size 6s fit her. A little tight was a good thing.

"'May I,' Nerise. For a bit, okay. You mind Caleb, now, you hear?"

"I will, Mama. Thank you."

* * *

Paul carved roast turkey, rubbed with butter, barded with bacon.

He asked the blessing, all said "Amen."

"I'm so thankful for this day, for a house full of family and friends," said Jack. "Most of all, I'm thankful for Melody, who opens the world up every day. And I'm thankful she said yes when I asked her. We're getting married, late August or September. When the new house is ready." He raised his glass to her.

Choruses of "Congratulations," "Be very happy," and variants.

"I'm *very* thankful. To be alive, to be home. For your happiness, Melody, Jack. For each and every one of you," Gwen looked around the table; Seth's eyes held hers the longest. "For no headache. And for this feast, which looks and smells absolutely gorgeous, thank you *so much*, Althea."

She raised her glass; Althea was toasted with enthusiasm.

Everyone was thankful Gwen was alive and with them, all were thankful on Melody's and Jack's behalves.

Each of them added their own personal reasons to be thankful, aloud or in silence. Some of Seth's were unspeakable, and went unspoken.

It wasn't the meal she'd planned, but it was wonderful. She'd been going to start with oyster stew; the oysters were in the stuffing, which was made with fresh cornbread. None of the sausage Gwen normally used, pecans instead of walnuts. She'd been going to make waffles with the mixture, for a change.

Maybe next year. But Althea's was delicious.

And the turkeys were tender and succulent, smoky with bacon, beautifully seasoned. Silky, deep-flavored gravy.

Althea had found a jar of Gwen's strained cranberry jelly. Almost like mother used to open, only much, much better.

"Girl, you should put this out there, too. I bet it'd sell like crazy."

"Thanks, I'll think about that."

Nerise took three scoops of jelly, one at a time, and consumed every bit. Gwen opened a second jar.

The pecan pie was better than her own, Gwen acknowledged happily. *It's fun, having someone else around who can really cook. She gets it.*

Happy Thanksgiving.

Dear God. Please, not a build-up like this one at Christmas. But a Christmas Day as good as this or better.

Please.

She yearned for that, she needed this Christmas.

She'd *earned* it. *Bought* it. With pain, with loss and its grief.

With will and effort—and with love. Those three in her pocket, she'd *make* Christmas turn out right.

* * *

After dinner the menfolk, with Nerise's help, cleared and loaded the dishwasher.

Althea had already run the loads of pots and pans. Gwen had helped, thoroughly approving. *Clean as you go. That's the way to do it.*

More than half of them felt like a walk afterward, shake off post-feast stupor.

Gwen didn't, Paul didn't, and Seth stayed behind with them. He could walk home. Later. Gwen was up to cribbage; she and Seth played quietly. Paul read a book.

Jack walked Melody home to her parents' house. Stayed a bit before heading home.

Nerise and Ken's boys ran ahead under the night sky; their respective parents walked together.

For a while, Althea Jones and Ken Pelletier strode in comfortable, companionable, silence.

"Miss Althea, it's been on my mind a while to ask—I hope you know how much I admire you, ma'am. I'd be honored if you and Nerise would come out to dinner with my boys and me, some time."

Althea looked at him levelly.

"You know what I wish, Ken Pelletier? I wish you'd asked just me. Then I'd say yes.

"But I wouldn't bring the kids into it. Not yet, anyhow."

She smiled into the grin breaking over his face.

CHAPTER 20

December

Gwen's assessment was accurate—most of the secrets Seth kept weren't his.

Most of them were entirely irrelevant to his own life; or the life of anyone he cared much about. Some of them were things he didn't want to know. Had no business knowing.

People did tell him things. Clients told him their business—sometimes what they told him would have been better unsaid, or told to a priest. Could get them in pretty hot water, if Seth told. But he didn't.

Women, too, told him things at the tavern a couple of towns up, and later.

He didn't have much to say to them, so he listened.

Seth preferred the quieter women. If she had a book, he watched. Those were the interesting ones. If she kept her eyes on the pages, he left her alone.

But the ones who—sometimes almost reluctantly—raised their eyes and looked around, from time to time—these he'd approach.

It had, in its way, been quite an education. Lot of unhappiness, in this world. People had troubles, and a surprising number seemed to want to talk about them.

They had needs, too, as he did; taking a few hours away from the trouble, he and they, filling the need. Anybody liked having someone pay attention for a while. A dance or two. Small moments of comfort in sad lives.

Seth hadn't been to that tavern since Paul Hardie had brought Gwen home. Didn't feel right.

* * *

The Hardie table, that evening, consisted of Paul, Seth, and Gwen. This was more and more often the case; Jack dined most evenings with his bride- and in-laws-to-be.

Gwen was busier than she'd imagined at this point in the year. Voluntarily—she'd decided to try jarring her cranberry sauce for sale, and was building up inventory for next season. She was also trying to come up with additional shelf-stable recipes.

Using her own figures, Tim Douglass had convinced Gwen to take the plant renovation over an extended period. One of the reasons she was building inventory.

She and Tim had discussed broadening her distribution area beyond Haven Point. Bar Harbor, other points up and down the coast. Another reason to stock up now.

It was Paul, that evening, who asked Seth for a game of cribbage; Seth set it up on a low table by Paul's chair.

A while, since they'd talked at any length.

"How much woodland do you have left, now, Seth? Enough deadfall to keep you heated?"

"About ten acres, enough, it's a small house. I'd like more, ten's not a lot to hunt."

"Son, you know you're free on our land, anytime. Not a

person in this house but would insist on it."

"You're all real good people, Paul. Best I've known. But . . ."

Paul finished, "But you'd rather own it yourself, if you're using it."

Seth shrugged, nodded. "Would you think about selling me some of yours?"

"I don't suppose you'd let me give you five acres? The cost wouldn't keep that foal fed for more than a year or three. Not taking vet bills into account."

"Couldn't let you do that. Two've got nothing to do with each other."

Paul suggested they move the discussion to his new study.

The big desk dominated the smaller room as it had not Paul's old study, in which he now slept.

"How many acres were you thinking?"

"Ten, if you're willing. Depending what you want for it, I should have the price now."

Paul thought. Finally, he took a fresh sheet of paper, dated it, wrote.

Signed the bottom, dated the signature, and printed his name under it. Scratched a straight-ish line to the right, and pushed the paper across the desk.

Seth took it, read.

"I can't accept this, Paul."

The price per acre was close to market. That was fair, and Seth had the money. But Paul's note of intent specified a mere 10% down payment, interest at 2% over a repayment period of 10 years, and a moratorium on both interest accrual and principal payments for five years.

"I don't feel like arguing, son. If you want the land, those are my terms."

The two men looked at each other.

Seth wanted the acreage. If the terms were a gift, at least the land itself wasn't. He could, he supposed, compromise. Since Paul insisted.

He signed, and wrote Paul a check.

He would pay it all off when the moratorium ended.

* * *

Haven Point's Christmas lights were up, wrapping Main Street at night in bright twinkles.

Private householders, from the town line to the point, decorated as they saw fit. Such displays almost invariably included wreaths—it would be positively anti-Maine not to display at least one balsam wreath. Even Seth Greenlaw hung one on his barn door, though this was the extent of his holiday decoration.

The Grays outlined windows, door, porches with colored lights. Colored lights in shrubbery, on trees.

The Hardie décor was similar, but the lights were white. Some were designed to dangle strands of bulbs; these were hung from the porch roof of the earlier of the two wings. Outside foliage was left unadorned.

There were, to be sure, some very vulgar displays. But these were few.

Year-round stores stayed open late; this coming Friday evening would bring the annual "Christmas Shopping Night." Stores would offer patrons alcohol-free punch or eggnog, or mulled cider; choirs from St. Aidan's (Anglican Catholic), St. Stephen's (Roman Catholic), First Congregational, and Trinity (Methodist) churches would carol.

Melody Gray sold more than a few party dresses—not the

more expensive vintage gowns, but pretty, and some pricey. Gwen bought one Melody had set aside for her the minute it came in. A lot of very small dresses came to her; people used to be littler. Gwen was one of the few Haven Point women who could fit into most of them.

Gwen had agreed to accept Melody's 50% family discount on any item that had been in the store more than a month. Melody felt no need to tell her that some of what she showed Gwen had been set aside for her over that month.

In addition to clothing, Melody offered vintage and local artisan jewelry. Costume and art glass to a few real gold-and-gems pieces; this late afternoon in early December, Gwen was looking at the latter.

"Go ahead and look, but let me just get out some stuff that came in yesterday. I haven't had a chance to price it yet, but if there's something you want, we'll figure it out."

Among that 'stuff' was just what Gwen hoped to find. She'd had to try Melody first, but Gwen had imagined she'd need another road trip. Probably she still would, for Melody's present, but at least one more name was crossed off her list.

Almost done. One more to go. Oh—and Patrick Riordan. He'd given her a whole lot of books, she really ought to get him something.

The Book Nook, Haven Point's second-hand bookstore, was three doors down; Gwen spent an hour poking into shelves, stacks. One small volume made her chuckle as she pulled it from the shelf. She dusted the cover off, checked the penciled price. It wasn't expensive, didn't look impressive, but that was beside the point. This would do nicely, she thought. A first edition, technically, though the eighth printing.

She exchanged holiday greetings with Robert Weed, the proprietor. Bought the book, plus several postcards reproducing works by Andrew Wyeth.

She deserved a little celebratory break, Gwen thought, before she headed back to prepare her family's dinner. Not that there was much to do, she'd make some rolls using a very handy quick-rising yeast bread recipe. The ingredients in a big pot of beef stew had been getting better acquainted overnight, and salad didn't take any time.

Gwen pulled her—*very own!*—car into the Main Street Tavern's parking lot.

Patrick Riordan, coming out of Cole's Pharmacy, noted the green Volvo. He had seen little of Gwen since before Thanksgiving; he'd spent some of that time in New York and California, in connection with a premium cable mini-series to be made based on a three-book narrative arc from his prior mystery series.

It pleased Patrick that Gwen's car was green—so was his Jag. He had no reason to know she'd relied on Seth Greenlaw to pick for her, only giving final approval to his choice.

He parked in the tavern's parking lot, went in, and made pretense.

"Gwen, my dear. What a pleasure to run into you. Do let me buy you a drink."

"Patrick. Hope your trip went well? Oh!" Remembering her manners, "please sit down."

Gwen was, disappointingly, drinking hot apple cider, non-alcoholic. She declined a refill; one glass was filling enough, before dinner.

"But I do want to thank you for the Robertson Davies books. I love him, I really do—*beautifully* formal prose. I like the hard-minded optimism, so serious and so funny at once. And that— the—awareness of the infinite. His writing feels like something I knew a lifetime ago, and am rediscovering.

"I'm even giving my father the books of speeches and essays for Christmas—he likes that sort of thing better than fiction," she smiled. "And then I can read them when he's finished."

"Gwen, I'm delighted to have introduced you to his work—it's indeed everything you say, or such is my opinion. We must discuss the books in greater depth, and soon."

"After Christmas, Patrick—I have the house to decorate, we still don't have a tree, and I'm not done planning the food."

"I hear the Christmas Eve Lord-Hardie gathering goes back two centuries, though they were not named Lord then. I would adore being part of that."

Patrick was confused by her reaction, which was—confusion.

"Oh, Patrick—yes, it does, so does their Boxing Day dinner at the Grays. But—I mean, it *is* a tradition. We've only added the Greenlaw boys—and that was when my father sort of—well, he was kind of semi-responsible for them for a few years, after their Dad died.

"Ben was only 12, and Seth wasn't 18 yet—we all wanted the family to stay together. Seth—he worked so hard. Too hard, much too hard. But he got smarter about *what* he worked at, and look where he is now. Best, most successful trainer in at least three counties, and everyone knows it." Gwen smiled. *He's done so well. Shown them all what he can do. What he is.*

Patrick did not particularly care for this avenue of discussion, and returned to the subject of Christmas Eve.

"Well, really, it'd be Mr. and Mrs. Lord, and my parents, who would have to approve. I'm not the hostess, just the cook."

Gwen's manner made it clear that, if anyone were to ask for his inclusion, it would not be she.

"I apologize for putting you in an awkward position. Please

let me assure you it was not intentional. And I will not do so again."

Gwen looked relieved.

As a rule, Patrick wasn't over-scrupulous unless it served his purpose. He thought he could charm the Lords into asking if they could bring him.

CHAPTER 21

Christmas Eve

Christmas Eve dawned cold and gray-skied with the threat—or promise—of snow.

Gwen had put pheasants in brine two days before. Julia Lord had mentioned how good they'd been, a few years back, and Gwen had asked Seth, who shot some, and brought four to her. Put a few more into his big freezer.

It was a pleasant distribution of labor—it had been quite some years since Gwen had hunted quail and snowshoe hare with Seth. He liked seeing his kills on the Hardie table. Worked into delicious meals by the woman he loved.

Gwen bustled happily. She'd have help, and Melody, to deal with tomorrow; tonight's feast was her own.

It was mid-afternoon, shadows already long, when Seth brought Ben over—driving, meeting the flight, getting Ben settled.

Ben had talked non-stop from Bangor to Haven Point. He still hadn't given a formal answer, but would not be accepting the Department of Defense's offer.

"We're going on our own, Sydney and Brian and me. We found a place in Richmond—their contracts are up in January, and they're getting it fixed up as we speak. There's a banker there—we met him in Arlington, and he's making interested noises about funding, once I'm out in April."

Ben talked on, things he and his going-to-be-partners were planning. He got going, his words were about as comprehensible to Seth as written Cyrillic. What Seth did hear, and understand, was that Ben, if genuinely excited over what he was speaking of, was talking around something else.

Around and around.

Eventually, "So, what *aren't* you telling me? Might as well get it said."

Ben flushed. Seth read him too well.

"Well. That banker. Name's Randolph. When he was in Arlington, and we met him. It was a business stop on his way to a family vacation. He's got—we met the family.

"He has—his daughter, she's—Seth, she's the one. I knew it the minute I laid eyes on her. Most beautiful thing I ever saw. Smart, funny, and—she's a Virginia girl, that Southern charm . . .

"She's a little younger than me—not quite a year, still in college, of course. The biggest dark eyes—I could just dive into them and never get to the bottom. I'm hooked, I'm sunk."

Ben was laughing, though, and sounded very happy.

"She feel the same?"

"I don't know—she's interested, though—I've been seeing her for two months, going to Richmond weekends. Don't want to freak her out, taking it very slow. Best not to rush things, important ones."

He'd learned that much, anyway.

"Her name's Abigail." Their mother's name. Did that mean something? Ben always denied any memory of her.

"I wish you luck, brother. Bring her up, some time."

"Come down and meet her. Spring, maybe. See the new lab, when we're all out of the contracts."

* * *

Patrick Riordan realized his mistake before Paul Hardie handed him a champagne flute.

He had, indeed, managed to charm the Lords into requesting he be invited, though he thought they hadn't been overjoyed about it. And here he was, a golden apple of discord on the hearth rug.

Of course, they were all very polite, but almost no-one was at ease. Not the Lords, not the elder Hardies. Certainly not Gwen Sinclair, who was too obviously trying to hide embarrassment. Elizabeth, blast her, was amused—she'd warned him, and she'd been right.

He'd wanted to take part in this, but there was no part for him to play. The cast of characters had been set long since. And he did not want salient memories in their minds of how he'd ruined Christmas Eve for them.

After one glass, and a very little small talk, which included reminding Madeleine Hardie of a previous meeting, a party in New York a decade past, Patrick declined a refill.

"I do hope you will all forgive me—it is perfectly clear I've barged in where I'd no business to, and I apologize from the bottom of my heart.

"If I may call again, perhaps the 27th or 28th?"

Madeleine said he was welcome between 11:00 and 3:00, either day.

"Then I will wish you all the happiest of Christmases, and take myself home, genuflecting and saying 'mea culpas' all the way."

Seth, close to Gwen by the fire, murmured, "Drive safe," and Gwen laughed out loud.

To atone, she saw Patrick to the door.

"Thank you, Patrick. I'm glad you understand."

"A bit late getting to it, but I do, I really do."

"Happy Christmas, my dear. I look forward to seeing you soon."

* * *

"Just marvelous, Gwen, dear. As ever. Aren't we lucky?" Julia Lord, setting down her fork after a last bite of cranberry-walnut pie, "To have you to cook for us."

"You're too kind, Mrs. Lord."

"Please call me Julia, dear."

Jack, Melody, Seth and Ben helped Madeleine clear the table; ten hands made quick work of it. Liz had offered help, which was declined.

Liz—and Paul Hardie—saw, amused, Gwen almost visibly extend antennae of watchfulness. Amateurs. In her kitchen. She'd gotten worse about that, Paul thought, since she'd met Althea Jones.

Dinner remnants dealt with, the party adjourned to the parlor.

The tree twinkled, Gwen's ever-shabbier angel atop it, Ben's increasingly numerous silver-wire ornaments glinting with flickers of firelight.

"This must be your recipe, Gwen," as Liz sipped eggnog. The first Christmas she'd spent in Haven Point in years.

"You know it."

It went down almost too smoothly; Gwen combined the sugar and bourbon, left it out overnight, covered with cheesecloth. This mellowed the sharp alcohol taste—almost eliminated it; the eggnog was slightly less lethal, also, due to evaporation of the alcohol. The eggs and rich Jersey milk—the creamline came almost halfway down the bottle—were local. Nutmeg fresh-grated, naturally.

Presents were opened. The Lords' gifts were, for 'the young people,' signed prints of Haven Point landscapes, the work of Jonathan Cohen, a New York artist who'd recently retired to their town. The images were sharp, poignant—for a city person, Cohen made nature—and weather—sing with energy on the parchment prints.

Seth laughed to himself at these. His gift to the Lords was a semi-abstract painting on a small wood board of one of the foals, now a two-year old in light training. Peter Lord had contracted for Melissa, and would purchase her when she was three or so and full-trained. A beautiful red roan; the painting suggested her red-and-white effectively.

The signature read "Sarah Morgan;" the artist had come to Haven Point in summer, to paint, for some years. Her unobtrusive presence at any property with horses had become a commonplace seasonal eccentricity. Haven Point was not, generally, aware of the prominence Sarah Morgan's work received in the art world.

Seth liked the paintings Ms. Morgan traded him for rides, every summer—she was quite a decent horsewoman.

She sketched for hours at a time—exercise, lessons, training. Never fussed, just did her thing and kept quiet. Sarah Morgan painted horses with seeing love—smooth power, animation. Nothing awkward, nothing static.

Sarah Morgan *got* horses, in her brushes and her hands.

"Seth, this is marvelous. I know Ms. Morgan's work, of course, but this will be a coveted item for collectors. Thank you *very* much—a fine gift, indeed."

Julia Lord echoed her husband's sentiments.

Seth hadn't imagined the painting would be the high-point of gift-opening, but so it was, this evening.

Presents were not the point, anyway—the company was.

Melody fit in immediately, as Seth and Ben Greenlaw had been made to feel they did, years ago, and as Patrick Riordan had not this evening.

Gwen had opened a little box with a pair of earrings in it—the Lords presented her with earrings every year since Julia Lord had removed hers for Gwen to christen her Greenlaw-made box with. A new sort-of-tradition.

This year's were made of metal-merged glass, an abstraction of blues, greens and golds.

Gwen looked at them until the little frown cleared from between her brows.

"I get it—they're peacock feathers, just sort of kaleidoscoped—am I right?"

Julia Lord laughed, "Gwen, dear, I've no idea—I just thought of you when I saw them. They do go so nicely with that dress." Gwen was wearing the deep-teal silk jersey she'd picked up from Melody, the first time she'd visited The Dress-Up Box.

And shoes—the Lords definitely counted as 'dress-proper' company. Tomorrow, she could go barefoot as much as she liked.

Patrick had at least gracefully rectified his error, Gwen thought. Everyone was comfortable, and this was the great thing.

Liz opened Gwen's two boxes for her—a silk scarf, white with a red border, a pattern of red lips. And a video of "The Rocky Horror Picture Show." Liz had shepherded Gwen and

Mark Sinclair to a midnight showing in Boston. Gwen had thought it marvelous, though Mark had been less enthusiastic; she and Liz had seen it maybe half a dozen times together.

"Gwen—very cool. Thanks. Let's watch it together, some late night—It'll be like old times."

Like old times. Gwen wondered if there were sweeter words. *This is 'old times,' just another of them. Bless you—bless us—all.*

* * *

Ben had fallen asleep on the floor, shortly after the Lords left; Gwen and Paul persuaded Seth they should stay the night. Gwen took far longer to return to announce a ready room than was usual, Seth noted.

She did, indeed—moving everything she'd set up to her own bedroom, removing the "Do not open" paper she'd taped up. She would, she thought, leave a light on so she didn't bump into anything. *No disasters. Not now, not so close.*

Gwen—and Paul—stayed up later than the rest, moving from the old parlor to the less-old living room.

"If you want, Daddy, you can go to bed. I'll get everything wrapped for both of us, once they're sleeping soundly."

Paul demurred; he put on a video of his and Gwen's mutual favorite 'A Christmas Carol,' a newer version, recorded several years ago, with George C. Scott as Ebeneezer Scrooge. Gwen paused it about 20 minutes in, and made trips upstairs and down.

It had been harder to find gift-type boxes big enough than finding what there was to put in them. Industrial-size wrapping paper hadn't been too difficult.

The real problem was the wrapping itself—the boxes were almost as big as she was. She couldn't manage without a lot of maneuvering.

Gwen maneuvered, and managed. Carried two unwieldy large boxes to under the tree. Next-to-under. And a number of smaller packages.

"Daddy?" Paul had fallen asleep; the film, again paused, had maybe half-an-hour left.

"Hm?" Waking drowsy and warm.

"You go on to bed, now. I've got it all done. Merry Christmas." It was after midnight.

Paul went to join Madeleine in his former study and new bedroom; Gwen curled up to watch the end of the movie. Fell asleep herself, on the couch, in her pretty silk dress.

She woke in the small hours. Took herself upstairs to bed, pausing to gently touch the door behind which her 'other brothers' slept. It was good to have Ben with them all.

Her baby brother. Gwen, almost four years older, had mothered him, a little, when he was a motherless little one. Aptly named—the biblical Benjamin had been Jacob's youngest son, as Ben Greenlaw had been the youngest of the four of them, Gwen, Seth, Jack—and Ben. The tag-along, then, but fortune's darling, now. Or soon would be, bless him.

Ben could have his horizons. Gwen would keep Haven Point.

It was *good* to have Seth in the house, always.

Happy birthday, Lord Jesus. Thank you.

CHAPTER 22

Christmas Day

Christmas morning, Gwen woke to butterflies in her stomach. Not, thank God, the really nauseating ones she still remembered from the time her mother had convinced her to take a role in a grade school play.

She'd been miserable. Gwen had an excellent memory, and had known when anyone got a line wrong after the first week of rehearsal. Which they did, a lot, and mostly were not corrected.

But it was the *worst*, standing in front of everyone, without a book to refer to, without anything to hold or use in your hands, trying to call up the words you knew you knew. Gwen had been unable to come up with most of her lines, been awful, and been glad to be. Her mother never put her through that again.

Jack, his one attempt, remembered his lines, but recited them as if he had no awareness of their meaning.

Madeleine's talent had not taken root in her children.

No, this morning's butterflies were like the flutters her first night serving tasting menus. She knew this, she *had this.*

God willing, and the creek don't rise.

Oh, God. She'd thought that commonplace the night before she married Mark. She'd thought she'd be happy forever. God had not been willing; the creek had risen and flooded.

My first widowed Christmas. Mark. Gwen let the tears come. Opened herself to welcoming the pain of her loss. What she and Mark had had, had shared, was—it was *theirs*—it was—special, and beautiful, and was gone. She was thankful to have known it; she was going to have to let it go.

Wherever Mark was, Gwen hoped the place had a good library.

* * *

Schedules had been adjusted; Jack had been the effective force. He—and Melody—needed to accommodate two family celebrations. Joanna Gray had come up from Portland with her new fiancé, Richard Prentice; Jason, who'd moved to the house and land his wife Rachel had inherited from an aunt, would of course be there with her and their three children, Jonas, Luke, and Michelle.

The Grays would, as usual, open gifts directly after breakfast, and serve Christmas dinner around 1:00 p.m.

Gwen had joined Jack in requesting that the Hardies put off presents until after *their* dinner at 6:00. That way, Jack and Melody could share in the Hardies' Christmas as well as the Grays'.

And leaving the presents until last—well, as far as Gwen was concerned, that just made the day's sparkle last longer.

Wrap it up with unwrapping.

* * *

The kitchen windows still showed dark, when she put on

the day's first pot of coffee. She was the first down this morning. Liked the feeling—for these moments, herself alone in aware possession of this dwelling—*lovely word*—she loved so dearly.

Gwen put on, also, a CD of Christmas carols. English carols, an English choir of men and boys. Newly recorded, in the most old-school of styles. She'd heard it Boston, one of the years she hadn't made it home for the holiday. Bought it on the spot. It was her favorite Christmas album, like a just-met-old-friend.

She hummed and sang along as she took eggs, buttermilk, etc. from the refrigerator, stuck butter into the freezer. Mixed up dry ingredients for biscuit dough, and set that bowl into the freezer, too. Cut a block of cream cheese into bits, chopped chives, wrapped them, and set both chives and cream cheese bits back in the fridge.

Squeezed two bags of oranges; the juice went into the refrigerator in turn.

Jack was next down. Gwen made an exception to her no-non-cooks rule mornings. You had to let people come where the coffee was. No way around that fact of life. And she could make breakfast with distractions all over the place. It was just breakfast.

"What time do the Grays do breakfast? Do you want some toast, or something, to keep you going?"

"No, thanks, coffee's all I need. I'll be going over in about an hour, they sit down around 7:30."

"Jack, I'm so happy for the two of you. It's—it's heartening, two good people finding each other. It's like springtime—it's so—it makes me feel hopeful."

"I'm glad you're starting to feel hopeful, Gwen. And thanks. Yeah. Can I say she makes my heart feel like spring? Without sounding too goofy?"

"It's okay to be a little goofy when you're in love. I won't tell on you."

They laughed, and Gwen, behind Jack's chair, put her arms around him. "I'll miss you, though. I wish it could work, bringing Melody here, but you probably know best. I don't really get it—I mean, I can stitch up a seam or hem, sew a button, but I'd never mess around in her workroom. That's where she's got me beat by miles."

The implication being that, as a cook, Gwen beat Melody by miles. Which was true. Melody cooked good, simple food. She didn't think up new things, but she took care with what she did, and the result was tasty and comforting and made with love.

"Kitchen's different. Melody's been cooking for her parents for years—like you used to, like you do now. She likes being in charge—also like you.

"I'm really glad you're friends. And no way I am going to let you two start fighting over whose territory what is."

Gwen said no more on the subject.

Jack did not ask his sister about the large—the enormous—box with his name on it. He thought he had an idea what it might be—Gwen had told him a little about a plan, asked him a few questions, and there was an identically sized box for Seth. She hadn't told Jack he was to be included, and he didn't want to—what did Sherlock Holmes say—"theorize ahead of the data?" Something like that.

Jack had decided to give reading another try. Paul Hardie had suggested Sherlock Holmes stories to start, and—surprise—Jack was enjoying them a lot. He thought he'd try 'Treasure Island,' maybe, next.

He did know what the boxes for Ken Pelletier contained. What Seth's big box held—in a general way, if not exactly. And highly approved.

* * *

Seth's was the third coffee cup Gwen filled.

"Merry Christmas, Gwen, Jack. Gwen—what's up with that big box?"

"You are *not* supposed to ask. But since you have, inside is a smaller box, all wrapped, and a smaller one, wrapped inside that. And more and more boxes, all wrapped. With lots of tightly tied ribbon and a ton of tape. By the time you get to the last box, which is about this big," Gwen held up two fingers half an inch apart, "it will be after midnight. But you'll find your present in that tiny one."

Both men were laughing; she was, too.

"Merry Christmas, Seth. Don't even think about presents, not yet—they come later."

Jack left for the Grays'.

"What do you say we get these slowpokes out of bed?"

"Start cooking—that'll get 'em up. Or down." Seth smiled at her.

"My thought, exactly." Gwen smiled back.

She flicked on a couple of burners, started heating pans.

Seth was the one person Gwen liked in her kitchen anytime.

Soon, the aromas of sausage, bacon, fresh biscuits spread through the house. Paul and Madeleine joined them in short order, and Ben followed soon after.

Even Althea Jones' down-South-home soul food, Seth thought, couldn't hold a candle to Gwen's Christmas breakfasts. Maybe it was the love Gwen put in that made the difference.

He hoped she hadn't done anything too silly about presents.

After breakfast, Ben walked back with Seth to their own land. Seth, among other things, wanted to check on Rosie, now five months old. He'd set up food and water dispensers, and she used the hinged panel in the kitchen door to do her business in the yard, but a puppy needed company, at least some of the time.

Ben wanted to help with morning stables, of all things.

"You think I could get back to an okay place with horses, all this time?"

"I expect, you want to. Your girl, she rides?"

"Yeah."

Ben was 21. He was still puzzled by the way his brother, never a good student, could be so damn' smart about some things.

* * *

The Greenlaws' departure left Gwen alone with her parents.

It was an awkward hole in the day, not opening gifts right after breakfast. The house seemed to rattle with lack of celebrants. *We'll have to get accustomed,* Gwen thought.

They'd been to Mass early Christmas Eve, would not go today.

Gwen re-wound the tape she and her father had semi-watched, semi-slept through. Wrapped through, in her case.

Paul and Madeleine took the sofa, Gwen curled up, bare feet tucked under her, in an armchair, and they watched the film.

It really was Gwen's favorite adaptation.

After, Madeleine spoke of different modes of fidelity to a literary original in adaptation.

Gwen thought the spirit more vital than the letter. If you got that right, you could make changes. She defended the excising of Dickens' lower-caste characters' obsequy—one thing, in the Victorian era. Another today—it blurred the wrong lines, made for a too-easy sympathy directed to the wrong people. Denied genuinely sympathetic characters any relatable *dignity* in modern eyes.

For once, she thought, her mother took her argument seriously. Still a little like an exam—Gwen had to support her view, Madeleine challenged her up one side and down the other.

It didn't shake her. Inside or out. This was new. And welcome.

* * *

Cousin Ken brought a station wagon-full of happiness—his boys, his new lady-friend Althea, and her daughter—around 1:00 in the afternoon. Along with the first whirling snowflakes. A foot or more was predicted, accumulating through the day, perhaps overnight.

Seth and Ben were not back—what took them so long? Morning stables had to be long over, and more than enough time for Seth and his two year-round hands, who lived above the garage, to give all the horses proper exercise.

The three kids—was Caleb still *properly* placed in that category? he was nearly as tall as Seth—had brought ice skates and, once holiday greetings were exchanged, laced up and headed for the patch of ice out back.

Gwen and Althea took to the kitchen, leaving Ken with Madeleine and Paul Hardie. They scrolled through television offerings, but ended watching the same "Christmas Carol" over again—Ken hadn't seen it.

"I'm trying something new with the dressing—you were the inspiration, Althea. Half cornbread—sorry, only a tablespoon of sugar—half biscuit. The rest is the way I usually do it, sausage, onion, apple, celery, dried wild blueberries, walnuts. And the usual suspects, of course—eggs, butter, stock.

"I liked your baking it in a shallow dish—more crusty bits, I'll be doing that from now on."

"What we got on the menu?"

"Grouse, Seth bagged them; they've been frozen and thawed, alas, but they're early-season young birds, hung a few days after. I've brined them, and boned them; the breasts are small, even as many as we have won't take much time to cook."

"Never eaten grouse. Quail, sure. What they taste like?"

Gwen shrugged. "Like—a very mild game bird. Not too dissimilar from wild quail—we have those here, too. Quail are awfully *little* for eating. I need at least two per person. Four, if it's Seth or Jack. I'm thinking maybe Ken and Caleb, too. Grouse are bigger. We'll cook one and a half per. I won't eat a whole one."

"Hard-working men put away a lot, for true."

"Don't they, just?"

"Mashed potatoes, to go with, and roasted Brussels sprouts with mushrooms and bacon. I found real Porcini at the marketplace. Frozen, but what can you do, this time of year? The flavor will still be there. I thawed and peeled them yesterday. And a clear, intense sauce, instead of gravy. Made a stock with the quail carcasses and legs, it came out very tasty. I'll reduce it down, add some wine and herbs, mount it with butter at the end."

"You don't do sweet potatoes?"

"Pie. They're made, I got that done yesterday, too. We've still got cranberry-maple-walnut to go, but that's quick and easy. Piecrust is in the fridge, already rolled and in the plates. We just have to make the filling, roll out and cut the lattice top."

"Speaking of pie, you got any of that mincemeat left?"

"You just bet I do. Think you can bang us out some tarts?

I'd like to serve them before, appetizers. With Madeira—the mincemeat's got that in it—or sherry. I found an amazing Amontillado in Portland a couple of months back, and ordered a case. You can take a bottle—you might try it in that cheese sauce you put on those wonderful shrimp fritters. It's *soooo* better than what we can get in Bangor or closer. And by the way, I want that recipe.

"Melody's bringing a ham. It should be okay—she gets her meat from Vince Morey, same as we do. She insisted." Both professionals shrugged at amateur quirks and foibles.

"Got that recipe from a book, didn't even tweak it much. I'll write it down."

Althea set to work on mincemeat tarts, Gwen busied herself with cornbread prep. Took the extra biscuit dough she'd prepped with breakfast, pressed it into one cast iron skillet, poured cornbread batter into the other.

* * *

Dinner was well in hand by 3:30; Althea and Gwen retired upstairs to change. They could protect dresses with aprons and their chef coats, for the final push.

Gwen put on the new green dress she'd got from Melody—that shop was a godsend. *Melody* was a godsend. Memory for her stock like a filing cabinet—with a good filing system.

Althea had brought a dress of topaz and green velvet. Almost a caftan, loose and flowing.

How do you get to look that queenly?

Honestly. Gwen adored Haven Point, all her family, was deeply fond of her new friends. But they provided a regular exercise in humility, when it came to looks. Gwen knew she was—what was that old line? "Pretty enough for all normal purposes." But with her mother, the Lord ladies, and now Althea Jones to be looked at, Gwen was a distant straggler. Pretty she might be. They were beautiful.

At least Melody was around the same level as she—pretty. Of course, Melody had a lot more in the curve department than Gwen, who was still struggling to gain back the last five pounds she'd lost in the wake of her accident. She wouldn't mind ten.

Gwen and Althea brought out boards with cheese, butter, bread and crackers. Orange segments, grapes. A bowl of shelled pistachios, another of smooth, skinless Marcona almonds, sheened with their oil, lightly salted.

They'd barely finished setting them out when Seth and Ben arrived. Seth's face was amused and pleased, Ben's was a cipher. Both were flushed with exercise; they'd spent the time on horseback—mostly—and had begun the walk back through four inches of snow, with another falling before they reached the Hardies'.

"You look real pretty, Gwen. I like that dress." Gwen felt herself color a little. Seth rarely paid personal compliments.

"Thank you. Melody—I kind of let her pick. She's got a good eye, if that's what you call it."

The dress was green silk jersey, heavy and with a dull sheen. Self-covered flat buttons down the front, from the wide neckline to the hem of the full skirt. Cap sleeves. The frock skimmed her figure gracefully. You could imagine she had a little more flesh than she did.

"What were you and Ben doing so long?"

He laughed. "Might be he wants it a secret. Seems Ben's got a girl he likes. It's to do with her—I'll say that much."

"Oh, I'm glad. About time—has he ever been serious about a girl before?"

"None he ever told me about."

Suddenly, "What about you, Seth?" He was 27. And he'd never spoken about a special girl, or woman.

Gwen, back in Haven Point for some six months, had heard rumors. Well, of course, he'd get his needs met somehow. Weird, if he didn't. She just hoped he was sensible about it.

She needn't have worried on that score.

But—"I mean, don't you want to get married, sometime? Have kids, to inherit what you've built?" Gwen wasn't up on real estate values, but Seth's working stable—and the horses, and the house he'd fixed up, and 50 acres, with the ten he'd bought from her father—had to be worth at least five times what the property left by his father had been. Less than ten years ago. Against the odds, Seth had prospered.

Not that she'd doubted him. Worry, she had. But doubted? Never.

"Don't worry about me. I'm fine the way I am. Seriously."

The last thing he wanted was Gwen trying to match him off with other women.

"What am I thinking, keeping you in the hallway? Come on—wish Ken and Althea a Merry Christmas. I think Caleb and Nerise and Kyle are still out back skating.

"Should I see if we can dig that—that huge *puddle* into a real pond, do you think? Blades would move better on it."

"Think it'd be worth doing? 'Less I'm missing something, only those three ever skate on it. And they're growing up." Fast. Caleb was almost a man. *Life just keeps moving.*

"Maybe not. But—down the road, Jack and Melody'll probably have kids—I certainly hope so. Nice for them, if it turns out they like skating."

"I'd wait, then. See what happens."

He was probably right. Seth usually was.

She took his arm, and they joined the rest in the parlor.

Jack brought Melody—with her ham—a little after 4:30; hot mincemeat tarts appeared, little glasses of Madeira and sherry were poured.

Christmas was toasted, the cooks were toasted, including a nod to Melody and her ham. Jack and Melody were toasted. Everyone toasted everyone else. Melody Gray was slightly tipsy by the time she sat down to dinner.

Gwen and Althea had stayed to toast Christmas, accepted the toast to themselves, and repaired to the kitchen to finish dinner; they were the soberest people in the house.

Tasted, making unobtrusive cuts, Melody's ham. It was quite tasty, if nothing special.

A little before 6:00, the Hardies and their guests sat down to a table crowded with serving plates—sliced ham, breast of grouse, bacon-mushroom-Brussels sprouts, mashed potatoes, dressing. Sauceboats full of intense, delicious-smelling liquid. Gwen's cranberry jelly, which was selling decently—for off-season—these past few weeks at the marketplace.

"Thank you for the birds, Seth. I think ruffed grouse might be even better than pheasant. And it's easier to cook."

"Sure. I'd be bagging them anyway, couldn't make them taste like this."

That was for sure.

"I remember you trying to cook me breakfast, once. I've always wanted to know—was that *real* axle grease you used to cook with? It certainly didn't taste like a food product."

"Never said I could cook."

"You know what? I am going to make a New Year's resolution to teach you how to cook a decent breakfast. You're not dumb, and it's not rocket science."

"You can manage that, hat's off to you. I'm game to try."

"Game *on*, then. New Year's Day, first lesson."

"Bright and early."

They grinned at each other.

* * *

Gwen, with an eye on the weather forecast, had made up bedrooms for everyone. After sherry-toasts, a good deal of Burgundy with dinner, and with more wine and eggnog being poured, she was doubly glad she had.

Caleb had been permitted two glasses, one sherry and one of wine. Kyle and Nerise half a glass each of wine, after one sip of sherry. Now they were the sober ones.

Gwen saw a new large box under the tree—not quite under, under was filled and spilled over. Her name on the tag, white paper, tied with green twine and with holly and balsam cones. That would be the last one she opened.

Another, small, with sparkling stars stenciled everywhere on shining silver paper. At least five colors of shiny curled ribbon tied up together. From Ben.

Gwen always wondered what those two would come up with. She'd open Ben's first.

She couldn't wait to see Seth's face, when he opened hers.

An informal round-robin of unwrapping.

Gwen had found Ben an oddity—an old computer once made by Xerox; she'd heard him talk about them—the first major 'what-you-see-is-what-you-get' interface. The most elegant of the early attempts, according to Ben.

A dozen had been found in an old warehouse in Ellsworth. In working order. And sold for almost nothing.

"Gwen. *Thanks.* I don't know *where* you came up with this, but I've been itching to take one of these apart as long as I can remember."

By 'taking apart,' Ben meant diving into the operating system's code, analyzing it. The ancient machine had nothing for him. Gwen saw only dismantled hardware.

"Merry Christmas, Ben. I got lucky. Make yourself all the unholy electronic mess you want."

His sparkly gift contained a necklace and earrings, handmade by Ben. The necklace was large gold wire links; dangling were miniature replicas in gold wire of all the tree ornaments he'd made over the years. From each of these depended a very small tumbled amethyst nugget, shining like petrified jelly, set with *tiny* gold-circled emeralds. The earrings were miniatures of the first and most recent ornaments.

"Ben, how beautiful. Thank you, dear little brother." She put them on. "Do they look okay? I never think I pull off different earrings. Some women can."

She was assured they looked lovely; checked in a hall mirror. Not bad, not ridiculous, anyway.

Took them off again, putting back her jade-and-pearl mistletoe posts. *The* Christmas earrings.

Ben had made gold earrings for Madeleine, and Melody, too. Matching ones—Madeleine's the first ornament he'd made, dangling unembellished amethysts; Melody's were this year's design, with sapphires.

Madeleine Hardie opened two flat parcels—reproductions in pencil and charcoal of John Singer Sargent's portraits in those media of John and Ethel Barrymore, respectively. Another package, containing a necklace of large tumbled amethyst chunks.

"How lovely, Gwen—all of them. Thank you, darling. Where did you find the sketches?"

Gwen laughed, and did not answer, except to say, "Merry Christmas, Mom." She'd had to hire an artist for the pencil portrait of John Barrymore. It hadn't even been close to her biggest expense. Which had gone into one of the two big boxes she'd wrapped last night.

Melody's was an antique necklace of rough-faceted sapphire beads.

"For your wedding, if you want—both old and blue."

"Gwen, they're—you *shouldn't* have. Thank you so much."

"Merry Christmas, Melody. I never had a sister before."

Paul opened his packages from Gwen. One contained several volumes, each individually wrapped in alternating gold and silver tissue. Speeches, essays, by that Robertson Davies fellow she'd been reading. Paul hadn't got round to any of the novels yet, but Gwen's description of the prose, the tenor of thought and approach, had interested him.

"I'll read these with pleasure, Gwen. Thank you."

The second was rather different. It was a signed copy of Arthur Conan Doyle's historical novel, 'The White Company.' Not signed by the author, alas, but by this edition's illustrator, Arthur Rackham.

Paul Hardie had read that book aloud, showed those illustrations, to Jack and Gwen uncountable times during their childhood. It had been one of their very favorites—a rare instance when their preferences matched.

"Oh, my dear. How lovely of you." Paul's eyes misted a little.

"Merry Christmas, Daddy. I love remembering you reading this."

The mandoline she'd bought Althea earned her a slightly reproachful look. It was the best one she could find.

"Gwen, I appreciate it, I don't guess I'll ever manage to break this one."

"That's the idea. Merry Christmas, Althea."

Nerise squealed over her running shoes. "Thanks, Miss Gwen! Mama, can I try them on right now?"

"Sure you *may*, honey." Perfect fit.

Caleb opened riding boots, Kyle new hockey skates.

Now, for it.

Ken Pelletier unwrapped a long-ish box. Seth, asked, had told Gwen Ken was looking for a new bow for his fiddle; the one he used was cheap and now old.

A bow of the best wood for the purpose. Pernambuco—a high grade of Brazilwood; the wood had what they called high sonic frequency—vibrationally, musically, this was desirable. Gwen had listened, had not understood much, and had purchased.

Gwen pronounced the name of the wood carefully, in response to Ken's question. His eyes lit up.

Ken's second box held high-grade green rosin, a new violin case, a tailpiece, also of Pernambuco.

"Cousin, this is one mighty fine gift. I'm much obliged."

"Don't mention it, cousin, Merry Christmas."

He tightened the bow strings, began applying rosin. New bows took a lot, to start them out. Seth had mentioned Ken might want to bring his fiddle. *Slyboots, the pair of 'em.*

Jack, glancing quizzically at his sister, began cutting bright red ribbon off his huge box. Gwen wore a mischievous mock-innocent face.

Seth watched Jack. The box for him was the same size, what had she gone and done?

"Ooh, Gwennie!" A solid guitar case, dark red, suitable for shipping an instrument via airfreight.

"Open it. And don't call me that—you know I always hated it." Gwen grinned at her big brother.

"Oh, Gwen-!" Even louder, stopping himself from adding

the extra syllable she disliked, as he un-snapped the case, took out what it contained.

Oh, Jesus. Seth hoped to God Gwen hadn't, like her father, got matching, or near-matching instruments for Jack and himself. That guitar had cost—he didn't know, but—plenty.

An old Gibson—legendary name. Sunburst on the sound board. *Rosewood* back and sides.

The guitar was more than twice Jack's age. "They don't know if the rosewood's Brazilian or Indian, and they don't know if the—soundboard?—is," she frowned, thought, "red spruce or—white?—do I have that right?"

She did. White, Sitka spruce was the most popular soundboard wood for high-end guitars. It didn't age—sounded as good out of the factory as it ever would.

It wasn't the biggest body available, but bigger than the ones Jack and Seth had been playing these years. Those were solid wood, too, a huge step up from the cheap laminate Seth had played for so long. But nothing like rosewood. Even if it weren't Brazilian.

Jack looked at it in his hands, and began tuning. Then he plucked, then picked, strummed.

Crisp and clear, bright treble, solid bass notes, both—*forward* sounding. A little retiring, in the mid-range. Sounding like nothing Jack—or Seth—had ever heard in person.

"This is amazing, Gwen. I don't know what to say."

"Just say 'thank you, Gwen, Merry Christmas,' and leave it at that. Glad to do it. I promise."

Sweet, crazy girl, Seth thought. She probably *had* got him something like that. It wouldn't be a duplicate, she wouldn't have found two just the same. But it would be comparable, and she *should not* have.

He was about to find out. Seth took his time, carefully

sliding off the curled green ribbon rather than cutting it. Jack was a paper-ripper; Seth was not. He carefully slit tape with his pocket knife, rolled the freed wrapping paper, set it aside.

Took the lid off the big box. The case wasn't a duplicate—even heavier-duty than Jack's. Dark green, like the ribbons.

Seth opened the case. "What did you do?" he whispered. Not looking at her, but at the guitar.

'C.F. Martin.' If there were a name to conjure with more powerful than 'Gibson,' that was it.

"What did you do," he repeated.

Dreadnought body. Bigger than Jack's stage-model. Shade top finish on the soundboard, similar to the Gibson's sunburst.

"*That* one definitely has red spruce."

Adirondack spruce. That might sound less good than Sitka to start. But it aged, improving in tone with the years. As rosewood did. Or so he'd read.

"They're the same vintage. Just like the two of you. When the guy in the store played them for me, that was the one that— it just—sounded like you."

Oh, God. Seth picked up the Martin. Not rosewood— mahogany.

A few dings in the finish, scratched pick guard, of course. In amazing condition for its age, though, maybe better than the Gibson. Mahogany improved, too, with the years.

He tuned, carefully. *Oh, God.* Even that was music.

As Jack had, Seth plucked, picked, strummed. *Oh, God.* The mahogany's resonance—deep and dark and rich, right through. Not the same brightness in the treble as the rosewood Gibson, but—oh, *God,* the *depth* of sound. Like musical thunder. The action was—he couldn't believe how easy the Martin was to play—the guitar itself made him play better. The sound was— it was—

A line, referent to music, from her beloved 'Much Ado About Nothing' flashed into Madeleine Hardie's mind—*Now is his soul ravished.*

Gwen saw Seth's hands start to shake.

So carefully it was as if he moved in slow-motion, he set the Martin back in its case. Whispered, "Excuse me."

Nothing slow-motion about the long strides that took him out of the room.

Exchanged glances all around. Except Gwen, who looked at the doorway. Ken Pelletier continued rosining his new bow; Jack played his Gibson, experimenting with bright sound. *What a sweetheart of a guitar. What a sweetheart of a sister.*

Gwen counted, slowly, to 200 in her head. Said, "Excuse me," herself, and went after Seth.

She found him in the hall, one hand on the stair railing, as if to brace himself. His face in the other.

Her bare foot creaked on a floorboard. Seth turned—in what seemed a heartbeat's space, his arms were around her. Holding her so hard she thought her healed ribs might re-crack. He was shaking, a little, as her arms went round him.

His face in her hair, kissing it. "Crazy girl," he whispered, "*Crazy girl,* what would you go and do that for. Oh, God, you *shouldn't have.*" Kissing her hair again.

A *long* time, Gwen thought, since he'd held her quite like this. Since they were—it couldn't be that long, could it? She held him. His face still in her hair, Seth felt her hand stroke his. She spoke, very softly.

"I *should.* If you want a 'why,' take your pick, Seth. I heard a lot of music in Boston—plenty of guys nowhere near as good as you make a living at it. They have good instruments, so should you.

"Then again, maybe I thought if I gave all of you *something* to do with your music, you might finally let me hear you play together.

"You gave me Belinda, she's beautiful, I love her. I wanted to give you something beautiful that you'd love.

"Most of all, I wanted to *thank* you. You saved my sanity this spring. You did. When I was in that horrible hospital. *And* since. You've been—everything. *Everything.*

"Now, tell me you aren't going to refuse it."

"I—*can't.* I'm—I'm in *love* with the blessed thing, and—I love you so much." He kissed her forehead, so hard she wondered if his lips left a mark.

"I love you more."

"No, you don't."

He wasn't shaking now. Still they held each other. Gwen wouldn't let go until he did, until he was all right.

Finally, Seth loosed his arms a little.

"You want some music? I think we can do that for you."

"Come on, then. Everyone's going to be wondering if we died or something."

Gwen took his hand, and they rejoined the others.

Ken Pelletier applied the new bow to his violin, fitted now with the new tailpiece. Played a neat, jaunty riff on "Sweet Georgia Brown."

Seth and Jack both started—it didn't sound like the same instrument. Sweeter, sharper, clearer, by miles.

"Oh, my land. And here's me was thinking I might be needing a new fiddle. Cousin, feels like you just gave me one. You're real sweet, Gwen. And I thank you kindly."

Seth said, "Gwen wants us to play something. I think maybe we owe her that, huh?"

"Anything you like, Seth. You don't even have to sing, if you don't want. Just let me hear you guys do your thing."

He looked at Ken.

Ken shrugged, "You heard the lady—your pick."

There were a couple of songs Seth would have given his eye teeth to sing her. Inappropriate, very.

There was one. Not out of place on the day.

Seth named it. "We can sing, Jack, 'less you don't want."

Jack didn't mind. He liked that song.

Seth took up the Martin—the beautiful thing felt so fine in his hands. Plucked the opening notes.

Jack picked counterpoint, the bright treble and hard bass touching up peaks and lows. In Seth's hands, the Martin's deep resonance searched out and filled corners under the ceiling, cracks in the baseboards. Flowed out open doorways. Flowed, Seth thought, like water over stone, like—red silk threads, through his fingers.

Ken's violin keened above, sweet and longing.

The song limned humans' burdens, and humans' faith. Melancholy and hope twined. Hope seemed to have the last word.

As they say, there wasn't a dry eye in the house when the final notes faded.

* * *

Further presents remained to be opened—maybe anti-climactic, but a measured winding down was probably wholesome, Gwen thought. She, at least, was keyed up by the music—the song might have been gentle, but the sound had wound her tight.

She'd praised Seth's playing to him, but she'd never heard him so—so *masterful* of his ability. It had been a while, to be sure, since she'd heard him play. He'd got better, a lot better.

And he'd been so good before.

Gwen thought she'd never, so long as she lived, have a better Christmas present than his reaction.

She hadn't opened Seth's gift. Big box, and heavy. She struggled with it.

"Here." Seth's hands took it from her, set it on the floor where she could open it. Gwen slid off the green twine, keeping the holly-balsam cone bow intact, as always. She'd brought home the ones she had stored in her Boston freezer, to keep the cones' blue-purple fresh and vibrant.

Inside was a large mirror, pivoted to tilt on side rods above its base. Meant to sit on a dressing table. The glass was old and fine and thick, the silvering only a little flaked at the corners.

Seth had found the old mirror, and a few smaller ones, at a house auction. Frames cracked, rotting, glass you couldn't get anymore, 'less you were very rich, maybe.

He'd reframed Gwen's in black walnut—it would match her jewelry box, and a few other things he'd made for her.

"Oh, Seth, it's gorgeous. I love old glass—where did you find it?" She looked hard at the frame. Couldn't see jointure. Even the plugs he'd used to cover screws were so closely grain-matched she could barely tell they were separate pieces.

"As beautifully made as that guitar. Thank you, dear Seth. And Merry Christmas. You're the best. The absolute *best.*"

He'd have liked to say she was, but not in company.

He'd made cherry-framed hand mirrors for Madeline Hardie and for Melody; Madeleine Hardie's 'thank you' held a note Seth hadn't heard her address to him before this.

Madeleine sang, almost as well as she acted. Her early convent schooling had trained her, she'd sung a good many solos in choir—an unusual number, considering her contralto register.

Hollywood had left this ability almost unused; nonetheless, she'd not only kept it up, but improved.

Madeleine Hardie recognized this evening in Seth Greenlaw, in her cousin Ken Pelletier, fellow musicians. Jack, her son, was surprisingly good, surprisingly musical. But Seth and Ken were artists.

Which she had never expected to find, certainly not in Gwen's darling Seth. To whom she'd never warmed— Madeleine found his dark intensity, his secret-keeping eyes, off-putting.

A re-evaluation was clearly called for.

Gwen had done right. Seth Greenlaw was a musician worthy of that instrument.

* * *

Further boxes for Jack and Seth, nominally from Paul Hardie—accessories, straps, flat and thumb picks, extra strings. Jack had mentioned Seth went through strings fast. Capos. The man at the store had mentioned guitars having different-width necks. It was perfectly possible the ones they had would not fit the new instruments.

A final box for Seth—from Gwen—contained a small humidifier which could be hooked up to the included monitor.

"You only heat with wood. The guy said too-dry air can ruin a guitar. I imagine you wouldn't want that. So—this will protect it. You keep it in the case, too."

Crazy girl. She was right, though—if he let this beautiful thing, which she'd given him—*die*—he should be shot, was all.

She hadn't gotten Jack one—radiant heat wasn't drying, and Jack had laid the tubing for his new house to be so heated.

Paul and Madeleine Hardie wished the company good night,

and retired—it was already approaching midnight.

Nerise, Caleb and Kyle were next; Gwen had made up beds for them—and for Ken and Althea—in the older of the two wings; Caleb and Kyle shared. Melody was in the old house, in Paul and Madeleine's former bedroom. In that section, also, were Gwen, Jack, Seth and Ben.

* * *

Obviously, further music was out of the question—Paul and Madeleine slept too close.

Gwen picked up frustration-vibes, and had a light-bulb moment.

The big library was at the far end of Martin Hardie's folly of a wing. Certainly enough space between to muffle sound.

No more eggnog, and the wine bottles were empty. Gwen, feeling happy and reckless, got two more from the pantry.

"I'll leave you to it," and Ben went upstairs. Ben wasn't musical—at least, not as his brother was. The notes Ben heard in his head were electronic, and were part of larger, complex visions.

He was exhausted, anyway. Wrung out by a day of fear and facing it. He'd have given it up as a lost cause a dozen times, if Abby weren't so special. And Seth had held him to his purpose. There'd been times, through Ben's life, he'd been glad to rely on Seth's willpower; this was one of them.

His own willpower was less reliable, on most subjects. *Not his work.* And Ben was determined he'd learn to apply it in his dealings with Abigail Randolph. He was, he thought, almost there. Just not so much, when it came to horses.

Thus halved, the remaining company repaired as Gwen suggested. The men brought their instruments, accessories.

Gwen had the wine bottles she'd opened, Althea and Melody carried glasses.

Affianced couple, lovers, and whatever Gwen and Seth were, Melody and Althea both thought.

Gwen filled glasses, and they settled in. Seth and Jack sat on the floor, as they had in the parlor. Ken stood, Gwen and Melody curled up in corners of the leather sofa. Althea took one of the matching chairs.

A queen from exotic lands. To Gwen, New Orleans was as exotic, as romantic as Africa. Her cousin was one lucky man.

The menfolk almost ignored their glasses; Ken and Seth called songs, and they riffed. Not singing, just hearing how the music sounded, how they played.

Seth and Ken got racy with prior arrangements—the new bow, the Martin's action, allowed for more than they'd been able to achieve before.

Jack struggled a little to keep up, but did so respectably, if not inspiringly. Gwen felt for him a little. Ken and Seth were superior musicians. Jack was quite good, though. And given who Seth and Ken *were*, she figured they'd bring him up to speed, or close as Jack could get, sooner than later.

The music wound her like a watch. Which Gwen could not wear; she was one of those who stopped every watch within a couple of days. Digital was a bit better than clockwork, but she'd stopped the longest-lived one at ten days. Seth was worse—nothing lasted twenty-four hours on his wrist or in his pocket.

They stopped to breathe, and to toast Gwen. She laughed, demurred. She'd given them no more than their due, and glad to do it.

Ken was the first to pick up his instrument again. "Sweet Georgia Brown," again, experimental, exploratory this time.

Althea Jones's alto lifted, joining the violin in the refrain. Ken, who sang as badly as she sang well at St. Stephen's on Sundays, was the only one unsurprised.

Tone almost like the Martin, was Seth's thought. *Rich and deep.*

"Y'all think we could ask Althea to sit in with us some?" Ken addressed Seth and Jack.

Seth didn't like the idea. If Althea joined them, she'd be the one to sing, his voice couldn't match hers. Songs would be chosen to fit her. The band, if you could call it that, would change, the music they played would change. His position in it would diminish.

"Sure," he said.

Althea looked at the three of them.

"Ken, I'd love to sit in once or twice, for fun. But what I sing ain't what you boys play." Alternative country, white-boy music. Good of its kind, which wasn't Althea's. "I don't think y'all need me squaring any triangles, here. Kind of you, though, I appreciate it.

"What we could do, Ken, we could work up a couple of jazz numbers, just you and me. And, Seth—I don't know if you'd care about it, but there's a song I love needs a good guitar, and I'm hopeless on any instrument but the one I sing with. I'd be real glad if you wanted to see what we could do with that number."

Nicely done, thought Gwen, who'd seen Seth's face shut. So, perhaps, had Althea.

Ken Pelletier was torn—he felt rebuked, but delighted at her neat management. Might be he'd spoken without thinking.

Althea named the song she meant. Seth knew and liked the piece, though he'd never thought of playing it. "We could try. You got sheet music?"

She, who didn't read music well, and mostly sang by ear,

did not. "I got the CD, and an old 45 single from when it first came out."

"Can you lend me the 45? What key we looking at?"

"A major. Same's the original."

They agreed she'd get him the single, he'd listen and see about the guitar line, they'd talk.

No-one had checked a watch; when Jack finally looked at his, it was after 2:00 a.m.

"Oh, wow, I'd better get myself to bed. If I don't want to throw my inside clock totally off."

There was general agreement, reluctant in a couple of cases, that it was time to call Christmas a day. Instruments were cased, accessories gathered neatly. Jack, Melody, Ken and Althea took themselves upstairs.

Gwen wasn't quite ready to do that. Still wound up. Seth lingered, too.

She poured herself half a glass of wine, looked a question at Seth, who shook his head.

The library windows faced east on one side, toward the wood and Greenlaw land, north, toward more wood, on the other. Gwen looked out at white—well over a foot of snowfall, and still coming down hard.

"You must be tired, Seth. Go on up, I'll clear the glasses and bottles. We can leave all the unwrapping debris 'til morning."

He ignored her, and helped clear; they turned off library lights. Seth put bottles in the reclamation bin, Gwen put glasses in the sink.

"Sure you don't want half a glass?" Seth decided he did, he was keyed up and wiped out at once. They sat on the wide, deep windowsill, looking at snow, not talking. The unwind finally set in.

Before they called it a night, Gwen ran water very cold, filled two large glasses, and produced aspirin.

"Drink it and take these. They'll help stave off hangovers," she instructed him.

"Yes, ma'am," Seth chuckled; they both took hangover-preventive measures, and climbed the stairs.

At Gwen's door, Seth hugged her hard, saying low, "Crazy girl. Thank you," again.

"I guess I've at least graduated from 'silly.' I'll take 'crazy,'" Gwen said softly.

"That was always a joke." *Sort of.* A catch-all, when she wasn't sensible. Too reckless, too trusting, too sweet. Too generous, or too loving.

"Was it? I can be silly, I own it. I don't mind being a little that way, but I'd rather 'silly' wasn't the first thing people think of me."

"Never was or will be. Not me, anyhow. What I think, you're the best person I ever knew."

"Back at you, Seth, double. Thanks for being here. Merry Christmas."

"Merry Christmas, crazy girl."

CHAPTER 23

Boxing Day to New Year

Paul Hardie, leaving his sleeping wife, found himself in an empty kitchen on Boxing Day. His first thought was whether Gwen had overdone, and worked herself into another headache.

Jack came down before Paul had poured his first cup of coffee. Which would be disappointing, compared with Gwen's.

"Was Gwen all right last night? It isn't like her to sleep so long."

Jack explained the late music, said she'd seemed fine. "I'd be sleeping, too, only I don't want to get off schedule. I can get by on four hours." It had been slightly less than that he'd slept.

"I'd let her sleep. She and Seth were still up when the rest of us went to bed."

Paul had not, in fact, thought of waking his daughter. She'd been in so high a state of excitement, she'd been so generous with them all. Add that emotion to the work she'd put in on food the past several days—she'd crash sometime. Not, he hoped, into headache or—he didn't know what 'or.'

As they'd readied for bed, Madeleine had remarked, approvingly, on Gwen's gifts to their cousin, and to Jack and

Seth. Startling Paul, who remembered her disapproval of his own present to Seth, four years back. Those guitars hadn't set him back but a couple-three hundred dollars for the two of them.

These new-old ones—Paul didn't know what high-end vintage guitars went for, but probably what he'd spent on his two wouldn't make but a *very* small percentage of the cost of either of these.

Paul, who hoped to see Seth their son-in-law, was relieved and gratified.

Caleb, Kyle and Nerise were next down. Caleb took coffee, with a lot of milk but no sugar; Paul made cocoa for the younger two. Gwen had found locally made dark-chocolate-dipped marshmallows at the marketplace; he cut two in half, dropped them, marshmallow sides down, into the mugs. Floating brown cartoon eyes in the lighter liquid.

Gwen was next in the kitchen. Looking like she'd barely slept, if at all, but deeply happy. She poured out a half-full pot of coffee, started a fresh.

The kids wanted to skate, they'd gone up before the snow got deep.

But almost two feet now blanketed the field and frozen puddle-pond.

Seth joined them before Gwen's first pot was down. His face like hers, sleepless, happy.

Paul watched Gwen set down Seth's cup; her arm went about his shoulders, she kissed the side of his head. Seth's arm encircled her waist, they smiled at each other.

If Paul's heart sped up, warmed, what, he wondered, did Seth's do?

Not yet, but she's getting there. I hope. That, roughly, was what went through both men's minds.

Althea Jones came down a moment after Ken; they helped themselves in turn to coffee. Madeleine made her appearance, every hair in place, makeup perfect. As ever.

Before coffee.

Gwen wondered how she did it. Gwen herself had slept with her hair still braided, and done nothing to it this morning. She'd brushed her teeth, splashed cold water, and left it at that.

Ben, first of the young adults to hit his pillow, was mildly mortified to find himself the last to wake.

Twelve people crowded the kitchen—the table, at a pinch, seated eight, chairs had been brought from the dining room. Caleb, Kyle, and Nerise sat on stools at the counter.

Ben got himself coffee, and took the remaining chair at table. Gwen and Seth sat in the windowsill, looking at white.

Their talk concerned the highly romantic topic of snow removal. And when the plows would reach Gray Way.

* * *

Gwen, deeply thankful she'd got plenty of eggs, took the last pound of sausage from the refrigerator, and thawed two pounds from her freezer in the microwave.

With this morning, she'd have cooked twenty-two breakfasts, all told, over three days. Almost like being back in a restaurant.

Althea, saying nothing, joined Gwen in breakfast prep. Gwen, silently, reached and squeezed her arm. *Althea Jones, I think I love you.*

Jack and Seth put their heads together. Like most Haven Point men—at least, those not living in town—they both fixed plows to their pickups after Thanksgiving, if not before. Route 226 would already be cleared by county plows; if they could open Gray Way enough, people could get home. And start shoveling.

Seth needed to get home, too. See to the horses, Rosie. And rent a plow, probably, to clear his corrals. Horses could be exercised, with care, in deep snow, but you couldn't let them stand around in it.

He called his own number; Sam Billings, one of the hands who lived over the garage Seth had built, answered. Sam had no immediate family, and had had some setbacks before Seth had hired him.

Sam, too, had a plow on his pickup; he and Frank Wiberg, who also lived in and normally took turns with Sam on light Sunday and holiday chores, had cleared the corrals sufficiently to turn the horses out. Fed, watered them, filled haynets, and cleared the stables by themselves. That would do, until better could be managed.

Sam and Frank deserved bonuses.

After breakfast, Jack and Seth set out. Cleared car space to 226, which was indeed plowed, though fallen snow still blew and drifted.

By agreement, they drove toward town; Jack stopped to clear Ken's driveway; Seth drove on, around the point up 226 to clear Althea's.

It had been a magical Christmas. But everyone, no exclusions, was glad to have their—or their guests'—way home open.

* * *

By instinct or serendipity, Patrick Riordan called on the 28th, which was much better than the 27th would have been, under the circumstances.

Gwen, happy but exhausted, had drifted for two days. Done little cooking; the Hardies' Boxing Day tradition of bringing their leftovers to St. Aidan's had been broken, for this year. Many families had been unable to get to the church; Gwen had written a substantial check to the pantry as part of her Christmas splurge, and felt less guilty than she might have otherwise.

She served up Christmas leftovers; this was an unusual luxury for the Hardies.

Jack spent much of his waking time with his prospective in-laws; Paul, Madeleine and Gwen read a good deal. Watched a few more Christmas films.

On the 28th, Patrick presented himself a little after 1:00 p.m., armed with presents, and was offered hot cider. Fortified with apple brandy, if he liked. He did like. Liked less that no-one else added alcohol to theirs. Long cinnamon sticks to stir.

He'd brought gifts for Gwen's family; as his Christmas Eve inclusion was last-minute, they had none for him. Patrick was left alone in the parlor with Gwen, which suited him perfectly.

He unwrapped Gwen's gift for him. A small, buckram-bound, unassuming old volume. Anita Loos' "Gentlemen Prefer Blondes." Eighth printing of the first edition.

Patrick laughed with delight. "Gwen, my *dear*. How *charming*. Where on earth did you come up with this?"

"I found it right here in town. Pure luck. You should visit The Book Nook, if you haven't. Robert's got some treasures, and the place is chock-full of wonderful Wyeth prints.

"It's nothing much, Patrick, I do hope you enjoy it. I'll be re-reading Robertson Davies a long time."

"I'm delighted to have brought you two together. Now –"

He handed her a small box, wrapped in shiny green, very similar to what Gwen used. Green ribbon and red.

Inside were a deep green stone, large and round-cut, gold-bound on a gold chain, and matching earrings. Simple and *very* elegant.

"Oh, they're *lovely*, Patrick. Thank you so much. What's the stone? Green quartz?"

"Perish the thought. They're emeralds."

Gwen looked at the stones. She was no judge, but the stones had to be three or four carats each, and looked flawless.

She sighed, shut the box with a snap. Handed it back to him.

"I'm sorry, Patrick. I wish they weren't. I can't possibly accept them. Please understand."

"Don't think that way, Gwen. It isn't as if I can't afford it—many times over. And, from what I've heard, you yourself were quite lavish this Christmas—allow a friend to treat you as you did others."

"Oranges and apples, Patrick. That was family—extended, anyway. I like you a lot, but really, we barely know each other.

"Please don't press me. They're beautiful, but I simply can't."

She could never put them in her Greenlaw-made walnut box; she'd feel uncomfortable every time she looked at it. And *that* was not going to happen.

He'd put his foot wrong. Again. How did one put one's foot *right*, with this girl? With these people?

"As you wish. But I want a favor in return for taking them back. Think of something I *can* get you. I promise, it shall be yours."

"I'll try to think of something, Patrick. I don't need anything. But I will try.

"Now, tell me, I've been wondering. How long, exactly, did you spend in Ireland?"

Patrick was taken aback. "How do you know I've spent

any?"

Gwen laughed. "I lived over seven years in Boston," *so long, so dreadfully long.* "I'd think shame on myself if I couldn't hear Ireland in a voice."

"I was there eight years and some, actually. My father took a contract job there when I was five, it blossomed into other work. We didn't return to New York until I was almost 14. Ireland's so lovely, Gwen—you really should visit."

"I'd like to. Some day."

They chatted a little longer, and Patrick, who sensed he had *not—yet*—outstayed his welcome, said his goodbyes.

That foot at least not wrong. He'd see her again New Year's Eve—he'd been invited to the Lords' party.

* * *

The temperature had shot up in the days after Christmas. By the 31st of December, much of the snow had melted, though berms left by the plows still mounded the roadsides, and here and there were other small white heaps, where trees disallowed sunshine at any hour of day.

The Lords' New Year's Eve gathering began at eight-ish, after-dinner hours for Haven Point locals. Invited guests ate lightly, drank sparingly or not at all, as the spread of finger foods and snacks would be lavish, the wine and champagne copious.

It was the eleventh such party to which Seth Greenlaw had been invited; he'd attended most.

When the Hardies arrived at twenty minutes past eight, the Gray contingent were already fitted with glasses and plates; the Greenlaws arrived about six minutes later.

Melody looked at the party with satisfaction. Every local

woman had been outfitted from her shop. Not particularly to be wondered at, she knew—they were either her blood or her in-laws-to-be. Still, it was gratifying. And Julia Lord's gown, watered green Fortuny silk, would, sooner or later, adorn her walls—Mrs. Lord was a major contributor to her stock.

Gwen wore the same green silk jersey she'd donned Christmas Day; the Lords had seen her other 'best' on Christmas Eve, and Seth approved this one. Melody had rummaged for green silk heels, an almost-match.

Gwen had debated jewelry, and decided to forego any of Julia Lord's earrings for Ben's new creations; they were fun and festive and beautiful. And deserved showing off.

Liz Lord, back from a post-Christmas emergency meeting in New York, to discuss 'Be Yourself's' planned Miami Beach location, wore glimmering gold satin. She could pull it off.

The men were all suited; Ben's three-piece gray ensemble had been tailor-made in Arlington. Melody had outfitted Seth with a very good dark grey-green suit; she'd taken down trouser and jacket cuffs, nipped in waistlines. The result fit fairly well. Neckties felt like slow strangulation, but he'd donned one.

Gwen, kissing cheeks with him, murmured, "That dratted thing looks like a noose. Here –" she loosened the tie, undid collar and two shirt-buttons. Electric shock as her fingers brushed his skin; she started back.

"Sorry—I should have made sure we weren't standing on the rug."

Was that all it was?

"*That* is *way* better."

"Thanks. I wouldn't've."

"I know you wouldn't. That's why I did.

"Shall we check out the food, get some wine?"

"'Less you'd rather dance."

The Lords' New Year's Eve formula never varied—a band, from Portland, as usual, since there were few good ones closer. In the old ballroom, food and wine set out in the adjacent formal dining room, which table seated 24, with leaves in. Locally hired wait-staff passed, here and there, with trays.

"Oh, *absolutely!* Let's see if it makes a difference, me wearing heels."

It made *quite* a difference—and they danced comfortably, happily, together.

* * *

By 11:45, Gwen was tired; it had been a very fun party, but she was ready for home and for bed.

She'd danced with Seth quite a few times; she'd danced with Ben, with Patrick Riordan—an exceptional dancer—two (three?) times, with Peter Lord. Even with her father and Jack.

Gwen was glad of Melody's tip—*two* drug-store insoles in each of her shoes. The green heels were a size large, to accommodate. Even so, her feet were tired, if not sore.

The food was excellent, the wine better. Gwen had sampled a superb white Burgundy, but stuck mostly to the California cabernet, which was, in her opinion, even finer. She did, as a rule, prefer reds.

But now it was time for champagne; deep popping sounds as bottles were uncorked, and waiters and waitresses carried trays of glasses round.

Super-pricey, vintage bubbly gold. Gwen sipped. She knew this a splendid, storied vintage, and still preferred the far less expensive wine her mother poured. Like Madeleine, and Liz Lord, Gwen liked the Pinot Noir grape's primacy. This was pure Chardonnay; while Gwen had absolutely nothing against a good wine from those grapes, champagne made of them exclusively tasted sharp, thin, over-acidic to her.

Liz Lord swung around at a question from her mother, and knocked into a waiter. Half a dozen Baccarat flutes shattered almost musically on parquet; hundreds of dollars' worth of champagne ran over wood into the Aubusson carpet.

"Oh, *damn!* Sorry," to the waiter, "Sorry, Mother."

"Don't give it a thought, Liz dear." Julia was annoyed, but that was the only proper response in company. The carpet could be cleaned; flutes replaced.

Confusion as guests and wait-staff alike tried to pick up glass shards, and the clock began to toll the year's passing.

As 'Happy New Years' went up, unmarried guests were novelly assorted. Gwen kissed Ben Greenlaw, Seth kissed Melody Gray, Liz Lord kissed Jack Hardie. Married couples, having made sure of one another, kissed—Paul kissed Madeleine, Peter Lord kissed Julia, Jake and Ann Gray, Jason and Rachel kissed.

Patrick Riordan seized an unencumbered waitress, kissing her with flourish.

Julia Lord had realized that Patrick Riordan's inclusion made an odd number. Liz seemed to have a soft spot for the man; Julia had conflicting impressions. Very charming, very handsome, a little mercurial for her taste. He was discordant with Haven Point, she felt.

She was glad he'd been odd man out, since one of the men had to be. Julia felt he'd handled that—well enough. A little showy. But his having managed to get a New Year's kiss in allowed her to feel as she did without guilt.

The party wound down in short order; Christmas, snow, had taken a toll on energy for most guests.

The Grays left first, together, only Melody remaining

behind with Jack. Which meant the Hardies had to stay a little longer. Couldn't have a general exodus. One more glass. The Greenlaws stayed, too.

Just a little while; once those final flutes were drained, the party felt quite done. And the Lords' remaining *traditional* guests departed, only Patrick Riordan left.

"Happy New Year, Gwen," and Seth kissed her cheek. Gwen kissed his, returning his wishes.

"Don't forget—you have a cooking lesson tomorrow morning."

"Be there right after stables," he smiled. "Looking forward to it."

"Me, too."

* * *

New Year's morning, Seth presented himself for Gwen's cooking lesson at 7:00.

"Have some coffee, first; then we'll get started."

He never said no to her coffee. She'd got everything out, or into the freezer—they'd need.

"First tip, measure by weight, not volume. Flour settles, volume can vary. Weight's a consistent measure."

Oven temperature, pre-heating time. A hotter pan for browning sausage; lower heat to cook eggs gently.

Paul, rising late, for him, came in for coffee. He felt odd. Fatigued, in his bones.

Seeing Gwen teaching Seth cooking skills warmed him. Coffee warmed him.

"Freezing all the ingredients, every step, helps. But if you don't, at least freeze the butter beforehand. Flakier biscuits, if you don't let it start melting."

Seth grated frozen butter into shreds, mixed the shreds carefully—and very quickly—into dry ingredients. The bowl went into the freezer.

Gwen put on another pot of coffee. Took a pound of sausage meat—she'd stocked up since Christmas—from the fridge.

"Crumble it up in the pan—and break any big lumps with a fork."

Seth followed instructions, and soon was draining a pan of nicely browned little sausage bits.

Learns fast. But she'd expected that. He just needed to put his mind to it; he'd do fine.

Paul loved the smell of sausage cooking—why was he nauseated? Cold sweat beaded his skin. Breathing, suddenly, was difficult.

"Gwen. Would you call Dr. Oliver, please? I think I –"

"Daddy!" Gwen—and Seth—looked at him, horrified. How was it possible to be so flushed, and look so *grayed?*

"I'll call—get your mother. Get Jack first." Jack, as a boat captain, knew CPR better than anyone else in the house. Seth dialed—the number was one on a list by the phone.

Gwen flew from the room—moving as quickly as she ever had in her life.

Dr. Nora Oliver arrived, with the ambulance, in less than ten minutes.

Paul was still conscious—just.

* * *

Madeleine rode in the ambulance with her husband; Seth, following with Gwen and Jack in Paul's station wagon, cursed its lack of speed (the ambulance was doing 75 in a 55 zone).

A bare five weeks since Gwen had been ambulanced to

Ellsworth, here they went again.

Please don't do this, God. Don't. Don't. Please. She wouldn't sob, but tears trickled down Gwen's face. Shaking with fear. The *thought* of—the very thought was too painful to touch, to contemplate.

Seth, eyes on the ambulance ahead, took his right hand from the wheel and stretched it to her. Gwen held it hard in both hers.

Jack's head spun. He'd never thought of his father as—as—destructible. Paul Hardie was a rock—his rock, Gwen's—hers maybe more than his. He wondered, suddenly, how much "rock" he was to their mother.

"Rock" was down to him. At least—temporarily. *Please, just for now.*

"Gwen, we got the ambulance fast, it's not far. That has to be a good thing. They're treating him already."

"Yes," Gwen said. But Jack's words held no comfort for her terror. Death happened. To people you loved.

The half-hour drive took forever. Seth swung the wagon into a parking space; they were at the ambulance before Paul was taken from it.

Awake. "Don't worry," he whispered. As if they could *not* worry.

But awake was better than the alternative.

* * *

They waited. Jack sat with his mother—he figured she needed him most. Gwen had Seth.

Madeleine's white, stricken face frightened him.

Gwen paced. Tried to sit a moment, jumped up and paced.

"Darling, please try to sit still. You're making me nervous," murmured Madeleine.

"I'll go get us some coffee—anyone want anything else?"

Madeleine requested tea.

Seth went with Gwen. He thought they'd go out, but Gwen steered them to the cafeteria. Which coffee would be terrible. He supposed they couldn't do too much wrong with hot water and a tea bag.

When they returned, Dr. Oliver and another doctor were speaking with Madeleine and Jack.

Paul had had a mild heart attack. He should make a complete recovery, the doctors told them; but they'd need to keep him a few days to run tests, determine the best course of treatment.

He'd have to give up his pipe.

Could they see him? Not just now, Paul was resting and would undergo tests beginning soon. They could come back later, in the afternoon.

Was it morning still?

* * *

No-one wanted to spend dispiriting hours on New Year's Day in Ellsworth.

Seth drove them back to Haven Point, Gwen beside him, Jack with Madeleine in back.

No one said a word the entire drive.

Gwen put on coffee and a kettle of water; having tossed the cooked sausage they'd left out, made them a quick breakfast, most of which was not eaten.

Coffee and tea were welcome.

This was how it was for them, when it was me, Gwen thought. Now she knew both sides. This side was worse.

The sudden access of gratitude and sympathy combined with present anxiety, starting tears. She fought them back. She would not be weak. It was awful for all of them.

"Mom, can I get you anything? More tea?" Madeleine shook her head.

The telephone rang; her manager calling from Hollywood. Normally she would have excused herself and taken the call privately. At the moment, Madeleine didn't give a fig for who heard her.

"Yes, I know. I'll be back as soon as I can. And my contract—remember, I won't be renewing it. I'm done with television." She pulled the receiver from her ear; they all heard the yelling.

"Don't say any more. We've had this out before, I'm quite determined. As soon as the covers are wrapped up, I'll be coming home for good."

Madeleine hung the phone up. Looked at her children. "Now you know. That was our plan, your father's and mine. I've more reason than ever to stick to it."

Gwen and Jack looked at their mother, at each other. This would be change indeed.

It wouldn't affect Jack much, or for long; he'd be marrying, and moving into his own home with Melody before summer was over, absent monkey wrenches.

Gwen had been mistress here—she'd felt that way even while she was in Boston, whether it had been accurate or not. No way she'd be so with her mother in residence, rather than visiting.

Except in her kitchen—not even her mother could challenge that ascendency.

She guessed she could live with that. The adjustment would not be easy.

Seth, watching Gwen, read her feelings clear as if she'd spoken them.

It was a strange and frustrating few hours—they couldn't even *worry*, legitimately. Not with the promise of Paul's full recovery.

But they did worry. All of them.

CHAPTER 24

January—Early March

Paul Hardie was back at home three days later. With pills, commands to quit smoking, a restricted diet.

And the sense that Gwen should be told what Madeleine and Jack knew—how he'd made out his will.

As he expected, Gwen argued. Paul wasn't being fair to Jack, she said. Which was foolishness—Jack was, if anything, better dealt with than she.

Paul refused to engage. That was the way it would be, he told her. Jack was fine with it, so was their mother.

Gwen accepted defeat. Probably she shouldn't have tried— her father didn't need upset.

What she *should* do was figure out how to make the diet he needed as delicious as possible.

Gwen copied the list for herself, evaluated the contents of refrigerator, pantry. Studied permissible ingredients, limits.

And went food-shopping. With a side visit to the hardware store, which sold also small appliances.

If yogurt were going to be a staple, she'd make her own.

Nice thing about un-homogenized milk—you could skim it yourself.

* * *

Paul did recover. *Mostly*. He was tireder than ever. He sucked on an empty pipe, wistfully, when Madeleine wasn't looking.

Gwen cooked superbly, tailoring meals to doctor's orders; lobster with peas in yogurt-and-lobster-stock sauce, flavored with lemon zest, dill seed, lemon basil, was delicious. Chicken braised with chickpeas in fat-skimmed stock with tomatoes and Zaatar spices was delicious.

Paul missed beef. Steaks, roasts, stews. Mashed potatoes. Fried potatoes. Gravy.

Gwen, after checking with Dr. Oliver, thawed venison tenderloin, roasted it together with root vegetables, made a clear stock-based broth.

Oven-fried potatoes, tossed in a single tablespoon of duck fat, for flavor.

The meal drew a smile from her father, but it just wasn't the same.

The diet annoyed him—the doctors had said his heart attack had not resulted from blocked arteries, but from a valve spasm. And he was put on a diet for those with arterial blockage, "just to be safe."

Why did he need to be 'safe' from a non-existent condition?

Madeleine, Gwen, and Seth Greenlaw all took CPR training. Just (for Paul) to be safe.

Paul's wife and daughter struggled with impulses to wrap him up in a big soft quilt, and duct tape it round him.

He found their ministrations trying. Tried, hard, to remember how well they meant, how much of this was the manifestation of love. Mostly, he kept in temper.

Madeleine flew back to Hollywood for two weeks of filming, and returned to Haven Point for good. She might—*might*—

consider guest shots or small film roles, if filming were on the East Coast. Might consider Boston or New York stage productions.

In a year or two. For now, she wanted to be with Paul. And her children, of course—she'd missed so much of their lives.

But right now, Madeleine most wanted time with her husband.

* * *

In late January, with Dr. Oliver's blessing, Paul and Madeleine set off for Halifax, Nova Scotia, to enjoy a leisurely train trip across Canada and back.

Paul booked the best package available (in winter, they were a bargain), which had stopovers every night, in some cases up to three days and nights, and included hotel rooms.

Madeleine bought two cashmere frocks and several sweaters from Melody, a new sheepskin coat from William Eaton, who worked in leathers and furs, from tanning pelts to dyeing to sewing garments. Will, whose brother Charlie did plumbing work for the Hardies, Seth Greenlaw, and others, shared a double-storefront with Sid Powers. Who repaired shoes and boots, mostly, but made them new to lasts for some better-off customers, including Julia Lord and Madeleine Hardie. He'd made boots, too, for Gwen Sinclair—her father's Christmas gift. With which he could not surprise her, the lasts needing to be made. Gwen loved those boots.

Paul and Madeleine would be gone at least three weeks.

Jack spent almost no time at home these days; when he wasn't working, he was with Melody and / or with contractors, planning for his new home.

Gwen felt she rattled in the house—it was too big for her.

Spent the lion's share of her time in the kitchen, and thanked God for Seth's company most evenings.

For him, she reverted to pre-heart attack cooking, for which Seth was thankful.

The stuff she'd cooked for Paul tasted great, same as everything she made. But, like Paul Hardie, Seth liked red meat, whether he'd shot the animal or not. And all that Gwen had, typically, served with it.

*   *   *

Mile upon mile of white. Broken with lakes, with evergreen, with cities and towns.

Paul and Madeleine enjoyed the slow pace of the train and the trip—the itinerary was leisurely, measured. Fellow travelers were pleasant and various—a post-graduate student from MIT; a young writer from Florida, who took copious notes and penciled a few sketches. Couples—newlyweds on honeymoon to one pair in their 90s, from Philadelphia, Sioux Lookout, Devonshire, Melbourne.

Autograph seekers were a minor annoyance—there were more of these than Madeleine had anticipated. Liz Lord's 'Be Yourself' ad campaign, combined with the series of which she'd wrapped up her last season and syndicated re-runs, kept her beautiful face in the public eye, the public mind.

They rose above irritation. Enjoyed the still, snowy land unfolding before them, fine food—though Madeleine policed what Paul ordered, and the doctor had limited his wine intake to one glass an evening.

Most of all, they enjoyed each other. This was the first trip they'd had alone since Paul had taken Madeleine to New York City for their honeymoon, nearly thirty years past.

Paul had brought the books of speeches Gwen had given him at Christmas; he and Madeleine took turns reading them aloud—they were humorous but not light, optimistic but tough-minded.

Both he and Madeleine felt they'd discovered a long-lost friend, a companion in perfect tenor with this journey.

They cupped happiness in their hands, held and beheld it.

* * *

"You been talking to Caleb 'bout not going to college?" Ken's voice was heavy, and not happy.

Seth had not been—Caleb had never once mentioned post-high school plans.

"Thinks he don't need it, 'cause he wants to work for you, learn your trade. Says you didn't go, why should he."

Hell. Seth did *not* want to be in the middle of this. Here he was.

"You want I should talk to him?" The boy shouldn't be taking *him* as any kind of role model.

"Maybe so, I'll try some more, first. Not your lookout. But if it comes up—"

"I'll say he should go." Caleb was a decent student, B average. College was good, if you had the chance. If you had the right sort of mind.

Seth's grades had bounced—he'd got all As in music and music theory, Bs in art, B to C in English and Cs in science. Mostly Ds in math.

Math was simpler in the real world. When it was money. *Money* he understood. Some, anyway.

* * *

Her parents had decamped for Boston shortly after New Year's. Liz Lord had been unwilling to close the house, and stayed, conducting meetings via videoconference and telephone, flying out and back when she needed to.

She'd found she *liked* Haven Point. Once she paid attention. Gwen was right—the Hardies, the Grays, the Greenlaws and Pelletiers—these were not trifling people. You knew where you stood.

This was strangely restful, Liz found.

Liz liked Patrick Riordan, too, and he showed no sign of giving up the house he'd rented. Like Liz, he flew out as called upon, and returned.

Minna Robbins, the local cook / housekeeper Peter and Julia Lord had hired, was glad to have her employment extended.

***

Gwen, thinking about her product line over coffee, heard a motor which was neither Seth's nor Jack's pickup.

The half-glassed kitchen door overlooked a small slice of driveway, showed a sliver of red fender.

She opened the door—"Come on in, Liz, how's the paint business going?"

Liz laughed, "Hot cakes are nothing to it. I've doubled production, and I keep getting these revised sales projections—up and up.

"Now, when are *you* going to get down to it, and bring that heavenly food you made in Boston here? Not that what you cook isn't always fabulous."

"Oh, Liz, I don't know. I did love it. But—it was sort of— imperative, in Boston. More like irrelevant in Haven Point. It doesn't make sense to spend my time on 'irrelevant.'

"Anyway, I like what I'm doing now, and I love cooking for my family and friends. Which, by the way, includes you, and you haven't come for dinner since Christmas Eve. Just drop in, if you want, any day."

Gwen had never lived alone, and didn't like the taste of it she was getting. No-one to do for, except when Seth came to dinner. Best part of the week, those evenings.

"Thanks, Gwen, I will. Speaking of getting together, how about we do that, and watch that video? I'll bet you don't remember half the lyrics."

Gwen laughed. "I'll bet you're right. I'd love a refresher."

"Shall we go all the way, and make it a midnight show?"

"Oooh. I'd like to, but . . . it'd kind of put me off-schedule. Let's make it earlier, if you don't mind."

Liz didn't. "Well, then, how about we set it up for after dinner. You can come to the house, or we can do it here—whichever.

"Let's do it here. Come for dinner, and the movie after. What would you like? Lobster? I've got some lovely short ribs in the freezer—they're off Daddy's diet."

"Surprise me. When?"

"Tonight, if you want. Seth won't be here, he's at my cousin's playing music. We'll have ourselves a girls' night."

Tonight it was.

Liz stayed a little while longer; the company welcome to both women.

And hour and a half after she'd left, Gwen picked up the ringing phone.

"Gwen? Sorry—Patrick's here—he wants to join us. Do you mind?"

That was annoying. "I kind of do, yeah. Does that man ever learn? If you can't say no to him, put him on the phone, and I will. No, I've changed my mind—can he hear me, Liz?"

Patrick could—Liz was calling on speaker.

"He can come, and we'll totally ignore him, and say exactly what we'd say if he weren't there. That'll embarrass the living daylights out of him."

Patrick said he'd leave them to it, and apologized. He knew he came on too strong; he was impatient. Gwen Sinclair remonstrated with him over gifts inappropriate to their level of acquaintance, and resisted his every attempt to deepen that level.

"Patrick," Liz admonished, "you'd do better to back off for a good while—you are absolutely making an impression on her, and not a good one, not anymore. Patience is a virtue—with Gwen more than most."

* * *

Patrick Riordan deflected, Gwen turned to thoughts of dinner.

Wondered whether Liz would get the joke if she made meatloaf. Gwen thought she would, but meatloaf and the name of Lord didn't sit comfortably together in her mind.

In the end, Gwen thawed venison, Porcini mushrooms, and prepped for Stroganoff over herbed spaetzle. Quick-pickled shallots, radishes and blueberries for spinach salad.

Sang snatches of remembered lyrics. A lot more came back to her than she'd imagined.

Late that afternoon, the phone rang again.

"Hey, Gwen. Ken cancelled—Kyle's sick, stomach flu or something. Want company?"

"Yours? Of course. Liz is coming, I'm making stroganoff—

your venison. You're more than welcome to join us. We're going to watch the film I gave her for Christmas. Are you up for that?"

"What's it about?"

"It's a musical comedy-tragedy about an alien transvestite mad scientist, the Frankenstein's monster he creates—who isn't a monster—his incestuous servants who are plotting against him, and some earthlings who get caught in the web.

"It's very funny. Really."

"Pass, thanks."

"Come for dinner, anyway. I'm sure Liz won't mind—she likes you."

Liz did seem partial to the two men who'd been strong-minded enough to turn her down, that one September. Which said interesting things about Liz, Gwen thought.

"You two have fun. See you tomorrow."

Seth, Gwen thought, might not arrange words as prettily as Patrick Riordan, but he'd a lot better grace—you never found Seth being pushy. It was a trait Gwen particularly disliked; the more so as pushing back, or at least managing not to be pushed *over*, had been a steep learning curve for her.

'Yes' had been her default; she was learning, still, how to protect the yesses that mattered—with noes given elsewhere.

* * *

Liz arrived around 7:30, bringing the video and three bottles of Chateauneuf-du-Pape.

"Liz, thank you! What a treat. But I am *not* opening three bottles—you should take one home. We can get sloshed enough on two. You don't mind eating in the kitchen, do you? We don't use the dining room much, except for special."

"Of course not. Don't be silly, Gwen."

Silly. She bridled a little, inwardly. It was one thing for Seth to call her that—and he hadn't used the word to her since Christmas. Not once.

Let it go.

"This is heavenly. Where do you get your venison? I don't see it available at any of the markets."

"You get venison by shooting it. Or knowing someone who does. Seth takes his legal limit, and he gets extra deer, as a landowner. And Daddy transfers his permit to Seth, too, so he can kill twice as many.

"That man puts more game on our table . . . has for almost a decade."

Every year, Seth grumbled about permits, registrations, regulations, kill limits. Telling a man what he could and couldn't shoot on his own land. Taxing you to pay salaries of people who did nothing but tell other people what to do and what not to do. Treating adults as if they were in nursery school.

And every year, St. Aidan's and other food pantries received venison to distribute to Haven Point's least fortunate. There wasn't much Seth could do to pay back Paul Hardie or Peter Lord; if you couldn't pay back, you could pay forward.

"We used to hunt rabbits, and quail, and squirrels. Seth and Jack and me. The two of them hunted deer together, later; I'm not sure why Jack lost interest. I probably couldn't even hit a rabbit, not anymore."

She should get back in practice. Accuracy with firearms was not a bad idea; she might, God forbid, need the skill sometime.

After dinner, the ladies took wine bottles and glasses into the big living room. It was two rooms, really, with a large, almost room-width open arch between; there were several distinct areas in addition to the grouping of couch, arm chairs, coffee table and television.

Another three armchairs by a double library bookcase, with small tables and a graceful old floor lamp. Game table and dining-style chairs. Two more bookcases framing the bowed picture window, with a deep window seat and a loveseat facing it.

Gwen had made little tarts of chocolate mousse in hazelnut shortbread shells.

Liz sighed over them. "All they need is a pansy and a little gold leaf on top, and I'd think I was back at Farmhouse Table. How do you get to *be* so good at this?"

"Same way you got good at your job, Liz. Aptitude, application. The second part is what we can control. The first is a crap shoot."

"Isn't that the truth? When you get lucky is when you love what you're good at."

"Here's to being lucky." Gwen raised her glass, Liz clinked.

"To being lucky," she echoed.

Liz handed Gwen the video; Gwen inserted it into the player.

They sang along, spoke the cult-call-and-response lines they remembered, laughing.

When Tim Curry made his first appearance, Liz murmured, "More woman than I'll ever be, more man than I'll ever get."

Gwen chuckled. That was the sort of thing that would *not* have been said in mixed company. "Don't give up hope, Liz. There's men around, and good ones. You never looked for the right ones, just the right-now ones. As for the first part, I *heartily* doubt it."

There was home-truth in what Gwen said, Liz thought.

"*Meatloaf again?*" Speaking the audience-ad-lib together.

"I almost made meatloaf." They laughed.

As the credits rolled their last image, "That was *fun*. Thanks, Liz."

"Thank *you*—for the video, and the reminder. And dinner. Shall we polish off the bottle?"

"Why not? Will you be okay to drive? Or do you want to sleep here? I could make up a bed. And Mom's almost your height— I can scavenge you a nightgown and robe."

"Thanks, but I only have to get across 226 and down the lane. I'll be fine."

"If you're sure."

Liz got home safely, leaving behind an unopened bottle of wine. Accidentally-on-purpose, as a thank-you.

It had been a *very* fun evening. She'd have to take Gwen up on the drop-in-anytime she'd offered.

Of course, Liz would call first. And remember *not* to bring Patrick Riordan.

* * *

Paul looked out the large corner windows of their suite at the Fairmont Chateau. Lake Louise lay frozen; skaters frolicked against the backdrop of Victoria Glacier. It might not make sense, on the surface, to holiday in a winter wonderland, when one left a wintery landscape, but Paul found it pleasant to see snow and leave it behind, untouched, undealt with. And not his lookout to do so.

Madeleine had all but stopped worrying over him, which he appreciated. As long as he kept to his diet. Paul did miss his pipe, but was learning to manage without it.

They'd called home the night before; Jack had not been there, he was at the Grays'. Paul had listened with amusement as Madeleine gave Gwen instructions about housekeeping. It sounded as if Gwen bore what she must regard as interference with at least a modicum of patience.

Full Circle

He spoke with his daughter, and with Seth, who was there also, having had dinner with Gwen.

Both Paul and Madeleine were finding the leisurely pace of their journey magical—they experienced it as a series of discrete moments, each extendable almost indefinitely. Freezable, in the frozen white landscape.

This was the second of three full days at Lake Louise. They'd taken a guided tour with a very small group yesterday morning, but had eschewed organized activities for the remaining time.

Long snowy walks, yesterday afternoon, this morning. Gloved hand in gloved hand.

Coffee (decaffeinated) or cocoa in front of the tiny, decorative fireplace in their little suite. Looking at the spectacular view, reading aloud or silently.

Paul had arranged for a compact stereo system at each hotel they stopped at; they found excellent classical radio stations everywhere, and the strains of Bach, Mozart, Schumann, Vivaldi gave grace to their hours.

More than three-fourths of the way across Canada, and the trip home would be shorter. Paul wondered whether he should change that, re-book the longer return. These days, alone with his beloved wife, were enchantment.

Almost a second honeymoon. Waking up beside Madeleine every morning—and that vista stretching before him.

He thought about their children, two thousand miles back, and more. In another country. Almost, from Paul's charmed present, in another world.

Jack was well settled, or near to being so. His future was secure, his wife-to-be happily and wisely chosen.

As for Gwen, she'd reported no headaches since Thanksgiving. Her future was less certain than her brother's, but her finances were sound.

269

Both she and Jack would be secured better still, in time.

For now, for these minutes and hours and days, Paul would drift in a white-clean world with Madeleine and be happy.

* * *

"They're changing the trip—taking a longer train back to Toronto, before they switch for Halifax. Daddy called last night from Vancouver to say. They won't be back for another two weeks, at least. Maybe longer—Mom said they might spend some time in Toronto before coming home."

Gwen was at Seth's stables. There'd been a decent bit of melt-off the last week, temperatures hitting unseasonable mid-40s almost every day; his corrals showed patches of dead grass.

The foal ring was near clear; Belinda with her fellow weanlings, under Seth's eyes and those of his aging chestnut mare, Gem, who babysat them. She'd been the second horse bought mostly with his riding-lesson earnings, back when she was five. He'd been fifteen.

Seth—and Caleb, weekends—had begun the next stages of light, careful training for the foals.

"Miss 'em? Or glad to have the house to yourself?"

"Oh, I definitely miss Daddy. Mom—well. Mixed feelings, I guess. I mean, I'm glad for Daddy she wants to spend her time with him. God knows, he's waited long enough for that.

"But she's telling me how to run the house! As if I haven't done as much of that as she ever did! She makes me dig in my heels, and the result is, I haven't vacuumed for two weeks.

"I can't even get motivated to cook for myself. I had a fried egg sandwich for dinner last night—I am, clearly, thoroughly demoralized. Please save me—tell me you're coming tonight, so I can get cooking."

He was laughing at her; she grinned back.

"Sure, I'll come. Can't have you not wanting to cook."

"My hero. Thank you."

Bound to be a more peaceful evening than yesterday's. Seth had been at Ken Pelletier's, but they hadn't played. One new song chosen, and then the fighting.

Caleb was stubborn about college. It was a waste of time, he knew what he wanted to do with his life—learn horse training properly, and open his own stable, in time. What use was college?

Seth, appealed to, had kept to the party line—Caleb should go to college, first; his plans would wait, and Seth would hire him when he graduated. If he still wanted.

"Main thing you need, 'sides ability, which you've got, is patience, Caleb. You show it with the horses—show your own self some."

But 18 was not, normally, a patient age. Seth, by that time, had learned patience, but he'd had to.

Caleb had yelled, his father yelled back, and Seth had left.

He didn't give Gwen details, but mentioned the issue, Caleb's stubbornness, and his own—tricky—position in it.

She thought. "Would it make sense—and would Ken accept it—for Caleb to take one of those on-line degree programs? Some decent universities are offering them, now.

"Caleb could do that nights, and work days. You and Ken could tell him he has to keep his grades up if he wants to keep working."

Fresh eyes on a problem. "I dunno. I'll ask Ken what he thinks. It's an idea. Thanks."

"Don't mention it." Gwen liked problem-solving.

* * *

Gwen wished she'd driven; the woods had deeper snow still than open land; warm temperatures made it wet, heavy. Snow, clumps falling from branches, wet her hair. She was sorry she'd removed her parka's hood.

Back home, she went into the house just long enough to towel her hair, pick up wallet and keys.

She drove over to Vince Morey, who raised pigs, cattle, and sheep. Vince also owned a licensed meat-processing facility; he not only butchered the animals he raised, but offered his services to other farmers, for a fee or for meat. And hunters— most brought their deer take to him. Seth did his own butchering; Gwen thought he did nearly a professional job, and she'd seen some good butchery, especially at Farmhouse Table. Gail Winthrop had been a stickler.

Luck was with her—a new butcher at Vince's had cut some ribeyes too thick on one order. He'd planned to offer them, with apologies, but was content to sell them to Gwen, and have more cut, at the proper thickness.

A full two and a half inches. Pan sear, oven roast. Daddy's favorite, one of Seth's. Her mother had forbidden it—too fatty a cut. Filet mignon, much leaner, was permissible, in small and infrequent portions. Paul did not like the substitution.

Nothing wrong with Seth's heart. Any way you looked at it.

* * *

After a week in Vancouver, a little sightseeing, a lot of comfortable hours reading and talking, good walks and good food, Paul and Madeleine Hardie set off on their return trip.

It would be the same trip, just in reverse. They'd had so

lovely a time, both looked forward to reliving what were already forever-fond memories.

Sometimes there was a scheduled tour they had missed but wanted to take, sometimes an activity would be revisited.

And they'd have their private nights. Dr. Oliver had given Paul the green light on more than travel.

* * *

"I'm a little concerned about Gwen, Paul," in Toronto, after dinner and theatre—'A Midsummer Night's Dream,' a magical production.

"It's been almost a year. I wish she'd start getting out more, mixing with other people her age. Not just family. Take one of these young men up on their invitations, perhaps. Do you think remarriage even enters her mind?" Gwen still wore Mark Sinclair's white-gold band.

"Likely not, yet. You know how—loyal—she is. And she's always—*always*, Madeleine—been content with Jack and the Greenlaws. I'd like to see her settled, in good hands, myself.

"But those boys asking her out, she'd wouldn't have them, and shouldn't. Madeleine, you don't know most of the Haven Point people well, anymore. She's far too strong-willed. Gwen wouldn't respect a man she could steamroll, and that's any of them."

"There's that writer friend of Liz Lord's. Patrick . . . Riordan, isn't it? He seems very interested in her. And he has—presence, at least. He's a good bit older, of course, but I don't think that would bother Gwen, if she found she cared for him. I know she enjoys his company, at least sometimes, and she's taken his advice on reading."

"I don't want her married to a 'summer people' sort again.

I'm afraid he'd try taking her back to New York—Boston made her so unhappy, remember. No matter how much she loved Mark."

"Who would you think of, for her, then?"

Paul considered. Chose words carefully—he could speak to his own hopes, without betrayal. "Frankly, I wish she'd think of Seth. He's a good man, they already love each other, and he can stand up to her." *Mostly.*

And Gwen rarely gave Seth cause; she deferred more to him than to anyone else. Including her parents.

"But, Paul, even if Gwen could—see him as other than her brother, could Seth? Their relation's been what it is for so long, could they change, even if they wanted to, without destroying it altogether? That would be devastating—for both of them."

Her first question, Paul knew the answer to. He hadn't thought of the second. It was fair to ask. And a disquieting thought. Under the circumstances, though, "I think they might well love—and trust—each other enough to make it work. If they both wanted it to.

"It would ease my mind, I will say that."

They went to bed, and to sleep. Paul was glad Madeleine had raised the subject of Gwen's future, glad he'd voiced his thoughts.

His eyes closed, for the last time.

CHAPTER 25

March

"Gwendolen Sinclair?"

"Speaking." And hardly awake; Gwen was on her first cup of coffee. Jack, of course, was out in deepwater, hauling lobster traps.

"This is Dr. Nolan Kenney, I'm calling from the Fairmont Hotel in Toronto. I'm afraid I have bad news."

Gwen listened. Her father was dead. Her mother had been sedated; the shock of waking to her dead husband had been overwhelming.

There would be paperwork to be done before bringing Paul Hardie's body home. Other . . . *things* would need to be done; Dr. Kenney did not believe Madeleine Hardie up to handling them.

"Either my brother or I will be there sometime today. Thank you for calling me."

Gwen felt nothing. Felt dead, herself. Her impulse was to call Seth, who would certainly need to be told. That call must wait.

She went to her father's new study; Paul kept a VHS radio for contact with his boats. Gwen selected the appropriate, non-distress-call channel; hoped someone was monitoring it closely.

"Calling vessel Whiskey November six three zero five P— Papa. Over."

She repeated the registration until, "This is Whiskey November six three zero five Papa. Over."

"Fred Wills, is that you? It's Gwen. Can you get Jack for me, please? Now? Over."

"Roger that, Gwen. One minute. Over."

A space, then, "Gwen? What's up?" Jack didn't bother with "over."

"Jack. I had a call, from the doctor at Mom and Daddy's hotel."

Gwen related the scant details—their father, it appeared, had had a second heart attack, in the night, and passed away in his sleep. Their mother was a mess.

"One of us has to go; I'll do it, you don't need to leave Melody."

A beat, then, "No, Gwen, we'll both go. That's what's right. I'll bring in what I've got now, you get us on a flight in about four hours' time. Over."

"Roger that, Jack. Over and out."

She could probably book tickets online, but Gwen called Jo Harris, who ran the local travel agency. "Oh, no, Gwen, I'm so sorry. I'll get you and Jack booked, we'll get the bereavement discount. How many nights at the Fairmont do you and Jack need?"

"Thank you. The discount isn't important, but thanks. Hotel, I don't know. Can you get us a little suite, or something? Mom can't stay in that same room, and it sounds like she shouldn't be alone."

"Of course. I'll bring all the information there when I've got it handled."

Gwen repeated thanks, and rang off.

Now she should call Seth. And now, first impulse past, she dreaded telling him. She poured out old coffee, made fresh. Had a cup, and half another.

Dialed. Seth had installed extensions in the live-in hands' space, and the tack rooms.

He picked up on the third ring. "Seth, it's me. Where are you?"

"I'm—here, Gwen, that's how we're talking." Her voice sounded strange.

"Sorry, what extension?"

"Tack room, main barn, why?"

"Can you call me back from the house? You'll understand. Just—can you do that, please?"

"Sure." Sound of receiver cradled. She waited.

Not long. "Gwen? What's the matter?"

"It's. It's—Daddy's dead, Seth. In his sleep, at their hotel. It was peaceful, they say."

Long pause. "For real, Gwen?" A lost boy's voice. Tears stung her eyelids. She could feel Seth's pain, if not her own.

"Yes. I'm sorry, Seth, I know you loved him. He loved you, too."

"*I'm* sorry. Didn't need this, did you. On top of—you okay?"

"I guess. I'm not taking it in. It's just a fact. Sitting there. Sort of.

"Jack's bringing his boat in, we've got to go to Toronto, help Mom get this sorted out."

"You need me? For anything?"

"Always. But there's nothing you can do now."

"Can I come over, anyway?"

"Don't ever ask that. Just come. Any time."

* * *

By the time Jack arrived, Jo Harris had brought information about their flights out, the hotel. Their return was open; Gwen would call Jo when they knew more.

Gwen had packed a bag for herself, and one for Jack; she'd put her father's address book in her purse. In case there was time to start making calls.

All Jack needed to do was shower and change his clothes.

Seth drove them to the airport, and would pick them and their mother up on their return.

Little was said over the drive; what was there to say?

A good man had left the world.

Poor Seth, thought Gwen. His loss almost as great as hers and Jack's. And they had occupation, steps that must be taken, things that must be done, and done by family. Narrowly defined. All Seth could do was wait. Wait, and grieve.

Propriety. Whatever. To hell with it. Gwen pulled out the address book. It was an old thing; worn leather; it had sat on her father's desk as long as she could remember. She'd got into the habit, back in Boston, of carrying a small notebook, in case Mark had wanted paper and not had any. It had come in handy, and not just for Mark.

She went through the book, jotting names and telephone numbers in her notebook, starring next to their originals in her father's hand.

Jack's time estimate had been long. On purpose, to be safe. Seth had not driven as fast as he normally did; even so, when they reached the airport, checked in, they had over an hour to wait before their plane would board.

Seth had parked, and come in, carrying Gwen's bag. "Can I wait with you?"

"Sure," from Jack, and

"Of course," said Gwen.

"Anyone besides me want coffee?" Everyone did, and Jack went in search.

"Could I ask a favor, Seth? I don't think we'll have time to make calls from Toronto, and people should be told. Do you think you could telephone these names for me? Tell them I asked you. It would be a huge help."

She didn't fool him for a second. This wasn't for her, it was for him. Something to do. Anything was welcome.

He clasped his hand over hers before taking the notebook from it.

"Sure. Glad to help. And—thanks, Gwen."

"Back at you. It really will be a help."

Jack brought back coffee. Milk for Gwen, milk and sugar for himself, black, no sugar, for Seth.

Minutes ticked by, enough of them, eventually, that it was time Gwen and Jack went through security.

Each embraced the brother they were leaving behind.

Gwen whispered, "I'll call when we get there. Thanks—for everything. I'm always saying that. And take care of yourself. *Please.*"

The men she loved were dropping like flies. Two, in less than one year. *Am I some sort of jinx?*

"Tell your Mom I'm real sorry. Got to be worst, for her."

On the plane, Gwen tried to read. She'd brought two books; 'The White Company'—not the signed copy she'd given her father, but the old volume he'd read to her and Jack from. Jane Austen's 'Emma;' there surely wasn't a *saner* novel.

Words swam, wriggling on the pages. Nauseating her. She put Jane Austen away. *Guess I'm not sane enough.*

Life's ironies. Jack was buried in 'The Adventures of

Sherlock Holmes,' and Gwen couldn't read.

* * *

Toronto was cold, gray, and forbidding. No-one met them at the airport; Gwen and Jack took a taxi to the Fairmont Hotel. Madeleine Hardie had been moved to a different room, and must now be moved to the suite Jo Harris had reserved for them.

Their mother's face was white and empty, she gave barely on-point answers, in too few words, to their questions, and Gwen and Jack gave up for tonight. Ordered room service, watched each other try to eat. Madeleine ate nothing, stared at nothing.

When she'd seen her mother into bed, with a sedative, Gwen called Seth; he'd reached about half the names. Would try the rest again tomorrow.

"When'll you be back?"

"I don't know. Mom's in bad shape. We'll have to deal with the funeral home, and the consulate, tomorrow. The hotel's done a lot, thank God—I'll have to write them a thank-you letter.

"Maybe the day after, but that's assuming Mom can at least sign some papers tomorrow, and I don't know whether she'll be up to it. I did give her your sympathies; she might not have grasped it, I don't know. I don't know anything."

I hate this! She didn't say it.

"Let me know."

"I will. Are you okay?"

"Yeah, I guess. I'll miss him. How're you doing?"

"We all will. I'm okay for now. It still hasn't hit me. I should go—thanks, Seth. I'll call you tomorrow."

"'Kay. Take care of yourself."

"You, too."

The morning saw Madeleine in slightly more composed mien; she accompanied Gwen to the U.S. Consulate, and Jack to the local funeral home to which Paul's body had been removed, and signed at Xs.

Paperwork was faxed from the Haven Point office of Taylor Jones, Esquire, who had been Paul Hardie's attorney. Paperwork was faxed to and from elsewhere. Authorities were consulted, the dragons of regulation mollified.

It was not the following day, but the day after that they flew back, escorting the embalmed body of husband and father.

Bobby Joseph's funeral home took Paul's coffin; Seth drove the living home.

* * *

"Jack. I'll take Bobby Joseph, if you deal with Father Trundy. I'm not exactly happy with God right now. I'd be sure to say the wrong thing."

Jack nodded. He got why Gwen could feel that way. She'd been through way too much for one year. And—their father's death was still sinking in. For both of them.

Could have used you around longer, Dad. He'd been running the boats a good while, and the back office for several years, but his Dad had been—a safety net. All on him, now, the family business. It was a weight.

"But let's stagger. I don't want Mom left alone."

Gwen agreed, and stayed as Jack went to make funeral, burial arrangements. Madeleine was still asleep; or at least had not yet left her bedroom.

She poured coffee; lights danced in front of her eyes. *Damn it*, she knew what that meant. Grabbed aspirin, took three. *Nothing stronger.*

Jack returned; the aspirin seemed to be keeping the headache somewhat at bay. There, but not overwhelming.

Gwen drove into town, to the funeral home which sat two streets above Main Street, down toward the eastern end.

Sat across from Bobby Joseph, talked logistics, made arrangements. Set viewing time for tomorrow.

"Can you call the paper, put the notice in?" Gwen handed him the paper Jack had scribbled on, noting the time of the service, day after tomorrow.

"We'll do that. I think that's everything, Gwen."

Not quite. "Can I use your bathroom?" He showed her the door; Gwen threw up, pain exploding in her skull. Rinsed her mouth—she hadn't thought to bring teeth-cleaning supplies. Rummaging in her purse, Gwen found a single, lint-covered breath mint. Rinsed it, quickly, steeled herself, and sucked on it.

"Thank you, Bobby. I should get home."

She drove carefully; didn't hit anything.

"What do you want to do with all of this?" asked Jack. He'd ordered the headstone while she was out.

Five casserole dishes on the kitchen counter. Neighbors, friends—including Althea Jones, bringing food to the bereaved household. There'd be more.

"Just—the fridge, for now. I can't deal, Jack, my head's killing me."

"Should I get your pills?"

"No. I'm not risking sleeping for two days. Not 'til Daddy's buried, anyway."

Not 'til Mom was more herself, either.

* * *

The headache parked itself like an unwelcome relative. Gwen consumed bottles of aspirin, which held the pain to almost bearable; ginger ale helped with nausea, and she managed.

The Lords drove from Boston for Paul's funeral.

Ben Greenlaw flew up from Arlington. He didn't bring Abigail Randolph; not the right occasion to introduce her. But he'd told her about Paul Hardie, and Abby had sent a letter of sympathy. He'd probably be back in Virginia before the Hardies received it. Mail being what it was.

Paul Hardie, like his forefathers, was interred in St. Aidan's churchyard; the plot next was reserved for Madeleine.

Mourners gathered at the house; Gwen and Jack reheated sympathy food, set it out with plates, silver, napkins.

Madeleine Hardie, ghost-white, tragic and beautiful, accepted condolences, barely noting who spoke them.

Gwen looked as ill as she felt, alarming all three of her brothers.

The elder two put their heads together.

"She won't take anything stronger than aspirin. Worried she'll sleep for days—you remember last time."

"Doesn't want to leave you dealing alone, I expect."

"No. But after this, it's just Mom to look out for. I can do that, I've got time off coming." Jack had rearranged his crews, and was covered for a week more, if needed. Which he guessed it was.

"She minds you better than me—maybe you can make her see sense."

"Both of us, then."

And Gwen, not as reluctantly as she made out, was put to

bed with two prescription tablets washed down. She'd tried to limit to one, but had been firmly overruled. By her brothers, who loved her.

The pills worked fast.

She slept.

* * *

As before, Gwen was out for a day and a half, give or take. Twenty minutes, half an hour, of waking, here and there.

Dreamt of her father. Dreamt of her husband.

And woke, finally. Free of headache, weeping with grief.

She'd never talk with her father again. Never see his face, smiling, sad. They'd see no more films together. He'd never read to her again.

Mark might as well have died all over again—his loss came fresh and sharp, shiny new pain.

Gwen cried until she had no more tears to shed.

Dressed, took herself downstairs. Yawning and empty.

Jack was up, had made coffee, the dregs of which pot she poured down the drain. Made fresh.

"I owe you one, Jack. And Seth, too."

"You don't—you were a mess, sis. Any decent person would have done the same."

"Thank God, I know decent people. Thank you, Jack. You're a good brother. How's Mom doing?"

"Better, a little, I think. She's not up yet. Made a call or two, on her own, yesterday. You know better than me what she's dealing with."

Gwen and her mother had both, within a twelvemonth span, lost their husbands.

"Four and a half years aren't almost thirty." As hard as

losing Mark had been, Mom's loss had to be worse. She'd been happy at the prospect of time with Daddy. He'd been happy.

And it had all been stolen.

Madeleine, dressed, perfectly groomed, joined her children. Gwen poured her mother coffee, added milk and a little sugar.

"Here, Mom. Sorry I was out of commission so long—how are you?"

A deep sigh. "I'm not sure, dear. I must learn to stand on new ground." Tears welling in beautiful lavender-blue eyes. "I loved your father. I hope he knows how much."

Gwen knew she spoke truth, and realized she'd spent her life failing to fully understand that truth. Had short-handed her mother's desertion, as it had seemed to her, into lack of love. She understood, now, suddenly and whole.

Tears in her own eyes. It came to her, and she said it, "He was happy, Mom. I could hear it in his voice every time he called. *You* made him happy.

"I hope I go that happy, when it's my turn. It's good you were with him."

She reached, covering her mother's hand with her own. Madeleine turned her hand over, clasped her daughter's.

"Thank you, Gwen. We were happy. I thought—I thought we had years of happiness ahead."

"It's rotten you had that taken away. I'm so mad for you."

"There's no point thinking of it that way, dear. I hate it, too. We must trust God has His reasons."

Gwen knew that was how she was supposed to feel, but she couldn't buy it. Wouldn't argue with whatever helped Mom, though.

Murmured something meaningless, in pseudo-assent.

* * *

Taylor Jones, attorney, sat at Paul Hardie's desk. Assembled were Madeleine and Jack Hardie, Gwen Sinclair, Seth Greenlaw, and four of Jack's employees, who'd been hired by Paul and had over twenty years each in the family's service.

Paul Hardie's will would be read.

Seth hadn't been too surprised; it was like Paul to leave him a keepsake. One of his guns, maybe. Kind, decent man, he'd been. A better father to Seth than nature had given him.

Paul's biggest asset was the lobster business. The house and land produced no income but what Gwen's sales brought in, and that was a new enterprise, not certain of success.

Jack was left 65% of the business outright. He'd earned that, on top of his salary, no question in anyone's mind. Gwen got 25%, Madeleine 10% for her lifetime; this would revert to Jack at her death.

Gwen got the house and land, Madeleine had usufruct—the right to live her remaining days there.

Gwen would receive, also, the proceeds of a substantial life insurance policy, which brought her portion almost into line with Jack's. Close enough, and with so much of it cash, to make Gwen feel guilty, a little.

Madeleine had the proceeds of another, smaller, insurance settlement. Paul's station wagon, his personal belongings, any books or keepsakes she fancied.

She was wealthy in her own right, and received substantial residuals on syndications—at present, there were three of her series in rerun on cable.

Paul's personal accounts, cash, investments, were split evenly among his wife and children.

Small bequests for the four lobstermen.

"To my good friend and neighbor, Seth Greenlaw, I leave ten acres contiguous with his own land," measurements and location specifications, "and this testament cancels any and all debt of his to my estate."

There was, also, an envelope. Containing a bank passbook, Seth's name on the account. His minimal down payment on the ten acres he thought he'd bought. Interest.

Damn. He'd already written a check in full payment of those acres; only the payee left blank. Seth had figured the lawyer would tell him how to make it out.

Gwen and Jack looked at him with love and approval. Even Mrs. Hardie looked—maybe philosophical was the word.

Seth had to accept one last kindness at Paul Hardie's hands.

CHAPTER 26

April

Madeleine found the house intolerable. Paul was both gone, and everywhere she looked. Nearly everything her eye fell upon brought tears.

She tried moving to an unused bedroom, in the older wing. Madeleine slept better there, but waking minutes wrung her.

"I can't stay here, Gwen, darling. I must look for another home. In town, perhaps. I'm so sorry to leave you, you'll be alone so much."

Gwen wasn't sure *she* was sorry. She'd be alone much of the time, yes. But, even with newfound sympathy for her mother, living with her, after so long, was not comfortable. They reminded each other of loss and pain.

Madeleine hunted, and purchased a small, late-Victorian house, well-built and pretty. On a hill near to town, with views of the ocean.

Furnishing and decorating, welcome distractions.

What will I do, now?

She'd given up her career to be with her husband. Who'd left her. Not willingly, but in the most final way.

Madeleine found she had no desire to return to Hollywood.

No heart even for New York or Boston stages.

Occupation, however, she must have. And would find it.

* * *

In mid-April, a wave of influenza hit Haven Point's peninsula, and the region. Schoolrooms were half-empty, lobster boats manned with barely minimal crews.

Seth woke with a cough, one morning. Colds were a nuisance. Nothing more—they never took hold of him, he fought them off.

But the cough didn't go away, it got worse, and he was light-headed. He worked through. Jim Marshall said he should see the doctor. For a cold. Seth didn't take his advice, or Gwen's, who urged him likewise. She was sweet, but she worried too much.

One morning, checking the hoof of one of his boarders who was picking with it, he stood up quickly. Too quickly—the world spun. Seth saw stars, passed out.

Jim, Sam, and Frank got him up, into the house, into bed. He was hot with fever. All thought of calling Dr. Oliver, but feared to. Seth Greenlaw, the man who signed their paychecks, had said they should not.

"Call Gwen Sinclair," said Jim. She was there in minutes.

She hadn't seen Seth for several days, and was frightened—his breath was so labored, he burned with fever in unquiet sleep.

"And not one of you thought to call Dr. Oliver." They spoke their objection.

"Well, he can't fire me." Which was why they'd called her. And who else should they call? She dialed.

Seth called *her* crazy.

Dr. Oliver arrived in short order. Listened with stethoscope, took samples of blood and what Seth coughed up.

"I'll have to send these for testing. It's either very bad bronchitis or pneumonia. I won't know the best treatment until I know which, and whether it's bacterial or viral. Is he allergic to penicillin?"

Gwen shook her head.

"Then I'll give him a shot. It won't hurt, and might help. See he takes aspirin to bring the fever down. Bed rest, plenty of fluids. I wouldn't worry. He'll have a bad couple of weeks, but he'll come round. Be careful, Gwen, you don't want to catch what he's got yourself, whichever it is."

As if she cared. She could see the doctor, too, if needed. And wouldn't need anyone to make the call for her.

But Nora Oliver was less reassuring than she hoped to be. Gwen's father had been supposed to recover, too.

Seth's mother had died of pneumonia.

Two of the people she loved best in the world were dead. The last, ill. Threatened. She'd never loved anyone more than Seth, never. Differently, yes. But no more.

He was not her father. Wasn't Prince Charming. Seth wasn't a fairy story, he was real.

What an odd thought. But Gwen had no attention to spare on fancies. She could wonder about it later.

She got Jim Marshall to sit with Seth, while she went home for things.

"You'll be staying here?"

"Of course I will. You think I'm going to leave him alone? He'll just find some way to make himself sicker. I know him."

Gwen loaded her Volvo with food, pots, pans, utensils. A small bag with a few clothes and toothbrush.

Was in Seth's kitchen within an hour of leaving. Making

chicken soup. With lots of garlic, which was anti-bacterial.

She'd rather be dead, herself, than lose him.

* * *

Seth Greenlaw was not an easy patient. For the first day or two, he wasn't awake enough of the time to know that Gwen slept on the floor beside his bed; when he realized this, Seth forbade it. Gwen moved her blanket and pillow to the hall outside his door. Which he made her shut.

He would not be bathed—not by Gwen. All right, then. She enlisted Sam Wiberg's help, Sam helped Seth shower, and that problem was solved.

Rosie, the redbone puppy Jack had given Seth for his last birthday, was shy of Gwen. Would not come close enough to be petted—not in the house, though they'd always got along outdoors. Gwen sighed to herself, and kept food and water dispensers filled. If Rosie didn't want to be friends, she didn't.

Tests came back; Seth had pneumonia. Gwen drove to town, picked up prescriptions.

For nearly two weeks, she hardly saw the house which was now hers; once or twice, she went back for supplies, fresh clothes. And books—there were very few at the Greenlaw residence.

The family King James Bible; a collected Shakespeare, cheaply made and dusty with years of shelf-sitting. An ancient tome on land cultivation, its advice doddering with age. One or two others, of no interest to Gwen as reading material. She'd read the Bible, knew her Shakespeare.

She brought over the books of speeches she'd given her father at Christmas. Her mother had told her how much they had been enjoyed, that last, happy journey.

A journey which ended in her father's grave. But she read them with more sweet than bitter, absorbed strength, determination, as well as pleasure. There would be no third gravesite she must weep over. That was not going to happen.

And Seth improved. Fever subsided; his cough grew less racking.

Gwen spoke with Ben Greenlaw daily; he was wrapped in disconnection from the Department of Defense and setting up, with his new partners, their own facilities. With more assurance than she felt assured of herself, she told Ben there was no need to drop things to fly North, promised to let him know if that need arose.

Came one morning, as she roasted beef bones for more stock, Gwen heard footsteps on the stairs, and Seth, dressed but barefoot, entered the kitchen.

"Well, *hello*, you. How're you feeling?" His color was certainly better than it had been. *Now*, she believed he'd be all right. *Thank you, God.*

"Fine. You been taking care of yourself? Hate to have you come down with whatever I had."

"Don't lie to me, Seth Greenlaw. You're better, and I'm so thrilled—and relieved—I can't tell you, but fine you are *not*. What you *have* is pneumonia, officially, until you've taken all the antibiotics. And if I were going to catch it, I'd have got it already. You're not contagious now."

"Gave you a hard time, didn't I? Sorry."

"So you should be. But I didn't expect anything else. I know you—you think you have to be tougher than God. You don't, you really don't. Hungry?"

He was; Gwen made him soft-boiled eggs and toast.

"Thanks. For this—and everything. For putting up with me."

Seth wasn't happy she'd seen him disgustingly sick, weak. *Against the nature of things, her being the stronger.* Or so he felt.

"I'd put up with worse, to get you well, Seth. A lot worse. I've lost too many people. You don't think I'd let you go without putting up a fight, do you?

"I love you better than anyone in the world."

He didn't mind hearing that one bit.

"Me you, too."

* * *

Madeleine Hardie, settled in her new home, thought of possible avenues of activity.

Mourned her husband less in the present than in their lost future. She had lived alone most of the past—nearly twenty—years, and was accustomed to being without him, day to day. It was the knowledge that no shared time would come again that made her want to howl with rage. With grief.

She did not do this; she wept. Quietly. Determined not to sit idly in self-pity—that was unseemly, unworthy of the man she'd married and buried.

She was not yet 48. There must be something she could contribute to Haven Point.

The community theatre she'd got her start at, long ago, had been moribund for some years. It had languished after Madeleine's decampment for Hollywood, picked up a little, and dropped again into a state of mediocrity, at best.

She could attempt to revive it. Perhaps, Madeleine thought, go further—a Haven Point Arts Center. Haven Point's beauty drew artists; several had small galleries, but these were isolated. Music, possibly—once in a blue moon, the Main Street Tavern hired a band, usually from away. Mostly its small stage was dark. But there must be *some* local talent. There were, she reminded herself, her cousin and her son. Seth Greenlaw. Were there others, gifted but unknown to her?

And could Madeleine gather and braid strands of art? She could try.

* * *

Melody and Jack planned to marry in late September, with a honeymoon cruise—Boston to the Caribbean—in October. It tickled Jack—the idea of being a boat's passenger, for a change. And Melody had never been far from Haven Point. The farthest she'd gone was Boston. With Jack, to see Gwen in the hospital.

Joanna Gray's nuptials had been celebrated in Portland, in February, quietly—Joanna was not willing to come home for a big deal of a ceremony. Ann Gray felt gypped of planning her elder girl's pageant, for Haven Point to see.

She took over Melody's and Jack's with a firm and determined hand and no eye at all. Melody took her mother in stride, philosophically. The point was to be married to Jack, after all.

She hugged Jack's love tight, when she needed patience. Jack—he was calm seas, fields of wildflowers. They laughed when they loved, for happiness.

"I'll try to talk with her, if you want, Melody—it's our wedding, you're my bride, it should be how you want it. After all," he grinned at her, "it's not like you'll have another one."

"Or maybe it would be better if I got my mother to do it?"

"Oh, don't do that! My mom's a little—I think yours kind of intimidates her. She'll resent her, and just dig in her heels more. It's okay, Jack, I don't mind. It means so much to her. Afterward—that's for us.

"At least I got her to back off on those awful bridesmaid dresses she wanted. Can you imagine goldenrod taffeta on Joanna? Or Gwen, for that matter, and she can wear almost any color but red."

Jack's house would be ready for them. New home, new life, evergreen joy.

CHAPTER 27

April—May

After seeing Seth well, back at work, Gwen was restless. A late-April feeling—snow still lined roads, plough-berms hulking, crocuses and leaves pushing through. Time for winter to go.

No need to ready product for the season. She'd filled almost every inch of shelf space she had already.

Gwen reviewed her plans for the old cannery. Maybe a greenhouse should come first. Tomatoes were a problem, and had been for months; she'd had to make do with hydroponic, roasting them to bring out flavor.

She wanted to act, and couldn't focus. The house, the land, were entirely hers, she could do what she pleased. Nothing seemed urgent.

When Madeleine had moved out, Gwen had taken over the new bedroom which had been her father's. If her mother found reminders of Paul Hardie unbearable, Gwen couldn't get enough of them. Couldn't feel the ghost of his presence too near for her liking.

It was comfort. Her father's love lived in the house, breathed through the walls. She could feel it wrap her, in her best moments.

The more she let him go, the closer he stayed.

It was harder, with Mark. When she loosed her grip, he went further away.

Perhaps that was what he needed. It had been a year, now. Perhaps it was what she needed.

* * *

Madeleine began looking for a new home for—either the theatre group by itself (currently operating in the high school's auditorium), or a more ambitious Arts Center. Her best option would be to renovate the old town hall, which had been put up for sale. A new one had been built further up 226; the old stood in town, one block north of Main Street.

A big, granite structure; room for everything she might want the Center to showcase. An auditorium. Madeleine spoke with contractors and suppliers, and—with the assistance of Tim Douglass' accounting acumen—developed a business plan.

She wanted this, but Madeleine Hardie, true to her French ancestry, was a practical woman. The lion's share of her Hollywood wealth was already tucked away, secured for Paul's and her descendants. She really ought to tell the children.

This was a community affair; she would not bankroll it all herself. The building's purchase, yes, that she could do. But she'd have to raise funds. Summer people, first; Julia Lord first of all. Julia, long-schooled in charitable fundraising, might well have some tips on the subject.

Perhaps an event, a small one, to draw local participation and, she hoped, enthusiasm.

* * *

"How're you doing, brother? Back in the land of the living? To stay, yeah?"

Seth laughed. "Fine. Yeah. You?"

"So busy, now we're all out, free. But I—could you come down for a day or two? I need—there's something I want to talk to you about."

"Sorry, Ben, can't, not now, I'm behind. Getting sick was a damn' nuisance."

Ben had known his timing wasn't good. He thought. "Well, you can expect a package from me, soon. Call me before you open it, okay?"

"Sure."

* * *

Patrick Riordan had been two months in Los Angeles, assisting with re-writes. Then ten days in New York, a couple of television interviews, meeting with his editor, and several dinners with Liz Lord, in New York for strategy sessions, expansion plans. Television interviews of her own.

"How is Gwen? Her father's death must have been a huge blow. I wrote to her, you know. And her mother. God, life's a bugger. The great Madeleine Hardie retires to spend time with her husband, and—there—he up and dies on her. Shall we laugh or weep?"

"She's—I think she's all right. Gwen, I mean. She did tell me losing him brought back her husband's death as if it just happened. That was at first. Not that it's been long. But I've been here a while, and before that she was—very occupied—I didn't see her for at least two weeks."

"Poor girl. She looks so fragile, you'd think she'd break under the weight of what she's been given to carry."

"That's looks, Patrick. Deceptive. Gwen's a real Maine girl—she's tougher than you imagine."

"She is a remarkable young woman. How long, do you think, before she yearns for her proper work? I can't believe she'll be contented to cook family meals and make pretty little bottles of things forever.

"I ate a good few times at her tastings. And so did you, Elizabeth. Don't you think she'd be fêted, if she came to take a bite of the Big Apple?"

"Oh, probably. But, Patrick, she's—I thought Gwen was happy enough in Boston, but it turns out she was miserable. She loved her husband and her work, but she's told me she felt eaten alive by city life.

"If she felt that way in Boston . . . I don't think New York City's going to make any sort of natural habitat for her."

"Ah, well. Perhaps not. Or she may just need time."

"She's in no hurry to get back to fine dining, I can tell you that for certain—she says she likes what she's doing, and what she did in Boston is irrelevant."

Patrick shrugged, "The talented are ambitious, as a general matter."

Liz nodded. Patrick was correct. As a general matter. Whether Gwen Sinclair's ambitions dovetailed with Patrick's idea of them was another question.

And, when considering Gwen, there was Seth Greenlaw to take into account. She didn't think Patrick took that wild-card-constant-factor seriously enough.

Liz heard her mother's voice in her head, "*Don't mix metaphors, darling,*" and chuckled.

"What?"

"Nothing."

* * *

Madeleine Hardie looked at landscapes. Autumn leaves blown in storm-winds, suffused, congested light. A worn path through woods just before twilight, hushed-looking, at once numinous and ominous.

Sounds from behind the door at the back of the tiny room which served as Jonathan Cohen's "gallery."

A voice, "I'll be with you in a minute."

Another painting depicted the night sky, stars, a not-quite-full moon. Clever, thought Madeleine; the faint asymmetry of the sphere unsettled the simplicity, created a sense of impending motion.

The door opened. "Sorry. Can't time art with a stopwatch. I was in the middle of a house, the light was special. Jonathan Cohen." Holding out what looked like a clean hand. He smelled of turpentine and oil paint.

Dark gray hair, some black still in his goatee. A face seamed and folded with years and life. Dark lively eyes. About her own height, in her high heels.

"Madeleine Hardie. Thank you for seeing me," shaking hands.

"It's not why I came, but I'd like to buy that night sky painting. For my daughter—she'd love that, or I'm much mistaken."

"I know who you are, of course. As for the painting, I haven't decided whether I want to sell that one. Everyone looks at it—that's why I moved it by the window.

"But why *did* you come?"

Madeleine told him.

"Interesting. Better if it were right on the main drag."

Madeleine nodded. "We'll need eye-catching signs on Main Street."

"Who else are you talking to?"

"Sarah Morgan—her reputation in the art world is next to your own, among our possibilities. Lily Hastings."

"The children's book illustrator? Why her?"

"Like you, she's here year-round. And, again, reputation. Name participation is key; we can add lesser-known artists, and local-grown talent, afterward. Also David James—he's only here in summers, like Sarah Morgan."

"I know his work. Potential. If you're looking for name recognition, though, you've left out your best draw. I'd call Catherine Strange, if I were you."

Henry Strange, British-born, had been, before his death three years past, an artist of the highest rank. Not a Haven Point resident; he'd bought a small island south of the peninsula's western coast as a young man and, eventually, brought his young bride and cousin there.

If Haven Point had thought 34-year-old Paul Hardie courting 18-year-old Madeleine Pelletier scandalous, it was nothing to this. Catherine had married 35-year-old Henry Strange shortly after her 15th birthday. There were rumors, disturbing ones, of abuse in her prior guardian's home.

Catherine Strange turned into an actress. Henry's brother, Charles, acted, directed, produced in their native England and in New York.

Two years after Madeleine, then 33, had won her Tony for 'Much Ado About Nothing,' she'd been nominated for a second. Rosalind, in 'As You Like It.' She'd lost to 18-year-old Catherine Strange's Juliet.

It was certainly possible she'd allow Madeleine to exhibit

Henry's work. Catherine had left Maine a year ago; with her brother-in-law, and another cousin, this one Canadian—Gerard Fielding, who had been her Romeo—started a theatre company in New Orleans.

"Good idea—I'll call her. But—can I count you in? Will you at least think about it?"

"You wouldn't require exclusivity? I'd want to keep this gallery open. I'll admit closer to town might drive sales, but that's not why I came to Haven Point."

"Certainly, we'd want you to keep your gallery. Cross-pollination of visitors. The Center will drive them to you, your gallery, to us."

"I think—give me a day or two. But I lean your way."

What a nice smile he had.

* * *

Sarah Morgan listened, agreed to participate. So did Lily Hastings and David James. And so, the day after her visit, did Jonathan Cohen.

Catherine Strange professed herself glad to hear from Madeleine, said she'd call the elderly couple who'd come from England with Henry Strange, and now acted as caretakers. Madeleine could exhibit what she liked from Henry's old studio—she'd have to arrange transport to and from the little island.

Catherine was also interested in Madeleine's planned event. Might come North to see it. Couldn't participate—"We're in rehearsal for 'As You Like It.' I'm Celia, Maggie—Marguerite—Therrien is Rosalind. She's absolutely marvelous—have you seen her work?"

"I have not. I ought to come down and see one of your

productions—I've heard your Jennet in 'The Lady's Not for Burning' was superb. I played her, long ago, you know."

Madeleine had already negotiated a take-over of the theatre group. Emily Butler, formerly an English teacher at the high school, was glad to relinquish the reins; for over five years, she'd directed it solely because no-one else wanted to.

Assembling her business plan, Madeleine made an offer on Haven Point's former town hall. On the low side, but she pitched the potential benefits, both community and commercial, of an Arts Center. A good theatre, perhaps music as well—depending on what talent she could find; a central art gallery, to showcase the painters who lived or drew inspiration here.

These would bring additional summer traffic, business to the hotels, restaurants and tavern, local merchants. Luster to Haven Point's reputation as a summer and autumn destination. And inevitably, tax revenue to the town.

It worked—the town's counter was only slightly higher than her offer.

Madeleine Hardie closed with Haven Point, and the old town hall was hers and her Center's.

* * *

Seth looked at the taped-up box addressed in Ben's impatient scrawl. Picked up the phone.

"Ben. It's here."

"Okay, put the phone down, open it, and we'll talk."

"Couldn't I have opened it and then called?"

"No."

He slit tape with his knife, opened flaps. Inside, a bunch of plastic bubble wrap. Seth took out the taped-up mass, cut tape carefully, unwrapped. Cut more tape, unwrapped the next layer. And the next.

A rectangular frame, some kind of clear plastic. Holding six glass rods, red, orange, yellow, green, blue, purple. Seth untaped a small remote control from the frame.

"Ben, it's unwrapped. What the hell is it?"

"Stuff my dreams have been made of, off and on. Years and years. Remember those turning helices I used to do on computer?"

Seth had got Ben a second-hand—desktop, they called it—for schoolwork; it hadn't been much, but Ben had souped it up like a hot rod, scavenged parts, code hacked and re-written.

Those spirals had been—they'd made Seth's brain go jittery. He'd seen them in his own sleep, sometimes. The strange buzzes Ben had matched them with were worse.

"This is where they were heading."

Great. "What'm I supposed to do with it?"

"It's mood art. You get a neutral default, light and sound pattern changes for anger, love, grief, happiness, sadness, humor, etc. Turn it on with the remote."

Seth clicked the 'on' button; the colored rods lit within, revolved, flashing brighter in some sort of pattern, emitted sound. Unbidden, pressed the button labeled 'Anger.' A different flashing pattern, different key, different arrangement to match the lights. Each color in each pattern had its own note.

The notes were—wrong.

"I need you—you know music. None of us does. Can you get the sound right for us?"

"I'm no composer."

"You did some, in high school. Got As, too." That was true. So far as high school went.

Seth looked at the thing, thought.

"Be easier if there were eight of those rods. Eight notes. Rainbow, right? You left out indigo, that's one."

"They don't count it anymore. And that only makes seven—oh, hell. You're a genius, brother. A clear one. For white. Send it back. Express. How functional do you need it? It'll take a while, longer if we don't cannibalize the prototype."

You could get whiplash listening to Ben's ping-pong thoughts.

"Um. Don't need the sound, that's what you want me to fix. The—patterns, yeah."

"Obviously. You need them to spin, or can I get away with just the patterns?"

"Better they spin." It changed the—perspective.

Ben sighed. "Okay, then. We'll get started, but get that baby back to me ASAP."

"Tomorrow morning."

They rang off. Big mistake, Seth thought. Investing time and money in something that—who'd buy anything so frivolous?

Maybe Ben needed to get it done, out of his mind, and could move on then.

That evening, Seth, second-guessing, borrowed a small tape recorder from Gwen. Recorded the various sound patterns. Just in case.

He wrapped the thing up, sent it back to Ben. And waited.

CHAPTER 28

May

In mid-May, like clockwork, Julia and Peter Lord officially opened the Van Leyden house, which had not really been closed. Liz joined them within a week.

Patrick Riordan followed. He'd missed too much time he might have spent persuading Gwen Sinclair to allow him to court her seriously.

He found he missed, also, Elizabeth Lord's company and conversation. Odd, that they'd become friends. It spoke a larger spirit in her than he'd credited, that night she'd put her moves on him.

It appeared she liked men who resisted her; perhaps it was a matter of respect. She'd confided in him about Seth Greenlaw. Patrick thought she might—possibly—have a little itch still for the man. But genuine regard, certainly.

She'd cleaned up her act, too, so far as he knew. And he knew a good bit.

Interesting, now he looked at it.

Patrick set his suitcase in the bedroom, showered, changed, and called Gwen.

"How are you managing, my dear? I have, of course, been

concerned. I'm so sorry I won't have a chance to know your father better."

"I'm all right, thanks. 'Managing,' as you say. Daddy was a good man. The world will miss him, if it has any sense."

"Which it so rarely seems to have. *You* will miss him enough for us all."

"Not just me, Patrick. Mom, and Jack, Seth and Ben Greenlaw—we all know how special he was, we'll miss him together."

Gwen's *family*, as she defined it.

"I'm glad you've family to share memory as well as grief. Is there anything I can do? To make anything—anything at all—easier for you?"

He did mean well, Gwen thought. And perhaps there was something he, uniquely among those she knew, could do.

She'd had several calls from the Sinclairs since her father's death. Ostensibly sympathy, checking in, but the last time, a hint less veiled than previously. And it was time, indeed, *that* was dealt with. Or, rather, *those.*

"There might be, at that, Patrick. Why don't you bring Liz for dinner, and we'll talk about it. Come around 6:30, I'll serve at 7:00."

"An invitation! I thank you, my dear—delighted—and, of course, I'm only too happy to do anything I may. I will call Elizabeth directly. Will we be your only guests, or are we a party?"

"I'm not sure. I think just you two. Mom might be here, she drops in for dinner sometimes." Seth had promised he'd try, but he was busy with something or other for Ben, when he wasn't at her cousin Ken's, playing.

Gwen couldn't object to Seth's enjoying the guitar she'd given him, but she missed his company—these recent weeks, he'd averaged one dinner in seven or eight days with her. She'd hardly see him at all, except for her visits to Belinda. Pretty thing. Over a year before she'd be ready for even the lightest riding—horses were a long-horizon commitment.

"If Liz can't make it, see if tomorrow works—if you're free."

"I will let you know directly."

Patrick was elated—his first invitation to Gwen's table. Better if she didn't want a chaperone, but he had also the possibility of doing her a service.

It had only taken eight months.

* * *

Patrick confirmed he and Liz would be there; Gwen thought about possible entrées. Radioed Jack to request half a dozen lobsters, invited him to bring Melody for dinner. She barely saw him, either, these days. These weeks.

She'd enjoy having company.

A drive to town, and she had the few components her larder lacked.

It would be the first time she cooked for Patrick, outside a restaurant setting. Gwen found she rather wanted to impress him—if he thought she'd lost all her edge, away from the restaurant world, Patrick Riordan had another think coming.

Back in her kitchen, Gwen prepped—mixing pasta dough, chopping garlic and shallots, juicing asparagus stems, microplaning parmesan. She chopped bacon, set a dozen eggs out to lose refrigerator chill.

Made a Caesar dressing. Pulled a homemade ciabatta loaf from the freezer to thaw.

After clean-up, her dough still had a while longer to rest before rolling and cutting.

Gwen steeled herself, climbed the stairs to the attic. Found the stacks of boxes labeled 'Mark's writing.' It was hard to look at them.

She fought waves of nausea. Opened a box, pulled out one notebook at random.

Gwen showered dust and cobwebs off herself, was back in her kitchen as Jack—home from the sea—brought her crustaceans, packed in seaweed. He declined her dinner invite; Melody was, as always, cooking at home, and Jack was expected at Ken Pelletier's.

Which meant Seth would not be coming, either.

Gwen boiled lobsters in wine and water with onion, garlic and herbs. Set several bottles of light Chardonnay and a sparkling white Bordeaux to chill. Washed and tore leaves of Romaine lettuce.

She shelled and chopped the cooked lobsters. Rolled out her pasta, cut it on the strung 'guitar' which produced the shape she liked best, which drew its name from the instrument it was cut on.

Wondered if she liked 'chitarra' pasta because of the name. 'Guitar,' of course, brought Seth, and a smile, to her mind.

* * *

At precisely 6:30, Gwen heard the first engine; the second followed close on its heels. Why two? She glanced out the window—fender slivers visible, the red Mercedes, the green Jaguar.

Opening the door for her guests, "Your cars look like Christmas. It's cute. You should always park them side by side."

They'd brought wine, Margaux, this time.

"Oh, thank you, wonderful—but we're having lobster, I've got white chilling, and one bottle breathing. So you're off the hook, you can put these back in your cellar. Or cellars."

Liz and Patrick murmured variants on 'hostess gift;' Gwen accepted the bottles. Margaux didn't take much persuasion.

She poured Chardonnay for her guests, gestured them to

seats.

"Liz knows we don't use the dining room except for holidays and such, Patrick. I hope you don't feel eating in the kitchen is too déclassé for you." Smiling as she spoke, turning up burners, sticking thawed bread in her warmed oven, to keep warm plates company.

"On the contrary, my dear, I'm honored—not to mention delighted—to eat at your family table."

Not that 'family' was in evidence. Which suited Patrick quite well.

Gwen melted butter, added chopped shallots. Roasted asparagus pieces in a second pan, turned flames up high, and doused them in their stems' juice, cooking in extra flavor until the juice evaporated. Added them to the shallots along with garlic, lobster meat, salt, white pepper. Separated eggs, whisked the yolks creamy.

Cooked her pasta in the ready pot of half water, half lobster stock, and lots of salt. Dressed her salad. Drained pasta, reserving some of the cooking liquid which she added to her sauce. Tossed pasta in the sauce, adding egg yolk and Parmesan off-heat, at the end. Sprinkled more parmesan, some chopped parsley, and tasted. Well-seasoned, needing nothing.

Gwen set hot, empty plates and cooler salad bowls before her guests, brought salad bowl, bread on a board, and a heaping platter of lobster carbonara to the table.

"Real family style, help yourselves."

They did so, and dug in.

"Good God! My dear, does your family eat like this every night? They are blessed beyond mortal deserving."

"*I* don't. Thank you, Patrick." Over the top, he always was, but a nice compliment. "It's just me, most nights. And I don't cook like this for one.

"I'll cop to making a little extra effort—but I'd like to think I don't offer my family any short-change on craft." Or love, which was—always—the most essential ingredient.

"I'm certain you never do. But you spoke of something I might do for you?"

Oh, God. But this was why she'd invited him.

"I did. My husband—my late husband," she could speak of him calmly, now, "I don't know how much Liz has told you. Mark was—a sort of scholar. On his own sort of quest. He read, he wrote on what he read, what the books pointed to. As he saw it.

"He hoped to get a book, maybe more than one, out of it. He didn't live to do that; I've got boxes and boxes and boxes of notebooks. And his parents—they've been hinting I should get on it for him.

"Do you know anyone who could maybe read them, and just—give an opinion on whether there's anything there to work with? I really would be grateful. I can't do it myself, I'm no judge."

"As it happens, I do know such a person. Not only does she do more or less what you're asking, she would be the very person I'd recommend to extract any book, or books, which might be in there.

"I cannot, though, ask her to read over cartons and cartons of writing without taking a look myself, to ensure it would be worth her time—I don't mean money, I assume either you or your in-laws are willing to pay for services."

"Of course."

"Would you allow me to read one or two of the notebooks? Let me assure you—I am not attempting to invade your—or your late husband's—privacy, but we are talking about a serious undertaking, and this woman is a friend of mine."

"I got one out for you. I haven't read a word in any of them. Thank you, Patrick. Either way, it'll get my in-laws off my back. Which I would appreciate more than you can imagine."

"Oh, I can imagine many, many things, my dear—

imagining is my bread and butter—as, in a different vein, it is your own. And Elizabeth's," raising his glass to both of them.

Liz had been very quiet; this evening, she did not mind watching Patrick and Gwen. Patrick was capable of charming almost anyone, up to a point. What, she wondered, was Gwen's stopping-point?

Liz thought Patrick was going to be disappointed, more likely than not. Wasn't sure why she thought this, but it didn't shake off.

Gwen set out lemon curd tarts in lemon-shortbread shells, a pitcher of blueberry sauce, and fresh glasses, into which she poured sparkling wine.

"Even better than the chocolate mousse, Gwen."

"Thanks, Liz. I love chocolate –"

"Who doesn't?"

"I know, right? But lemon's my favorite."

Ring went the telephone.

"Excuse me." Gwen picked up the receiver.

"Good evening!" She felt good, relieved, she'd taken some action, anyway. And Patrick, at least, was cheerful company. *What's up with Liz?*

"Hey, Seth. How're you musical geniuses doing these days?" Laughing.

Liz and Patrick pretended not to listen.

"We should go, Patrick."

"Must we?"

"I'd advise it. You're ahead—let that do you for the moment."

Gwen, on the phone, "Sure, I *told* you—you never need to ask. See you."

She rang off, turned back to her guests, "Seth's coming over for a bit. Anyone want more tarts, another glass?"

"My dear, I think I shall take myself off to begin on your late husband's notebook. Thank you, Gwen for a lovely evening, and the most delicious meal I have ever eaten in a kitchen."

"Thank *you*, Patrick. By the way, this counts as your Christmas present to me—so that's square. And thanks for coming, both of you. I need people to cook for."

Liz said, "I promise I'll come more often. I always mean to, and something comes up. I won't let it."

"You're sweet, Liz, and I'd appreciate your company any time."

Liz and Patrick left. Gwen waited, happily, for Seth.

She hadn't long to wait; Seth arrived shortly after Liz's and Patrick's departure. Guitar case in hand, looking tired, stressed.

The music had gone well; he and Ken had worked up some new arrangements for Jack, who was so much better now than he had been; he needed more challenge. They'd worked more into their own arrangements, too, since Christmas.

Caleb Pelletier was a happy young man, and no longer fighting with his father. Seth had proposed Gwen's on-line degree program notion to Ken; it wasn't ideal, but Ken had offered it to Caleb, who'd said yes before his father had finished speaking. He'd done his work, selected a program, got Ken's approval for it, applied and been accepted. Promised to keep his grades up.

A couple of weeks away, Caleb would graduate from high school, and start full-time at the stables.

"You look tired to death. What's Ben got you working on, that's so awful? Can I get you a beer, some wine?"

"Thanks, I'll take a beer. Can't talk about it, Ben made me promise. Says it's 'proprietary data,' or something. God, I keep seeing—what it is, what it does. Got it behind the eyeballs, dream about it. Feel like I want my brain washed."

"That sounds terrible. What can we do to clear your head? I'm assuming music doesn't quite cut through it, or you wouldn't be saying."

"Don't know. Maybe—you want to watch a movie? One I

don't know, have to pay attention."

It wasn't late. "Sure. Let's go pick."

They looked through titles; Seth had seen most of the best ones.

"Oh! Do you know this?" He didn't. "Liz turned me on to it. It's weird, but very funny. And serious. The acting's great."

"Anything."

Gwen turned on equipment, started the video; they settled on the couch to watch.

Sure didn't start funny, Seth thought. But it got there, sly, ironic, and he laughed. Sort of twisted. Crazy lead actor—hell of a performance.

The actor, the star, wasn't the hero—madman-ex-machina, master of ceremonies at a dark carnival. Beautiful voice, the cadence singing, hypnotic. It soothed Gwen; she was emotionally wrung out, dealing with those damned notebooks. Taking steps toward, anyway. She would call her in-laws—tomorrow.

Sleepily, she murmured that the actor had been nominated for an Oscar.

"Hey, Gwen." She woke with a start. The film was over.

"Oh, sorry. I didn't mean to fall asleep on you. How'd you like it?"

"It was good—and I had to pay attention." The revolving colored lights were there, but they'd receded a lot. He had the default; the moods were harder. Grief, anger, happiness, the others. Some of them hurt to touch, was the real problem.

"Better get back, you should get to bed, too."

"I will. I just have to see to the dishes, it won't be a minute's work."

Seth helped; it was more than a minute's work, but not many minutes'.

"Get home safe. See you tomorrow?"

"Hope so. 'Night, Gwen. Thanks."

"For what? Come anytime. For anything. Sleep tight."

CHAPTER 29

June

Gwen had done nothing to the cannery this spring. Nor built greenhouses. She was glad she'd fixed the structure, and run the pipe to the well. Water, however the building might be used, would be necessary.

But her grand thoughts had shrunk, like a swelling going down. The reality was—orders were not what she'd hoped. Not what sales last summer had signaled. And it was already well into June. Maybe they'd pick up after Independence Day—the 'official' start of the season. Memorial Day was the 'soft' opening.

Gwen had built—or, rather, paid Kyle Pelletier to build—a big raised bed for tomatoes and another for strawberries, bought and planted seedlings. Before that, she'd had Tommy Hutchinson lay tubing for radiant heat, in case she did want heated greenhouses. Kyle was happy to get extra spending money; he'd used it to buy a new hockey stick.

Even if sales slowed to nothing, tomatoes and strawberries would be used. Berries, purees, would freeze.

Gwen didn't need the income, not anymore. But—some activity, some focus—that she did need. Maybe she could make wine, strawberry, tomato. Experiment with vinegars made directly from those wines. Even if she didn't sell them, it might be interesting work. The first crop of strawberries was nearly ripe. But not quite

One gray morning in late June—rain was expected, and would be welcomed by farmers—she treated herself to breakfast at Downeast Bayou. Gwen missed Althea, who was busy with her restaurant, whose leisure was consumed in romance. A handsome couple she and Ken made, thought Gwen. And the kids were happy.

"Good to see you, girl. How you making out?" Althea had made sure to check in on Gwen frequently, the first couple of months after her father died; she'd slacked that off, since. Too much, she thought. She missed cooking with Gwen—and Gwen looked lonely.

"I'm okay, Althea. Don't need to ask how you are, I can see for myself."

Althea laughed. "Can't complain, I surely cannot."

"How're sales on the vinegars and oils going?"

"Steady, but slow. Think people buy them, use them once and save them for special. And then they sit on the shelf. Better, maybe, once we get the summer people, tourist traffic coming in."

Of course, that would be the way of it, for locals. And Althea got it before she did. Funny thing, that.

"You wouldn't want to bring your tribe to dinner at my place, some time, would you? Jack's never home, Mom's wrapped up in that Arts Center thing she's planning, Seth's got just about zero time for me these days, and I'm going nuts with no-one to cook for."

Now Althea really felt guilty. "Think we'd all love that, Gwen, you're real sweet. I'll talk to Ken about when. Be fun—kind of miss cooking with you."

"Me, too. Any night—just say when. Thanks."

Althea brought her plate, a fried egg over a biscuit and sausage gravy.

"Ain't like yours—best be upfront about it."

Gwen took a bite. "It's really good Althea. Lots of flavor. I told you—you couldn't make mine pay in a restaurant."

"For real. Worked it out myself."

Gwen let Althea attend to her other customers, finished her breakfast, slowly. In no hurry to get back to her empty house.

After, she drove to town, visited other stores which sold her wares. Same story as Althea's. Steady, but slow. If she were going to stick with this, she'd have to look into expansion. Branch out deliveries.

Gwen hadn't had heart for of it, in the wake of her father's death. Still didn't, truth be told.

Caring for Seth, when he was ill—that had been an imperative—she'd focused everything in her to make sure he stayed alive and got better. With him well, and busy, she was back to restless listlessness.

* * *

Liz Lord also felt unfocused. When she wasn't working. She'd set up an efficient office in an unused bedroom, computer, dedicated two-line phone, video-conferencing equipment. Sales rocketed. Liz was arranging models for a new ad series.

After her morning conference, she decided to take a drive. Nowhere. Just to clear her head.

"Liz?" As she passed her father's office. "If you are headed out, I wonder if you'd take a commission for me?"

So Liz drove somewhere instead. Livestock feed dealer, two towns up the peninsula.

Matthew Babbidge was behind his counter, conversing with his sole customer besides Liz. Who waited patiently—or trying for patience. Small town custom, etiquette.

"Sorry to hear you're selling her, Andy. Fine mare, no doubt. Got a buyer?"

"I was hoping Seth Greenlaw might take her. He trained her."

Matthew Babbidge laughed. "Barking up the wrong tree there. You ain't selling that mare to Seth Greenlaw, don't matter how fine she is."

"How you figure that? Only ever said good things about her."

"Wrong color. Your Maxie's gray. Look at his stock. Chestnuts, red roans, sorrels. Blood bay stallion's the only one with even a dark mane and stockings. Seth don't buy nothing ain't red."

Andy looked crestfallen. "Never noticed. Guess maybe you're right, now I think on it. Why's that, you figure?"

"Wouldn't know." Gossipy guesses weren't Matthew Babbidge's style. Especially about his best customer.

Liz hadn't noticed that, either. She'd seen Seth's horses among others boarded by his clients—mixed in, their colors hadn't registered. Not as a theme.

It wasn't a light-bulb type thing. More like a tiny blood vessel bursting behind her mind's eye. Spreading red. Theme and variations.

So Patrick was right. Liz had bantered about it, but hadn't been convinced. Now she was. Buying horses to match his beloved's hair. Romantic—and it meant the feeling was long-standing.

The thought soothed her ego. His heart already a shrine to another woman—that would have been armor. No, he would not want to be known to have trifled with—or been trifled with by—a Liz Lord, even if she weren't the daughter of a neighbor and client.

Poor Patrick. Liz couldn't imagine what Seth was waiting

for—Gwen had been a widow for over a year. But if he perceived Patrick Riordan as a genuine threat, he'd step up. She was sure of that. Given the lady in question, Patrick's suit was probably doomed.

A good thing. Liz liked Patrick a lot, but he and Gwen were nothing like an ideal match. He persisted in thinking she belonged in a big city, that her ambitions would eventually require such a setting. Liz was certain he was wrong. Even if he realized that, Patrick Riordan—city-bred, city-raised—might be charmed by Haven Point, but could never be truly local, even by adoption.

Gwen was all Haven Point, firmly, finally.

Poor Patrick. Liz smiled.

Placed her father's order, when Andy finally left the store.

* * *

Liz drove to town, with no particular object. Parked the Mercedes, walked down Main Street, gazed into store windows.

She hadn't been inside The Dress-Up Box but once, when it first opened. Liz didn't buy second hand clothing, even high-end. Didn't wear vintage. But the store looked inviting, and had been beautiful the time she'd seen it. She went in.

Melody Gray was talking with Gwen at the counter; several other women browsed clothing racks.

"Hello, ladies. How are Haven Point's nicest entrepreneurial distaff making out?"

"Great, Liz," said Melody.

Gwen sighed. "I wish I could say the same. My early sales aren't what I'd hoped. Althea Jones thinks people buy my infusions, use them once and then they sit. Waiting for 'special.'"

"People are stupid. Carpe diem—they should use them up and buy more."

"I won't argue with that, Liz. That's what I'd like. But people do what they do, not what we want them to. If I keep on, I'll have to expand distribution. Thank God I can wait until this season goes to decide."

"I hope you do keep making those vinegars—Mother loves them, and so does Dad, and I do, too."

Gwen assured her that she'd keep the Lords supplied, whatever the fate of her business.

"How are the wedding plans coming along, Melody?" Liz remembered to ask.

"Oh, my God. Don't even go there. Mom has the absolute worst taste—especially in bridesmaid dresses. I nix one awful idea, and—bang—there she comes with another. Her latest pick is lime green organza. I found something pretty, but she thinks they're too plain."

"The simpler the better—tell your mother I said so. And that I heard first it from *my* mother," commented Liz.

"Thanks, I'll do that. And my matron of honor—my sister, Joanna," to Liz, "is pregnant. And Mom thinks Jack should have Jason as his best man, which, why? They weren't ever close, too big an age gap."

Gwen raised her eyebrows. "Jack asked Seth, back when you announced it—but you know that."

"Of course he did. Mom's gone off the deep end. Jack was wonderful, actually. He told Mom that if she wants prospective in-laws as principal attendants, I should have *you* for my maid of honor. And then he'd think about Jason."

"Good for him—but I wish he'd left me out of it. Do you have to have real 'bridesmaid' dresses? I'd think you could mix it up and supply them beautifully from here."

"Gwen, I only wish. Mom would have kittens, puppies, and probably badgers, too. I told you, right off the deep end. I switch between being furious with Joanna for letting me in for this, and totally sympathizing."

"Melody, you're a trouper, as *my* Mom would say. I'm sorry. It sounds like a nightmare."

"It is, but when it's all over, I'll wake up and be married to Jack. That's what matters, in the end. At least, that's what I keep telling myself."

"I'll say it again—my brother's a lucky man. I hope you two will be every bit as happy as you deserve."

"Oh, I think we'll be plenty happy," said Melody, a little smile breaking on her face, like sun through clouds. "He's the sweetest, dearest man I ever met."

"And on that note," said Liz, "I'll say goodbye—I'm looking forward to your wedding, Melody. It sounds as if it will be interesting, at least. Gwen, do you want company for dinner?"

"Absolutely. I should go, too, Melody. I'm ready for fitting, though, whenever you and your Mom get on the same page about our dresses."

Melody sighed.

* * *

"You're not done yet? Jeez, Seth. What's taking you so long?"

"Getting it right. You worked on this how long, yourself?"

That was fair, Ben thought. Almost.

"How much longer, you think? We've got people wanting to look at it. Money people."

"Don't know. It's coming. Want it faster, get someone else. I'll send it back tomorrow."

"Don't do that."

"Don't rush me."

Seth hated to be rushed. Personally, Ben liked the exhilaration. Not that Seth couldn't move fast, on those long legs of his. Got plenty done, too, working steady, measured. They just lived by different tempos, Ben reminded himself.

"Sorry. I'll wait. Call me."

"'Kay."

Seth hung up the phone. The note-patterns, couldn't call them tunes, were indeed coming. Slowly. Painfully, sometimes.

He'd thought 'love' would be the easiest. Until he'd tried, and realized the pattern needed to sound happier.

Seth put 'love' on the back burner, tackled the others. A metaphor of his life.

* * *

Gwen thawed duck breasts in cold water. More notice, duck rouennaise would have been wonderful, but she hadn't time.

The marketplace had frozen porcini this week; Gwen peeled them for roasting. Made butter pie crust, using vodka to moisten it—the lower water content made the crust shrink less when baked. Chopped mirepoix—onion, carrot, celery.

Bones never went to waste in her kitchen; the freezer held various concentrated stocks which Gwen froze in ice cube trays. She pulled out the container labeled "duck."

By the time Liz arrived, a thick stew of duck and mushroom was simmering warmly. Gwen brushed piecrust cloches with egg-wash, popped them, plus scraps, into the hot oven. Sautéed washed spinach in butter with shallots, garlic.

Liz had brought two bottles of Amarone. "Thanks—I've got two of the Margaux you brought last time breathing. I love Amarone—don't they call it 'wine to think by?'"

"*Vino da meditazione*, yes."

"I'll make osso bucco to go with it, next time. If you give me a little more notice. And assuming I can find veal shanks."

Gwen poured wine, served up semi-deconstructed duck pie, lining soup plates with baked crust scraps, ladling stew. Topped the plates with the cloches, now golden, shiny. Set them out, then side plates of spinach.

"Heaven. And great with the wine."

"Thanks, I thought they'd pair."

"Tell, me, how's Patrick doing on that book of Mark's?"

Patrick had been summoned to Los Angeles, rewrites again needed.

"He said he'd read it while he's in California. I haven't heard from him since."

Liz looked at Gwen. "You do know he's terribly smitten with you—since you two first met. Frankly, I've never seen anyone hold onto a crush so long with so little encouragement."

"Don't say 'you two' like that, Liz. Patrick and I aren't any sort of 'us.' I like him, he's tons of fun, but—I don't *know* him, and no matter if we spend time, I don't know him *better*. Is there any getting past that surface? He's charming, but it's hard to see who he is underneath."

Interesting question. "I suppose I haven't tried. I enjoy his manner, frankly."

"Oh, I do, too. But—he looks at me like he wants to be the big bad wolf and I'm Little Red Riding Hood. I don't want to be eaten up."

Which was a fairly good metaphor, now she thought of it.

If you married someone—and romantic involvement, for Gwen, meant at least looking toward that resolution—you ended up being married to their job. She had, her father had— to some extent. Her mother hadn't; hers had been the consuming career. Which Patrick's would be. No, she thought, that wasn't a good hand of cards for her to play.

"Let's talk about you, Liz. Don't you ever, ever think about something that lasts longer than a couple of weeks? And, if you don't have kids, who will your parents leave the property to?"

"I know, I know. Mother gently hints. Not too often, thank God. I honestly don't think I'm cut out for it, Gwen.

"Mother just may have to leave it to some Van Leyden cousin or other. After I'm gone, of course—I know she'll let me have the use of it. But I'm not ruling anything out of the question."

"It'd be a shame to break the line—it runs back over 200 years here."

"You're so fixed on family, Gwen—what's wrong?"

"Nothing, really. Just—I came back to *be* with family, after—after Mark died, and—I got smashed up. Now it feels like I've got no-one. Daddy's gone. Mom's moved out, and she's all wrapped up in this benefit thing for the Arts Center—which is a great idea. Jack's never here except to sleep and have coffee. And Seth—he's practically a stranger, all spring since he got well, and the summer so far. If I didn't visit Belinda, I wouldn't have seen him in almost two weeks."

"But the benefit and Seth—that thing he's working on— those are temporary, no?"

"I guess. Maybe I'm still shaky from losing Daddy. I just feel so damn' lonely. It's not fair, I know, but I feel as if everyone's abandoning me, and I'm all alone.

"I can't even focus on business, not that there's any need— I've got shelves full of product, and people aren't buying fast. I can't seem to tackle any kind of project."

"Give yourself—and your mother, and Jack and Seth, too— a little time, Gwen. You've all been through a lot. It's just bad luck your family's preoccupied at the moment. Wait until the season ends—there'll be people at your table every night. You'll like that."

"You're probably right. And yes, I will." *But that was too far away.*

"The real solution is taking a page from your brother's book. If you want perpetual company, you're going to have to marry again yourself.

"When are you going to take off that ring?"

"Oh." Gwen looked at her wedding band. An anachronism. "I really just keep it on as—protection. It helps keep the dateimportuning minimal. Who would I marry? I adore Haven Point, but it's pretty slim on eligible men. Jack was probably the best catch in the town, but he's my brother, not to mention engaged. And Ken Pelletier—my cousin—he's great, but he's taken, too. I expect he and Althea will marry before a year's out. Talk about smitten."

"If you gave Patrick a chance . . ."

"I don't know him well enough. And I don't think we want the same things out of life."

"Well, Gwen, if it's Haven Point eligible you're looking for, there's always Seth Greenlaw. He isn't your brother, whatever you say."

"Liz. Seth would never look at me that way—I'm just his silly—no, tell a lie, since Christmas I've been promoted to crazy—kid sister. He'll love me all my days, he'll take care of me when I need it—and that runs both ways. He'd kill for me, he'd die for me, if it came to that—so would I, for him. In a heartbeat. But what you're suggesting? The very idea would shock—and embarrass—him."

"Are you sure? Patrick thinks not."

"What would Patrick Riordan know about it? He's barely seen Seth and me together."

"He's a writer, Gwen, and a good one. He picks up on things."

"Writers invent things, and this is one of them."

"Have it your way. I'll say this, though—if I were you, I'd make sure. And if Seth Greenlaw does have feelings for you, I wouldn't let them go to waste. Because, in case you're haven't noticed, that man is *hot*.

"What's for dessert?"

CHAPTER 30

July

He was beginning to be angry. Melody could say everything was fine, but it wasn't fine, and it wasn't right.

Jack had started to sit in with her and Ann, his mother-in-law-to-be. On planning sessions.

"Mom, Liz Lord said so herself. 'Simpler is better.' Don't you think she'd know? And she got the idea handed to her by her mother. *Julia Lord*, Mom."

"That's all very well for places like Boston. We do things different, here. Every bride wants her attendants to wear those dresses. And any girl loves a bridesmaid dress."

"*No-one* loves them, Mom. I don't know what it was like when you got married, obviously, but those dresses—they're a bad joke, on every girl who has to buy one and wear it. On every girl who has to tell her friends to shell out money for those monstrosities."

"You'll thank me later, Melody. I want you to have a real, proper wedding."

Jack broke in. "What she's going to have is an elopement, if you don't stop, Mother Ann. You've got just about the sweetest daughter anyone could have, and she's let you have your way plenty. But this is supposed to be her day, not yours, and if you don't start giving her at least *some* say, we'll just run away and get hitched. Done deal, no fuss, no muss.

"Melody? You down with that?"

For answer, much-tried Melody burst into tears, and threw herself into his arms.

Between sobs, "When was the last time I told you you're wonderful, Jack, darling? Let's just do it, anyway. Please?"

Ann Gray backed down. Anything was better than them eloping. Melody's choice of bridesmaid dresses it would be.

* * *

She'd take no chances. Melody ordered the dresses, was swiftly reimbursed by her attendants, and would make alterations herself. Joanna's size 10, Gwen's size 2, Susie Pashley's size 8. Susie had been in Melody's—and Gwen's—class at school, and Melody's closest school-friend. She ran Fine Grind, Main Street's coffee house.

Gwen presented herself at The Dress-Up Box, dutifully, for her fitting. She'd been a bride, but never a bridesmaid. Melody's pick of dress was very pretty, indeed.

Her sister-in-law-elect pinned seams. Didn't stick her, not once. So skilled, so deft she was, Gwen thought.

"Oh, you should have heard that brother of yours! He'll keep Mom in line. Really laid down the law to her. You'd have been so proud—I was just *bursting*."

Well, there. Gwen hadn't known Jack had *that* in him. "Oh, I *am* proud of him. And so happy for *you*. Mom did *all* the planning for mine."

"Yes, but she's got *good* taste! And you were in college, and I'm not. I'm not 19, either."

"No, you're 26 this month." It was early July. "What do you

want for your birthday? And what are you doing about a shower? I can't throw you one, it's not proper."

"Susie's seeing to it. End of the month, we're looking at. And I don't know—with a new house, we kind of need everything. I'll get china from Mom, she's got three sets."

"Kitchen equipment?"

"I'd love one of those slicing things, like you gave Althea at Christmas."

"Mandoline. Sure—I can get you one. But what else? You've got gifts plural coming, not just birthday."

"Anything you think of. Knives?"

"Leave it to me—I'll pick you good ones. And a stone to sharpen them.

"Think about it, let me know what else you need. Or want."

* * *

Seth showed up for dinner. As she'd bidden of late, he did not call first. But,

"Sorry I didn't call, impulse."

"Any time you have that impulse. You don't have to call, or ask. Or apologize."

A sight for sore eyes, Seth at her kitchen table. Pushing three weeks, and how long since that happened? Not in the year she'd been back. But she hadn't planned for him.

"You'll have to take potluck. Let me see what I can whip up."

"Anything. Came for company, mostly. Been missing you, Gwen."

"Me you, too. Something awful."

The words came easy. *Normal*, for them, for her with him. Which she did not quite feel. Gwen had seen him so little, lately. So sweet, seeing him smile. So easy, smiling back. Something in her was not easy.

Gwen checked her refrigerator, freezer. Ran hot water over a container of sauce Bolognese, slipped out the frozen block into a skillet, turned the flame low. Set a pot of salted water over a high flame.

As she opened wine to breathe, "It will have to be boxed pasta, I'm afraid. Fresh takes so long, what with resting." Not that Seth would care. Or even know the difference, probably. She glanced at him; he was smiling at her. Unsettled, Gwen swiveled her gaze to her sauce, turning the block on its side, turning up the flame a little.

Seth liked watching her. Gwen was getting graceful again. Natural, he guessed, it'd show first in her kitchen. Slower than she'd been, before the accident. But easier, more confident in motion, at the new pace. Good to see.

She chopped garlic cloves, separated the results. Put half into her stone mortar, forked anchovies in, and ground them together.

"What are you doing for Jack's bachelor party? Strippers from Bangor?" *Damn.* She'd meant it for a joke. Had her voice sounded a little sharp? Maybe it was all in her mind. Because he laughed.

"Nothing like that. Wouldn't know where to find 'em, Jack wouldn't want 'em if I did.

"Probably take him to the Tavern. Jason Gray, Ken, whoever of his crews. Think it's what Jack wants—he sort of hinted."

"I love it he threatened Ann Gray with elopement if she didn't back off poor Melody. I think that girl would be glad to run off with him this minute. Can I pour you some wine? Or would you rather a beer?"

"Heard some stuff about dresses. Wine, thanks, if that's what you're having."

Gwen poured two glasses. "Oh, God, the bridesmaid dresses. I have to say I'm glad—I only heard about two of Ann's ideas. Melody said they weren't the worst—and given what she *did* tell me, I shudder to think of what she didn't."

He chuckled, but didn't answer, he was looking at her, and she felt odd. *Off.* Words—one of her best things—were tangling in her head. Gwen fell silent, and cooked. Took elaborate care of her melting sauce, turning it, adjusting the flame, much more frequently than was needed.

Tore up some croutons onto a sheet pan, tossed them in oil, salted, peppered, and shoved them into her oven. Accidentally banged the oven door hard, shutting it, and set napkins and silver out.

"Tell me about what you're training this summer."

Non-specific and open. She'd let him talk; on this subject she wouldn't have to answer much.

Seth looked at her; the way she'd worded that wasn't like Gwen.

He told her a few stories—the bay mare that kept kicking her shoes off. The blue roan gelding, a little old to start training, that had almost thrown him day one, but was now learning well.

"Glad it was me, and not Caleb on it, that day."

"I'd imagine so." *Lame.*

Blast Liz Lord, anyway. Filling her head with wrong notions. Setting cats among pigeons. Serpent in the Garden, more like. Shoving bits of apple so far down her gullet she, Gwen-Eve, couldn't dislodge them.

Sauce melted and simmering, Gwen pulled toasted croutons out of the oven, dropped a boxful of tagliatelle into her boiling pot. Tore up romaine leaves, shaved a little Parmesan, microplaned more. Put the rest of the bread loaf she'd torn croutons from, plates, and a bowl of store-bought ricotta in the oven to warm. Ricotta was better added cold, for her; she liked the contrast, but Seth didn't.

Gwen tossed salad in Caesar dressing, topped it with croutons and shaved cheese, set the bowl on the table.

She set warmed plates at her place and Seth's. Topped off his glass, refilled her own, which—goodness—she'd finished in the kitchen.

He smiled, she smiled back. *That* reflex worked as it should.

Liz was wrong. He was as always—his smile, if anything, sweeter, more open than usual. All right, she wasn't wrong about everything—Seth just got better and better looking. Being a grown-up suited him. Gwen wasn't at all sure she could say the same for herself. And felt a little small. Stunted. Just his crazy kid sister. Well, that was as always, too. Wasn't it?

They ate in near silence. Except for Seth commenting, with pleasure, on her sauce. Which was a very good batch, if Gwen said so herself—the texture velvety, meat melted down to smoothness.

But the silence between them wasn't its usual peace. At least, not for her.

And when they said good night, and hugged, Gwen felt uncomfortable, self-conscious. *Liz, what have you done?* This wasn't—right.

He kissed her forehead—which he kissed, lately, more often than her cheek. Probably because he didn't have to bend quite as far.

The kitchen door shut behind him and his parting "'Night, Gwen."

Damn. *Damn.* A precious evening in his company, and she hadn't even been able to enjoy it.

And if you're Eve, what does that make Seth? Her own metaphor. She should wash her mind out with soap. But she'd never have thought it if Liz had kept her damned mouth shut.

Gwen did not want to swallow apple-bits.

What was the psycho-emotional equivalent of sticking a finger down your throat?

* * *

Madeleine Hardie, with the assistance of Taylor James and Tim Douglass, set up the Haven Point Arts Center as a non-profit organization. Co-opted both men, with herself and Julia Lord—so far—as Directors. Charmed funds from summer people's pockets and pocketbooks.

Catherine Strange sent a very generous check.

The benefit, however, was a thornier path than she'd imagined. She should have realized, but hadn't, that amateurs were, by definition, unprofessional.

Madeleine had held auditions. Learned quickly to tell 'talent' there were limited slots and many applicants. Talent. That was a laugh, if she'd had laughter to spare. Mayor Thomas Haskell's granddaughter, Lindsay, whom she'd agreed to let spout a poem from Jack London's 'The Iron Heel'—one highly inappropriate to an eight-year-old female. A good verse, though.

Three elderly and one young church organist were itching to show their piano and vocal skills. The former they all had, to a reasonable degree. If they thought they were singers, they were mistaken. Madeleine, sighing, assigned slots to Taryn Sommers, the young organist from Trinity Church, whose voice was relatively inoffensive, and St. Aidan's own ancient fixture, Billie Billings, who played superbly, and whom Madeleine was able to intimidate out of her desire to vocalize.

Madeleine herself would appear twice; a comic song, and Patrick Riordan had importuned her to play at Beatrice and Benedick—a scene from 'Much Ado About Nothing'—with him. The temptation to relive her New York triumph in that role had over-mastered Madeleine, but Patrick, while assuring her by telephone he knew his lines, had been out of Haven Point for almost a month; they'd had no rehearsal whatever, yet. An unopened gift-box; would Saint Nicholas have left coals for her?

Cousin Ken's diffident suggestion that he, her son, and Seth

Greenlaw might play had been so much more than welcome she could have kissed him full on the lips. She had given him a light hug and kissed his cheek. They would play well. And would—probably—behave like adults.

Another adult, Jonathan Cohen, auditioned, privately, for her. He played piano quite well, accompanying comic song-patter.

Two children, high-school age, Madeleine was glad to acknowledge as possessing the seeds of talent. Matilda Small, 16, tiny, thin, and pale, auditioned a monologue; in the role of an adolescent's mother, she was sharp, funny, emotional, and dead-on.

And Artie Babbidge, just 15, from two towns over, had written his own comic piece. It was not full-baked, would not do, professionally, but Madeleine had laughed several times, aloud, at the end of a long and unpleasant day.

Althea Jones' voice had been a blessing to hear and include.

And the roster was filled.

Madeleine, sighing over a mock-up proof of her programme, rather hoped Catherine Strange would find herself unable to fly up for it.

It was an uneven mix.

***

"We're neglecting her. *I'm* neglecting her. She's been through so much, Melody. I feel like a bad brother. And Seth said she was—well, weird, last time he was there."

"I know Gwen's feeling off, these days. Off her feed, or maybe just off 'cause she's not feeding people—we both know she doesn't like that. I feel kind of bad, too."

"Then we'll have dinner with her tomorrow. Your parents can eat at the tavern, our treat. We should send them out more often. They'll have to get used to doing without you anyway—

once we're married, I'm keeping you to myself."

Melody knew that "our treat" meant Jack's. But any 'our,' 'we,' 'us,' was soul-music.

She was a very bad girl for thinking it, but Melody was a little bit glad they had to move the wedding up a month. It would keep her mother scrambling, Joanna would be less visibly pregnant at the ceremony.

Not that she was glad of the reason—her father had been diagnosed with arterial blockage, and Dr. Oliver had recommended angioplasty. Sooner rather than later. Jake Gray was older than Paul Hardie by a decade, and they were all uneasy, Melody not least.

She prayed and hoped for her father, but couldn't be wholly sorry she'd be Jack's wife that much sooner.

* * *

Gwen prepped dinner for four—Vince Morey had slaughtered several young pigs, and she'd scored some lovely hind shanks. Slow-roast over onion, carrot and apple. Mashed white sweet potatoes with butter and salt. Roasted brussels sprouts with bacon and garlic.

Having dropped off Jake and Ann Gray at the tavern, Jack and Melody arrived a few minutes after Seth, who thought he'd best keep a closer eye on Gwen.

She'd been so unlike herself the other night. He'd have thought her preoccupied—except she kept looking at him. As if he were a problem she had to solve.

Which might be his fault. Seth was trying to walk a tricky line—neither to display nor actively hide what he felt for her. Habits, long-standing, were hard to break; he might well be confusing Gwen. He'd been keeping his feelings from her since before she turned thirteen—still a little girl, too young to tell.

He hadn't been unhappy, holding his secret, not for years.

Seth had planned. Jack had been 15 then, and was looking forward to 16, when his father would let him date. Seth figured Gwen would be allowed at the same age. Three years, then, and a little, to wait. Then, he could tell her how he loved her, speak to her father. And, soon as she turned 18, they could be married.

God laughs at our plans. Hank Greenlaw had chain-smoked four packs of cigarettes a day. Seth thought it had been less, when his mother was alive, but wasn't sure he remembered right. Another poor choice of his father's, and there were many of them. An expensive habit, too, for a man with two sons to keep. Who didn't make his land pay what it should, even with Seth's help.

Dead, of lung cancer, at 42. His responsibility toward his younger son falling like a stone mantle onto Seth's shoulders. Seth had known, of course, that he'd have to help out with Ben and college. But the whole burden shouldn't have been his.

If it hadn't been. If Gwen hadn't gone off to college. If she'd come home after, still single. If there'd been no Mark Sinclair.

If wishes were horses.

If horses were wishes, come to that.

"Give you a hand with anything?"

Gwen, startled, knocked the wooden spoon she was mixing mashed sweet potato with onto the floor. Felt herself turn pink.

"No, thanks—I'm fine." Stupid thing to say, and a lie at that.

"At least let me clean that up—my fault you jumped." Without waiting for permission, he rinsed a rag under the tap, wiped up the yellow blob.

Gwen looked at his dark, bent head, saw each lock of heavy hair distinct. Wanted to smooth them. Comb her fingers through.

Oh, no, oh, no, no, no. This—*she*—would spoil everything between them.

The punishment for eating apple-bits—banishment from

the Garden.

Gwen set out hot plates, bowls of sweet potato, brussels sprouts. Took one roasting pan from the oven, remembering just in time to use potholders.

Four hind shanks, brown and crackling, stood to jaunty attention on their bed of vegetables and apples.

"There's another pan just like this keeping warm, guys, you'll get enough."

Melody always felt a little jealous, and guilty for it, when she ate Gwen's cooking. So much better than her own, though her own was good . . . enough. She could leave off the 'enough,' usually. But not here. One reason she and Jack came rarely to Gwen's table.

Jack watched his sister and Seth Greenlaw watching each other. If he didn't love them both so much, it might be funny. Too close-up, those two, to see each other without distortion. Not Jack's job, adjusting their focus. Not a good idea, either, meddling with what belonged to them.

Gwen picked at her food, eating even less than was normal for her; this was noted. It was not commented on.

"You said there's more? This is great." Seth's plate was empty.

"I did." She brought out the second roasting pan. Let her hand touch his shoulder, after setting it down. Mistake. Hard muscle, harder bone beneath, warm through cloth under her palm. He smiled up at her. She wanted to kiss him. Or curl up in his arms and cry herself to death.

Jack and Seth polished off the remaining pork; Gwen was setting out lemon tarts with her own home-grown fresh strawberries as the phone rang.

"Hello?" Gwen listened. "Okay, sure, I'll tell them. Thanks."

"Jack, Melody, I'm to tell you Jake and Ann are ready to go home. Do you want to take them some tarts? In case they didn't order dessert."

"That's so thoughtful, Gwen. I think they'd love that, thanks," said Melody.

Gwen took a pie plate from the cupboard, filled it with tarts.

"Leave a couple for me, will you?" asked Seth.

"There's more in the fridge." She covered the pie plate with foil, handed it to Melody, hugged her, hugged Jack.

"Thank you for coming—it's good to have you here. Drive safe, now."

Left alone with Seth, which she probably should avoid. Now. *Oh, God, take this away.*

Seth watched as Gwen bustled, cleaning up. More unsettled even than the other night—and it centered on him. Might be a good sign, if she were re-evaluating her feelings. Might not be, if she saw his. He'd never seen her so—*uncertain*—and couldn't read her.

"Braid's getting long, Gwen. Think there's more of it than when you were twelve."

"It's time I cut it. Too long—it's a nuisance when I leave it down." No time like the present, in fact, and Gwen got sewing—not kitchen—scissors from the drawer of the little table by the door.

"You cut it yourself?"

"Yes. I'll just snip off a few inches and call it good."

"Can I?"

Gwen, stomach suddenly full of butterflies, felt it would be safer to refuse. Heard herself say, "If you want."

Handed him the scissors, turned her back and stood, waiting.

She felt him take hold of her braided hair. Run it through his hand—gauging where to cut, no doubt.

Seth wanted to turn her round to him, slowly wrap his hand in that braid, pull her head back—gently—and kiss her breathless.

Gwen heard the metallic sound of scissor blades parting, felt the pull on her scalp as they sliced through the thick rope of her hair. Flinched, as blades came together.

"That hurt? Sorry." Seth tucked three inches of braid into his shirt pocket.

"N-no."

"Want me to try evening it up?" He wouldn't mind unbraiding that red rope—it was coming undone already—and playing with her hair some more. He'd kind of liked the way cutting it felt.

"That's okay, thanks. It'll have to be seen to properly for the wedding, anyway."

She looked tired, Seth thought, and it was late. "Won't keep you up longer. I'll head on home."

They hugged. Gwen didn't want to let go, despite disturbing, *wrong* feelings crowding in with familiar, safe ones. She felt his lips on her hair. Looked up at him.

Her eyes filled with tears.

"What is it, Gwen? Tell me."

She shook her head. "Just—some stuff I'm trying to get past." Absolute truth, and, she hoped, absolutely misleading.

"I'm okay. Really. Get home safe."

"'Kay. If you're sure."

He left.

Gwen poured herself a glass of wine, and wept salt tears into it.

* * *

Jack and Melody, having dropped her parents off at the home that would—so wonderfully—soon not be Melody's, drove out Gray Way, and North.

Construction on their new house was complete; Jack, in consultation with his bride-to-be, had furnished it with a mix of old and new, comfortable and cozy. The master bedroom, of course, had been first; they'd spent hours on happy hours in that bed.

"That was weird."

"Not that weird," responded Jack. "Not if you break it down. We knew how Seth felt already."

"Yes, but what's with that sister of yours? I don't think I've ever seen her so nervous. She's been moving better, I'd noticed, but she was almost—*clumsy*, a couple of times. In her own kitchen."

"That's what would make this funny. If I didn't care about them. Don't you see it? Gwen's either falling in love with him, or realizing she already is. All he'd need to do is reach out— she'd fall right into his hand. And he doesn't see it. Just like she doesn't see what he feels."

"Sort of—romantic myopia, you mean?"

"Yeah. Sort of—too close to see each other clear. I hope to God they get it straight. And soon.

"I don't like thinking of Gwen alone over the winter."

CHAPTER 31

July

Rows of unsold oils, vinegars, on her shelves. Cranberry jelly, which would sell well at holiday time, but not much before. This was not working out as she'd hoped.

Gwen was beginning to feel Haven Point—her beloved home—almost *withdraw* from her. Estrangement. A good word. An awful feeling.

Patrick Riordan, back in New York, called her one morning. "My dear, I've read the notebook at last—I apologize for the delay. Actors. They don't really want new lines, they want attention."

Gwen laughed. Patrick's voice cheered her, unaccountably.

"I think there's something there. Your husband has a genuine voice. He must have been an unusual and interesting man."

"He was." Mark was gone, now. A lovely memory. A ring on her finger. Which she should probably take off.

"I'd like to read a bit more, before I take all of it to Laura. I think you'd like her, Gwen. Perhaps I can persuade her to come up. Or—perhaps—you'd like to visit New York?"

"Thank you, Patrick—you can read as much as you like.

Shall I send you a couple more notebooks?"

"No, my dear, not necessary. I'll be back in Haven Point by Friday. Will you have dinner with me? You owe me the chance to return your hospitality."

"No need for that, Patrick, I love cooking for company."

"Oh, but I insist. Proper protocol, you know. Do say yes."

In the end, she did.

* * *

Althea brought Ken and their children to dinner with Gwen. Too late to help cook.

Nerise just grew like a weed, almost as tall as Kyle Pelletier, and was looking at state championships in fall. An arrow in flight—Gwen had enjoyed watching her race, once or twice, this spring and summer. Cheering along with Althea, Ken, the boys.

Gwen served up chili and fixings. Cornbread, coleslaw. She'd added cumin, a dash of paprika, was fairly sure by now that was Althea's secret. Most of it. Not quite all. But she liked the additions.

Althea, tasting, laughed. "Almost."

"I know, not quite. I'll get it right, though, you just see if I don't."

"Any beans this time, Miss Gwen?" asked Nerise, hopefully.

"Sorry, Nerise. I make it Texas-style, like I told you. No beans."

"I wish you'd try them sometime, Miss Gwen. If they don't go with Texas, could you try some other state?"

"I'll think about it," Gwen laughed, but made no promises.

"Are you coming to Melody's birthday party this weekend? Golly, 26. I'll be that in September. Where does it go, all that time?"

No-one had an answer for her last question, but Althea and Ken were invited to the party.

It was easier, focusing, without Seth there. Which realization was, itself, almost beyond bearing.

She was a terrible person. An ingrate. He gave, had given, so much—and here she was, not content with everything she had from him, wanting more. She was ashamed, mortified. Miserable, when she couldn't box it away. Which was almost all the time.

She was falling in love with her brother. Some terrible kind of sin—it had to be.

She deserved her misery.

* * *

Seth looked at revolving glass rods, flashing patterns of light. Listened to the tape of note patterns he'd put together. They worked, they were right. Or at least he thought they were, and what more than that could he do?

The last was not done. He had one idea of what might set him on the right road. He shied from it, bone-deep reluctance. It would hurt. And it had been so long.

But he'd promised Ben. And it was something, he thought, he ought to conquer. Along with his resistance. Re-conquer.

He thought, deliberately, of what had only come unbidden to his mind these nine years and more. Since his father was pronounced terminal.

A clearing in his—now his—woods. Sunlight, moonlight, stars, variously. A boy of 11, a girl of 9. And later, and older.

Seth got out sheet music. In case he couldn't remember. Took his Martin from its fortress of a case. The guitar Paul Hardie had given him sat in its own, lighter case; his first, hidden in cheap cardboard, cracked, crushed here and there, he kept too. His mother had given it to him for his 7th birthday. She hadn't lived to see Christmas.

His mother, Paul, Gwen—all gifts. Of love.

He tuned up. Took a deep breath. Three minutes, not even. He could face three minutes.

The most difficult piece he'd tackled, until he'd started playing with Ken Pelletier.

The happiest music he'd ever made.

A little rusty, but it came back. The happiness of it hurt. Some. He played it again. And again, and again, until it ran, tumbling, pinging, singing. Sounding, mahogany and red spruce resonance, better than he'd ever made it sound before.

Rust rubbed off, mastery cracked pain. *Good* to play this again. Good to hear it sound so; the two instruments he'd played it on were—well, compare a convenience store hot dog with Gwen's holiday feasts.

He took staff paper, pencils. Turned to Ben's absurd contrivance (which, he had to admit, had its beauty, fascination, even).

Pushed the remote button labeled 'Love,' opened his mind to the pattern. Felt the notes, waiting.

They would come, now.

* * *

"So, I asked him, flat, what *he* thought the character would say in those circumstances. He turned an interesting shade of red, and stammered that that was *my* job. I rejoined that I'd done it already, to my own satisfaction, and if he wanted change, he had to tell me how and, more important, of course, why."

"What did he say to that?" Gwen, laughing.

"Nothing, my dear. Nothing at all. He did turn a deeper red, and took himself off.

"Ah, well, 'all's well that ends well.' As the Bard tells us."

"'Still the fine's the crown.' Act four, scene four." Gwen finished the line, placed it. "They don't make act breaks like they used to."

Patrick laughed. *Clever girl, lovely girl.* "Indeed, they do not." Try finding one play, nowadays, which had more than a single intermission to break the action.

Gwen was enjoying herself. Being with Patrick was *beautifully* uncomplicated, compared with . . . she wasn't going to think about that. She was having fun. *Be here, now.*

Patrick talked around bites of ribeye; Gwen, not terribly hungry, had ordered an appetizer of mussels in white wine-cream sauce. She made this dish herself, and had given the recipe—slightly simplified—to Amelia Betts, the tavern's co-owner and its chief cook and bottle washer.

He'd brought from New York a minion of his publisher's, who'd checked packaging, labeled notebook boxes for shipping to Patrick's New York loft. Made arrangement for pickup and transportation to the airport.

"It is a nuisance I must be there so much. But duty calls, and one must answer."

"Oh, I know." But what was her duty, now? She'd loved being a dutiful daughter and sister. But her father was gone, her brothers too busy for her.

It was true, Seth put in appearances. Sometimes staying for dinner, mostly just checking in. He was stretched awfully thin, these days, Ben's secret project, best-man-duties, rehearsals. And a full stable.

But he was as sweet as could be. Kinder, more thoughtful than ever. Every day he did not stop by, he called. Which was new.

Gwen was further unsettled by this. Change—any change—was—precarious. Precipitous. *Dangerous.*

Change took him away, a little, and she was trying to keep him close. Without letting him see what she felt. Which, if he did, he would politely and lovingly refrain from laughing at. *Oh, God.*

"My dear?"

She'd promised herself *not* to think about Seth.

"I'm sorry, Patrick, I missed that. What were you saying?"

"Only that I'd like to show New York to you—and you to the city—it must be years since you've been there."

"Oh, Patrick. Don't. Please. I can't think about it right now—my brother's getting married, then there's Mom's benefit thing—you should get in at least *some* rehearsal with her, if you can, while you're here. She's having conniptions.

"And the Lords, for reasons best known to themselves, want to throw me a birthday party. Mom's letting them, because it's so close after the benefit.

"My head's just *crammed*."

"May I raise the subject again, when your calendar is clearer?"

Gwen looked at the ceiling. "It's a free country."

* * *

Melody had opened birthday presents, enjoyed informal catering from her guests' kitchens, including Althea Jones' and her soon-to-be-sister-in-law's. She'd seen her guests thanked and out. And thought this year she would have two bridal showers, and no birthday at all.

No girl-gifts, no jewelry, no pretties. Only household items. Well, 26 wasn't a girl, properly speaking. And the things she really needed were for the house. That Jack had built for her.

Gwen had got her the—slicing thing, what did she call it, sounded like some musical instrument. Knives. And a standing mixer, with an extra bowl and a lot of attachments.

Joanna, up from Portland, gave Melody a generous gift certificate to a big chain store that would provide a huge selection of home items, when Melody had time to get to Bangor. Which would probably not be until after her honeymoon cruise.

Susie Pashley presented her with a good solid cast iron stove-top grill.

Althea's gifts were a handwritten notebook of recipes, and two old majolica oyster plates. Gwen whispered, later, that these were hard to find, highly collectible, and she was pea-green with envy. Smiling, as she said it.

Melody hadn't expected Liz Lord to accept her invitation, but she had, and brought an enormous marble slab, like a great big cutting board, for rolling pastry.

Gwen, looking at it, made a mental note to get one of those.

The biggest monkey-wrench Melody and Jack had encountered, moving the wedding up to late August, was that Madeleine Hardie's Arts Center benefit came the following weekend. And Jack, understandably, spent a good bit of time rehearsing. He hadn't, nor had Seth, performed in public, ever. Both were nervous. Ken was less so; he'd sat in with a couple of bands in Portland occasionally.

* * *

Madeleine had calculated; the old Town Hall auditorium would be unlikely to fill up—not yet; she'd arranged with George and Amelia Betts to hold it at the Main Street Tavern. It hadn't hurt that Amelia was well-inclined toward Gwen, who gave her tips and recipes here and there.

Tables—and the Tavern would add a few extra—looked like selling out in short order.

Curiosity might kill cats, but it also sold tickets.

* * *

July wrapped up, for Gwen, with a decent uptick in sales and Melody's shower. Which went well enough, although Gwen squirmed, internally, at the silly games Susie made them play.

Patrick had flown back to New York. He'd spent some time rehearsing with Gwen's mother. Not enough, not nearly enough, for Madeleine. But his promise of being letter-perfect had been no lie, and his fluency with Shakespeare's dialogue was impressive. For an amateur.

Seth, finally, got the note patterns recorded, and sent the contraption back to Richmond, safely wrapped. He'd had to refuse Ben's insistence that they needed him there, at least for a few days. He had too much still on his plate.

Ben could find out the hard way—Seth still thought no-one would buy the thing. Maybe a few rich weirdos. But it was no longer his worry.

He thought he'd earned an evening off, and went to Gwen's for dinner. She wasn't as nervous as she'd been for a few weeks. But something had changed. She seemed—sadder than when she'd come home from Boston. Accepting of sadness, like she'd given up some fight. He heard it in her voice, saw it in her smile, felt it in her body when he held her.

Giving up was so unlike Gwen he didn't know how to deal with it. Had what she'd been through—loss of her husband, injury, pain, topped off with her father's death—smashed her so badly? She'd said she was trying to get past something. Maybe it was so hard she'd stopped the effort.

Seth couldn't know. She was—shut off from him, somehow. Her manner was so gentle, so tender toward him. But she didn't banter, riff, with her old ease.

It just about killed him, not knowing what was wrong. How to fix it for her. For both of them. He couldn't stand feeling like an onlooker in her emotional life.

He'd been an active participant in that life so long—even while Gwen was in Boston, she'd made him feel that—he'd taken it for granted.

Kept his love—part of it—hidden, to hold on to what that

closeness gave him. The price had been steep, but worth paying.

Life without at least emotional intimacy with her was too bleak to contemplate.

* * *

Ken Pelletier, in the midst of benefit rehearsals, work, fatherhood and love, sought guidance from Father Peter McCaughey.

He wanted to marry Althea Jones. In church, specifically St. Stephen's. Motherhood notwithstanding, Althea had never been married, and was free to wed according to the tenets of the Roman Catholic church.

He did not know whether he was or not—Ken was a divorced man. His former wife, Kathleen Parmenter as was, was not Catholic, had not wanted a church wedding, down in Portland, and he had not insisted. Would he need an annulment to have the wedding he wanted for—with—Althea?

Ken thought he had grounds enough—during their marriage, Kathleen had demonstrated so much disregard for what the Church held essential to marriage, he hoped a petition might be considered.

The issue was Kathleen—canon law held that both spouses must have knowledge of any formal annulment proceeding. And he had no idea where she was. Had made efforts to find her, as divorce law mandated, which had turned up no clue as to her whereabouts.

Father McCaughey hemmed. Hawed. "Write it all down for me, Ken. Everything you can think of, I'll review it. I hope I can find some way out for you—glad to hear you want to do it right, this time."

Ken, hopeful, typed up pages, turned them over to his priest.

And continued to hope. Kept the fingers of his mind crossed.

CHAPTER 32

Early August

The little clearing stood where it always had. About a mile in, west. Hadn't changed much, though it seemed smaller than before. Not as much as he'd changed, ten years and more, nearer eleven, it had been, and what the hell was he doing, anyway?

Setting himself up, almost certainly, foolishness. But the notion had been unshakeable, the impulse too strong to resist.

It had been his place, his retreat from a house as loveless as motherless, to sit and think. To play.

Seth sat on a rock; it felt almost the same. For a while, all he did was sit, shadows lengthening in the dawning twilight. Feeling foolish, feeling other things.

She wouldn't come, he told himself. Hadn't always, even those years, and now—almost a decade, and she'd changed more than he had.

But if she did, if the magic still held . . . maybe it would set things straight between them. Maybe even set them *right*.

He opened the case, took his guitar out. Never yet played any but his first—couldn't really dignify it with the word 'instrument'—not in this place.

Seth tuned the Martin. Picked a song from the many in his head, took a deep breath, and played. Ran through that piece twice, played another, once. A third, a fourth. Not singing, pure wood-and-steel sound.

She didn't come. He hadn't really believed she would. Good to play here again, anyway. Take his refuge back.

He'd had a hard time picking a song for the benefit—Mrs. Hardie had allowed them three, which was neat—Ken, Seth and Jack each got to choose one. She'd set them last, which was flattering and alarming. Even warned they might want a fourth number, in case the audience asked. She must think they were pretty good.

Ken had known exactly what he wanted; it was a number they hadn't played before, and the devil to arrange, but a great song, heartbreaking, heart-mending. Jack's was new, too, and he'd sing lead. It was a sweet, upbeat number, a little quirky, and suited him, both his voice and who he was. His and Seth's arrangements were easy, Ken's had been much less so.

Seth had changed his mind twice. And still wasn't sure, but he couldn't switch a third time; not fair to Ken and Jack. At least, all had been songs they knew well.

He played the number he'd settled on, singing the lyrics, this time. He hadn't done more than play, here, all those years, all those years ago.

Then the first he'd chosen and rejected. And the second.

Seth thought of the first time Gwen had—just shown up, while he played. Sixteen years ago, give or take a month or two.

She'd sat and listened, her back against a tree; they hadn't spoken. Hadn't even looked, directly, at each other. They never talked of it, after. As if any acknowledgement would break some spell.

She'd come again, and again, unasked, unannounced. Not every time he'd taken to the clearing to play, but more and more often, as months, years, came and went.

Not this time.

Seth played a song he'd put on the shelf last spring. After the accident, after Mark Sinclair had died. He'd never played it with Ken and Jack, a little too—revealing. Any song was, of course, if you played it, sang it, right. But some cut too close, this among them.

He didn't sing, not these lyrics, not now.

Sound of movement, in the woods. His quick glance caught the flash of red, and there she was. Gwen sat against a tree, not looking at him. He took breath, and played. Not looking, not singing. Song after song, in the deepening shadows.

Gwen had been sure the clearing's pull had been, not instinct, but a trick of her mind, a trick of her heart. She'd resisted, certain she'd find an empty clearing, and proof of her idiocy. The utter, abject foolishness of what she felt.

But the impulse had proved too strong. And here he was. It couldn't mean anything beyond her sensitivity to him. At least he was here, and the music was fire to warm her hands at. If not her heart.

She watched Seth's hands make music. Saw, double-vision, those hands as they'd been, when he was a boy. So fine and strong, those long fingers. Work had roughed, but not coarsened them. Fine hands still, he had.

Seth watched her sidelong. Here she was, and now what? He played.

Finally, the old, difficult piece he'd taken out, polished up for Ben's project. He'd been working on it that first time, so long ago. Three-four more years, before he really had it.

The last notes still hanging in the air, he looked at her face. Gwen met his gaze. Tears in her eyes, welling, spilling. He wanted to kiss them away. Maybe he'd do just that.

Seth put the Martin back in its case. Stood up, and she did, too, standing as she'd sat, back against the old maple. In a couple of months, its leaves would be red as her hair. He took a step toward her; she didn't move a muscle.

A flurry of large wings in the wood, a small animal's dying shriek, startled them—ironic that it was breaking their gaze which broke the spell.

Gwen whirled and bolted. Back through the woods she'd appeared from.

Maybe he should have chased her, but he didn't.

* * *

Patrick Riordan bounced from Haven Point to New York and back, and back again.

He found some time, in each Haven Point instance, to see Gwen, to at least run lines with Madeleine. Who was never satisfied. Patrick—who had performed in amateur theatricals in his early 20s, before his writing had caught, and before that at school—found her fierce work ethic as off-putting as it was admirable. He did acknowledge the latter; but she was going to throw shade all over him, if he didn't step up his game. That was something he hadn't contemplated. He should have.

Gwen, finally, accepted a second invitation to dinner. She even allowed him, as she had not the first time, to pick her up at her home.

"I had Laura to my flat, to look at what she'll be dealing with. I'm sorry to say she found the sheer volume a bit daunting—but I've offered to categorize them a bit for her. I hope you won't feel it intrusive of me? I will have to at least flip through them all."

"Oh, wow, Patrick—I didn't mean to put that sort of burden on you. No, I understand if you need to glance them over. If you're willing.

"Really, I could just tell my in-laws it's too overwhelming for the expert, and we'll have to call it, or they can deal with the whole thing themselves. That would be fine with me."

"No, no, Gwen. I confess to feeling a bit—invested—myself in this. I never met your late husband, but some of his insights, some of his sentences, recur to me. I rather feel his voice should be heard."

"Mark was—I don't think my family ever really 'got' Mark and me. Maybe Mom did, a little."

"I *loved* his mind. I never met anyone who could *read* the way he did, or get what he got from what he read. I don't think he cared much whether there ever *was* a book, it was the process that mattered. What he did—it was, well, like a *quest*. Worth the doing, for the right person—and he was that person."

Worth the helping with, and she had been the right person for that—if only it hadn't had to be so *citified*.

Of course, thought Patrick, any man who captured Gwen's imagination would have been remarkable.

"Will you dance, Gwen? Let's choose some music."

It was comfortable, being with someone for whom what she felt wasn't full of tangles. Patrick danced so well. A good height for her, with or without heels, about like Jack. So handsome, too, in that black-Irish fashion, bright dark eyes, his wicked, conspiratorial smile.

And Gwen was grateful—he was giving his time, his attention, to Mark's work. She knew he'd started for her sake, but—now he appreciated Mark, for the qualities she herself had loved.

A man—two men—of unusual quality. But 'city fellas,' both. She'd done that. She would not, again.

Patrick drove her home. "Gwen, forgive me, I *must*—have you at all thought of coming to New York? A week, a month, a weekend, if that's all. Even if you've no chef-ly ambition yourself at the moment, you'd *love* the food. And theatre, and lively, bookish minds," he added, slyly.

"I actually have, Patrick. I just—can't see it." She should say this, "I honestly—I don't think I'm at all who—or what—

you think I am."

He pulled the Jaguar, sharply, off the road. Stopped the engine.

"I think you are Sleeping Beauty, Gwen. Wake up."

He seized her shoulders, pulled her to him, kissed her lips. Hard and quick, and again, softer, longer.

Her skin fizzed, like champagne poured all over her.

Breathless, Gwen broke the kiss, pulled away.

"Wake up, sweet girl. The world wants you."

"How do you know what the world wants?"

"Ah, well—perhaps I put myself into its person, and so give it out. Identify that one for me."

Gwen smiled. "You've totally bastardized that quote. It's 'Much Ado,' Benedick, Act 2, Scene 1. I won't give you the correct line."

Patrick dropped her at her door; Gwen managed to avoid being kissed again. Did not invite him in.

She was *very* confused.

He flew back the next day to New York.

CHAPTER 33

Late August

Jack and Melody would be married on Saturday; their wedding rehearsal was the Thursday before.

Had this not been her son's wedding, Madeleine Hardie would have grudged, bitterly, the time taken from fine-tuning the benefit performances and set-up. As it was, she chafed only a little, inside, and showed a serene and happy face to the rest of the wedding party.

Acting was a useful skill in the real world, too, sometimes.

Madeleine glanced at her daughter; fresh and pretty in a crisp cotton frock, white striped with turquoise and violet (one of the first three dresses she'd bought at Melody's shop), Gwen looked sober and decorous; very appropriate.

Her son looked, as grooms often do, nervous and unsettled. Some looked downright scared; Madeleine was glad Jack didn't.

Madeleine was escorted down St. Aidan's long aisle by Jonas Gray, 16 and Jason Gray's eldest. Ann Gray followed on the arm of Richard Prentice, Joanna's husband. They took their seats, left and right, respectively.

Jack Hardie, Seth Greenlaw, Jason Gray and Ken Pelletier took their stance at right before the altar steps.

Billie Billings played Pachelbel's Canon in D, and Susie Pashley, first bridesmaid down the aisle, tripped on a crease in the carpet.

Gwen Hardie Sinclair followed Susie, without incident, nor did Joanna Prentice, née Gray, suffer or occasion any mishaps.

The ladies all in place at left, the organ lurched into Wagner and 'Lohengrin.' Gwen, whom her father had escorted to these strains, made a mental note that, were she ever to marry again, she'd find a less—*bombastic*—piece of music. Not, she thought, that it was likely she'd have occasion. Given all the circumstances, she didn't see it happening for her.

Michelle Gray, Jason's six-year-old daughter, forgot all her instruction, flinging handfuls of pink and white rose petals in crushed clumps. Corrected, she burst into tears, upended her basket, dumping remaining petals in a heap, and sat down in the aisle, wailing.

Rachel Gray, her mother, picked Michelle up and removed her from the proceedings, murmuring "I am *so* sorry," to her father- and sister-in-law as she passed.

Billie Billings struck up 'Lohengrin' again, and Melody, holding her father's arm, proceeded down the aisle. Madeleine noted, with approval, that Melody walked stately, in time with the music. And had got Jake Gray to do the same.

No mishaps attended the motions of rehearsing the ceremony—which was not itself rehearsed at all. Nor should it be, in Madeleine's opinion, but still. 'Rehearsal' meant what it meant.

Seth Greenlaw produced rings as prompted.

Father Trundy, "Then I will say, 'you may kiss the bride,'" and Jack, knowing it wasn't proper, kissed Melody soundly, producing a few chuckles.

Melody took his arm, smiling up at him, and they marched up the aisle to well-worn Mendelssohn.

Seth and Joanna followed. Jason took such long strides

Gwen had to scurry to keep up, stumbled, and almost lost her balance. Ken and Susie kept pace together far better, and Susie knew just where that carpet crease was, now.

There were no additional missteps.

* * *

The Gray's dining table could not seat a wedding party of fourteen, and the rehearsal dinner was held at the Main Street Tavern. Tables had been pushed together to accommodate them.

Melody and Jack were at the jukebox, ostensibly picking out songs, but in fact discussing a much more important matter.

"I didn't, and still don't mind, Melody. If it kept her off your back a little."

"Well, I *do* mind. You really should have shown me sooner, we can't actually *change* it now. But I don't want my wedding pictures showing you looking less than your best—and those cravats *have got to go*. Not one of you but will look—I don't care what Mom thinks, or what she says after. You take those off, all of you, before you come in on Saturday. And open a collar button or three

"I mean it. I'll peek, or have Joanna do it, and if you're wearing those things, I won't come down the aisle. Well," softening, "I will, of course I will. But I'll give you a piece of my mind later."

He'd meant to laugh with her over those collars, those cravats, when he showed her the picture Ann had taken at the last fitting. Instead, she'd been horrified. Jack, and all his attendants, had well-muscled necks, and the billowy cravats, with high-buttoning collars, would be—unflattering was too mild a word for it.

"If you mean it, Melody, we will. And thank you, darling. Don't ever think I don't know how lucky I am. You're the best thing that ever happened to me." He kissed her, in front of anyone who cared to look.

There were more women than men at the table; Melody was seated between her father and her future mother-in-law.

Madeleine murmured, "Don't worry too much, dear. There's a saying in the theatre—'bad dress rehearsal, good show.'" Properly, the word "rehearsal" wasn't said, wasn't necessary, but Madeleine wanted to be sure the meaning was clear, for non-theatre-person Melody.

"Thank you—I hope it holds true for us, Mother Madeleine."

"I think just "Madeleine" is fine, Melody, dear. You might consider cutting the flower girl—it's just a bit part, really. And, frankly, she looked flushed to me—make sure she isn't coming down with something."

Including Michelle had been Ann's idea, not Melody's. At this last minute, Melody was feeling rebellious.

Rachel admitted several of Michelle's friends had late-summer colds.

After dinner, Melody informed her mother there would be no flower girl, and cut off protests.

"One more word—just *one*, Mom—and Jack and me will run off tomorrow. I swear we will."

And Ann Gray, scowling, backed down.

* * *

Gwen sat in her kitchen, drinking coffee, thinking of Seth. She'd come to terms—to peace, almost, with being in love with him. It was only addition, not change, to what she'd always felt. She wasn't even sorry. She wouldn't embarrass him, she'd never ask for more than he gave her already.

But Seth deserved to be loved as much as was possible— even if he never knew. And who knew better than she how worth loving he was?

Gwen knew it would be anything but easy—she'd never been good at hiding her feelings. Hadn't much practice trying, even. She had to regard this as a secret—Seth's secret—and keep it for him. It *was* his, really. And it wouldn't be the first she'd kept. She knew a few—a very few—things he'd never told her. And she'd never told him she knew.

She should build, in her mind, in her heart, a box to keep them in.

What Gwen did do was put her wedding band in the box Seth and Ben had made for her.

* * *

Saturday dawned fair, with a gentle breeze. St. Aidan's, that afternoon, filled with ceremonial participants, invited guests, curious locals, and a few who found the Mass time convenient.

No hitches in the processional, this time around. But Melody, on her father's arm, glanced sidelong at her mother, who was slightly purple as she beheld the unclad necks of her almost-son-in-law and the men standing with him.

Melody bit her lips to keep a straight face. To keep from laughing out loud. Dear, darling Jack.

She was pleased with her dress. Her mother had wanted Melody to wear the gown she had worn, that Ann's own mother had worn. That Ann had wanted to see Joanna wear. It might have been doable for Joanna who, like their mother, was thin. There wasn't fabric enough in the seams to accommodate Melody's curves.

So Melody had picked her own gown, and on that score had refused to budge. Very simple, heavy white silk, strapless; tiny pearls embroidered in clusters here and there. Organza veil, under a pearl circlet, borrowed from Madeleine.

Her bridesmaids were *very* pretty in high-waisted pale

peach silk chiffon, also strapless. Hair held back with combs decorated with peach chiffon flowers. You had to scrutinize Joanna closely to tell she was pregnant; the color and cut of the dresses flattered all three ladies.

"Dearly beloved," began Father Trundy, and the old words, time-honored rite, took the congregation.

"Ernest John, wilt thou have this woman to thy wedded wife, to live together after God's ordinance in the holy estate of Matrimony? Wilt thou love her, comfort her, honour, and keep her in sickness and in health; and, forsaking all others, keep thee only unto her, so long as ye both shall live?"

"I will!" Jack's emphatic assent.

Melody, in turn, said her own "I will," fervently.

Melody and Jack had wanted Madeleine to read from Paul's Epistle to the Ephesians; Ann Gray had been most uncomfortable with this, for reasons she could not articulate.

They'd compromised—Gwen, who read well, took the passage, concluding, "Nevertheless let every one of you in particular so love his wife even as himself; and the wife see that she reverence her husband. The Word of the Lord."

The congregation responded, "Thanks be to God," as she left the lectern and rejoined her fellow attendants.

Father Trundy read from the Gospel of John, and began the communion service.

Finally, Jack and Melody made their vows, were joined, blessed, and Jack was permitted to kiss his bride—his wife, now. Thanks be to God, indeed.

To Mendelssohn's 'Wedding March,' they walked smartly and in step, attendants following, and parents after them, to form the receiving line or not, as appropriate.

Gwen, as bridesmaid, wasn't truly necessary, but Jack and Melody had both felt she should be with them—she was family. Jack had rather wished to have Seth in line, as well, but adding groom's attendants was so non-traditional he hadn't pressed the point. Jason wasn't included, either.

Jack's attendants, therefore, mingled with guests out front; Seth mostly talked with Ben, who had managed to fly up that morning for the ceremony, but must turn around and head back to Richmond, and would miss—and be missed at—the reception.

By the time the last congregant had run the receiving gauntlet, right hands were near-numbed from handshake after handshake.

Time for more pictures.

* * *

The reception was held at the Haven Point Inn. Gwen had offered the Hardie house, but this, like so many suggestions not hers, had not been well-received by Ann Gray.

That morning, early, Gwen had instructed—and supervised—the Inn's kitchen staff in the preparation of strawberry shortbread tarts. Melody had asked her, as a favor— she adored those tarts, and they were Jack's favorite.

Gwen made them rarely, as they required a lot of work, took forever, and seemed so simple when presented that the work and time were discounted. To look right—and to make sure the texture was what it should be—strawberries must be fine-diced, precisely, by hand. No corner-cutting. *None*.

Prep cooks groaned. But diced, finely, precisely.

Patrick had called her, yesterday; Gwen had said she was too busy to talk. He was here, though, and talk with him she must, at some point. Here was safest.

Food was buffet-fashion only; no wait staff, no composed plates—this last was Gwen's thought. Even the wedding party would help themselves. There was an open bar, featuring wine, beer, cider; only champagne, for toasts, would be offered at table.

Very usual, very proper—round tables with place cards, a raised platform with a long table for the couple, principal attendants, and parents. Dance floor at one end, adjacent to French doors leading out to the patio and grounds.

Haven Point Inn had hosted hundreds of wedding receptions; it was a significant revenue stream.

A pretty setting—the old, old converted mansion, just out of town, set high. Ocean views, prettily landscaped grounds. At sunset, there would be more pictures with the photographer from Brewer.

Melody and Jack would spend their wedding night at the Inn; that had been Madeleine's idea.

They'd hired a good disc jockey. Trevor Joyce was a local boy, originally, but had moved to Bangor, and was making a name for himself. It was a lucky thing he'd been able to accommodate the date change.

Everyone found their seats, got food, what drinks they wanted.

Gwen, Susie Pashley, Jason and Rachel Gray, Ken and Althea made up one table near the platform which held the center-of-attention folk.

At the next were Julia and Peter Lord, Liz, Patrick Riordan, Mayor Haskell and his wife, Linda.

Gwen thought they should have done better on the food. Both as to choices and preparation. They'd overcooked the chicken *and* the shrimp. And the white sauce on the chicken—she wasn't sure what it was supposed to be—had separated in the steam tray.

No-one but she seemed to notice—people were eating with gusto.

She wasn't hungry, anyway.

Jack and she had sat up, a while, last night. Both he and Melody were to sleep at their family homes; he mustn't see his bride the night before their wedding.

He'd had his bachelor party, such as it was. They weren't a rowdy bunch, Jack's internal clock was set for earlier hours than most, and they'd broken up before midnight.

Gwen wasn't sleeping well, these days, and was still up when Jack came in; they'd talked a while, played a few games of cribbage. And grieved, together, that their father would not see his son married.

Jack thanked everyone for coming, Melody added her own thanks. Jake Gray toasted them, then Madeleine, then Seth. Very brief, all.

Well done, thought Gwen. And Seth looked so good. Good enough to eat. *Shut up, SHUT UP!* she told that voice. She must not let her thoughts go down that road.

What she should do was find a minute to speak with Patrick, and a place to do so.

Dancing—Jack and Melody, of course, and didn't they look like the definition of happiness.

Melody and her father, Jack and his mother. The general invitation to the floor.

Gwen slipped out of the banquet room; there were armchairs and small tables in the anteroom. That would do, she thought, and turned back to find Patrick.

She hadn't far to look—he'd followed her.

"Just the person I was looking for. Can we talk a minute?"

"An hour, a lifetime, if you wish it."

"You are so *florid*, Patrick. No-one could talk a whole lifetime."

"May I hope you've reconsidered New York?"

"No. That's just it, Patrick. I hope I haven't led you on. But—just—stop. I won't come to New York. That just isn't happening."

He looked at her. "Are we, Gwen? Is there any possibility? I'd fall madly—and I do mean madly—in love with you if you gave me a milligram of encouragement."

"I don't think so. No. I like you a lot, Patrick, you're about as much fun as anyone I know. And if I said I wasn't attracted to you, I'd be lying. But I'm not in love with you, and I'm not going to be. I'm sorry, but there it is."

"Can you be so sure, Sleeping Beauty? Ah, wake up, Gwen. You're in the wrong fairytale. Come to New York with me, and be Cinderella."

What had he said? Gwen looked at him, smiling very strangely.

"Been there, done that, Patrick. Let me tell you a little about being Cinderella.

"Cinderella went to the ball. She wasn't really 'Cinderella,' she was Ella. She didn't sit in the cinders, didn't have a wicked stepmother and stepsisters. She had a mysterious mother who wasn't home very much, but her father was there, and her brothers, and she loved them and they loved her.

"She didn't need a fairy godmother, her father provided the gown, and the glass slippers, and he and her brothers kissed her goodbye.

"So, off she went. And the castle was very glittery, and the prince very handsome; he asked her to be his princess, and of course she said yes.

"And she had all new duties. Princess ones. She was good at some of them, even loved a few. But the prince didn't have much time for her—he had his own duties to attend to. And the castle was full of people she didn't know. They all called her 'Princess,' but that wasn't *who* she was, only *what* she was— 'Princess' could be anyone.

"And she began to miss her home in the country, very badly. And her father, and her brothers. Who knew her, and for whom she was just 'Ella.'

"One last thing, Patrick—glass slippers hurt like the dickens, after you've worn them a while."

"That is *lovely*, Gwen. You are the most adorable—I won't

say 'princess.' Is this your final word? Must it be?

"Is it that you've someone else in mind? That," Patrick checked himself—he'd been about to say 'hayseed'—"horse-training friend of yours, perhaps?"

"Patrick, this isn't about anyone but me. I don't need another ball. I don't want another fairytale. And, forgive me, I don't think you really do, either. You've got castles *way* up in the air, and they've no foundation.

"Maybe it's you who needs to wake up, Patrick. I wish you every happiness, truly, but you won't find it with me."

He argued, but Gwen had said what she had to say, and, eventually, left Patrick to argue with himself. She returned to the ballroom.

Seth, properly, danced with Joanna Prentice first. Would have liked to dance with Gwen, next, but didn't see her, and sat it out.

Noted her return; that Riordan guy shortly after. Looking put out. *Fine by me.* Gwen was inspecting the food; Riordan made straight for the bar.

Seth headed toward the food tables, and Gwen. Liz Lord interrupted progress.

"Seth, it's been ages since I rode, and with Dad's stables filling up, I've been thinking I'd like to—could you squeeze in a few lessons, one-on-one?

"No, no, don't worry," at his narrowed gaze, "I promised my father—he made me—you're *strictly* off-limits. Unless my intentions are honorable, and honestly, can you see *that?*"

That was so outlandish a notion Seth laughed out loud; Liz laughed with him.

People looked at them. Including Gwen.

Seth and Liz looked so good together. Tall, strong, and—beautiful. *They*, really, looked a little like brother and sister, dark hair, blue eyes. A fine-looking couple.

Gwen was jealous—not that way, she knew Seth wasn't

looking for a Liz Lord. But jealous of Liz's beauty, the picture she made with him.

Look at him—Melody had told her about the cravats—his neck so strong. Her fingers wanted to trace the line of it, stroke his beard, play in his hair. Best to keep her awareness on her fingers, not the rest of her.

Liz was right—he was just so—*desirable*.

He made her mouth water. Both of them. She was wet.

Seth looked at her; she turned away. Blushing to her hair-roots. If she couldn't keep her feelings to herself . . . something earth-shattering would happen.

She looked, Seth thought, like the kid who didn't get invited to a birthday party. Not quite. *Like the only girl who didn't get a valentine.* Looking at him, looking like that.

Sweet Jesus. Was this what she'd been struggling with? How had he missed it?

"Excuse me." He left Liz open-mouthed, mid-word. Rudeness wasn't like Seth; curious, she watched.

Gwen, abstractedly, took a bite of strawberry shortbread, and left the bitten remains on the tablecloth. There was a glass of wine in her hand—she didn't know how it had got there. She sipped.

A hand on her arm—a hand she'd know the feel of, anywhere, blindfold.

"Dance with me." When had she taken off that damn' ring? He'd swear she'd been wearing it two days ago, but her fingers were naked and beautiful.

"Okay—I mean, thank you, of course I will." He was looking at her oddly—a smile she'd never seen.

He took her hand, led her to the floor. The song was easy, slow.

Make small talk. *Be normal.* Whatever *that* meant.

"They look so happy, don't they?"

"They do. Come with me to your Mom's benefit, next

Saturday?"

Normal would be to say of course she'd be there, he could drive her if he wanted. But—something made her wait, think; she tripped over her own feet. Blushing harder,

"You mean—like—a *date?*"

"A date." She was *flustered.* It was so cute. Also exciting. His heart beat faster.

"Sure—I mean, yes. Thank you." Her mind raced and spun. Asking her on a *date???* That meant—Seth would cut off his arm before he'd trifle with her, and didn't *that* have to mean—

"How long have you felt this way?" Her voice a whisper.

She was so damn' *quick.* Softly, "Long enough." Look how she looked at him. Blushing, starry-eyed, wondering. *Softened.*

Gwen could hardly believe the way he looked at her. *Hungry.* She was tense and weak-kneed at the same time. Quivering, inside and out, *yearning.*

"Meet me outside, five minutes."

"Okay, but why?"

The look he gave her said *do-what-I-tell-you.* "Yes." Suddenly she felt a little shy of him. A little scared, even—not of him, not exactly.

Gwen waited, trying to count minutes. Kept losing her count. Guessed, and left the ballroom. He'd gone that way, not out the French doors. Side exit, past the restrooms. She slipped out into dark.

His hands caught hers before her eyes adjusted. Pulled her between two potted, cone-shaped conifers—out of view of windows. In moonlight.

He'd wanted this forever. Seth put both his hands into her hair, knocking the combs holding it to the ground. Gripped handfuls of red silk. Combed his fingers through, scalp to ends. Soft, satin-smooth.

The pull of his hands turned her face up to his; Gwen stroked his cheek. He kissed her palm, the inside of her wrist;

felt her pulse leap and race against his lips. His heart hammered. He took her face in his hands, her cheeks fiery with blood-heat. Kissed her, very gently.

Her lips returned pressure, gentle as his. *Sweet, so sweet.* They separated, a little; he looked into her magic eyes. Stars and more stars, love and more love in them. All for him. He took her in his arms, hands crushing the fragile fabric of her dress, feeling the soft skin of her naked shoulders. So slight in his hands, but he knew her strength. Kissed her again. Her mouth opened on a sigh, breathing it into him, drawing it back. A moist little sound in her throat as his tongue found hers—and she answered him.

His arms tightened round her, they pressed close. Her heart beat against his, hummingbird wings. He felt her hands in his hair. Her tongue whispered wordless secrets. Kissing him with her whole sweet soul. Oh, she was water, and he bone dry so long. He drank.

"All right, break it up, kids." Jack's voice.

Startled, Seth and Gwen broke their embrace, and looked at him.

Later, Jack would tell Melody, "They looked at me like they weren't sure *what* I was, let alone *who.*"

His sister's face was red as her hair, which was all mussed. Seth looked downright *dangerous.*

"Melody's tired, she's going to throw her bouquet and then I'm taking her upstairs. She wants you guys there."

Gwen bent, picked up her hair combs. They'd stepped on one; it was cracked through.

"Give me a few minutes—I'll make myself—as presentable as possible." Her voice shook.

As she passed Seth, her fingers couldn't keep from brushing his. His curled round and gripped. She stopped, their eyes met. Held.

"Gwen."

"I'm going." Seth, slowly, let go her hand, and she went.

"Where do you get off calling me 'kid?'" His voice wasn't steady, either.

Jack grinned at him. "I'm 28, you're not, I'm a married man, you're not—I outrank you. For once.

"You courting my sister, now?"

"Something like that. You mind?"

"Hell, no, Seth. About damn' time you staked that claim."

"You knew?"

Jack nodded. "Since Christmas. You, that is. Her—she was close, then, but this whole summer she's—if I didn't love you guys, it'd have been funny, the two of you not seeing each other clear.

"Glad you're sorting it out. I'm guessing I won't be ahead on the 'married' part much longer than the age thing."

Seth would be 28 in a little over two months.

* * *

Gwen, thankful she'd used the side door, ducked into the ladies' room.

Looked at the mirror. Liz hadn't exaggerated the smudge-proof qualities of her cosmetics. Her lips were swollen, but no smears whatever.

Her dress was creased, crumpled, her hair was a mess. Gwen did her best to smooth the hair, comb it out with her fingers. There was a real comb in her purse, but she'd left it on the table she'd sat at.

Gwen looked at her hair combs. Carefully drew back hair with the intact one, the two pieces of the other.

Best she could do.

* * *

Jack left Seth to collect himself, rejoined his bride. "Melody, honey. Could you try to aim for Gwen?"

Melody looked at him. "You mean to tell me—?"

He nodded. "You couldn't have slipped a *thought* between them. He was kissing her something *serious*."

Melody beamed. "Well, *there*. We're role models for romance. That is so cool."

"Isn't it? What does Althea call it—something extra you don't expect? *Lagniappe*, that's the word."

"Darling Melody. I didn't think I could *get* any happier."

"There's Gwen. Oh, my Lord, look at her. There'll be talk tomorrow, Jack. I'll try to see she gets the bouquet. I don't really suppose it matters, though."

He shook his head. "I don't, either. But it'd be nice. She did the best she could—you should have seen her a few minutes ago. And there's always talk. Haven Point, Melody."

Seth was back. Eyes like lasers on Jack's little sister. Jack was enjoying feeling the elder—which he was—toward both of them, for a change. Enjoying it *immensely*.

Single ladies gathered at the Inn's carved stair, Melody went up a few steps. Noted Gwen's position, turned, and hoped she aimed right.

Too right, and too enthusiastic. The bouquet, white lilies, hit Gwen square in the face; she had to pick it up off the floor. Involuntarily—no will needed, none possible—she looked for Seth. He was leaning against a column, watching her. Gwen dropped her eyes—his gaze made her shiver. She blushed.

Gwen handed the bouquet back to Melody, who hadn't had an extra made—she felt she should toss the one she'd carried, or it wouldn't 'take.'

Jack and Melody thanked their guests again, went upstairs to their bridal chamber.

No need to stay longer. Gwen retrieved her purse, went out to the parking lot. If she wasn't okay to drive, it wasn't alcohol.

She hadn't had two full glasses of wine. There'd been a much headier draught, though, and she'd drunk deep. Her head spun, still.

"Need a lift home?" He'd followed her, and wasted no time doing it, she thought.

"I think maybe I do." Her voice was shaky still—or again.

"I'll drive you back in the morning, you can pick your car up."

"Okay." She wasn't sure there was *any* suggestion of his she'd say different to, just now.

Seth drove, one hand on the wheel; the other laced fingers with hers. They didn't speak for a while.

"You're playing at that benefit, right? You and Jack and Ken?"

"Yeah. Your Mom seems to think we're pretty good. Got us closing, anyway."

"So . . . I'm dating the lead singer-guitarist in a band? That's *way* glamorous."

He laughed. "Don't make too much of it. One-time thing."

"It *is* glamorous—for Haven Point."

Their home.

Seth pulled into her driveway.

"Do you—want to come in? For . . . anything?"

"You know I do. But it's not a good idea."

"Why ever not?"

"You're a nice girl, Gwen. A decent man takes a nice girl out, 'fore he tears her clothes off."

And he needed to be able to focus on his music. Until the benefit. That was going to be hard enough, as it was.

They kissed good-night, not going as far as they had earlier, but not chastely, either.

"See you in the morning?"

"Count on it."

CHAPTER 34

Late to End-August

Gwen closed the door behind her, turned and watched the sliver of fender. It was a minute, maybe two, before Seth reversed, and drove away.

She was dazed, shivery. Ached, pleasurably, in places she hadn't known were even *there.* Her body *alive* with longing.

She loved him, and there he was, waiting for her.

If she couldn't hide her feelings, she remembered thinking, something earth-shattering would happen. And so it had.

She could conjure sense-memory of the shape, the pressure, of palms, each finger. Could feel his hands in her hair, through her dress, on her skin.

He kissed her as if he knew *everything* about her body. Like he could kiss the soul out of her. She'd almost come, just kissing him. Never, never had she felt anything like this.

More. She needed *more.*

Gwen had read romances, quite a few of them. Jane Austen, mostly.

Jane Austen did not write of anything remotely like what she was feeling now.

Patrick had been right—she'd been sleep-walking, part of her, anyway—through her life.

Wide-awake—awakened—now.

It was marvelous. It was terrifying.

She'd crossed some Rubicon, into an unfamiliar landscape. There was no road back.

If you went exploring strange places, best you didn't go alone. And if what you needed was someone to have your back, no-one better than Seth Greenlaw.

Suddenly, Gwen knew the scariness would be fine, maybe even fun.

Seth. Brave new world, indeed, that hath such people in 't.

* * *

Seth, for his part, took a long, very cold shower, and slept much better than he'd any right to, the way he looked at it.

Early, he drove next door; Gwen's smile, soft, eager, turned his heart over. They kissed. At last, they'd come right. This, he thought, was going to be one tough week.

As they drove to the Inn, to retrieve Gwen's car,

"Will you come by tonight, when you leave Ken's? We need to talk—there are so many blanks I need filled in."

"Do we? We're on the same page, now, does before matter so much?" He knew her answer, though.

"I need to know—at least—more than I do. Like—why you never told me. For one thing. Don't answer now, this isn't the time, but I want to—need to—understand."

"Okay, we'll talk. Probably not tonight, gonna be a long session, I expect."

He pulled into the Haven Point Inn driveway.

"Can I take you to breakfast?" The Inn's dining room opened at 6:00 a.m.

Gwen was startled. "If you're hungry, come back to the house and I'll cook. Wait a minute—I never *did* teach you how to make breakfast. My New Year's resolution."

"Got four months and a bit, think you can do it in that

time?" He grinned at her.

"You just bet I can. We'll start when you say."

Easy again. Even with—with—*this* looming hugely, they were themselves, together. *Thank God,* as heartfelt a prayer as Gwen had ever offered up.

"Soon. And I'd like to take you to breakfast."

"If you insist. Is this an official date?"

"I'd say so. Magic number's supposed to be three, right?"

"Depends on who you ask," softly, "it can be as many or few as you like."

He heard '*I'm yours*' and couldn't keep from kissing her. Her hair was braided, he couldn't mess it up much.

She was still bright pink as they ordered breakfast.

It was going to take a hell of an effort to keep his mind on his work.

Good thing there wasn't much to do, Sundays.

* * *

Seth finished evening stables, and drove Caleb Pelletier—who still biked over—home. Caleb was saving for a car. Part of his agreement with his father was that he'd live at home until he graduated—Ken, still unsettled by his elder son's sudden rebellion, did not quite trust him to complete his degree program.

Caleb didn't have to work Sundays after church, but usually he did. He was learning, and he loved it. Seth hoped he would put in the same effort on his college work this fall. Doubted it—not quite as much, anyway.

Ken Pelletier's neat little house, just outside of town, was full of his sons, Althea and Nerise Jones, Seth, and Jack Hardie—the last looking the very image of satisfaction.

Althea had cooked—chili *with* beans, cornbread—with plenty of sugar, her signature coleslaw. Seth liked the coleslaw, and everything was real good. Just not as good as Gwen's.

They all ate, crowded around the table, and the younger generation was sent to do course work and homework. The spare bedroom had been set up for Nerise, when she and Althea overnighted.

Ken and Althea looked like they had a happy secret of their own.

"Had me some real fine news at church, today." Father Peter McCaughey had told him his first marriage was invalid in the Church's eyes.

"And this lovely lady's allowed as how she'll marry me." Next spring, before the summer season. How they'd manage a honeymoon was a question, but they'd figure it out.

Seth and Jack offered Ken sincere congratulations, wished Althea happiness.

Althea, who'd taken note, yesterday, of Gwen's dishevelment when Melody Hardie tossed her bouquet, looked closely at Seth.

"'Pears to me somebody else got an early birthday present. Want to let us in on it, Seth?"

"Birthday and Christmas, too." He felt shy of speaking Gwen's name, like it was his secret.

Jack helped him out. "Seth and Gwen are courting. Finally, and I couldn't be any happier."

"Been wondering 'bout you and her," said Ken.

Jesus. Had he fooled *anyone* but Gwen?

"You're going to kill me." He'd changed his mind about what song he wanted. Again. Told them which one.

Loud "No!" in chorus from Ken and Jack.

"It's not new, we've done it. Just—can we try it a couple of times? Three? Ten minutes. You aren't comfortable we can get it right in time, I'll shut up."

Seth's indecision—so unlike him—notwithstanding, they'd spent much more time working out arrangements and learning each of the new numbers Ken and Jack wanted than they had on his.

Ten minutes wasn't too much to ask.

The song came easily, but neither Ken nor Jack thought the new pick as good a number as Seth's prior choice. Nor did Althea, who was a frequent audience at their sessions.

Ken was the only one to say so.

"Better strategy. Get people dancing, maybe. Can't dance to yours, or Jack's. Or the one I had before."

Which might get people wanting the fourth number.

Althea liked that song better than most they played. It was upbeat, but with an almost blues-y swing under it. She'd caught herself singing it, and Seth—!—had invited her to sing along, once –

"Just don't drown me out." But he'd smiled, saying it. And after that, they'd do an extra run-through for her to join in.

Her own numbers needed the Tavern's karaoke machine; the instrumentation wasn't suitable for the boys, and they hadn't had time to work up both her and their own new arrangements.

Haven Point might be world enough, but there was never enough time.

Until winter. When you had to make yourself get out of the house, or risk stir-crazy.

* * *

Patrick had flown back to New York that morning, in a bit of a temper. No-one likes rejection, and why should he be different?

Even if she were probably right. He had to concede it—he believed, now, that Gwen knew her mind, knew what she wanted. It was not Patrick.

Nor had he, truly, envisioned Gwen as wedded so firmly, so

faithfully, to a small town and its life. She'd graced Boston, she'd been better known than she realized.

It made no sense to Patrick, but Gwen was simply less ambitious than he'd assumed. A talent like that, buried in a tiny town, mostly employed in the cooking of family fare. Content to be so. More or less—those condiments of hers were delicious, but that was frivolous stuff.

Perhaps frivolous was the way Gwen now looked upon her exquisite, expensive little Farmhouse Table plates. Hadn't Elizabeth said Gwen considered that food 'irrelevant?'

He might have brought a clearer reason to bear on this entire infatuation.

Elizabeth had made very sure to tell him everything he'd missed, and she'd seen, after he'd made an early exit from the wedding reception. He rather thought she'd enjoyed doing so.

Look it in the face. The woman who preferred a country hayseed to himself wasn't a princess to be put in a castle.

Maybe the fantasy itself *was* wrong. Gwen's charming, funny, turning of 'Cinderella' on its head had rung with truth.

Patrick turned to the piles of still-unsorted notebooks filled with Mark Sinclair's writing. It did not occur to him to throw in the towel in a snit—he'd spoken the truth when he'd told Gwen he felt invested.

He sorted through several. Picked up one, which had a title. None of the others he'd seen had. Frowning, he opened it, read a couple of paragraphs. Patrick flipped through the pages, slowly.

Well, I am damned.

He must see if there were other notebooks requiring special handling.

* * *

Gwen sipped her vanilla malted. She hadn't seen Seth in

almost two days, and was having trouble eating; this was at least a way to get some calories into her. She didn't want to lose weight, she needed what she had, or she'd get weak.

He called, of course, but she wanted his presence. His embrace, his kiss. His vitality, and his strength.

That, if she went way back, had been key. Seth was—more *alive* than other people. Even a very little girl could feel that.

She'd heard it in church—St. Aidan's had no Sunday School, and small children attended Mass with their parents—Jesus said, "I am come that they might have life, and that they might have it more abundantly."

He had wrought that in Seth Greenlaw.

She'd adored him. Absorbing that vitality, feeling it kindle her own to challenge his.

Even Seth couldn't keep up with her over the rocks. She'd loved—so much—the sure-footedness she'd lost. Sometimes, she could outrace him on horseback. Only because she was lighter. Or on a faster mount.

She'd taken any advantage she could get.

* * *

They'd wrapped it up early, tonight. Mrs. Hardie had warned them of the dangers of over-rehearsal, and they'd got all four numbers in good working order.

Before he left Ken's house, Seth called Gwen.

"Want to talk?"

"Yes, please. And to see you."

"On my way."

He'd thought, a lot, about what to say to her. This had been his own secret so long. Hard to think about speaking of it. Even to Gwen. But she had the right to ask, and to the truth.

She was standing in the kitchen doorway before he'd switched his engine off. Couldn't know what it meant to him, what it did to him, her eagerness.

Seth didn't hurry. Much.

He lifted her with one arm, pulling them both into the house, closing the door behind them. They kissed, feverishly.

She wanted to take him back to a sad past. He wanted to yank her into the happy present.

Her bedroom was maddeningly close. Hell, there was a perfectly good kitchen table right in front of them.

Thickly, "Can't talk here. Let's get a drink."

"Yes." Gwen couldn't think. Except how near her bed was, how fiercely she wanted to lie naked with Seth in it.

He took her hand, practically dragged her outside.

"Lock up." He held her from behind, hand on hers as she turned the key, kissing her hair. She leaned back against him, sighed.

"I love you," it came out of her on its own.

"Me you, too." The familiar response just about burst her heart into pieces.

* * *

They looked at each other, looked into glasses of red wine. Met each other's eyes again.

Gwen began, "It feels like I've been living a censored edition of my own life. That may not be fair, but it's how I feel. I want the uncensored version. How long have you been *not* telling me?"

"I told you, long enough."

"Not an answer, Seth. Two years? Five?" She thought. No, it had to be longer. Since before she married Mark. Which explained their encounter the night before her wedding. "How long, Seth?"

He couldn't look at her and tell her, it still seemed a little shameful. "Since before I turned 15. Late that summer." A memorable one, for that reason, and others.

"I was 13?"

"About to be. When you took that damn fence bareback."

"And you were so mad at me."

"I was. You were stupid, reckless. But you stopped laughing, and said you'd mind me. And you never wanted me to be hurt.

"Turned my heart over. I was still—hot—from being angry—I wanted to kiss you, bad." That hadn't been all he wanted, either. Paul Hardie would have shot him. And should.

"Why didn't you?" She made it sound so simple. It had been anything but.

"You were—a little girl, Gwen. I could wait 'til you were older. Thought so, anyway."

"I thought you stayed mad at me, a little, anyway. Until . . ." she stopped. Looked at him.

"You swiped my .22 and shot that vixen," he finished for her.

"Remember what you said?"

Not her exact words. "Something like I tried to do what you'd do. Because what you'd do would be the right thing."

"Nobody said *anything* like that to me. Ever. I was always getting in hot water. Teachers, my Dad. Guess I never did have much use for rules."

"You never had much use for *other* people's rules. But you always, *always* had your own. *I* got in hot water for not minding *your* rules, more than a few times, if you recall."

One way to look at it, he guessed. Generous way, but that was Gwen.

"It was like you thought I was some kind of hero. Made me want to be what you thought. Live in that world. With you."

Big picture stuff, she thought. And he was way out of focus.

"Seth. You don't—you really—look, let me introduce you to a friend of mine.

"He was kind of a loner, when he was a boy, but he let a

couple of neighbor kids tag along on his adventures, took charge of them, made sure they didn't get hurt. When his baby brother got old enough, he got to tag along, too.

"Then his father died—his mother had passed long before, and my friend had helped raise—mostly did raise—his brother. And this friend of mine put any ambitions he had, any hopes," her voice caught a little, "on the back burner, and worked himself half to death to make sure his brother got into college.

"That man is a hero, Seth. Anyone would say so. And I love him—I love you—with my whole entire heart."

He shook his head. "Anyone'd have done the same."

"No, a few—a very few—would. Heroes would. Most would not."

So, now we come to it. "And all these years, you never said a word. Why, why didn't you?"

"Meant to, when you turned 16. Your Dad would have let you date, then; I could've told you, and him.

"But *my* Dad died before that could happen. And then it couldn't."

"I don't see why."

"Don't you? Your Dad sure did."

"Daddy knew? You told him and not me?"

"I didn't tell. He—guessed, saw, I don't know. But—he talked about you. After he helped me keep Ben at home.

"What he wanted for you. Wasn't me. He wasn't—direct, but he made sure I knew."

"What was he thinking? He always liked you. Until he loved you."

"Didn't like the idea of you tied down, waiting. I didn't have money or—or *time* for a wife. Looked like I wouldn't a long time."

She was silent a while. Men and their chivalry. "I could have helped you. When it was bad. That's what a wife does."

"Wasn't your lookout. Couldn't put it on you."

"I wish you'd spoken, Seth. When I was 14, 15. I'd bet my life I'd have got round Daddy—he did think well of you. I'd have married you, after high school. Or waited. If that was what you wanted."

She hadn't known that was true until now. God, what a mess for him. For her, too—she just hadn't known it. *Men.* Keeping her from making *informed* choices. To protect her. She hadn't needed protection, she should have had the truth.

But they'd loved her. And they'd meant well. Mostly Daddy's doing—she understood Seth's obligation to him, how difficult it would have been to stand against his will. At least, after Hank Greenlaw's death.

Before that . . . Seth had been a young boy. She could wish he'd handled things differently, but you couldn't measure a boy's decision against a man's standard. He'd done the right thing, as he saw it at the time. As he always did.

His turn at silence. Then, "Mark Sinclair –"

Gwen put her hand on his. "Truth, Seth. If I'd been your girl, I wouldn't have looked at him the same way. I wouldn't have been available, so he wouldn't have been, to me."

That, too, was a new truth to face.

Oh, Jesus. "For real, Gwen?"

"For real, Seth."

He believed her. She was true as they came, no question.

Life, God, maybe, had mocked him. Didn't matter, now. Spilled milk, water under the bridge. They'd come together, at last.

"Don't be upset with your Dad. Think he was sorry, later. Gave me his blessing, too, for when you got over—everything."

"I wish he'd trusted me. And bet on you. I would have."

Gwen had what she needed. Time to let him off the hook.

"If I put money in the jukebox, will you dance with me?"

"That's a yes. Anytime."

* * *

Patrick Riordan, having informed his publisher he would be unavailable for several days, flew back to Haven Point for last rehearsals with Madeleine Hardie, and the benefit.

With two notebooks to deliver to Gwen.

Main Street Tavern opened at noon, seven days in the week. Mornings, this particular week, saw Madeleine supervising her performers, a few each day, making sure microphones worked, and how many of what sorts were needed.

Pianists needed vocal mics only, as did Althea Jones.

A stand-up vocal mic would do for Lindsay Haskell, the mayor's granddaughter.

Clip-on mics for herself and Patrick Riordan, for Matilda Small, and Artie Babbidge. Madeleine would not have needed one, herself, in a venue that size, if one could count on a silent audience. Which she knew she could not.

Five standing mics for Ken, Jack and Seth—two vocal, and one each for their instruments. A couple of wireless hand mics, in case.

Ruthie Wakelyn, who wrote a regular column for the weekly Haven Point Gazette and sold jams and pickles at the marketplace, had volunteered to assist Madeleine, take notes, coordinate, and had made herself indispensable.

She scurried after Madeleine, stenographer's book and pen in hand, extra pen and pencils stuck through her light brown bun. Which, by 11:30, would be a mess.

***

On Thursday, after leaving Madeleine and the Tavern, Patrick drove up Gray Way. He did not call first—Gwen might be unwilling to see him.

He was uncomfortable, himself, but this, he thought, was

an in-person matter.

Her Volvo was not in the driveway, nor the garage, which was open. Patrick debated leaving the notebooks in her mailbox, with a note to please call him.

Decided against it. She might not call, and he wanted a chance to explain. He'd try again, later. Before dinner, perhaps—Patrick was expected at the Lords' at 7:30 that evening.

Unfortunately, a call from his agent—post-production snarls in Los Angeles—held him hostage, and Patrick arrived at his hosts' home ten minutes late, without detouring.

Friday, fairly early, he tried again, and found Gwen at home.

"I know I am probably the last person you want to see, but—please let me have a moment. It concerns your husband's writing."

"Come in, then. Patrick, I apologize—I—you don't need to continue this, if you don't want to. It's good of you, but I do *not* want to impose."

He waved this away. "I'll see it through—as I told you, I feel involved."

"Thank you, so much, Patrick. Would you like coffee? Tea?"

"Coffee would be lovely."

Gwen poured two cups. "Milk, sugar?"

"Just milk, please."

She set a cup before him, and sat, herself. Waiting.

Patrick placed the two notebooks on the table between them.

"In categorizing your husband's notebooks, I came across these, which defy categorization. I confess, I looked at them rather more closely than the others, for that reason. And read enough to feel I should not have read in them at all. I've invaded your privacy, without meaning to, truly.

"You will not, I think, want what is in them made public. Read them or don't, put them in the fire, the decision is your own to make."

Gwen took the notebooks. Unlike the one she'd pulled out for Patrick at the start of this, they were labeled. 'Gwen,' 'Homes and Homings,' in Mark's neat script.

"Thank you, Patrick. It's—very good—very thoughtful, of you, and I do appreciate it. I'll look at them."

She didn't want to. She had other things—happier, *exciting* things—to think about.

"These are the only two that—?"

"They are. I looked quickly through them all. There are no other such."

"Thank you again."

They fell silent, sipped coffee. Uneasily.

Patrick, unable to stop himself, burst out, "You are a most singular person, Gwendolen Sinclair. A Michelin chef turns her back on her career for a life of barefoot-pregnant-and-in-the-kitchen." *Why, why had he had to say it?*

Gwen burst out laughing. "See, that's just my point. You don't *get* it—or me. I *love* going barefoot, I'm in my kitchen most of the day barefoot—it's one of my favorite things. And I *want* children.

"For what it's worth, that star was Gail Winthrop's, and the restaurant's. The most you can say for me is I didn't lose it for her."

"My apologies. I—truly—should not have spoken, I knew it as I heard the words. And on that note, I will leave you."

She saw him out, thanking him again. A *decent* man, he was, not to dump the notebooks back on her.

Looked at Mark's notebooks. Picked up 'Gwen.' Read two sentences, and closed it.

Gwen took the notebooks to the library, set them on the long table there.

She'd leave them sit a while.

CHAPTER 35

End of August

Gwen spent the rest of her morning checking refrigerator and freezer and pantry, making a shopping list. Two ducks went from freezer to fridge, to thaw. Several ribeye steaks, as well.

She was low on all kinds of produce—except tomatoes, which she had aplenty. Some second-crop strawberries still ripening, too.

Gwen drove to town, picked up vegetables at the marketplace—fresh porcini, first of the season, yay.

Her mother had always been hungry after performing, and had said musicals made her hungrier than straight comedy or drama. Singing, Mom said, took it out of you.

Breakfast Sunday, drinks Tuesday. Tomorrow night would make three. Food would perhaps not be the first thing on Seth's mind, after, she smiled to herself.

But it might be the second. And she would answer that hunger, as well as the other.

Anything he wanted.

Saturday morning, Gwen rose early. She prepped and cooked duck-and-mushroom stew; pie crust dough, which she wrapped in plastic and set in the fridge. Parboiled marketplace Katahdin potatoes for frying, in case Seth wanted steak.

Lemon-shortbread tart shells with dried wild blueberries worked in. Lemon curd to fill them.

Gwen picked fresh strawberries to go with.

All done, and the morning gone, Gwen took herself back to bed. It took a bit of unwinding, but she slept.

Dreamed. Seth and she, at the cove up north, he fishing, she with a book. Daddy, reading to her. Mark, smiling regretful and distant. Prince Charming, love of her young girl's mind. That mind, not a girl's, now, blew him a final kiss. *God speed, Mark.*

Seth in the clearing, playing the intricate, lovely song he'd worked so long and hard to master, that sounded, when he played it, like a blessing on their shared world. In the dream he was a boy, but his guitar was the one she'd given him.

Oh, holy Moses! When Gwen awakened, it was after 3:00 p.m. Sleep-fogged, she made coffee, drank two hasty cups. Bathed, washing her hair, in the enormous old clawfoot tub Daddy had put in his—her, now—new bathroom. She could lie flat on the bottom with almost a foot to spare.

Clean, herself, she made up her bed with fresh sheets. Blushing with anticipation, like a high school girl.

Who should have been Seth Greenlaw's girl long ago.

* * *

The evening air was warmer than usual for late August, humid and electric. A storm was expected from seaward, tonight or tomorrow.

Seth was to pick her up at 6:30, food would be served at 7:00, and performances at 8:00-ish. Probably closer to 8:30.

Gwen was ready by 6:15, dressed in her green silk jersey.

She'd never worn it without Seth saying he liked it on her. It was the only piece of clothing she'd ever known him to mention.

Green silk heels, with insoles in. Hair loose, no makeup.

She heard Seth's pickup at 6:23, grabbed her purse, opened the door.

He got out, came to her. Kissed, held her lightly, briefly. Her inside went all fluttery.

"Can we take your car?" Seth had realized his pickup had insufficient space for her, himself, and his guitar. Which normally he buckled into the passenger seat.

She locked the house, handed him her key-ring, car key foremost. Seth took it, and her hand.

"You look real good. Like that dress." Seth touched the top button, gently. One reason he liked it, those buttons, what they made him think. He'd undo them one-by-one, later.

Take what was his.

Gwen was handed into her own passenger seat; Seth carefully buckled the Martin case into the back seat, both seatbelts—which provided protection more to her car windows than the guitar itself; that case could withstand almost anything.

The engine's ignition jolted her heart into high gear. Top of the roller-coaster.

They drove, silent, for a bit.

"That writer guy –"

"Knows where he stands. And that it's not with me. What he wanted—it wasn't real. And even if it had been, he didn't have it to offer, and if he had I wouldn't have wanted it."

Not how he'd meant to do it, but, "You want real, Gwen, you could marry me. I do real."

No-one better. But—he hadn't even *looked* at her. "Seth

Greenlaw, is that supposed to be a proposal?"

Now he did glance at her. "Brace yourself." He braked hard, tires squealing.

Seth got out, slammed his door, opened hers. Reached, unsnapped her seatbelt, and pulled her out of the car.

Took her hands, dropped to one knee.

"Gwen. I love you. I'll never love anyone else. Will you marry me."

"Yes, yes I will, yes. I'll be thrilled—and proud, Seth," her voice barely sounded like her own, she was *so* all shivery, "*so* thrilled, *so* proud, to be your wife."

He rose, fished in his shirt pocket. Brought out a ring—he'd come prepared.

"I'll hold you to that, crazy girl."

"Do." Her whole heart in her eyes, as she smiled.

Gwen took the ring, looked at it, turning it in her hand. So long Seth felt a little uneasy. "If you—Ben said it wasn't right, you'd want a diamond or something."

It was rose gold, the band small, overlapping maple leaves, very finely detailed. Two leaves branched out from either side, holding a little, bezel-set emerald.

"Ben's a fool, thou art another. I'll wear none but this." He wouldn't know the quote; it had come out on its own, and was perfect.

"It's the most beautiful ring I ever saw."

"Story is my great-granddad made it for my great-grandmother." Adam Greenlaw had been a goldsmith and jeweler. One of the more successful Greenlaws.

"Doesn't have his hallmark, can't be sure." The only stamp was a double "G" on the inside of the band. Which could have meant Gabrielle Greenlaw.

"Oh, I totally believe it. Look at the workmanship, the detail.

Greenlaw handiwork, if I ever saw it. If you were a jeweler, or Ben, you'd make something like this. It's just *gorgeous.*"

"Hope it fits. Thought it might be small enough."

She handed it back to him. "Let's find out." He slid it onto her finger; both felt the erotic shiver. It fit. Good thing—no resizing possible.

"Better get going. Don't want to be late."

"I got George and Amelia to hold us a two-top. You never know."

Now he kissed her, for real. Turning her knees to jelly, her inside to sweet ache.

* * *

The Tavern's parking lot had overflowed; Main Street was lined with cars. Seth pulled the Volvo into a spot a block and a half away, on a side street.

"Do you want me to take it off? Everyone will know, if I don't."

He shrugged, "They'll know, anyway. Like seeing it there. Leave it."

"I do, too."

He kissed her, gently.

* * *

The Tavern was crowded, noisy. Wait staff, extra hired for the occasion, bustled between bar and tables. One showed Gwen and Seth to the only empty table, right by the stage. Whipped off the "Reserved" marker.

Gwen asked for cabernet and a glass of water, Seth water and draft beer.

They waved at Jack and Melody, who had a booth to themselves, at Ken and Althea, who sat in another with their kids crowded in.

Patrick Riordan sat with Liz Lord; Gwen sent a smile their way, Seth nodded.

Their glasses arrived. Mostly, Seth and Gwen drank the water. Looked at each other. Love, desire filled the space between them, curled round them, joined them.

Those who'd been wedding guests the week before, and those who'd heard the gossip, nodded, knowingly.

There were those who said they'd predicted those two would get together long ago. Most of those predictions were current, just backdated.

Madeleine Hardie busied herself, checking with her sound technician, a volunteer from the theatre she'd subsumed into her new Center. Checking that all her performers were present. They were.

There was no suitable space for a greenroom, performers could tune up, sing scales, run lines, collect themselves, in the Tavern's storeroom.

The sound tech, Harry Waits, had some concern over the karaoke machine, but thought he would likely be able to fix it.

Madeleine hoped so. It would be a pity to lose Althea Jones' contribution. She said nothing to Althea, yet.

Food was served, simple, and, Gwen thought, better prepared than Jack and Melody's wedding dinner. Fried chicken (Amelia Betts had got pointers from Althea), mashed potatoes, salad dressed with Gwen's blueberry vinegar and sage-infused olive oil.

Sales to the Tavern and Downeast Bayou represented most of Gwen's business, now. What she had already on her shelves would keep them supplied for two or three years.

No performer ate much. Nor did Gwen. Noting how little Seth ate, was glad she had food waiting.

Homemade chocolate ice cream, with shortbread cookies.

Tasty enough, but Gwen put her spoon down after one bite, and Seth left his untouched.

Non-performers ate with relish; it was almost 8:30 by the time places were cleared.

Drink orders were filled, and Madeleine, more nervous than she'd been in decades, took the stage. Thanking everyone, performers and audience, for their participation.

A celebratory, rallying speech—Haven Point and what the center would do for their town.

And Lindsay Haskell, granddaughter to the mayor, started them off.

Madeleine had found her odd, and undirectable. The girl, scowling with focus, delivered her poem in rehearsal with forceful off-beat stresses which somehow managed not to be wholly unsuitable to the energy of the piece.

Not tonight. Lindsay looked fixed with terror, and Madeleine crossed her fingers, whispered a brief prayer.

The words came out—she did know that poem—in a light, taut voice, almost stressless. The story of Man on earth, a girl-child's rendering. The effect was eerie, unsettling. It made Madeleine's hair stand.

Lindsay finished, looking ready to cry. Madeleine started the applause, Gwen right behind her, and the audience, prompted, followed suit. Mayor Haskell's puzzled frown cleared; he clapped, beamed. His granddaughter smiled uncertainly, bobbed a curtsey, and fled the stage.

Artie Babbidge's comic monologue was next, to be followed by Taryn Sommers, Trinity Church's organist, who'd play and sing two songs. Both had been consistently acceptable, in rehearsal. She had to trust that.

Madeleine and Patrick Riordan retired to the storeroom to prepare. They would close the first act.

Artie's piece got laughter and loud clapping, Taryn Sommers' songs drew a respectable round of applause.

It wasn't going badly.

Madeleine was up. Patrick spoke his opening line, and they were off.

Off, indeed. They'd rehearsed, though nowhere near enough, Patrick was letter perfect, kept to the blocking she'd given him. But this had been a mistake.

She hoped the audience would not pick up too much. Gwen would know.

They were ill-matched. It wasn't the decade or so between their ages. It was the difference between a gifted and trained professional and a persuasive amateur. Her polish made him seem callow, his spontaneous energy—more than he'd shown in rehearsal—made her look over-studied.

As a whole, the audience seemed pleased, the applause was quite healthy.

"I'm sorry, Madeleine. A bad idea, and mine." Patrick had been almost as sensitive as she to the disconnect.

"I should have known better. It isn't your fault."

"You are too kind. I think I have made one single right move in this town, and no other. And that only on specific request."

Madeleine reassured him again, and excused herself—she had to make sure that karaoke machine was in order again.

It was not, and would not be tonight, Harry Waits informed her. It was probably toast.

Madeleine sighed. The second act would be longer than the first, even without Althea Jones. The hole would be artistic—set Madeleine aside, and Althea's was much the best voice on the programme.

She took Althea aside, gave her the bad news. Which Althea accepted with grace, commiserating with Madeleine, rather than fixing on her own disappointment.

"'Pears I'm out. Karaoke machine's busted," she told Ken. "Wish we'd worked something up, like we meant." They'd started, many times, but other interests took them over, and they'd always ended in bed.

"The number you and Seth got together on?"

Althea shook her head. A sad song, a small-town girl, hopes of a better, a city life, turned to ashes. *Not* a song a big-city transplant could sing to a group of small-town locals who'd welcomed her.

She was simply out of luck. "Happens. No use fretting." Althea wasn't going to let her disappointment spoil Ken's, or the kids', evening.

Ken excused himself, gathered Jack, whom Melody kissed soundly for luck, and Seth, who put his arm round Gwen, kissed her cheek. She rubbed her face in his beard.

Their instruments waited in the storeroom.

Madeleine went to Gwen's table; she hadn't yet spoken to her daughter.

"Are you well, dear? You're very flushed." Gwen's eyes, too, looked fever-bright.

"I'm fine, Mom." Gwen slipped her left hand under a fold of her dress. She did not want her mother knowing, yet. Whatever Seth said.

At her son's wedding, Madeleine had been too preoccupied to notice what others did. She'd been so much out of Haven Point she wasn't on the gossip party-line. And, even if she had been, no-one would gossip about her daughter to her.

Madeleine Hardie announced, sadly, that Althea Jones

would not perform.

The audience sat through Billie Billings' rendering of a Mozart sonata. Out of place for this crowd, but lovely playing of lovely music.

Madeleine took the stage again, to, she hoped, redeem herself in her own estimation.

* * *

Tuning up, Ken told them about the karaoke failure.

"Damn. That's not *right*," said Seth. Electronics. He didn't trust them.

"Didn't you ever put anything together, you and Althea?" asked Jack. Ken shook his head. No need to tell them why it hadn't worked out—that was private.

Seth didn't mention the number he and Althea had practiced. He knew she wouldn't sing that, here. And why. But —

"Get her in here, Ken. I know what we'll do."

* * *

Madeleine Hardie launched, in broad New York accent, into 'Adelaide's Lament' from 'Guys and Dolls,' and had her audience in stitches. She was once more in good standing with herself.

High-schooler Mathilda Small, exuding quiet confidence, was dead-on as the mother earnestly offering advice to a teenage daughter, earning the laughs and applause she received.

Jonathan Cohen's clever piano-and-comic numbers kept the laughter coming.

Seth felt as if he'd broke through to the other side of nervous. After all, this wasn't the high point of his evening. Things went well, he'd have some celebrating coming to him. They didn't, world's best consolation prize.

Ken introduced them. With their individual names—maybe they should come up with a name for them, as a group, but they hadn't. He was, by tacit consensus, the band-leader. The eldest, and instigator.

If Ken hadn't proposed Seth and he play together, they wouldn't be here. While he was booking Seth. For beating up Amos Boyd, for making nasty remarks about Gwen. If Amos Boyd hadn't mouthed off like that, would they be here now?

One row of dominoes after another, life was.

Jack, "This number's for Melody, my one-week bride. Who I love an ocean more every day."

Gwen turned to smile, big, at Melody, who was looking like she could just hug herself with happiness. Turned back to the men onstage. Seth looked like he belonged up there. Like a rock star, Gwen thought.

She wanted to hear them, but was impatient for the moment they could leave. The moments that would come after.

Jack's song, a big hit some years back, was happy, sweet, with an off-beat, quirky slant. Gwen knew it, loved it, and sang along. The audience clapped in time, by the end, and the applause was loud with enthusiasm.

Ken spoke again, "Just so all y'all know, Miss Althea Jones, the lovely lady who's brought down-home Louisiana cooking to downeast, has agreed she'll be my wife, and I'd like to sing a song for her," loud groans from the audience made him laugh.

"See we have a St. Stephen's contingent here. Was saying, I'd like to, but I can't. So Seth's gonna."

They held fire for the laughter, began as it died out. Slow, intricate instrumentation, simple lyric. Love, polished shiny, offered in gift.

A good song, words and music should speak for themselves. Seth didn't try to fancy up the vocal line—he never did.

Madeleine noted this with approval. Not a voice to write home about, and untrained, but his phrasing was remarkable. Her son, too, had sung *very* well. The audience was enjoying itself, was *involved*. She'd been right to put them last.

Applause even louder this time. Ken's intro maybe hadn't hurt.

Seth didn't introduce his number; nods exchanged with Jack and Ken, they swung into the two-four rhythm.

Calls from the audience, "You gonna tell us who she is, Seth?" and variants. If anyone thought to add, "as if we couldn't guess," it wasn't loud enough to hear.

They stopped, Seth laughed. "You asked for one of the happier ones. Here it is." He looked at Gwen, but wouldn't name her, not for everyone.

Started over.

Gwen thought she might possibly dissolve. He was absolutely wonderful. *And hands off, ladies. He's mine.*

Patrick Riordan muttered, "Nursery-rhyme-nouveau-country."

Liz shushed him. "I'm trying to listen."

A number of couples did dance.

Cheers, a few, as well as loud clapping. Calls for more.

Well. Seth glanced at Ken, who said, un-mic'd, "Your idea."

Seth shrugged. "Althea, come on up here."

As good—and fun—a number as they'd ever played. Upbeat, like his other, and Jack's, slower, but with real swing to it. A little swagger, even, the way Althea sang it, and Seth stepped it up to match her.

He took the first verse, she the second. The bridge was his, the third verse hers. Each joined Jack for backup, as called for.

Instrumental, and Seth wrapped it up with the last half-verse, joined by Jack and Althea for the final refrain.

They could have played longer, but Ken thanked the audience, and wished them good night.

In the storeroom, as they cased instruments and accessories, Ken said, low, "You best take that girl on home, make her happy. Looks like she's 'bout ready to tear your clothes off right here, and I don't wanna have to arrest the pair of you on indecent exposure."

Seth grinned. That was the plan. And he'd bet he wasn't the only one of them with that on his mind, either.

He *liked* performing. He'd loved mastering music, always, but hadn't known the live power of playing for an audience. Taking that many people where he wanted them to go. The excitement was damn' near erotic.

Madeleine Hardie thanked everyone for coming (applause), thanked George and Amelia Betts for the venue and the food (applause), thanked the performers, "Isn't it wonderful how much talent we have right here in our own town?" (loud applause).

But the four who'd closed it out were not in evidence. Two empty booths, an empty little table.

Liz Lord, a near-full glass of wine in front of her, turned to Patrick Riordan.

"Now, what were you saying?"

"Just that it was a stupid song to sing for a girl. Not even about *her*. And barely a word over a single syllable."

"You don't get it, Patrick. That song said, plain as day, 'this is who I am, this is how I love you.' And I think the message got through just fine—did you see the way she looked at him when they left?"

He had, and the way Seth Greenlaw looked back, as well.

"That," said Liz, "is as psycho-emotionally naked as you will ever see that man. In public, anyway. And frankly, I never thought I'd see that much."

"I think you are a bit in love with him yourself, Elizabeth."

She shook her head. "No. Just melancholy, maybe, that I'm not the sort of person who gets what they have. And feeling a little old."

"If I were clever, I'd adopt your stance. I suppose I will forgive her. Sooner or later."

"Word to the wise, Patrick—you got the fairytale ass-backwards. You *wanted* to be a prince, and fell for what you thought was a princess to make you one. But in the stories, it's Prince Charming who bestows the title. And married—or widowed—titles don't carry over.

"You know the name of my brand, take that to heart. You're a terrific writer, and some of the best company I know—when you're not sulking. You're smart, handsome, and extremely attractive. Be content to be the man you are. Lots of men would give their eye teeth to be you."

Patrick said nothing to that. It was kind of her, perhaps, to build him up after tearing his fantasy—yes, it had been a fantasy—to shreds.

"Do you know what I want? I want a terribly seedy tavern, smelling of stale beer and sad lives. And to get very drunk in it."

Liz smiled. "Do you, now? I know just the place."

He looked at her. "I don't suppose the offer you made me once is still open?"

"Buy me some shots of cheap tequila, a few bad margaritas to wash them down, and ask me again."

* * *

Both hands on the wheel, eyes on the road. That's what he told himself, but Seth couldn't help glancing across at Gwen. Looking fixed at him, eyes big and sparkling. The still-sultry air tightened the waves of her hair to almost curly.

Gwen resisted the impulse to unsnap her seatbelt, slide over, press close, put her hands on him. Mustn't distract the driver. Even if he drove her to distraction.

The only sound their breath.

Seth pulled into her driveway.

Gwen's hand shook so it was hard to unlock her kitchen door. His hand on hers didn't help. But open it did, and strong arms swept her inside.

She giggled, breathless, as he scooped her up in his arms. *So* strong—he carried her as easy as if she'd been a couple of coins he'd picked up to put in his pocket.

Her bedroom door was open, one bedside lamp on. As she'd left it, deliberately. *Welcome.*

He kicked the door shut; the slam made her heart shiver. This was really happening, she had no idea what to expect. Her only experience had been with Mark. Seth was a different animal entirely. All she could be sure of was that this would be—new.

What she felt was also new, though it went by the old names. Love. Desire. A priest might be named John Smith, so might a prizefighter.

He set her on her feet, a confusion of kisses and buttons, bootlaces and zipper and touch. He pushed her down, they were naked in her bed.

His hands were everywhere, hardened palms, callused fingers scratching, quickening her skin, defining the shape of her. She kissed his neck, his shoulder, put her hands in his hair, so thick, *weighty*, almost alive.

So many *textures* of sensation—hands, skin, hair, lips, tongues, teeth. His beard and her skin doing *naughty* things together. His hair tickled. Her juices soaked the sheet beneath her.

Good thing the Commandments didn't say *thou shalt not covet thy neighbor.*

It hurt, a little, when he entered her, it was nothing, this was a *true* thing, truth sometimes hurts, her body needed this, and her soul.

He was slow, gentle, his body asking questions, eyes locked into hers, deeper, scarier penetration; he took all her soul's clothes off. Like dancing, she followed his lead in the rhythm. And then pushed it.

Maybe he'd found his answers, maybe she'd given them to him—he wasn't gentle, now. Rough, hard. *Wild. Yes.* The last corner of her mind surrendered.

She'd known *violent* pain, she needed pleasure to match and to counter.

His breath was ragged as torn cloth, hers came in gasps. The slap of sweating flesh colliding. Wordless sounds came from both of them.

Tumbling in strong currents. He'd gone too deep, touched a fault line, he was starting an earthquake that would tear the world to pieces, she could feel it, see it in his eyes. Mountains burned. Cities crumbled.

It *wasn't possible*, how could she feel so much, no release could resolve this, it would spiral up and in until it killed her.

He groaned, shivering a little, his mouth open on her neck. She raised his head tenderly, kissed him. Looked into his eyes.

Saw herself there. She was known, she was loved. She was

taken.

Sensation honed to knifepoint, pierced through her body to the quick of her soul. And suddenly it was all *possible*, she knew his truth, she knew her own. Heard herself cry his name as she shattered, cries turning to shrieks, drowned in the deep sound that tore out of him. He shuddered violently, she felt the hard jet. All his weight fell on her.

The press of his body was sweet.

He lifted off her a little, his murmured "Gwen" met her sighed "Seth." They kissed their names on each other's lips.

Seth withdrew, rolled on his back, taking her with him. Gwen stretched against him, in the crook of his arm, head on his shoulder. Her hand found his heart; his fingers played in her hair.

Good thing he'd never let himself imagine this. He'd never have done it—her—justice. He knew her now, the root of her sweetness, the fire that burned in her. Worth the waiting.

Gwen sighed happily, pressed her palm against his heartbeat. "Check. And *mated*."

He laughed, softly, "*Oh*, yeah."

. . .

See the mountains kiss high heaven,
And the waves clasp one another;
No sister-flower would be forgiven
If it disdained its brother;
And the sunlight clasps the earth,
And the moonbeams kiss the sea:
What is all this sweet work worth,
If thou kiss not me?

Percy Bysshe Shelley, *Love's Philosophy*

ACKNOWLEDGMENTS

My thanks to, first and foremost, my best friend and editor, Jessica O'Connor. Without her inspiration, I would not have written this book. My thanks, too, to Paula Guice, my proofreader. I hope I have not caused her to pull out too much hair. I am profoundly thankful to all the people who have given me support, encouragement, and feedback. To those many souls who have made the internet the resource it is—making the massive amounts of needed research possible for me. And special thanks to the folks at "Peanuts" for allowing me to use Lucy Van Pelt's name and quote.

Made in the USA
Middletown, DE
22 December 2018